# ABOVE GROUND

S0-ABB-193

*To those who give...*

# ABOVE GROUND

A Jack Taggart Mystery

## Don Easton

A Castle Street Mystery

**THE DUNDURN GROUP**
TORONTO

Copyright © Don Easton, 2007

All rights reserved. No part of this publication may be reproduced, stored in a retrieval system, or transmitted in any form or by any means, electronic, mechanical, photocopying, recording, or otherwise (except for brief passages for purposes of review) without the prior permission of Dundurn Press. Permission to photocopy should be requested from Access Copyright.

Editor: Barry Jowett
Copy-editor: Jennifer Gallant
Design: Jennifer Scott
Printer: Webcom

National Library of Canada Cataloguing in Publication

Easton, Don
    Above ground / Don Easton.

(A Jack Taggart mystery)
ISBN 978-1-55002-681-8

    I. Title. II. Series: Easton, Don. Jack Taggart mystery.

PS8609.A78A63 2007          C813'.6          C2007-900088-6

1   2   3   4   5       11   10   09   08   07

Conseil des Arts du Canada    Canada Council for the Arts    Canada    ONTARIO ARTS COUNCIL CONSEIL DES ARTS DE L'ONTARIO

We acknowledge the support of the Canada Council for the Arts and the Ontario Arts Council for our publishing program. We also acknowledge the financial support of the Government of Canada through the Book Publishing Industry Development Program and The Association for the Export of Canadian Books, and the Government of Ontario through the Ontario Book Publishers Tax Credit program and the Ontario Media Development Corporation.

Care has been taken to trace the ownership of copyright material used in this book. The author and the publisher welcome any information enabling them to rectify any references or credits in subsequent editions.

                                                    *J. Kirk Howard, President*

Printed and bound in Canada        www.dundurn.com

Dundurn Press                Gazelle Book Services Limited        Dundurn Press
3 Church Street, Suite 500            White Cross Mills              2250 Military Road
Toronto, Ontario, Canada        High Town, Lancaster, England        Tonawanda, NY
        M5E 1M2                            LA1 4XS                    U.S.A. 14150

# *chapter one*

H olly saw the flash of headlights in the carport and knew that Jack had arrived home. She checked the pot of simmering tomato sauce and turned up the heat. Their daughter, Jenny, at four years of age, was snuggled deep into a corner of the sofa watching television. Charlie, who'd recently had his first birthday, sat on the kitchen floor entertaining himself with an empty pasta box. Spaghetti was what Holly thought her family was going to eat tonight.

"Jenny! Go wash your hands for dinner, sweetie. Daddy is home."

Jenny was too absorbed in *The Simpsons* to pay attention.

Holly turned back to the stove, where the pasta sauce was beginning to boil. She felt Charlie's hug on her leg as she stirred. "Charlie! Daddy's home! Go see Daddy! Go on!"

Charlie knew the routine, and Holly smiled as he squealed with delight and hurried, taking a few awkward steps before landing on his diapered backside, then scrambling to his feet and disappearing around the corner and down the hall to the door.

Holly caught a glimpse of the cracked window over her kitchen sink. *Not much longer.* They had lived in the modest rented home for the last four years while her husband went to the University of British Columbia to earn his degree in computer science. *Only one more month to graduation! No longer a dim light at the end of a tunnel — it's a shining star!*

The dark green van with tinted rear windows did not draw any attention where it was parked on the street. Apartment buildings and low-rental housing made it a neighbourhood where unfamiliar vehicles were the norm.

Ray sat alone in the back of the van and waited. This was not the type of work he felt he should be doing. He had received his masters in business administration at Cambridge, but right now their resources in Canada were limited. Only twenty-one people, counting himself, for the entire lower mainland. Not much of an army ... but that would change.

Ray knew that The Boss was right about one thing. Corporate takeovers are easier when they are unexpected. First they must ensure that their own position is fortified before domination can begin. He was also confident in his research. British Columbia was the best place in the world for his type of corporation. The judiciary was so lenient that, for the most part, judges wouldn't even need to be bought. The power and wealth they had elsewhere made local crime groups look like petty thieves. It was time to quietly establish a new power in Canada.

Ray watched as a car slowed, then stopped at a driveway. He squeezed the transmit button on his portable radio and quietly gave the orders. Ray saw his target get out of the car and move the garbage can that had been placed to block his driveway. The target then returned to his car and slowly drove into the carport.

Ray saw the two Suzuki motorcycles zoom past him before braking hard and parking near the garbage can. One passenger got off each motorcycle and headed toward the carport while the drivers stayed and revved their engines.

"Jolly good," said Ray aloud, as he made his way back to the driver's seat.


"Where's my boy? Where's that Charlie?"

Charlie let out a long, high-pitched yell as he hurried toward his dad, then gasped when he was swept off the ground. Charlie giggled when he felt his dad nestle into his neck and pretend to blow bubbles.

Charlie was too young to grasp the danger when two men appeared in the open door behind his dad wearing motorcycle helmets with dark shields covering their faces. His father also did not understand when he turned around, still holding Charlie in his arms. But he saw the gun in each man's hand and started to close the door. He was too late.

One assassin calmly fired a shot that passed through Charlie and into his dad's heart. Jack's brain was momentarily still alive and he spun around to try to protect Charlie. He took one step before collapsing on the floor with Charlie under him.

The noise of the gun, equipped with a silencer, was drowned out by the television. The television did not, however, drown out a piercing cry from Charlie.

Both Holly and Jenny arrived on the run from different directions. Holly looked in horror, and upon seeing the two men she instinctively grabbed Jenny. One of the assassins stepped forward and fired another shot into the back of Jack's head before taking the time to stare at Holly and Jenny from behind his visor. The assassins did not know that their intended victim was already in a graveyard.

Constable Danny O'Reilly hurried to keep up with Corporal Jack Taggart. Being tall and lean, Jack tended to take larger strides. His metabolism was also high, and the strides were not only longer but also faster. Danny found himself in a position where jogging was too fast and walking fast was too slow.

"Damn it, slow down, will you?"

"We're late," replied Jack, quickening his pace.

"Only a few minutes. Lance has kept us waiting before."

"*Our friend* has kept us waiting before."

Danny sighed, then said, "Yeah, sorry. Our friend."

As they continued, Danny noticed the inscriptions on the tombstones they passed and the ages of some of the people. He thought of his own life, the past eleven years of which he had been a member of the Royal Canadian Mounted Police. Last year he had been transferred from Manitoba to work on the Intelligence Unit in Vancouver.

That was when he had met Jack Taggart, a man who was both his partner and his boss. He was also his best friend. Working with Jack was not easy. During his first shift with Jack, Danny had been attacked from behind by a junkie with a knife. Later, both he and his family had been targeted for assassination by a splinter group of bikers from Satans Wrath. This group had been led by a corrupt Crown prosecutor by the name of Sidney Bishop.

When the first assassination attempt had failed, Bishop had ordered the bikers to set up an ambush. The bikers were subsequently killed in a shootout, but Bishop fled the country. Danny ended up with a 40 percent loss of vision in one eye as a result of bullet fragments from the skirmish. He looked at one tombstone and did a double take before realizing the name he saw was *O'Brien*. He gave a wry smile. *Not even close to O'Reilly!*

His thoughts brought him back to his family. His daughter, Tiffany, was now fourteen months old. The latest arrival to their family, James Patrick O'Reilly, was two months old. Susan was a great mom. An even greater wife. *Working with Jack does make you appreciate life … as long as you're still alive to appreciate it.*

Danny glanced at Jack. *He's been with me through a lot of scrapes. Then again, he's also the asshole who got me into them!*

Jack was a specialist as an undercover operator and had received special police schooling for the task. At the moment, Jack was clean-shaven. Although Danny was now sporting a goatee, he was not a trained operator. His job was usually to remain in the background and try to keep Jack alive when things went wrong — or to identify the right culprits if Jack was killed. Not an easy task.

Satans Wrath was one of the top organized crime families in the world. Things had changed since the seventies. Long past were the days when they were just a bunch of thugs on wheels. Control of the drug industry brought immense wealth and sophistication to the bikers. The club expanded into twenty-one different countries. Now it was one of the most dangerous and insulated organized crime families in the world. Partly,

Satans Wrath could thank the police. Years of police
work and international cooperation had decimated
much of the mafia, and Satans Wrath had been more
than willing to step in and take over.

In Vancouver, police intelligence units estimated
that Satans Wrath had ninety-two members split
between the east-side and west-side chapters. There was
a president in charge of each chapter. The national president of the club, Damien, also lived in Vancouver.

With approximately ten hard-core criminal associ-
ates connected with each member, in Vancouver alone
Damien was in control of an army of approximately one
thousand. Across Canada, there were twenty-one other
chapters, all with their own armies — and no shortage
of recruits.

Satan's Wrath was actively seeking recruits at the
moment. Competition was deadly. The Indos were of
particular concern to Satans Wrath, followed by Asian
gangs. At the moment, the Indos were still fighting
amongst themselves to gain a share of the drug market,
but it would be only a matter of time before the pecking
order was established and the Indos turned their attention to Satans Wrath.

It was Satans Wrath that Jack and Danny focused
their attention on, and Lance was the key to their success. Satans Wrath was importing tonnes of cocaine from
a vicious drug lord in Columbia by the name of Carlos.
Lance had let Jack and Danny know about the intended
arrival of the last ship, with a cargo that included one
metric tonne of cocaine. To divert suspicion from Lance,
Jack had tipped off a friend in the American Drug
Enforcement Agency, who had then seized the ship before
it ever reached Canada.

Lance, along with two others, had tried to kill Jack
once, believing that he was a police informant. Jack had

escaped with Danny's help. Danny grimaced when he thought of how close Jack had come to dying. That was one of the first lessons he had learned from Jack about seeing the big picture.

Danny would have arrested those involved. Jack had another idea. He knew that Lance was a family man with four children and a lot to lose. He used this as leverage to convince Lance to become their informant. Having an informant in Satans Wrath was almost unheard of.

Unfortunately, the same was not true in reverse. Satans Wrath routinely developed informants of their own. In short, Lance was in an extremely precarious situation and Jack insisted that Lance's real name never be used. He was simply referred to as *our friend*. It also left Jack and Danny in a position where morality had to be carefully weighed and sorted out. It was a task that Danny found difficult. *How much evil do you allow on the prospect of stopping a larger evil?* There was something else that had bothered Danny since he had begun to work with Jack. *The law and morality may not coincide when your own family is threatened.*

Danny thought back to the ambush attempt on their lives and the biker who had threatened his family. It was someone he could have arrested ... but didn't. Danny was lucky. Lucky to have survived the ambush and lucky that Connie Crane in the Integrated Homicide Investigation Team purposely ignored evidence indicating exactly how the biker had died.

Danny had become a changed man since working with Jack. His understanding of right and wrong was now a tangled mess. Jack had brought him into a world where the rules were different and the laws of society were held in contempt. A world where the strong murder the weak. To survive, you have to be strong. If you're not strong, you die ... or someone you love dies. Jack had survived for a long time. Danny hoped he would too.

Lance nodded as they approached, then said, "Got some news for ya that ought to make ya happy. Our chapter had our elections. I made it. You're now lookin' at the new president of the west-side chapter."

"Excellent," said Jack, giving him a thumbs-up. "Way to go. Next thing you know you'll be national president."

"Not a chance," chuckled Lance. "I know my limitations. Damien is a lot smarter than I am. I don't know anybody that could replace him and do as good a job, including the guys back east."

"How did it go with us taking down the labs today? Any heat?"

"No heat, but you screwed up. You missed two of 'em."

"We tried. I think they were tipped."

"Warned ya. Told ya you had a narc talkin' to the club."

"Would be nice if you found out who. We had over sixty cops involved."

"You two go to all seven places yourselves?"

"No, Danny and I just coordinated and sat back. My name is on all the search warrants for providing the information, but we try to keep out of court as much as possible."

"Heard on the news you arrested thirteen. Word is you got Petro."

"He received the money. Case on him is weak but we charged him anyway."

"Serves him right. He should have stuck to arson. That's his specialty."

"Explains the nickname. We also nailed a striker. He collected the coin from the labs and gave it to Petro."

"Silent Sam?"

"Yes. Charges on him should stick."

Lance nodded.

"You've been doing well," continued Jack. "Still no problems with that ship being taken down in San Diego?"

"Not a bit. Your buddy in the DEA did it right. What with all the security for terrorism these days, everybody figures the cops in the U.S. just got lucky."

"I told you he would protect you. I wouldn't have used him if I didn't trust him."

"Yeah, well, I guess you were right."

"You told us that Damien fronted half the money for that shipment — $3 million U.S. He must be a little agitated."

"He did get a lot of heat from the club until Carlos said he would eat the loss. Carlos says the money has been applied to the second shipment. Everyone is okay with Damien now."

"A metric tonne of cocaine is a lot to eat," added Jack.

Lance shrugged. "Not for Carlos. He runs one of the biggest cartels Colombia has. He's sending two more ships our way. Our deposit was just applied to the second ship. We pay the other half when it gets here. Then we get a couple of weeks to pay another $3 mil for the third ship and the rest on delivery. This time the ships are coming direct to Vancouver. A place where we got some control of the docks. Might be a bit dicier for me then, as I'll be in charge of the initial warehousing."

"We'll look after you. I'd let the coke go rather than burn you."

"Yeah, I know that. I trust ya."

"I want to nail Damien, though."

"Forget it. He won't be anywhere near the action."

"I don't care!" said Jack, trying to control his anger. "He's still pulling the strings."

The tone of Jack's voice did not go unnoticed by

either Lance or Danny.

Lance frowned and said, "A lot is happening in the club now. Damien seems more obsessed with what the Indos are up to. Now that I'm prez, I'll be in the know a lot more."

"It's great what took place today," said Danny. "You did good!"

"That you did," added Jack. "I'm pleased. A tonne of coke three weeks ago and five labs today. We make one hell of a good team."

"Don't know if being drafted makes me a good team member or not. I'll just be glad when I've paid my dues and am finished with all this."

"You figure out a way for us to take down these other two ships and I'll say we're even. Might even buy you a gold watch as a retirement gift."

"Forget it! Not if it's got 'For loyal service to the RCMP' stamped on the back of it! Besides, as I said, I'll be in the middle of things. I'd rather follow through on our agreement and work for you for another four and a half years." Lance gestured to the tombstones and added, "That would be better than retiring early and ending up in here."

Jack's cellphone vibrated and he answered it. It was Connie Crane. Connie had once worked for the Homicide Section in the Major Crimes Unit. Now the homicide sections from the B.C. lower mainland, with the exception of Vancouver and Delta, had combined into what was known as the Integrated Homicide Investigation Team, or I-HIT, as it was commonly called.

"To what do I owe the pleasure of a call from I-HIT?" asked Jack. He heard Connie's sigh.

"Just called to let you know that I think there was a consequence to you taking down all those biker labs today," she said.

"What's that?"

"You were just murdered!"

"What are you talking about?" Jack let out a chuckle and added, "I might have one foot on a grave right now, but I assure you, any rumours of my death are premature."

"I'm at a homicide in Surrey. Looks like two professional hitters. Silencers used along with motorcycles for their escape. Shot a guy through the heart and then through the head. Also wounded his infant son, who is in critical condition at B.C. Children's right now."

"What's it got to do with me?"

"The victim's name was Jack Taggart."

Jack gave Lance a hard stare as he continued to talk. "Maybe it's a coincidence. Surrey, the guy is probably a —"

"He looks as pure as bottled water. No record. Not even a speeding ticket. Was about to graduate from UBC. Left a wife and two kids. If the little one survives, that is."

"He was just a student?"

"Older than most. He held a management position with a company five years ago but it dissolved with the economic times. He then went to university to better himself. They were struggling but they both held down part-time jobs and saw it through."

"What are the mom's and kids' names?"

"Holly is the mom. She has a toddler by the name of Jennifer and the baby is named Charlie."

"Not related to me."

"Holly said she hadn't intended to get pregnant with Charlie, as it added to their money worries, but from what I can tell they were still thrilled with Charlie's arrival."

Jack didn't respond as he stared at Lance's face, waiting for any sign that he knew about the hit.

"Jack? You still there?"

"I'm here, CC."

"Taking down five labs today — can't see that being a coincidence. Your name was on all the search warrants."

Jack watched Lance closely as he spoke into the phone and said, "If Satans Wrath tried to kill me today..." He saw the surprised look on Lance's face and added, "Hold on." He walked away so that he could talk in private. "I can't see Satans Wrath screwing up like this," he continued. "They know what I look like! It's either amateurs or just a coincidence."

"These weren't amateurs. They were too calm. They've done this before. Two guys, each with small-calibre pistols equipped with silencers. Both wearing motorcycle helmets with face visors. Two accomplices were waiting on motorcycles out front. The dad was holding his toddler. They shot through him to get the dad, then took their time and put one in his skull right in front of his wife and four-year-old daughter."

"But the bikers know me," was all Jack could think to say, as he looked over at Lance, *our supposed inside man at Satans Wrath!*

"If it's not Satans Wrath, it has to be somebody you know! Who is it, Jack?"

"I don't know."

"Bullshit! I know you. What have you done?"

# *chapter two*

*What have I done!* The words echoed in Jack's head as he walked back to where Danny and Lance were standing. He told Danny what CC had told him, while staring at Lance for his reaction. He didn't have to wait long.

"Jesus Christ! It wasn't us! I'd have known!"

Neither Jack nor Danny replied.

"Maybe some stupid fuckers connected to the lower end of the labs. We'll whack 'em ourselves if it was."

"I believe you," said Jack. "Do some digging. If it was meant for me, find out who is behind it!"

"Maybe Bishop is behind it," offered Lance. "I know he left the country, but that doesn't mean he didn't come back or isn't pulling the strings from someplace else."

"It's not Bishop," said Jack.

"You can't be sure. Just because —"

"I'm sure," said Jack firmly. He gave Lance a look that meant there was no doubt about the words he spoke.

Lance had seen that look a few times before. It had been given by men he knew in Satans Wrath. It conveyed a message that could not be said aloud.

Jack and Danny watched Lance leave before heading back to their car. "What do you think?" asked Danny. "You sure it's not Bishop?"

"Satans Wrath wouldn't make a mistake like that. I bet when CC digs a little deeper she'll find out the guy owed money for drugs or gambling or something."

"We going to call it a night?"

"I was going to drop in on Lucy at the lab. Tell her I appreciate all the extra hours she's putting in. I heard she already found speed residue on the money that was seized from Silent Sam's pockets."

"Let me do that. With what just happened, maybe you should get home to Natasha."

Jack hurried inside the office as soon as Danny dropped him off and placed a quick call to Natasha. She was concerned but accepted his explanation that he thought it was a coincidence.

"I've only been married to you for five months," she said. "You better not be coming home with any bullet holes in you!"

"Hey, you're a doctor. You could patch me up." Her silence told Jack that levity was not an option. "If, by some remote chance, it wasn't a coincidence, it had to be a moron to make a mistake like this. We'll find out who did it. In the meantime, make sure nobody pulls into the underground parking behind you. Check the camera before buzzing anybody in."

"You on your way home?"

"I'm going to drop by B.C. Children's. Meet the victim's wife. See if I can get a feel for all this. If her husband is dirty, she'll know."

"Jack..."

"What is it?"

"I love you."

"I love you, too."


Jack made his inquiries at the hospital. Charlie Taggart, barely a year old, was in critical condition in the operating room. His mom and sister were both in a private room talking with a hospital counsellor.

The room was not difficult to locate. Jack could hear the crying and sobbing from within. He stood outside and waited. *Even if the guy was dirty, listening to this is bloody awful.* He decided to stroll down the hallway.

Eventually, Holly, with Jenny wrapped under one arm, left the room. She anxiously glanced at a doctor who approached, but he continued past. She could have stayed in the room with the counsellor but thought it would delay news of her son. Jack watched as she nervously stood in the corridor. When she noticed Jack approaching, she pulled Jenny closer.

*Her face ... she hasn't a clue what is going on. Her eyes are as innocent as her little girl's. This is somehow a terrible mistake. Her husband shouldn't be in the morgue ... or Charlie on the operating table.*

Jack's brain screamed at him like two separate entities. *They were ripped apart because of me! It's me who should be in the morgue!*

*No! It can't be. This is all a coincidence ... nothing to do with me.*

Jack didn't give his name to Holly but showed her his badge while introducing himself as a member of the

Royal Canadian Mounted Police. He ushered Holly and
Jenny to a waiting area and gently asked for the details
of what happened.

Holly's response was in a monotone as she stared
past Jack down the hall. She had told the other officer
everything, she said. She opened her purse and handed
Jack a business card. *Integrated Homicide Investigation
Team — Cpl. Connie Crane*. Jack gave her the card back.

"I'll talk with Connie," said Jack.

"Are you a policeman?" asked Jenny.

"Yes," replied Jack. He tried to smile at the child
but felt awkward to be smiling in front of Holly.

"My name's Jenny. What's your name?"

"I should be going," said Jack, looking at Holly. He
stood up.

"I'm sorry, I didn't catch your name," said Holly.

Jack took a deep breath and then let it out as he sat
down again. "My name is Jack Taggart."

Holly shook her head and said, "No, I asked you
what *your* name is."

Jack swallowed, and then explained that Jack
Taggart was his name, too.

"That's my daddy's name," said Jenny. "That's
funny!" She laughed and then said, "Isn't that funny,
Mommy?"

Jack looked at Holly and said, "I don't work on
Homicide. I work on an intelligence section dealing with
organized crime. Corporal Crane called me to tell me
about your husband. She thinks he may have been murdered as a result of mistaken identity."

"Oh," Holly said, and then stared past him down
the hall. Jack wrote his own phone numbers down for
her, including his cell, his office, and his home phones.

"If there is anything, anything at all, that I can do
for you. Please ... please call me."

Holly nodded and gave a perfunctory smile before slipping the information into her purse.

Jack saw the counsellor watching from across the hall and spoke with her as he was leaving.

"I'm a policeman," he said. "Where's her family? Why isn't someone here?"

"Jenny and Charlie are her only family now. Neither she nor her husband had siblings. Her husband's parents are in a nursing home and her own parents died several years ago."

"Neighbours? Someone?"

"I asked. She said she didn't live in the sort of neighbourhood that was conducive to making friends. Sounds like she didn't have the time or the money to go out. She was either waitressing in a coffee shop or looking after her children while her husband went to school."

"There has to be somebody!"

"Apparently not. I'll watch her. She won't be going anywhere as long as her son is in OR."

"And if he doesn't make it?"

The counsellor bit her bottom lip and didn't reply.

Jack reached for his wallet and said, "If that happens, please call me. I'll help." He gave her his business card and included all his numbers.

Jack was just leaving the hospital when he met Connie Crane coming in.

"What are you doing here?" she demanded.

Jack looked at her and said, "That sounds familiar. Think you've asked me that before."

"I did on another investigation, and you didn't mind your own business then, either."

"I just wanted to see her. See what she looked like."

"Did you?"

Jack nodded.

"No tattoos," said Connie. "No weathered face. If her makeup wasn't smeared all over she would look like what I think she is."

"How's that?"

"Innocent!"

Jack sighed. "That's my read too."

"So I'm just having a hard time believing your crap that it's all a coincidence. I want names. Who do you suspect?"

"That's just it, I don't suspect anyone."

"You take down a bunch of Satans Wrath labs today and think it's all a coincidence?"

"They know me. They also know Natasha and they know we don't have any children. It's not them. I have a good source. If it turns out to be some low-level punks working the bottom end of the labs, I'll find out."

"These guys were professional. Cold and calculating. They shot him in the heart first. Didn't care that he was holding his baby. That's when his wife and daughter showed up. Then they stepped forward and shot him in the back of the head. After that, they just turned and walked away. These were no punks. These bastards have killed before."

"It still could be a coincidence. Completely unrelated to me."

"Could be, but I want you to think about it. Tomorrow morning I want a list of possibilities. After that, keep your head low and butt out this time!"

"If this isn't personal, that is exactly what I intend to do."

"And if it is?"

Jack turned on his heel and walked away.

# *chapter three*

It was nine o'clock in the morning when Staff Sergeant Luigi "Louie" Grazia strode across the carpeted floor in Assistant Commissioner Isaac's office and then stopped in front of his desk, waiting for him to look up.

For management purposes, the Royal Canadian Mounted Police was broken down into four regions Canada-wide: Atlantic, Central, North West, and Pacific. Assistant Commissioner Isaac was the criminal operations officer who oversaw all the operational investigations in the Pacific Region.

Louie knew that Isaac deserved the respect that went with his position. He was a shrewd and tireless worker. He could quote policy and legal matters to the point that Louie wondered if it was true that he had a photographic memory. Isaac was also unbending when it came to policy — something that made Louie uncomfortable. His section tended to have many grey areas when it came to what was right or wrong. *Well, actually some things are clearly wrong...*

Eventually Isaac glanced up and said, "How long have you been in charge of Intelligence, Louie?"

There were three leather upholstered chairs facing Isaac's desk, but he did not gesture for Louie to sit so he remained standing. "Coming up ten years, sir," replied Louie casually, trying to get a read on Isaac's disposition. As usual, Isaac's face revealed nothing.

"Still plan on retiring this coming summer?"

"Yes, sir. I'll have my thirty-five years in this July."

Isaac nodded before continuing. "What can you tell me about this Taggart matter? Is the Jack Taggart who works for you the target of someone who wants to kill him?"

"Not that I know of, sir. I-HIT is investigating. I spoke with Jack and he thinks it might all be a coincidence."

"I want I-HIT, you, and Taggart in my office in one hour for a meeting."

"Yes, sir. I'll arrange it."


Damien, at fifty-three years of age, had done well for someone who had started out with nothing. His home, protected from view by a stone wall, was situated on an estate in one of the most prestigious areas of Vancouver. From the street, one could see only the roof, which was peppered with satellite dishes and antennas. Closed-circuit television cameras mounted in strategic locations outside led to a fortified panic room inside the mansion. A large cast iron gate, electronically controlled, blocked the entrance to the driveway. Damien did not become national president of Satans Wrath Motorcycle Club by being careless ... or weak.

Damien sat at his kitchen table and read the newspaper. It was a quiet time of the day that he enjoyed. His wife, Vicki, who was thirty-five, had borne him three children. Buck was thirteen, and his two sisters, Sarah and Kate, were eleven and eight years old. Damien enjoyed bantering with his children at the breakfast table, but now that they were heading out the door to school, he also enjoyed sitting quietly and catching up on the news.

Vicki had already skimmed the paper today and she watched with interest as her husband flipped to the local news.

Damien let out a snort when he read about the speed labs being connected with Satans Wrath and how the arrests and seizures would have a big impact on the crystal meth supply in the city. *Good excuse to raise the price.*

Vicki gestured to the article and asked, "Is it a problem?"

Damien shook his head. "They're always trying to pin crap on us. Actually it's funny. They think it's a big deal … shows how small their cerebral cavities are. I might have to do the usual PR routine to the media. No big deal."

"The paper said that two members were taken down. Silent Sam and Petro."

"Silent Sam doesn't even have his full patch yet. No worries. Leisure Suit Larry will have them out today."

Vicki suppressed a smile. *Leisure Suit Larry* was Damien's pet name for Lawrence Leitch, a lawyer that Satans Wrath kept on retainer.

Vicki noticed Damien turn another page and scan the paper for something else to read. His eyes settled on an article. Seconds later, he slammed the paper down on the table. She saw the pulse beat on the side of his temple and his fist close momentarily. He abruptly stood up and headed for his communications centre in the den.

She knew from experience that this was not the time to ask why.

Vicki reached for the paper. The article was about the murder of a man called Jack Taggart. He was gunned down, leaving behind a wife and two children. One child, an infant, was wounded and still undergoing surgery. His condition was listed as critical. *Jack Taggart ... I've heard that name before. Isn't he one of the cops who was in a shootout with the club last year?*

In his control centre, Damien rapidly sent a BlackBerry message. Pussy Paul received the message immediately and understood its importance. Pussy Paul controlled the strip clubs for Satans Wrath, but more importantly, he was also responsible for recruiting people who worked in a variety of positions that could benefit Satans Wrath.

Damien's anger was evident. The message noted that an RCMP Intelligence officer was named Jack Taggart. Not just any officer, but one that had considerable past conflict with the club. Damien capitalized his point: *SOMEONE DOES THIS THE SAME DAY AS THE LABS ARE TAKEN DOWN! We don't need the attention — not now of all times! Contact the mole and find out what Taggart thinks. Are they blaming us? I want the info included with the other delivery. Arrange for me to meet LSL personally.*

Pussy Paul knew that the "other delivery" was a copy of an RCMP intelligence report that they were expecting to receive by Thursday. That only gave him two days to find out about this other matter.

Lawrence Leitch checked his watch as the judge released two of his more important clients. They were to return in a week to enter a plea. Leitch was pleased. They had been in jail less than a day. Silent Sam and Petro smirked at each other before giving a curt nod to Leitch. In a week they would enter a not guilty plea and a trial date would be set. With delay tactics, such as having his clients fire him just before the trial, Leitch was confident that he could drag the situation on for at least two years. They would then hire another lawyer from his firm and the games would continue. Who knew what could happen to witnesses during that time?

The court recessed for morning coffee. Leitch used the break to browse through the information he had on the other eleven clients arrested in connection with the speed labs.

Jack shifted in his seat and glanced at Assistant Commissioner Isaac. Operational meetings in his office were rare. The murder of his namesake was drawing more attention than he wished. Also present were Louie, Danny, Connie Crane, and Randy Otto, who was Connie's boss in I-HIT.

After a nod from Randy, Connie took a report from her briefcase and quickly read the details of the murder and the inquiries being conducted. She noted that the victim had never been in trouble with the police. He did not carry life insurance, and his wife was definitely not a suspect.

Jack fielded the questions as best he could. He was adamant that it was not in retaliation for yesterday's raids on the speed labs. He reiterated that he and Danny had a reliable source who would have known if that was the case, not to mention that Satans Wrath knew what he looked like and where he lived.

Isaac studied him closely and then said, "You were also responsible for the DEA seizing a metric tonne of cocaine in San Diego three weeks ago. Perhaps Satans Wrath found out that you were involved? Your name was on the warrants for the speed labs here. Did the Americans use it on their warrant for the cocaine in the ship?"

"No sir. It was left out intentionally to protect my informant. Lots of people knew about the speed labs, but not too many new the details about the ship. I called the DEA agent I dealt with over that matter. I've known Jim-Bo for years. I both trust and respect him. He assured me that he never divulged my name and simply identified me in a search warrant as a confidential informant. He didn't even indicate that I was Canadian."

"That much cocaine, it must have made someone angry," said Isaac.

"Sir," said Jack, "after 9-11, everyone knows that there is more security at the ports. I think the cartels expect to take a few hits once in a while. Even if Satans Wrath did find out, it still leaves us with the fact that they know what I look like. They also know what my wife looks like and that she's a doctor. The victim in this matter lived in low-rental housing and was obviously poor. Satans Wrath wouldn't make a blunder like that."

Isaac leaned forward, resting his elbows on the table with his hands up by his lips, almost like he was praying. The room became quiet as everyone waited for him to speak.

Isaac stared at Jack, and then he concluded the meeting by saying that it was possible it was a coincidence but that he wanted to be apprised of any new developments.

As Jack headed back to his office, Connie came up from behind.

"Jack! Hold on a minute. I want to talk to you about a few things. I need some names."

A few minutes later they entered Jack's office, which consisted of his desk butting up to Danny's desk. Danny offered Connie the use of his desk and left. Connie put her briefcase down on Danny's desk and took out a pad of paper.

"I've thought of a few names," said Jack, "but more to appease you than anything. None that I really think would do this."

"I have to go to the lady's room," said Connie. "Think hard. Try and come up with a few more while I'm gone."

As soon as she left, Jack slid her briefcase across to his desk and took out her file. He found a manila folder and dumped out numerous glossy photos of the crime scene. The horror shocked him. *Blood on Holly's face and hands from having dropped to her knees to hold her dead husband. Her eyes look blank — like they're dead. More blood on Jenny. Something a four-year-old should not have to experience. Something nobody should have to experience.* He was spared the pictures of Charlie, who had already been rushed to hospital when the photos were taken.

His phone rang and he was glad for the opportunity to look away.

"Jack? It's Laura Secord. Just got back from Bangkok last night and didn't hear the news until this morning. What's going on? Was it meant for you?"

"Don't know," replied Jack. "Maybe just a coincidence. What were you doing in Bangkok?"

"Playing the role of a dumb bimbo being used to body-pack a couple kilos of heroin. Why do I always have to play the dumb bimbo? Drug dealers are so damned sexist. They all have over-bloated egos. Wish I could play the parts you get just for once."

Jack knew that Laura was anything but dumb. He had teamed up with her on the occasional assignment and found her to be one of the best operatives he had ever worked with. She had long chestnut-coloured hair, an attractive figure, and a face that was as sweet as her name. It fooled a lot of people. Underneath her pretty face was a mind that was extremely sharp. She was also pragmatic, and it served her specialty well. Bad guys often didn't discover her real abilities until much too late. Her reputation was top-notch and her talents were in high demand.

"You didn't play a bimbo when we did that operation in Edmonton a few years ago."

"No, but that was unusual. Normally I'm there to show a little T and A and pretend to be someone's girlfriend."

"Look at it this way, you shock the bad guys a lot more when they find out what you're really all about. That has to give you some satisfaction."

"True. I do enjoy that part. Enough about me. What is going on with this other Jack Taggart being murdered? Any leads? Is it connected with you? I'll be glad to help."

"Doesn't your husband still work in Internal Affairs?"

"Sort of. Elvis is on the Anti-Corruption side of it. What's that got to do with anything? He's a good guy! Oh man, not you too. Just because —"

"No, I'm just teasing. I know he's a good guy. He's got a good rep. He turned out pretty good for coming from such cruel parents."

"His parents aren't cruel! Where did you hear that? They're nice people."

"Naming your child Elvis is not cruel? Come on! He had to be either a fighter or a runner."

Laura laughed and said, "He's never been a runner."

"That's good. Listen, I really appreciate your call. Right now we don't know what is going on. If I need…" Jack's voice choked when he flipped over a photo and saw a close-up of Holly. Her anguish and helplessness was vivid on her bloody face. *Am I responsible for this? Was this family ripped apart ... because of something I did?*

"Jack? What is it? Jack?"

Jack shook his head to clear his mind and then said, "Sorry, Laura. Just looking at some crime scene photos from last night. It's pretty bad. I should go."

Jack hung up the phone just as Connie returned. She saw the photos on Jack's desk.

"What the hell you doing? I can't even go to the can for a minute without you snooping in my briefcase! I told you last night to stay out of this..." She caught the stricken look on his face and stopped.

Jack stared up at her. His eyes were watery and he said, "If this was meant for me ... I thought there might be some clue only I would recognize. There wasn't. I really don't have any names for you right now. Let me think about it. Maybe later. If I have any ideas, no matter how remote, I promise I'll let you know."

Connie nodded and said, "Good enough. In the meantime, keep a low profile."

"I hear you. I will."

"Got your word on that?"

"Yes."

Danny entered as soon as she left. He took one look at Jack and said, "What is it? What did she say to you?"

Jack shook his head. "It's not her. It's me. I'm afraid ... that it's all about me." He stood and said, "I need some fresh air. Think I'll go for a walk."

"I'll come too. Could use the exercise."

"No. Thanks anyway. I'm okay. Just give me a few minutes."

Jack breathed deeply as he walked outside the building. *I just need a little time to...*

His cellphone vibrated and he answered. It was Holly calling from the hospital. Her voice was a monotone. She had some news about Charlie. Wanted to tell him in person.

# chapter four

Jack saw Holly talking with a doctor in the hallway near the nurse's station. Jenny clung to her mother's leg. Jack's heart sent a silent message to his brain. He knew then that the murder had been intended for him. His brain had rationalized and tried to deny it, but in his heart he knew.

Jack waited until the doctor left before approaching. An orderly pushed a cart of lunch trays past and he tried to read Holly's face as she looked at him from over the cart.

Jack was good at reading people's faces and body language — his life had often depended upon it. With Holly he drew a blank. *Is Charlie alive or dead?* Her eyes looked dark from the puffy lids and bags in the skin. There were no tears. Perhaps, for the moment, she was cried out.

"I came as fast as I could," he said.

"I want you to have this," she said, taking a photograph out of her purse. "It was taken two weeks ago when Charlie took his first steps."

Jack swallowed and took the picture from her hand. Charlie's joy was evident as he beamed up at the camera, proud and delighted with his accomplishment. "Did … did he survive the surgery?"

"Oh … yes, he did."

Jack realized that he had been holding his breath and let out a sigh of relief.

"But he was left paraplegic," continued Holly. "He won't ever walk again."

Jack felt like a wrecking ball had just taken out his guts. For a moment, he felt his legs buckle and looked for a chair.

"I'm afraid to go see him alone … with Jenny. You said you would help me. Please come with me."

Jack went with Holly as if he was in a trance. He saw Charlie, his body being kept alive by tubes and machines.

Jack didn't remember returning to his car or driving back to his office. Danny had not returned from lunch yet and he sat alone at his desk. His mind felt numb and he looked at Charlie's picture again. He opened and closed his eyes a few times to try to regain control.

"Hi, Jack! How's it going?"

Jack looked up as Dick Molen entered his office.

Molen worked as an analyst, more commonly known as the circle and squares job. He would take lengthy intelligence reports and bring clarity to them by encompassing names of people and organizations in various circles or squares. Adding connecting lines made it easier to analyze and understand at a glance how everyone was connected.

"I heard what happened," continued Molen. "Sure glad it wasn't you that was killed. Lucky mistake, eh?"

Jack looked down at Charlie's picture. He felt both anger and tears swell from within. "Lucky!" he yelled. "Look at this picture and tell me you think it was lucky!"

Dick stepped back, shocked by the outburst.

Jack closed his eyes momentarily, then said, "I'm sorry, Dick. It's not your fault. You just caught me at a bad time."

Dick coughed, then nodded and said, "That's okay. Guess I'd be a little upset too if someone tried to kill me. Who's the kid?"

Jack explained the situation to him and Molen said, "I can't see it being a coincidence after you took down all those speed labs. How did you get on to them? Maybe that's where this came from."

Jack grimaced and said, "You're not alone in your thinking. Everyone else is pointing a finger at the bikers too, but I don't think it's them. They know what I look like. They wouldn't make a mistake like that."

"How did you find out about the labs? Wiretap? Maybe there is something there that you missed?"

Jack shook his head and said, "Not wiretap. Just surveillance."

"Well, if you want me to take a look at the work you've been doing, I'll be glad to analyze it for you. Maybe something will jump out. Lately all I've been doing is analyzing reports on the Indos. They've got so many common names that it's a nightmare trying to sort everyone out. Would be nice to get back to good ol' names like Smith and Johnson."

Louie wondered why he had been summoned back to Isaac's office. Isaac was alone and motioned for Louie to sit down. Isaac held a report in his hand and said, "I have some information concerning someone your office was working on last year in regards to Satans Wrath."

"Yes, sir?"

"This just arrived from Ottawa a few minutes ago. We need to discuss…"

Isaac's secretary then came to the door and said, "Your one-thirty appointment is here, sir."

"Tell him to wait," replied Isaac. "I don't want to be disturbed now. Or better yet," he said, putting the report down on his desk, "let's set another appointment."

Louie risked a glance at the report while Isaac spoke with his secretary. Reading upside down was not easy, but some words caught his eye. "A small unnamed settlement near Barra de Navidad, Mexico" … "Sidney Bishop" … "deceased, November" … *Damn it! Taggart got him!*

Louie saw Isaac turn his attention back to him, so he smiled politely and said, "You said you received some information, sir?"

"Yes. But first, how long has Corporal Taggart been working for you?"

Louie thought for a moment and then replied, "About six years. He worked undercover on Drug Section for about six years prior to that. Is there a problem?"

"Wasn't it last November when he married?"

"Yes, sir. Is there a —"

"And they went to Mexico on their honeymoon."

"I believe so. Costa Rica too, I think."

"It's been almost a year since Taggart's niece and nephew were murdered when they happened upon those bikers meeting with that corrupt prosecutor, Sidney Bishop. Three or four months after that when the culprits were identified."

"Yes, sir. Sidney Bishop is still at large for that."

"I'm sure Bishop's escape must be constantly on Taggart's mind. How has he been handling it? Is he spending a lot of time trying to find him?"

"I don't think he has any leads to go on at the moment. He won't give up, though. Last week I saw him pound his desk in frustration, muttering that someday he would bring Bishop to justice."

"He did?" said Isaac, sounding surprised.

"But you know Satans Wrath," said Louie. "Chapters all over the world. I'm sure Bishop is living under an assumed name someplace. The prospects of finding him don't look good."

"Taggart has an informant in Satans Wrath. Surely by now he could have found out something."

"Taggart's informant wasn't high enough up the ladder to be privy to the information. It isn't the type of organization where you can ask questions. If you do, you're liable to receive a bullet as an answer. Taggart's rather protective of his informants, and quite frankly, when it comes to Satans Wrath, I don't blame him."

Isaac slowly nodded in agreement, then said, "Well, Louie, I've got some good news on that issue. I've just received a report that Bishop was located in Mexico."

"That's great! Taggart will be elated to hear this! We'll get an extradition order and —"

"Hold on," said Isaac, gesturing with his hands for Louie to stop. "Bishop is dead."

"Dead?"

"It happened last November. The Mexican police say he tripped and fell beside his swimming pool, knocking himself out and falling into the water and drowning. He was living under an assumed identity from the U.S. Things didn't match up there and it took until now for a fingerprint search to reach Ottawa, where he was properly identified."

Louie let out a deep breath and said, "I see. Well at least that wraps things up. Connie Crane from I-HIT was handling the case, but with your permission I would like to tell Taggart. He'll want to inform his sister and brother-in-law."

"Not a problem. I've discussed this with Staff Sergeant Randy Otto."

"I-HIT doesn't mind if Jack breaks the news?"

Isaac shook his head and said, "Staff Otto said he had no objections."

Louie stood to leave, and Isaac said, "By the way, just out of curiosity, do you happen to know where in Mexico it was that Taggart spent his honeymoon?"

"I believe it was around Mexico City. I'm not sure."

"Bishop was living on the Pacific side. Some little settlement that doesn't even have a name. Near a village called Barra de Navidad. Quite a coincidence that Bishop died during the same week that Taggart was in the country."

Louie briefly allowed his mouth to droop open in surprise and then said, "Good God! You're not thinking that Taggart had anything to do with…?"

"It certainly crossed my mind, but I feel reassured that you said he is still upset about not finding him. Go and tell him now. Maybe it will help provide him some closure to all this."

Isaac waited until Louie left his office before dialling Staff Sergeant Harry Legg, who was in charge of the Anti-Corruption Unit and was waiting for his call.

"Louie just left," said Isaac.

"Taggart is still in his office," replied Legg. "How did it go with Louie?"

"Not good. He scanned the report when I gave him the opportunity. Later he feigned surprise when I told him that Bishop was dead."

"Louie is in charge of Intelligence. It's his nature to be nosy. He might have been covering up that fact."

"I considered that, but I still don't like it. I asked Louie where Taggart went in Mexico. His reply was, *I believe it was around Mexico City. I'm not sure.*"

"That's the opposite side from where Bishop was."

"It's also a vague response. Hard to pin down. Just like Taggart not using any credit cards in Mexico, yet you say he did in Costa Rica."

"Could be he started with cash, then used his Visa when the money ran out."

"Or he didn't want to leave a paper trail. You sound like you support his innocence?"

"Sir, I'm not saying that. I'm just considering other possibilities, or what Taggart could say if he was interviewed."

"You said that Louie's nature is to be nosy. Yours is to be suspicious. I want to know for sure. If Taggart is responsible, find out how he knew where Bishop was. Was it his informant in Satans Wrath? Louie said the informant wasn't in a high enough position to know at that time. From what I know of Satans Wrath, I believe that to be true. But if Taggart is responsible, how did he find out where Bishop was? If only the top dogs in Satans Wrath knew the location … Taggart might have not only committed murder but could now be working for them."

"All this is purely speculation, sir. We don't have grounds for a wiretap, and surveillance, except for today, isn't likely to shed much light and could jeopardize Taggart and his investigations if he is innocent."

"I know, but see if you can find out exactly where he went in Mexico. Also give the Combined Forces Special Enforcement Unit a call. I know they're also monitoring Satans Wrath."

"CFSEU? They're independent. Do you really think we should be passing on our suspicions about Taggart this soon? He could be entirely innocent, and even if he isn't, it might jeopardize our —"

"No need to point fingers. Just say that we're investigating potential leaks and would like to be kept apprised should they become aware of any involvement between any of our members and Satans Wrath."

"Yes, sir. One moment, please.... I just got word that Taggart is leaving the office," added Legg.

"See if the news was a surprise."

"We're on him. Will let you know."


Jack was glad that he had the rest of the afternoon off as he crossed the Port Mann Bridge and headed east on the Trans-Canada Highway. He replayed the scenario in his head from when Louie had broken the news. Danny had been excited and anxious to call his wife, Susan, and let her know. She too had almost become a victim of Bishop's assassination plot.

Louie had then taken Jack into his own office and told him about Isaac's concern. Louie's advice was welcome but something Jack would have done regardless. Naturally he would want to tell his sister and brother-in-law that the man responsible for their children's murders was dead.

At first, Jack was careful not to move his head while scanning his rear-view mirror. *Advertising paranoia could be construed as evidence of a guilty mind. Then again, if someone is trying to kill me — who wouldn't be paranoid!*

He decided to make no pretence of hiding his actions and carefully studied all the vehicles around him. Nothing aroused his attention.

It was almost three-thirty when he arrived at the farm. He gave his sister a big hug and a kiss as she came to the door.

"What a pleasant surprise! Come on in. Where's Natasha?"

"Still at work."

Elizabeth hollered to Ben and he appeared from out of the barn and came over.

"You have time for tea?"

Jack nodded, then asked, "Is Marcie home yet?"

"Her school bus should be along any minute. Why?"

"Nothing. Just haven't seen you for a while. How's she doing?"

"Doing great. I was worried when she turned thirteen that her hormones would kick in and maybe give us a challenge. Just the opposite. She's now top in her class. Not bad for a kid who was on the street last year and ... you know, getting into that sort of life. The adoption is coming along great. She'll soon be officially ours."

"That's fantastic, Liz. I needed to hear some good news for a change."

Once Liz had plugged in the kettle, the three of them sat at the kitchen table.

"When you called this morning," said Ben, "you said a guy with your name was murdered. You here because of that?"

"Are you in danger?" asked Liz.

Jack shrugged. "Nothing new on that. The infant who was shot is going to live, but..." Jack stopped. He knew he couldn't finish without losing control of his emotions.

"But what?" asked Liz.

"But ... that's not why I'm here. The brass received a report today that the Mexican police found Bishop's body. They suspect accidental drowning."

"Good," said Ben.

"Glad, that's over," added Liz. "Do you want a cookie?"

Marcie burst through the kitchen door. "Hi, Jack!"

He stood as she came, and she gave him a strong hug and a kiss on his cheek. "You here for dinner?" she asked, taking a seat.

"No, I can't stay long. Natasha will be off work at five. I want to be home."

"Those your friends out on the road?" asked Marcie.

"What friends?"

"Two cops driving by in an unmarked car. Really eye-balled our mailbox. Either cops or Jehovah's Witnesses, but this is only Tuesday, not the weekend, so they gotta be cops."

Everyone exchanged glances and nobody spoke for several seconds. Then Jack said, "Heard it's supposed to rain tomorrow."

# *chapter five*

$J$ack awakened feeling groggy. The memories of Bishop had been reawakened and it had been a long, restless night. He knew today wouldn't go any better when Natasha looked across her breakfast and said, "I hadn't told you before ... but I bumped into a Mexican policeman less than a kilometre from Bishop's home the day before he died. I used the opportunity to practise my Spanish."

Jack felt a piece of egg rise from his stomach and swallowed again before asking, "Why?"

"I didn't know at the time what you were up to. I thought we were just on our honeymoon."

"No. Why didn't you tell me this sooner? After ... it happened?"

"I didn't want you to worry. Now that they've said it's an accident, it's no big deal, right?"

*Wrong! It is a big deal!* Jack looked at Natasha and

thought, *Why let her worry?* "You're right. I think it was just routine to follow me out to the farm. Tying up loose ends."

"Do you think they will continue to follow you?"

"No. It wouldn't gain them anything. As far as Ben and Liz go, that makes sense."

"I just thought … what about the phones? Would they —"

"They would never get grounds for a wiretap. It's hard enough to get grounds on people with criminal histories, let alone us."

Natasha let out a deep breath and then smiled. "It's finally over," she murmured.

Jack nodded, but his stomach continued to churn. The black coffee and eggs seemed more infused with grease.

"You still look like something is troubling you," said Natasha.

"I just have a lot on the go. I'm okay."

"You don't look it. This thing with Bishop — it could exacerbate the stress from last year. Now this thing with Holly's husband…. I'm worried about you."

"I can handle it."

"I've heard that before. Usually from people who are on their way to a nervous breakdown. You should take some time off."

*Boatloads of cocaine due to arrive any day. Lance now president of the west-side chapter. A debt to be repaid to Damien. A family destroyed who shared my name. Take a holiday! Don't I wish!*

"I'm fine! If you want to worry about someone, worry about Charlie. That's the little guy who needs help."

"No need to snap at me."

Jack stared at her and then said, "I'm sorry."

"It's okay. But it proves my point. You are under a lot of stress."

Jack sighed. "I know you're right. I'll watch myself, but there is too much happening right now for me to take a break. There is nothing going on that I can't handle. I still have control. You've taught me that."

Natasha smiled and said, "The advice I once gave you about post-traumatic stress was simplified. It's more complicated than that."

"Duly noted," said Jack. "I'd love to stay and talk, but I have to pick up Danny. We're meeting a source this morning. See if he can help shed some light on things."

Natasha followed him to the door, where she gave him a passionate kiss and said, "Just remember. I love you. I also know you're not made out of iron. I wouldn't love you if you were. I love you because you are human, and all humans have a breaking point. Just look after yourself, if not for you, then for my sake, will you?"

Jack kissed her again and then left.

Staff Sergeant Legg walked into Isaac's office and got right to the point. "He went straight to his sister's place. Everything seems legit."

"He may have suspected that he was being followed," said Isaac.

"Always possible. Do you want us to bring him in for interrogation and see if we can wrap it up, one way or the other? Shouldn't take long to corroborate when and where he went in Mexico."

"Not yet. Get your ducks in line first. Obtain photos of him and his wife and send them to the Mexican authorities. They can check with the local police where Bishop was staying. The place is so small that any gringos are bound to stand out."

"I doubt that there are more than a couple of police-men there to show pictures to," said Legg.

"Then there's also not much of a population base. Shouldn't take them long. If Taggart was there, we'll find out soon enough."


Jack and Danny crossed a small knoll in the cemetery and saw Lance waiting at the usual location.

"Any heat over the labs?" asked Jack.

"Not a bit. Too Mickey Mouse to worry about. Besides, we still have two labs going full tilt and it's a good excuse to jack the price way up."

"Anything on the Taggart murder?" asked Jack.

Lance shook his head. "Don't think it was con-nected. The dumb schmucks running the labs are too stupid to keep something like that quiet. We would have heard."

"What about the cargo ship taken down in San Diego?" asked Danny.

"Not a peep about it. Everyone thinks it was just a casualty from the war on terrorism. Our money is rid-ing on the next ship, which should arrive soon. I'll get a couple of days' notice to find a stash site and make sure the deliveries are lined up."

"Anything else?" asked Jack.

"Whiskey Jake and I are to meet with Damien tomorrow. Said something about having to see Leitch in the morning and then he wants to meet us right after."

"Bet Leitch wants to talk to him about the labs," said Danny.

"Naw, I don't think so. Damien is worried about the anti-gang legislation but nobody was charged with that. The labs will probably come up, but Damien wouldn't concern himself with something as trivial as that."

"What do you think it's about?" asked Jack. "Money laundering?"

"Leitch could be his Maytag agent, but these days Damien seems to be fixated on the Indos and what they're up to. He told Sparks to take whatever funding he needs for bugging and put him in charge of selecting surveillance teams. I think we might be going to war."

"With the police?" asked Danny.

Lance frowned at Danny, then said, "No, of course not. With the Indos. I got no idea where that thing came from about someone killing the other Jack."

"I want you to try and identify the dirty narc for us," said Jack.

"Yeah, I know, but it isn't the sort of thing I can ask about. Maybe now with my new promotion, things will come a little easier. Damien mentioned there will be some restructuring taking place. Maybe that's what he wants to talk to Whiskey Jake and me about tomorrow."

It was later that afternoon when Ray parked his green van with the tinted rear windows and went for a stroll in Stanley Park. It didn't take him long to find Leitch, who handed him a manila envelope. Ray opened it and withdrew a report.

"It's yours to keep," said Leitch. "I made a copy."

Ray was pleased as he glanced at the report. It gave him names, addresses, criminal histories, and a complete picture of the hierarchy of organized crime as it related to the Indo community in Western Canada. It also listed their affiliations with other groups worldwide. He was particularly pleased to see that The Boss was not included. Canada's federal police force was sadly lacking in its assessment!

Ray read in the report that there was speculation about a war in British Columbia between the Indos and Satans Wrath. *Interesting. Who will win? The bikers are much more organized yet seem to lack the propensity to remove obstacles related to the judiciary — something I just can't comprehend. On the other hand, the Indos use violence without hesitation but are not as well organized. If there is a war, which side will win and work for us?*

Ray looked at Leitch and asked, "Has Damien received this yet?"

Leitch shook his head and said, "The copy for Damien has been locked away as usual. I'm supposed to give it to him tomorrow morning."

Ray snickered to himself. The report was from a police officer that Satans Wrath had cultivated, yet it was he who saw it first. Leitch knew his place. The amount of money he had been paid was minuscule in the overall scheme of things. *Of course, a bloody fool like Leitch thinks the amount I gave him makes him wealthy. Small men ... small dreams.*

Ray saw another sheet of paper in the envelope and pulled it out. "What's this?" he asked.

"Some Mountie that Damien wanted checked out. An officer by the name of Taggart. Someone by that same name was murdered. The note says the police officer with the same name is almost in tears over it."

"Really!" Ray paused for a moment, lost in thought, then asked, "Tell me, is Jack Taggart a common name in Canada?"

Leitch shrugged and said, "Not really."

"I have never heard of such a name. It didn't occur to me that there would be two in one city. Perhaps it is fortunate for the policeman that his name was not in the telephone directory."

Leitch smirked when the meaning of Ray's words became clear. "I suspect The Boss will not be happy," he suggested.

"I'm hardly concerned. I will let him know. This is nothing that can't be fixed."

# chapter six

On Thursday morning, Jack felt more agitated as he thought about the funeral he would be attending tomorrow.

"Maybe you shouldn't go," suggested Natasha. "Why put yourself through that?"

"Holly thinks it has something to do with me. It would be cowardly not to show up."

"But at the funeral, it —"

"I think of them all the time. Holly ... Jenny ... Charlie. I need to go."

"You're tormenting yourself by being involved in something that may have nothing to do with you."

"How could I not be involved? Do you really think I could just forget about it, not knowing if it was because of me? Every time I see a little kid running or playing, I'll think of Charlie. There's no way I'll ever not be involved."

"Fine, then I'm going with you."

"Thought you had to work."

"You're more important. I figured I wouldn't be able to talk you out of it. I already booked the morning off. I also talked with Susan. She and Danny are going as well."

"She doesn't need to do that. Tiffany is barely a year old. Jimmy is less than two months. She should stay home. Danny and I will go, but it's not necessary for —"

"It is necessary! For all of us! Don't shut out the people who love you when you need them." Natasha then softened her voice and said, "We're all worried about you. Quit trying to shoulder everything yourself. You're not alone in this. It's imperative that you remember that."

The banks had just opened when Damien met with Leitch outside. Leitch watched his secretary go in, then turned to Damien and said, "The Crown's case against those arrested inside the labs is strong. Same goes for Silent Sam for picking up the money. Petro is in a better position. They saw Silent Sam hand him the money but can't prove that Petro knew it was the proceeds of a criminal venture."

"Just do your job," said Damien. "That's what we pay you for."

"The Crown does have a weak link. One person in toxicology examined all the exhibits. A Lucy somebody … I've got her name at the office. If something were to happen to her at the opportune time, everything might get tossed out of court. She would be easier to get to. She doesn't carry a gun."

"Forget it!" said Damien. "There's no need to whack anyone. This is B.C. What are my guys going to get? Probation? Maybe a couple of months?"

Leitch first shrugged that he didn't know but then admitted, "Probably."

"You read in the paper about someone by the name of Jack Taggart being murdered?" asked Damien.

"Yes. Unfortunately it wasn't the same Jack Taggart who provided the grounds for the search warrants."

"I think someone thought they were killing him. Whoever it was made a huge mistake. I've met Taggart. Had a chat with him last year in my basement after a couple of my men stepped out of bounds. Those men are now dead. Taggart saw to that. You can bet some sorry bastard will pay for trying to kill him."

"Too bad whoever tried didn't succeed."

Damien shook his head. "Killing cops makes martyrs — and more cops with a vengeful attitude to replace them."

Their conversation came to a stop when the secretary returned and handed her boss a brown manila envelope. She then continued down the street to her office.

Damien accepted the envelope and opened it. He caught a glimpse of the RCMP crime report. It was dated yesterday. *Hot off the presses.* He then read the note about Jack Taggart. *Upset about the murder … but doesn't suspect Satans Wrath.*

Moments after Leitch left, Damien sent a BlackBerry message to Lance and Whiskey Jake. Two hours later, when he finished meeting with them, he sent another message: *Mister Taggart, we need to meet!*

The reply was fast. *Excellent idea! How about now? This time, not in your basement!*

Damien sent his response. *Montrose Park — by Second Narrows Bridge — 30 minutes.*

Danny looked across the desk as Jack deleted a message on his BlackBerry and asked, "A message from our friend?"

"Different friend. I want you to drop me off and wait in the car. I'll call you when I'm done."

"Holding out on me?" said Danny light-heartedly, trying to be funny.

"It's Damien," whispered Jack.

"Christ! How did he get your number?"

"I gave it to him."

Danny was taken aback. "You're not meeting him alone. It could be a trap."

"It's not a trap. But you'll keep your trap shut and do as I say."

Danny's heart quickened and the blood vessels in his face revealed his anger. "We're partners. You think you're being macho meeting him alone? Think he'll respect you more? That's not the way to —"

"It has nothing to do with that. It's a personal matter. One I hope to resolve soon. Maybe you should just stay in the office."

Danny paused and then said, "Personal matter?"

Jack didn't respond.

"Damn it, okay. I'll wait in the car. At least I'll be closer if you need help."


It was late in the afternoon when Jack met Damien and they went for a stroll around the small park that faced the Burrard Inlet.

Jack was blunt and to the point. "What the fuck is going on? I knock off a few of your labs and someone tries to kill me!"

Damien let out a snort and said, "Why do so many of you cops feel you have to lard on the tough talk?"

Jack pointed an accusing finger at Damien and said, "I know who was getting rich from those labs!"

Damien smiled briefly and then said, "I understand your thought process. It's logical. There may even be a certain degree of verisimilitude to what you say, but I assure you that I had nothing to do with trying to kill you and don't know who did. You owe me a favour, remember?"

Jack eyed him suspiciously and said, "I haven't forgotten. I've still got your get-out-of-jail-free card tucked in my wallet."

"Good. Then think about it. I can't collect if you're dead."

Jack nodded. "Okay. I just wanted to hear it from you."

"Now you have," replied Damien.

"Speaking of favours, Bishop's body was identified."

"Really? I hear that swimming pools can be dangerous. Are you warm?"

"A little heat. Probably just routine. I think I'm okay now. Made sure I was clean before meeting you."

Damien snorted, then said, "Good. Glad you got a taste of it. I deal with that all the time. Bugging too."

"Don't think I have to worry about that. They would need grounds. But contacting you is a concern."

"The BlackBerry I'm using now is safe," replied Damien. "Doesn't hurt to be cautious, though."

"If you know nothing about whoever tried to kill me, I guess there is no reason for me to contact you." Jack eyed Damien carefully and said, "Unless I catch you doing something illegal and can rid my wallet of your card."

Damien smiled and said, "Good luck. Nailing me isn't going to happen. As far as some of the bros go, think about this. Speed labs are easy to replace — that's if we were in that business. Whacking you isn't a consideration."

Jack received another message on his BlackBerry. It was the code name for Lance, followed by 911. Lance had never used the code before. *Someone's life is in danger! Someone worth saving...*

# *chapter seven*

---

Jack and Danny drove into an underground parking garage and Lance scrambled into the back seat.

"You got a high-level rat!" said Lance, panting as he spoke.

"Tell us something we don't know," replied Danny. "Someone tipped off a couple of those speed labs."

"Not the narc! High level. This one has access to your intelligence reports."

Jack felt the back of his neck tingle. "Details," he asked. "Who? How did you find out?"

"Remember I told you that Whiskey Jake and I had to meet Damien this morning after he met with Leitch?"

Jack nodded.

"Damien showed us a secret RCMP Intelligence report. It was dated yesterday! It was all about the Indos. Laid everything out."

"The Indos?" said Danny.

"What if it had been about the club? I'd be dead right now!"

"Lance, you're forgetting something," said Jack quietly.

"What's that?"

"I said I would always protect you. Bishop wasn't the first guy your club corrupted. He won't be the last. Any reports I write are designed to protect you. I write them as if Damien is already reading them. I don't trust our judicial system not to order them released to some defence lawyer. Trust me on this. Besides, the team working on the Indos has nothing to do with us. At least, not at the moment."

Lance let out a deep breath and sat quietly.

"You okay now?" asked Jack.

"Yeah ... I'm okay."

"What can you tell us about the report?"

"Lots of names, addresses, and stuff. Some in boxes with lines going to circles. Damien refers to the leak as *The Mole*. I think it came via Leitch because he just got it. I read it a couple of hours ago but was with Whiskey Jake and I couldn't call you until now."

"Where is the report now?" asked Jack.

"Damien kept it, but I think he might hand it off to Pussy Paul for safekeeping. That's not all the meeting was about. Damien is setting up our corporate guidelines. He laid it all out. I suggest you make notes or you won't remember."

Jack glanced at Danny and gave a slight nod of his head. Danny removed his notebook and pen.

1) *Lance and Whiskey Jake to be project leaders responsible for overall day-to-day operations.*
2) *Union control, especially at the ports and airport, to be handled by Brutus.*

3)  *Elite mobile hit squad for Western Canada to be formed and run by Rellik, who also has president status. They will be their own chapter unto themselves with no official clubhouse.*

"Rellik?" asked Jack.

"Yeah," replied Lance. "Got that nickname because he's dyslexic."

Lance continued and Danny kept writing.

4)  *Surveillance and wiretap to be done/overseen by Sparks. Top priority is the Vietnamese.*

"The Vietnamese," said Danny. "I thought Damien was interested in the Indos!"

"You guys are doing a pretty good job on the Indos for us. If we go to war and the Indos form an alliance with the Vietnamese, then Damien wants to be prepared."

5)  *Strikers to recruit mules in southern Alberta and Saskatchewan — U.S. border may be easier for smuggling there.*

6)  *Pussy Paul to continue handling strip clubs and prostitution and is in charge of intelligence. Actively recruits people with no records to get jobs with the police, judiciary, Motor Vehicle Branch, telephone companies, etc. Handling of police and judiciary sources will be decided on a case-by-case basis. Important ones will always have a go-between so they won't be caught dealing with any club members.*

"How are they recruited?" asked Danny.

"The usual. Sex, money, blackmail, gambling debts, intimidation — whatever works."

"Intimidation?" commented Danny.

"Yeah. Some coppers are intimidated so they kind of suck up to us. We start them off by being friendly and maybe getting them to do small favours. You know, dropping some chicken-shit ticket or something. Takes time, but then we work our way up to more serious matters. Pussy Paul recruited The Mole, but I don't know what was used as incentive."

Danny put the cap on his pen, but Lance said, "Don't put your pen away yet. I got some more leaks to warn you about, but I don't know their names. All being handled through Pussy Paul somehow."

7) *One Supreme Court judge — financial incentive.*
8) *One RCMP narc — unknown recruitment method.*
9) *A secretary with VPD — thinks she's in love.*
10) *Close to turning a VPD detective working Vice — sexual inducement.*

"That pretty well wraps it up for now," said Lance.

"What about drugs? Who looks after that?" asked Danny.

"We try to keep that down to individual cells as much as possible. That way if a couple are busted they won't be able to link it to the rest of the club. There is some overlapping. Big projects like the ships coming in ... well, that's treated a little different."

"How so?" asked Jack.

"All the chapters in Canada are invested in those, but smaller amounts are divided into smaller groups. Naturally, we are all brothers and stand behind each other. If someone is having a problem with distribution or competition, the club name in itself is usually enough to see that we get our way. If our name is not enough, then anyone who is needed will step in to do whatever needs to be done."

"Like Rellik," said Jack.

"Exactly. So what do ya think? Enough to keep ya busy for a while?"

"Not enough to keep us busy. Just food for thought," replied Jack.

"This won't keep you busy?"

"We'll try to identify them, but I don't see a lot that we can do without risking you getting burned."

Lance nodded and said, "Appreciate that. I wouldn't have known this stuff if I hadn't just made president. You start a witch hunt and Damien would put it together in two seconds."

"You think you'll be going to war with the Indos soon?" asked Jack.

"Damien says it's inevitable, but with two more ships arriving in the next couple of weeks, he doesn't want the war to start any time soon."

Danny gestured to the last four entries in his notebook and asked, "Does Pussy Paul handle these sources direct?"

Lance glanced at the notes and said, "Naw, he would stay insulated. Most of the communication would go through someone else. Usually someone of the opposite sex, but these days, who knows."

After some further discussion about union affiliation for targeted interests and overseas expansion, Lance opened the door to get out but stopped and said, "Oh yeah, almost forgot to tell ya. There's something else." He waited until Danny retrieved his notebook again.

11) *Damien to handle public relations in the event*
    *of any bad press on the club. Might also arrange*

*some charity drive as a result of the bad press
from the labs being taken down.*

Jack and Danny arrived back at the office and Jack
said, "Take out your notebook, I want you to make
another entry."

"Sure," said Danny, pulling out his notebook. "Okay,
what?"

*"Source advises he might be able to set up Lance
and Damien but is concerned about being identified."*

Danny grinned when he understood Jack's comment. If his notebook ever fell into the wrong hands or
was ordered revealed by some judge, then the bad guys
would think Whiskey Jake was the informant.

Moments later, Jack and Danny told Louie what
they had learned.

"I think the report on the Indos came from Dick
Molen," said Jack. "The Mole ... Molen. Think about
it. The report is fresh, and two days ago Molen asked
me how I knew about the speed labs."

"What did you say?" asked Danny.

"I told him it was through surveillance. He volun-
teered to assist. I thought it strange then because I
hardly know the guy, but I passed it off as someone else
wanting to help."

"What can we do about him?" asked Danny. "If we
do anything, we risk burning our friend."

"First let's confirm it's Molen," said Louie. "If it
is, he will slowly have to be neutralized. All reports
to him will have to be sanitized. I'll speak to Isaac. If
it's him, then down the road we could have him
transferred someplace — like Highway Patrol on
Baffin Island."

"This will have to be handled with extreme care,"
said Jack. "Our friend's life depends upon it."

"I fully understand. We could start by submitting a false report and see where it ends up. Something juicy to demand immediate action."

"I like that idea," said Jack. "Maybe indicate the Indos are about to do a hit next week. Speculate that it might be on the bikers. A day or so later, follow it up with another report to indicate that the hit is on some low-level trafficker behind on his debts."

"Good," said Louie. "I don't want to scare anyone into starting a war."

"That would get messy," said Jack. "Satans Wrath has generally learned to be precise, but the Indos have a flair for drive-by shootings. Innocent people could get killed."

Louie reached for his phone and said, "I'll try and meet with Isaac now. Tomorrow is Friday. If Isaac agrees, we could provide Molen with the fake report first thing Monday morning."

"Good enough," said Jack, "except I have a funeral to go to tomorrow."

Louie understood. "No worries. I'll look after it."

"There's always worries," replied Jack. "Our friend is in a hell of a position."

"Yeah, a great position for us," said Danny.

"See if you feel that way when he starts fulfilling the responsibilities associated with his position," replied Jack.

Louie gestured for them to be quiet as he spoke with Isaac. He hung up and said, "All of us have an immediate audience. Wants to hear a shortened version now, with a written report to follow."


Jack sat forward in the stuffed leather chair and quickly provided Isaac with the organizational structure and history of Satans Wrath.

Isaac listened carefully to Jack's words. "They have their own hit squad, surveillance teams, and intelligence unit ... which is highly funded," Jack added.

A flicker of Isaac's eyes told Jack that his point had been heard. He then continued, "For their intelligence unit, corruption and knowledge of the enemy is the name of the game. They are actively targeting transportation systems. Currently, they have some influence over the unions, particularly at the docks, and are working on the airports, railways, and trucking firms. They're also expanding elsewhere."

"Such as?" asked Isaac.

"Anything to do with import and export. Downtown Vancouver is the western terminus for CN and CP Rail. We have Canada's largest deep-sea ports and are the gateway to the Orient. Deep-sea freighters exchange products from all over the world here. With Seattle just spitting distance away, large amounts of goods are shipped back and forth by truck and rail."

"These fellows certainly aren't sluggish when it comes to expansion," commented Isaac.

"There's more," said Jack. "The Trans-Canada Highway and U.S. Interstate Highway system are also vital links. Vancouver airport is continually expanding to provide international air cargo and passenger transportation across the Pacific and to Europe. Feelers have already been put out with the Russian mafia for potential partnerships. On the home front, they've set their sights on politicians. Control of the unions helps with that, since politicians don't like strikes."

Leitch sipped on his Starbucks cappuccino and listened carefully as Ray passed on the instructions from The Boss. The anonymous note to RCMP Homicide would be sent immediately. Leitch was all too familiar with police investigative techniques. *No prints. Leave no DNA under the seal. Use common bond paper.*

"So you see," said Ray, "the mistaken hit is no longer a mistake. It has worked in our favour. Who would have guessed that such a minor error would cause a policeman to grieve? You would think he would have been pleased that it was not him. It's really quite extraordinary how the police react in this country."

Leitch politely nodded his head in agreement, but his thoughts were still on delivering the message.

"I must admit, The Boss has come up with an excellent idea. We will make it look intentional. Murdered simply because he had the same name. Ensure that the police realize that no harm will befall Officer Taggart. Soon, it will be someone he works with or perhaps a friend or loved one. He will become a pariah. Let it be warning to any other officer who is energetic regarding organized crime that they may expect the same."

"Organized crime is so general," said Leitch, "that they won't —"

"Precisely! They won't know who to blame. Is it Satans Wrath? The Indos, Russians, Vietnamese — who? I think it is quite entertaining, really. Who cares if they do blame any of those groups? It won't really affect us. The Boss is right. Why turn Taggart into a hero?"

"This will cause quite a stir," said Leitch.

"Fear: it is the first step in making the law ineffective. The judiciary already appears indifferent. Why, as a policeman, would you want to risk your life or that of your loved ones? They will be both afraid and demoralized."

Leitch thought about it. *The police will concentrate on criminals at the bottom end, who will flourish as a consequence. Legal aid will pay well!*

"Are you listening?" asked Ray.

Leitch put his dream on hold and quickly looked up and nodded.

"Naturally," continued Ray, "we will follow up quickly by disposing of someone connected with Taggart. With his feelings of sympathy for the widow, I bet the chap shows up at the funeral tomorrow."

# *chapter eight*

T here were only a few days left in April. The leaves
had been out on most of the trees for a month and the
Japanese plum trees were in full bloom. Despite an
unusual surge of cold weather, it was a beautiful, sunny
morning. *Too nice*, thought Jack, *to be put in a coffin at
the age of thirty-two and lowered into the ground.* He
felt Natasha put her arm around him and he did the
same with her.

The church had been crowded, mostly with people
who had read about the incident and felt a need to
show compassion.

The news media made up the rest of the crowd.
He saw Holly clutching Jenny to her side. *They look
so all alone...*

He thought of Charlie in intensive care. *Maybe just
as well. To see him sitting here ... in a wheelchair at his
father's grave ... I couldn't handle it.*

As the casket was lowered deeper into the earth, he heard Susan sob and instinctively put his other arm around her shoulders, but felt Danny's arm and withdrew his own. He glanced down at Tiffany, who was clinging to her mother's leg. Susan was holding Jimmy close to her breast and Jack knew Tiffany felt left out. He nudged her and held out two fingers. It made him feel better when she latched on.

At the conclusion to the service, Jack, Natasha, and the O'Reillys walked down the street toward their cars. Jack's cellphone vibrated and he answered.

"Oh, I say, ol' chap, who have I reached here?"

"Jack Taggart."

"Dreadfully sorry, I think I have the wrong number."

Jack hung up and saw Holly approaching. She was pushing an elderly woman in a wheelchair and Jenny was walking beside her. She gestured for Jack to wait.

"Thank you for coming," she said. "I appreciated seeing at least one face in the crowd that I recognized."

Jack introduced Holly and Jenny to Natasha, Danny, and Susan.

Holly looked at the elderly woman and said, "This is Jack's mom. Mom, this is..." She stopped, not knowing what to say.

Jack was taken aback for a moment as the realization sunk in, then he stuck out his hand and said, "You're Jack Taggart's mother..."

She politely took his hand and tearfully said, "George couldn't be here today. He's too sick, you know. I must get back to him."

"I understand," said Jack.

"I think we should go," said Holly. "Thanks again for coming. Thanks to all of you."

As Holly wheeled Mrs. Taggart away, Jack heard her ask, "Who was that, dearie? You didn't tell me his name."

Jack felt a flood of emotion at Holly's response. It made him feel better but also caused him to bite the end of his tongue to keep from crying.

"A friend of the family, Mom. Just a friend."

Natasha kissed him on the cheek and whispered, "Guess you were right, coming here."

Jack's cellphone vibrated again.

"Sorry, have I dialled the same wrong number again?"

"You have," replied Jack, and hung up. He then walked Natasha over to her car so that she could drive to work.

"Jack!" Susan yelled. "Why don't you come to our place now? I'll make sandwiches for lunch and you can stay for dinner. We're having a roast with Yorkshire pudding. There will be lots."

Jack's reply was interrupted by a car horn. He saw that the driver had protested his annoyance at being cut off when a green van with tinted windows pulled out from the curb in front of him. A fist, with the middle finger pointing upward, briefly extended out the van window.

Jack accepted Susan's invitation before kissing Natasha goodbye and walking back to his own car.


Albert Dawson stood beside the bed and brushed the hair back from his wife's face. At eighty-six years of age, Esther was two years younger than her husband. She couldn't ignore the pain in her hip any longer and reluctantly decided to follow the doctor's advice and stay off it for a few days. It was almost noon and the warm sun coming through the window added to her dismay.

Albert saw the frustration in her face. "Won't be long, Essie, and you'll be up and about. I'll make you some soup and tea when I come back. Then I'll read to you."

"Take your time. I'll entertain the mailman while you're gone," she replied, sounding gruff.

Albert gave his wife a look of loving devotion brought on by sixty-seven years of marriage.

Esther stared back. She was legally blind and could not see his face, but she remembered the look well and sensed it. She imagined it more as his warm hand squeezed her shoulder and in the gentle kiss that followed. Albert then stood upright, using his cane to steady his balance.

In 1944, Albert had been a rear gunner in a Lancaster flying over Germany. He was smaller and thinner than most men, which suited his cramped quarters in the Lancaster just fine. Unfortunately his position also caused him to receive a fist-sized piece of shrapnel to his knee. Pain was something he had long learned to live with.

"Mailman, aye! If he's here when I get back I'll kick his ass."

Essie chuckled as Albert left the room.

Moments later, Albert carefully locked the door to the house and headed down the street.

The mall was only two blocks from their house, but Albert was the sociable type. What would have been a quick stop at an ATM and a drug store for most people took him considerably longer. It was an hour before he returned home and stepped inside.

"Essie! What's this mail bag doing in the living room?" he yelled.

"Quick, my husband's home! Hide under the bed!" came her staged whisper from the bedroom.

Albert's eyes twinkled as he was about to reply, but he was interrupted by a knock on the door. It was a man with a knife.

# *chapter nine*

---

Jack was glad that Natasha was off for the weekend. They spent it together, trying out a few new recipes that they paired with an appropriate wine. It gave them a chance to talk and unwind a little. For a brief period of time, Jack's brain overruled his heart and told him that the funeral was linked to him in name only.

By Monday morning, Jack was feeling somewhat refreshed and was waiting when Louie arrived at work.

"You're early," commented Louie, hanging up his jacket on a hook behind the door. "How did the funeral go on Friday?"

"It went," Jack replied, then paused and asked, "Molen ... is it set?"

"Told you I would look after it. I did. He'll get the fake report this morning. Anti-Corruption is handling the investigation. How do you feel about the meeting with Isaac last Thursday?"

"It was okay. I agree with the game plan for Molen, but we need to tread carefully."

Louie looked at Jack and quietly replied, "I think *you* need to tread very carefully."


Connie Crane didn't arrive at work until almost noon. She had worked all weekend. The murder of an elderly war veteran had enraged her. She knew she might as well work because she was too angry to sleep.

The media clamoured for every ugly detail they could learn. Connie was generous with what she gave them. The details would sicken the public. Anyone with a shred of humanity who knew anything should call. She was right. One tipster was not satisfied to talk to someone handling the tip line. She wanted to talk to the investigator in charge.

Connie took the call and listened to the woman. She sounded like she smoked six packs a day.

"Listen, I'm just an addict," she said. "I know nobody will believe me, but..."

Connie rolled her eyes. *Crack whore! You're right. I'm busy; let's get to the point.* She interrupted and said, "How much money are you looking to be paid? I don't work drugs. Not sure what a rock sells for these days."

"Listen, bitch! I don't want no money for this! Just because I'm a fuckin' addict don't mean I don't have a conscience! I'm also dying of fucking throat cancer so I really don't need this extra crap. If you ain't interested in me telling you who did it, then I'll hang up!"

"Don't do that," said Connie. "Please. I'm sorry. You're right. I haven't slept all weekend and I'm feeling grumpy. What do you have to tell me?"

Connie hastily scribbled notes as the tipster talked. *Is this some hooker with a grudge against her pimp — or someone else?* She took the details and handed them to a colleague to check out. Wasn't much to go on. Just a nickname: Spider. The tipster said he hung out at a skid-row bar on East Hastings called the Black Water. *A long way from where Essie fell out of bed, crawled over to her husband, and felt his gurgling windpipe. Then heard a man laugh and felt him rip the pendant off her neck...*

Connie saw a sealed envelope addressed to her at the office. She opened it and read the typed letter. It was about another murder. Details of how Holly's husband was murdered, including hold-back information that had never been revealed to the media. It talked about Jack Taggart and how people associated with him would soon be dying, along with acquaintances of other organized crime investigators. She carefully placed the letter down on her desk and reached for her phone.

The meeting was held in the boardroom and included Isaac, Louie, Jack, Danny, Connie, and several I-HIT investigators, including Randy Otto.

Jack heard what Connie had to say and briefly closed his eyes as a corner of his brain said *I told you so! Holly's husband ... Charlie ... because of you.*

"Sir," said Louie. "If Jack is transferred, this threat will only perpetuate. We're dealing with a terrorist. It will only get worse if we capitulate."

Isaac didn't respond.

"The note warns anyone working in Intelligence," said Jack. He paused to take a deep breath, then continued, "With the number of people in our office, there's no way we could protect everyone, let alone their families and friends. Even if we did, it would effectively shut down our office. We have to continue working the way we are."

"I agree," said Isaac, "but I want you in particular to keep an extremely low profile until we solve this matter."

Jack knew he would not be able to convince Isaac otherwise so said, "Yes, sir. I agree that would be prudent. The note indicates that the victim was killed simply for having my name. That doesn't make sense. We're dealing with someone whose ego is so big that they simply won't admit it was a mistake."

"I agree," said Isaac, "and someone with an ego like that will likely try to carry through with his threat in order to authenticate this letter."

"Sir, it goes without saying," said Randy, "that I have every person in my office working on this."

"Good. Don't worry about the overtime. Consider it approved."

Jack thought for a moment and then glanced at Danny and said, "Maybe I should go solo for a while."

Danny shook his head and said, "I don't scare that easy. Besides, as you said, the note threatens our whole office. We would have to either shut the whole office down or stay inside and play solitaire — exactly what this person wants."

"Who do you suspect is behind this?" asked Isaac.

"Not Satans Wrath," said Jack, wondering if he had blurted that out too soon.

"What other crime families have you been actively pursuing?" asked Randy.

"I've been working entirely on Satans Wrath."

"If you believe they are not involved with this … threat," said Isaac, "who do you propose as an alternate suspect, then?"

Jack grimaced. His answer was not something that Isaac would like to hear. "I don't know, sir."

When the meeting was over, Jack and Danny returned to their office.

"Forget the low profile," said Jack. "Holly's husband was definitely murdered because of me. This just made it personal! Not to mention, we've got two shiploads of cocaine due any day. This isn't the time for low profile!" Jack grabbed his jacket.

"Where we going?" asked Danny.

Jack shook his head. "I'm going alone to see Holly. Let her know that I am to blame. I'll be back after lunch."

Staff Sergeant Legg called Isaac's secretary, who transferred his call.

"Hello, Harry. What's up?"

"Just heard from my people, sir. Constable Molen is in a coffee shop right now with Lawrence Leitch's secretary. He just handed her an envelope."

"It would appear that Corporal Taggart was correct in his assumption," replied Isaac. "Frankly, I'm a little surprised."

"Why is that, sir?"

"I was in a meeting with him this morning. He was almost protective of Satans Wrath. Tried to assure me they had nothing to do with a threat the office has received. I really would like to find out what Taggart is all about."

"The photos have been passed on to our liaison officer in Mexico City, sir. We should have an answer fairly soon."

"Excellent. Let me know as soon as you hear from the LO."

"Yes, sir. As for now, I'll have my people follow the envelope that Molen handed over. I'll notify you as soon as anything develops in that area as well."

\* \* \*

"Holly doesn't live here anymore," said the landlord. "Who are you?"

Jack showed the man his police identification and was relieved that he didn't notice his name.

"She couldn't hack staying here after what happened. Can't say I blame her. Didn't mind that she didn't give me thirty days' notice. Feel bad about keeping her damage deposit, but the damage to the carpet wasn't my fault."

Jack obtained Holly's new address and then asked, "How much was her deposit?"

"Half a month's rent. Four-seventy-five."

After stopping at a bank, Jack met with Holly, who was living in a one-bedroom apartment just two blocks from her previous address.

Jack was invited inside. He saw Jenny sitting on the sofa watching television with her thumb in her mouth. Holly pulled it out as she walked past and then sat at the kitchen table with Jack. Jenny immediately put her thumb back in.

"She quit doing that two years ago," said Holly. "Just started again after…" Her voice trailed off and she looked around the apartment and said, "I know it's not much, but it's close to Jenny's daycare and I can still walk to work."

Jack leaned across the table and squeezed the top of her hand and said, "It's only been a week. Don't you think you should take some more time off?"

Holly pulled her hand away. "I can't afford to. Sitting around doesn't help. Keeping busy seems to. Between driving back and forth to visit Charlie, looking after Jenny, and going to work, I don't have time to feel sorry for myself."

Jack swallowed, and then said, "Our office received an anonymous letter this morning. It looks like your husband was murdered by mistake. It should have been me." Jack knew his voice sounded shaky. He put his palms down on the kitchen table in an effort to stop himself from trembling.

Holly just looked at him and didn't speak.

"Did you hear me?" asked Jack.

"Yes," she replied, shrugging her shoulders. "It wasn't something I didn't know. My husband was a good man. It wasn't a robbery. It had to be you. I'm glad that you know it too. Maybe now you'll find out who did it."

Jack paused and glanced at Jenny for a moment before turning his attention back to Holly. "I think I knew it the first night I met you. I could see you were decent people, but it … it was … I didn't want to admit that I was responsible."

Holly stared at him as she asked, "What did the letter say? Why would someone commit murder and then write to the police? Are they thinking of confessing?"

"No. They indicated that if our office keeps doing our job, then other police officers or people they love or know will be murdered. I work on an intelligence unit for organized crime. There are lots of potential groups of suspects."

"You mean to say that the people who murdered my husband are also threatening the police?"

"Exactly."

"They must be insane! How do they expect to get away with that?"

"If I have anything to do with it, they won't."

"Quite a few people in your office?"

"Quite a few."

"All with different names, I suppose. Like Smith, Adams, Jones, or whatever."

"Not exactly but … what are you getting at?"

"That enough people in Vancouver share names with people you work with that it would be ludicrous to try and protect them all. You're not to blame for what happened to my family. Do you know that there are at least a half-dozen J. Taggarts listed in the phone book in the lower mainland? Except for you, mine might have been the only Jack."

"I'm not listed in the phone book."

Holly paused and then said, "That figures. But you see what I mean. Taggart isn't even that common of a name."

"Maybe that was the problem."

"Maybe." Holly reached across the table and patted Jack's hand. "I admit that a few days ago I felt like smashing you in the face. Especially when I found out about Charlie. I know it was really mean of me to call you to the hospital that day."

"It's okay. I wanted to know."

"But the way I told you ... that must have been awful."

"Don't worry about me. I understand your anger."

"It wasn't just you. I have moments where I feel angry at the whole world. That day you just happened to be a convenient target to lash out at. In my heart I know it's not your fault."

*Funny, in my heart I think it* is *my fault...*

"What I guess I'm trying to say is that I'm not blaming you. I just want you to catch them."

Jack felt like some of his sorrow had been lifted, but it didn't ease his stress — nor his own anger. He put his other hand on top of hers and said, "Thank you. I promise ... I will get them."

Jack left the apartment after promising Holly he would keep her informed as best he could. She assured him that she would call if she needed help and thanked him for delivering the envelope from her previous landlord.

"Something to do with it being covered by insurance," said Jack.

"Hey, Connie, that name you asked me to check — Spider — got something on him."

Connie took the report and saw that it was an Intelligence report submitted last year by Jack Taggart. It described an individual he identified only as Spider who was a low-level speed dealer in the Black Water Hotel. *Jesus Christ! Did Taggart know the war vet?*

Jack had just arrived back at his office when Connie entered.

"You hear the news about the war vet murdered on Friday?" asked Connie.

"Heard about it on the news."

"Albert Dawson. His wife's name is Essie. Do you know them?"

"No. Why?"

"I'll tell you why. We're approaching close to a hundred murders a year in the lower mainland. Do you know how many murders last year took place at the front door when the victim had just arrived home?"

"No."

"None. Last week, in a period of five days, we've had two."

"What's it got to do with me?"

"You're connected to both murders!"

Jack felt stunned. "I've never met this Dawson fellow! I'm sure of it. If he was murdered because someone thought he was my friend, then they're completely wrong!"

Connie gave Jack a copy of the report he submitted last year about Spider.

"Sure, I know *him*," admitted Jack. "We met last year when I worked undercover in the Black Water.

Doing an Intelligence probe. Bought an ounce of speed off him. Never did find out who he really was. I was after someone else. Spider was just a stepping stone."

Connie told him about her phone call from some raspy sounding hooker who swore Spider killed the vet.

"Spider doesn't even know I'm a cop. I'm sure he didn't do both murders," said Jack. "Besides, he should remember what I look like."

"Holly's husband didn't look that much different than you. He was holding his baby in front of him. The killers were wearing visors. They might not have been able to see all that clearly."

"Spider is no professional. He could donate his brains to the field of scatology."

"So he could be dumb enough to kill the wrong guy? Like Holly's husband?"

"Dumb, yes. But not sophisticated enough to pack a piece with a silencer. Didn't I hear on the news that the vet was stabbed?"

"He was. Small amount of money and a piece of jewellery taken."

"That's something Spider would do, but Holly's husband was a professional hit. Robbery wasn't the motive there. This bit about being killed at the front door is a coincidence."

"And you said that it was a coincidence that your name matched Holly's husband's."

Jack sighed but didn't respond.

"When you were working in the Black Water, wasn't that to work your way up to someone connected with Satans Wrath?"

"Yes. It worked, but that was several steps above Spider."

"Maybe some of those steps have since disappeared. Spider could be more connected than you realize."

Jack shook his head and said, "I don't think so, but I'll go down to the Black Water right now and find out."

"This is what you meant when you told Isaac you would keep a low profile?"

"I said it would be prudent to keep a low profile. I didn't say that I was prudent!"

Connie smiled, then said, "Guess it's your neck. I'd appreciate you coming with me to identify him."

"You'd be made in there. Let me go in alone. Pair up with Danny and wait in a parkade across the street. If Spider's not there, I could wait or ask around without drawing heat."

"That is one sleazy hotel, but if you're okay with that, then so am I. When you find him, let us know and we'll come in and grab him."

"Do you have any evidence on this case?"

"Not really. He did take some cash and a gold pendant in the shape of a heart. It was engraved on the back from when Albert and Essie got married. He ripped it off her neck. Being blind probably saved her life."

"If Spider did it, I doubt that he'll be carrying it around with him. With all the heat he might even be afraid to pawn it right now."

"If he is as dumb as you say, maybe I can get him to confess."

"Right. You know how that goes these days. He'll be sitting on the lap of some legal aid lawyer. How about DNA or prints?"

"No prints. Recovered a single hair that we can't identify. Could be from the perp, but it could also be from someone else. Grab Spider and hope we get a match."

Jack smiled politely, then turned and grabbed his jacket.

Connie stared after him. *The son of a bitch has no intention of grabbing Spider!*

# chapter ten

Jack, Danny, and Connie were leaving the office when Danny saw Elvis Secord approaching and whispered, "Uh-oh. ACU."

"You got a moment, Jack?" asked Elvis. "You too, Danny? It would be better if we talked in Louie's office."

Connie smiled and said, "Take your time, Jack. A moment with Internal Affairs usually means an hour. I'll just sit at your desk and browse through *your* briefcase while I'm waiting."

"It's Anti-Corruption," muttered Elvis under his breath as he turned and headed for Louie's office. When Louie, Jack, and Danny were listening, Elvis told them about Molen.

"We did surveillance. Had people from our unit and I-HIT. Molen met Leitch's secretary in a coffee shop at noon. He gave her a large envelope and left."

"You follow the envelope?" asked Louie.

"Both. We split up the surveillance teams. Some went with Molen and the rest stayed with the envelope. Molen returned to the office and the secretary went to a park and handed the envelope to Leitch."

"Which park?" asked Jack.

"Nelson Park. Corner of Nelson and Thurlow. She then waited while Leitch took a walk in the park. He showed the envelope to an unidentified man, then returned and gave it back to his secretary. She then took it to her bank and put it in her safety deposit box."

"The guy in the park didn't get a copy of the report?" asked Jack.

"No, but it was pretty short. Juicy enough, but short. Might have been able to remember what was in it."

Jack nodded and said, "Well I'm sure that the guy in the park was either Damien or another Satans Wrath member who goes by the name of Pussy Paul."

"One of them a dark guy with a British accent?" asked Elvis.

"No."

"I walked past when they were meeting. I'm sure I heard him say 'jolly good.' Then they looked at me real hard and I just kept going. I'm hoping I didn't get burned."

"I hope not too," said Jack. "Let me show you some pictures."

Elvis spent the next half-hour looking through pictures of Satans Wrath. "Sorry," he said, "don't believe it's any of these. The fellow was quite dark. Maybe Indo. We'll do another report for Molen tomorrow. See what happens then."

"Good luck," replied Jack. "Is Laura still around? Or is she off to Bangkok or someplace again?"

"She's home. Why?"

"Nothing. Just tell her I said hello."

* * *

East Hastings was swarming with a variety of the drug addicts, low-level dealers, pimps, muggers, and prostitutes who laid claim to the area. Drug overdoses, murders, and AIDS took a severe toll, but the population continued to grow.

Jack felt dirty just walking into the Black Water Hotel. Even the regulars considered it a dirty, dangerous place. *I'll be showering tonight as soon as I get home. Maybe after the first shower, Natasha will join me for the second...*

The place had not changed any since last year. Pot lights marked a stage in the centre of the bar where a stripper was performing. She wore only a variety of tattoos and stood gyrating her crotch against a pole that ran up to the black ceiling before disappearing amongst the broken cardboard tiles. She didn't have much of an audience.

Jack sauntered to the rear of the bar where the pool tables were located. He didn't see Spider but did recognize the face of someone he had continually lost money to when he played pool last year. The man recognized him and was eager to continue making money.

The waitress came along a few minutes later. She also recognized him but didn't know his name. "Hey! Mister Kokanee, right?" she said.

Jack smiled. Like most waitresses, she knew her clients by what they drank.

"Haven't seen ya around for a while." she said.

"Ya, you know. Been travelling around the world. Staying in my penthouse suites as I go."

The waitress laughed, then said, "Good one. You'll be able to drop me a tip then."

Halfway through losing at pool, Jack casually asked if Spider had been around.

"Was here about an hour ago, don't know where he went."

Jack continued to sip beer and continued to lose at pool. Numerous hookers made eye contact with him but a subtle shake of his head indicated he wasn't interested. His mind drifted to what Elvis had told him about Leitch's contact in the park. *Is Leitch playing both sides? Wanting to represent the Indos and the bikers? Dangerous territory for a lawyer to be in.*

Spider did not return and it was long past midnight when Jack arrived home. Natasha was sleeping so he quietly slipped into the shower. When he stepped out to reach for a towel, she was standing in the doorway wearing a fluffy white bathrobe. "Remember me?" she asked.

"You sort of look familiar. Did you follow me home from the Black Water?"

"Noooo. Guess again."

"Your face is familiar, but I'm not sure. Maybe if I was to see a little more of you."

"Like this?" said Natasha, slipping the robe off her shoulders and letting it droop to reveal the tops of her breasts.

"Exactly ... but I still can't quite put my finger on it."

The bathrobe fell around her feet and Jack took a moment to reflect upon how beautiful she was ... *and how lucky I am that she loves me.*

"Perhaps you can't put your finger on it," said Natasha, "but it would appear that another part of your body is rising to the challenge."

Their bed was only a few steps away, but it was a few steps too far. They made love on Natasha's bathrobe. When they were finished, Natasha snuggled in with her head on Jack's chest. He covered her with part of her robe, and then they both fell asleep.

In the morning Natasha put on a pot of coffee. She did not have to be at work until after lunch. She was pleased that she had convinced Jack to spend the morning with her.

Jack walked into the kitchen and used the phone to call Danny. Susan answered and said that Danny was in the shower.

"Tell him that we're not starting work until one-thirty today," said Jack.

"Great. I've got shopping to do and he can look after Tiff and Jimmy for me."

"You say he's in the shower?" said Jack, loud enough for Natasha to notice. "Hang on, I should let you speak with Natasha. She'll tell you what you should do when he gets out."

"Jack! Damn it!" said Natasha, as Jack tried to pass her the phone. "No! You are such a turkey!"

"A turkey?" Jack started to laugh, then said, "If I'm a turkey, then so are you for marrying me!"

It had been too long, decided Natasha, since she had seen him laugh. She laughed as well. Not so much over what Jack said, but simply because their life seemed normal again ... at least for now.

They had a leisurely breakfast and Jack told Natasha about his visit with Holly yesterday and her response to what he had told her.

"Now you know it's not your fault," commented Natasha.

"Part of my brain tells me that. Sometimes another part makes me question the consequences of what I do."

"You do what you think is right. You weren't born with crystal balls ... thank heavens."

Jack smiled and said, "I know. Things just don't turn out as I plan sometimes. I need to think more about potential consequences."

"How about the potential consequences of another shower?"

It was mid-afternoon when Elvis arrived and motioned for Jack and Danny to follow him to Louie's office.

Elvis ignored Louie's greeting and said, "Things didn't go well. This morning Molen received the second report and delivered it to the secretary. Then he started to act real kinky. Maybe burned the surveillance. Later when the secretary showed the report to Leitch he sent a note on his BlackBerry and then burnt the report in a garbage can."

"Son of a bitch!" said Danny. "Leitch and Satans Wrath are on to us! They'll change how they get the info."

"This could draw some heat on our source," added Jack.

"Listen, fellows," said Elvis, "I'm really sorry if these guys burned our surveillance. I feel pretty bad about it."

"I've been burned on surveillances too," said Jack. "It happens. It was a chance we took when we decided to try this route. I'm not blaming you."

"Appreciate that."

"What are your plans now?" asked Louie.

"I'm going to talk with Legg and recommend that we back off him for a little while. I've checked his file. He has a history of alcohol-related incidents. Maybe people won't put a lot of faith in his paranoia."

"Is he married?" asked Jack.

"Was. Divorced four years ago. No children. What about the other leaks? Anything more on the narc who was recruited?" asked Elvis.

Jack shook his head and then said, "Did you ask Laura for suggestions?"

"We usually agree not to discuss work at home, but this time I made an exception. She said she doesn't know."

It was early evening when Jack walked back into the Black Water. He felt a surge of adrenalin when he saw Spider sitting with a hooker near the pool tables. He walked directly up to him and sat down.

"Remember me?" asked Jack, leaning across the table.

Spider looked a little surprised but sat back in his chair and said, "Yeah, I remember you. Where ya been? You lookin' to score?" he added, before Jack could respond.

*Surprised by my abruptness, but not scared. Just as I thought. He's not involved with anything to do with Holly's husband.*

"Hey, Mister Kokanee! Another?"

Jack nodded to the waitress and tried to turn his attention back to Spider but was interrupted once more by the tap of a pool cue on his shoulder.

"Hey, good buddy! Want a chance to win your money back?"

"Maybe later," said Jack. When the man left, he looked back at Spider and said, "I'm lookin' for somethin', but..." He stopped and gave a subtle nod toward the hooker sitting beside Spider.

Spider waved a hand for Jack to relax and said, "Don't worry about Ophelia here. She's solid. What do you want? Crystal meth?"

"Not now," replied Jack. "Do need to talk to you in private."

"It's okay, guys," said Ophelia, her voice sounding hoarse. "I'm gonna hit the street for a while. Can't even afford a smoke right now," she added, harshly.

Her raspy voice was not lost on Jack. *She's the tip-ster who called Connie!*

"So what ya after?" Spider asked before looking past Jack and yelling, "Hey! Freddy! Hang on!"

Jack turned and saw a man on the other side of the bar yell, "I'm leavin'."

Spider looked at Jack and said, "Hang on. Be right back." He then walked out of the bar with Freddy.

Jack stayed where he was and the hours slowly went by without Spider returning. Jack decided not to play pool tonight and sat waiting. He watched three men, all wearing cheap sports jackets, stagger inside and take a seat closest to the stage. Two had their ties loosened around their necks while the third man had his tie half hanging out the side pocket of his sports jacket. As the night wore on, their catcalls became louder. Occasionally, one or the other would throw loose change at the strippers.

"How ya doin'?" croaked Ophelia, taking a chair beside him.

"Doin' fine. Waiting for Spider. Know where he went?"

Ophelia shrugged and said, "Nope." She pointed to one of the three men hassling the stripper and said, "See the fat guy there?"

"Yeah."

"Flashed his wallet when he bought the last round of beer. Figure he's got at least forty bucks in it. Seein' as you're a friend of Spider's, thought I might let you in on it. We're gonna jump him in the alley. Could maybe use a man. Want in? We'll split it three ways."

Jack shook his head and said, "Thanks. Appreciate the offer but I don't need any cash at the moment."

"Suit yourself," said Ophelia.

Jack watched her speak with others in the bar. Eventually she ended up at a table talking to a skinny junkie. *Fellow looks like he's about to die at the ripe old age of twenty-two*. Then both of them got up and walked past Jack a few steps to the fire escape door at the rear. They stepped outside, letting a girl into the bar as they did.

It didn't appear to bother any of the clientele that the girl was about twelve years old, but it bothered Jack. He had seen child prostitutes before, but that didn't make it any easier. He watched her head straight to the fat man and bend over and whisper in his ear. Then she knelt beside him and ran her hand slowly up the inside of his thigh. Moments later, the girl walked out the back door.

The fat man leaned forward and said something to his two friends. They all laughed, and then the fat man stood up and made his way toward the back door.

*Should I bump into him and pick a fight? Deck him and save him from being another victim in the alley?* Jack felt his frustration grow. *Who is the real victim here? Him ... or the girl?*

"To hell with you, asshole," said Jack under his breath as the man staggered past him. Jack watched as he opened the rear door, blinking his eyes and staring into the darkness.

Immediately a tire iron smashed his face. The sound of his skull crunching above his eye and upper cheekbone was slightly audible. Before he could collapse, a hand appeared out of the darkness, grabbing his collar and jerking him off the back step. The door swung shut.

*God! They didn't even wait for him to step outside! He didn't even get a chance to yell!*

Jack was no stranger to violence, but the sudden brutality in this instance caught him by surprise. *Must not show my feelings...* He looked around the bar. Some of the junkies were looking to see if anyone would react.

Several glanced in his direction. He smiled and held his beer up in a silent toast before taking a sip.

Minutes later, Ophelia and the skinny junkie walked in through the front of the hotel and went straight to a table where a dealer had been busy all night. The skinny junkie hadn't bothered to wipe the spray of blood off his face. Jack watched them make an exchange under the table.

He could feel the knot in his stomach tighten as the crunch of the man's skull continued to echo in his own head. The only ones who hadn't noticed the attack were the two drunk friends up near the stage. One jostled his buddy with his elbow as he stood up and put some money between his teeth. The stripper squeezed her breasts with her hands to grip the money and take it from his mouth.

"Hey! You're still here," said Spider, sitting back down in his chair. "What's up?"

Jack's thoughts returned to the reason he was there. "I'm lookin' for a piece. Have to have it by the day after tomorrow at the latest."

"Don't have a gun." Spider paused as the waitress yelled that it was last call, and then he asked, "What's the rush? Maybe I could help ya if I thought it was worthwhile."

"I've been bangin' this chick for about four months now. She's kinda high class. Got lots of money and a rich husband."

"I'm listenin'."

"She wants him dead. Said there's ten Gs in it for me."

"Ten grand!"

"Keep your voice down," said Jack, looking suspiciously around.

"Why in two days?"

"It's her birthday. She's gonna take the ferry over to Victoria in the morning to visit her mom. Her husband works at home by himself. Does some sort of book-keeping thing. I've sort of been jerking her around for a couple of months. Now she says if it's not done, she'll find someone else. I swore I would do it."

"What's been takin' ya so long? Tryin' to work up the courage to do it?"

Jack looked down at the table as he toyed with his beer and said, "Yeah, I guess. Figure if I get a piece I could just pop him through the window and run. You come up with a piece and I'll pay ya a grand for it."

"Oh, man! That ain't the way to do it! You gotta get up close and personal. Popping him through a window ... you could miss or maybe just wing 'im. Look him right in the eye and take him out. That way ya know ya got him."

"I don't know if I could ... I mean, I think my way is better."

"Forget the piece! You should use a blade. Knock on his fuckin' door, an' when he opens it, thrust deep into his lungs, just under his rib cage. Twist hard a couple of times and pull out. It'll knock the air out of his lungs and he won't be able to yell. He'll grab his gut and bend over. Then bring it up and do his throat. No fuckin' noise. No gun goin' off to freak out the neighbours. I tell ya, that's the way it should be done."

Jack put his hand up to partially cover his eyes and said, "Oh, man. I don't think I could do that. I need a piece."

Spider smiled and said, "Just wait here. I'll do some checkin'. I know everyone in here. If there's one around, I'll find out."

Jack watched as Spider quickly moved amongst a few tables, occasionally glancing back at Jack. Two people at different tables glanced at their watches. *Spider is just asking them the time, pretending to look.* It was what Jack had hoped he would do. He really didn't want him coming back with a gun. *The hook is set.*

Jack went into the men's room and used his cellphone to make a call.

A groggy Elvis answered. "Yeah, she's here. Just a minute." In the background Jack could hear Elvis say, "Hon, wake up, it's Jack Taggart." A moment later, Laura was on the line.

"You offered to help," said Jack.

"What's up?" asked Laura, checking the time. It was after one.

"Need a quick undercover tomorrow."

"I've got court in the afternoon. This the guy who killed your namesake?"

"No, I'm fairly certain it's the guy who did the war vet."

"Oh, man! Glad to be a part of that! What do you need?"

"A girlfriend at about ten o'clock tomorrow morning. Won't take long."

Laura sighed and then asked, "A bimbo?"

"No, a couple levels above. Play the bitch. I want him controlled."

"Waking me up this time of night ... that should come easy tomorrow."

Jack returned to his seat as Spider came up to him. Spider said he couldn't find a gun, but he was able to convince Jack to let him meet Jack's girlfriend tomorrow morning at ten.

Jack checked his watch as he left the bar. It had been twenty minutes since the sound of a crunching skull had started echoing in his head. He crossed the street to the parking garage and jogged up to the second level. He told Connie and Danny about his meeting with Spider and described Spider's recommendation on how to murder someone.

"It's him," said Connie. "That is exactly how Albert Dawson was killed. We've never released that information. Nobody knows that except the killer."

"Good," said Jack, still distracted by what he knew was in the alley behind the hotel.

"Jack!" continued Connie. "This is great! You've got the son of a bitch! I had a feeling that you had something up your sleeve."

"Laura will do a number on him tomorrow morning," replied Jack. "Then he will be…" The sounds of sirens and a police car racing past, accompanied by squealing tires as it turned at the corner and then again into the alley behind the bar, interrupted Jack's conversation.

"Wonder what's going on?" said Danny, as both he and Connie looked at Jack.

Jack shrugged to indicate that he didn't know.

# *chapter eleven*

It was nine-thirty in the morning when Jack and Laura walked into the coffee shop and took a seat. Jack ordered a coffee, black. Laura ordered tea.

"So tell me," said Jack. "What's it like, you being a narc while being married to someone in Internal?"

"Elvis is on the Anti-Corruption Unit."

"Right. ACU ... the serious stuff members are investigated for. IA's big brother."

"You got it."

"Do you walk around the house constantly checking to see if he is watching you? Come on, a narc and ACU ... that's like trying to mix oil and vinegar."

Laura chuckled and said, "Actually, that makes a good salad dressing. I think the expression is oil and water." Laura took a sip of tea and said, "You're right, our marriage is a little like an oxymoron. I'm not sure about ACU, but I'm sure half of the files IA has come from Drug Section."

"Pretty wild bunch sometimes. Work hard, play harder."

"You ought to know. As I recall, you were one of the wildest when you were on the section. I was a little freaked out the first time I met you."

"Come on, I wasn't that wild."

"You were! Tell me, are you still drinking tequila?"

"No," replied Jack. "Decided it was too hard on my stomach. I've switched to olive soup."

"Olive soup?" Laura paused, then smiled and said, "More commonly known as martinis."

Jack nodded.

"Sounds like that new wife of yours has brought a little culture into your life."

Jack smiled but didn't reply.

"You're right about Drugs," said Laura. "It hasn't changed much. Sometimes I think IA is needed to tone things down a bit. Unfortunately, ACU is also needed on occasion."

"Hope you know I was just kidding about Elvis. Believe me, I know they're needed. I gave Elvis a little work just the other day."

Jack saw Laura look at him sharply and quickly added, "Not me! I mean I gave him a good target. Someone leaking information to a biker lawyer."

"Leitch?"

"That's the one. I hope Elvis nails him."

"If someone is dirty, Elvis will get him. He's good at what he does."

"Your husband seems like a good guy ... just don't tell anyone I said that. Ruin my rep."

Laura snickered and then said, "He's a *great* guy." She stirred her tea and said, "I have to admit that the work has affected our relationship a little. We always used to talk and made a rule not to go to bed with any unresolved issues. Now, with the differences in our work, minor stunts that some of the narcs pull, we try not to discuss our jobs. I like to think I'm a good operator, but I can't fool Elvis. He's pretty observant. He picks up on things. Seems to know whether I'm upset with work or with life."

"With life?"

"I was upset the other night and tried to hide it. Know that old expression 'a penny for your thoughts'?"

Jack nodded.

"We use it sometimes. When I went to go to bed the other night I found a penny on my pillow. Elvis just looked at me ... then I lost it and cried. I hadn't wanted to talk about it, but it was good that I did. I was upset that I had started my period. It was late and this time I thought I was pregnant for sure. He just held me and we talked. Think we'll go the adoption route."

Laura stared into the bottom of her teacup and added, "I really love the guy." She was quiet for a moment before asking, "So how's it been going with you? Your face looks a little gaunt. Actually you look awful. Everything okay at home?"

"Natasha and I are getting along great. I love her so much. Still feel like we're on our honeymoon ... even better. More relaxing than the honeymoon was."

"The job, then?"

Jack nodded. "It bothers me that a family was destroyed because some psycho thought it was me. They were a great family. Now Holly's on her own, barely scraping by and trying to raise a four-year-old. Both of them are suffering from post-traumatic stress. Meanwhile, her other baby is in intensive care and will end up in a wheelchair when he's big enough to handle one."

Laura's face showed her sorrow. "Jack, I don't know what to say to —"

"Hang on, here he comes," said Jack.

Laura took a deep breath and assumed her new role. "He does have an attitude, doesn't he?" she whispered, as Spider swaggered over.

Jack smiled and gestured for Spider to sit down.

"So this is him!" said Laura sarcastically. "Doesn't look like you described!"

Spider looked a little taken aback, but before he could respond, Laura said, "So you two have known each other for over ten years, is that right?"

Jack quickly interjected, "He's okay, sweetie. Honest, we go way back!"

"Really? Tell you what, babe, I'll talk to him alone for a few minutes. Go sit on the other side for a bit."

Jack hesitated, and then Spider leaned over and whispered in Jack's ear, "It's okay, man. It'll be better this way."

"You sure?" asked Jack.

"Yeah, I can handle her. I trust my instincts."

Jack took his coffee and moved to another table. He watched as Spider talked earnestly with Laura. Less than two minutes later, Spider reached into his pocket and handed Laura a gold chain and heart-shaped pendant.

Laura motioned with her finger for Spider to lean forward so she could whisper something to him. When he did, she grabbed him by the hair and smashed his face into the table while sticking the barrel of her 9mm in his ear.

Jack was on his feet, as were Connie and three of her colleagues who had been sitting at a couple of other tables.

They need not have rushed. Spider was too shocked to move. He would never trust his instincts again.

* * *

Late that afternoon, back at the office, Connie called
Jack to thank him.

"The dumb shit gave Laura the pendant he stole.
Told her it was a birthday present for her. Tried to file
off the numbers on the back but the lab will pull them
up. He's confessing to everything he's done, hoping to
get concurrent time."

"That's good. Obviously he doesn't have legal
aid yet."

"He waived it. The judge will probably be pissed off
that we didn't force him to get one. Makes it easy for his
lawyer to say he was intimidated and rule it inadmissi-
ble. Hope the DNA pans out. I know his lawyer will tell
him to say he bought the pendant from someone else."

"You've still got Laura and me to give evidence."

"Yeah, but you know how that goes. They'll say he
made up the story, either to impress you or because he
was scared of you."

"The normal defence to an undercover operation
on a murderer. If the jury believes it, they deserve to live
with spiders."

"I know. Still, I prefer to see justice."

"Me too. Sounds like you've done everything you
can. Let's hope the DNA is a match."

"That would be nice. Unfortunately your good friend
Spidey had nothing to do with killing Holly's husband."

"I figured that."

"He said he hopped the commuter train to go to
the suburbs and do some break-ins. He saw Albert go
to an ATM and picked him because he was old. Said he
needed the money because the price of speed went up
after all those labs got taken down last week."

Jack briefly closed his eyes and massaged his temple
with one hand. *So if I hadn't taken the labs down,
Albert Dawson would still be alive...*

"Anyway, I have one other thing to ask," continued Connie. "Don't know if you heard the news this morning on the radio, but there was a murder outside the Black Water last night. I called City. That was what the sirens were about when we were leaving. It had to have happened when you were there. Do you know anything that would help?"

Jack let out a long sigh, then said, "I might have a possible lead. Let me check it out. I'll pop down there tomorrow. There might be someone I could chat with."

## *chapter twelve*

The next afternoon, Jack told Danny he had some personal business to take care of and left the office. He stopped at a red light and thought about why Albert Dawson had died.

A blast from a horn behind him caused him to jerk, and the tires squealed as he drove through the intersection. When he arrived at the Black Water, he parked in the rear alley. *If Ophelia isn't here, I'm not waiting around!*

Jack strolled through the bar. He saw Ophelia and motioned her to come and sit with him at table near the rear exit.

"Yeah, what do ya want?" she asked.

"Have you heard from Spider?"

"Naw. Haven't seen 'im yet today."

"You're not going to," said Jack, showing her his identification.

"Oh, fuck," said Ophelia, her voice sounding like the blade of a snow truck on a bare street.

"You know why I'm here?"

"Can't believe I was that stupid to ask you to pipe that guy with me. That's my fuckin' luck!" she added.

"The young girl with you. What's her —"

"Aw, man, leave her be. She had nothing to do with it. Didn't know what was going on."

"Yeah, right. Do you think I'm blind?"

"Come on, man. Give her a break. She's just a kid. Here, take me," she said, holding her wrists out over the table to be handcuffed. "I won't cause a fuss."

"I know you're the one who dropped a quarter on Spider."

Ophelia's eyes widened. "Fuck! Don't say that too loud," she said, glancing around. Then she admitted, "Yeah. Glad you got him." She slowly put her hands down and then asked, "You did get him, right?"

"We did. So tell me, why did you turn him in ... for free?"

"He's scum. What the news said he did to that old guy…. Just because I'm an addict doesn't mean I don't give a shit about people."

"Where was your compassion when you killed an innocent man two nights ago?"

"Innocent! That fucker wasn't innocent! You see the age of the girl he wanted to fuck?"

Jack nodded.

"And she was older than some of the ones he's had. Do you know what that's like for a kid to go through?"

"I can only imagine."

"Yeah? Well you're lucky, cuz I do know what it's like to turn tricks at that age!"

"That's what I figured," said Jack.

"Yeah, well ... life sucks." She held out her wrists

again and said, "Go ahead. For the time I have left, maybe three meals a day won't hurt."

Jack shook his head and said, "Child molesters aren't high up on my Christmas list. As far as I'm concerned, justice has been served. See you around."

Jack stood up to go, and Ophelia said, "You mean you're not going to arrest me?"

"No, but keep this conversation between the two of us. Have a nice day."

"I owe ya one," she said.

"Yeah, I'll hold my breath waiting for the phone to ring," said Jack. He pushed open the rear door to step outside.

A woman with two preschool children stood in the back alley. She was weeping while placing a bouquet of flowers on the ground.

"Ophelia, come here." Jack motioned her over.

Ophelia came to the door and looked out.

They listened as the woman explained to the children that Daddy was in heaven now.

"Fuck," whispered Ophelia. "Her ol' man paid extra to ride bareback. That's why he liked them young. Thought he wouldn't get AIDS. What a chump. I know the kid has it. Maybe you should tell his ol' lady there to get checked."

Jack watched as Ophelia turned and walked back to her table.

He was just stepping out the door when he received a call on his cellphone.

"Hi ... uh, it's Holly," she said, not wanting to say his name. "You said you would help me, so..."

"What is it, Holly?"

"I'm sorry. I'm at the hospital but my car won't start. Then I went and locked my keys inside. Jenny needs to be picked up from daycare. They won't wait. Can you ... I don't know what to do."

"Stay at the hospital. Call the daycare and tell them I'll pick up Jenny. We'll meet you at the hospital. If we can't get it started, I'll give you a ride home."

"You sure? If you're busy..."

"A taxi would cost a fortune and buses would take longer. I'm not busy. I'm really glad you called. I need a break from work."

"Thanks." She gave Jack directions to the daycare. When she was finished, she said, "There's one other thing."

"What's that?"

"Is it okay if I don't call you Jack? Like ... do you have a nickname that you wouldn't mind being called?"

"My middle name is Bruce. Sometimes my friends call me J.B."

"Like the scotch?"

"Yes, like the scotch," said Jack, watching as the woman led the children down the alley.

"Well, guess I'm your friend ... so that's what I'll call you."

Jack paused for a moment, then said, "Thanks."

"For what?"

"I think you know."

Jack's thoughts were on Ophelia and the woman in the alley as he drove to the daycare. He grabbed his cellphone and called Connie Crane.

"I checked out the Black Water regarding the guy found in the alley," said Jack.

"Any luck?"

"Dead end."

"Well, thanks for trying."

"Victim Services involved with the wife?"

"I presume so. It's a City case. He was married?"

"Yes. His wife and two kids were laying flowers where his body was found."

"Too bad. Hope they solve it."

"Pass on to City to have Victim Services contact the wife's doctor. She should be checked for AIDS."

"I know the bar is sleazy, but just for having a beer?"

"It was more than beer," Jack said, then hung up.

Connie stared at the telephone still in her hand. *Tell me again it was a dead end ... lying son of a bitch.*


Jack picked Jenny up on schedule and explained that they were going to meet her mommy at the hospital.

The trip was uneventful as Jenny tried to impress Jack with everything she knew, including her ability to count and to sing nursery rhymes.

They were just pulling into the hospital lot when Jenny asked, "Are you going to be my new daddy, now?"

Jack felt a pang of guilt, then said, "No, I'm married to another lady. But if your mom says it's okay, I could sort of be like an uncle to you."

"What's a dunkle?"

"Not ... never mind, there's your mom now."

Locked cars were something that Jack was experienced with. It took him only a few seconds to gain entry.

"Why do I even bother to lock it?" asked Holly.

"Keeps the honest people out," replied Jack.

"Not that. I mean it's just a piece of junk. No decent car thief would want to be seen in it."

Jack made a quick examination under the hood and discovered that the battery was as old as the car. He told her that she would just need a boost and that he would call a tow truck. He suggested that Holly and Jenny wait in the hospital. It was rush hour and the tow truck might be a while.

Jack sat briefly in his own car to use his cellphone. A tow truck would be along in an hour, as soon as the new battery was charged. He gave them his cell number and told them to call when they arrived.

Jack met Holly in the reception area and they went to see Charlie. Jenny clung to her mother's leg, sucking her thumb as they walked.

Jack heard Charlie before he saw him. He was under enough medication to stop him from crying, but not from whimpering.

Tears filled Holly's eyes. She desperately wanted to pick him up and hold him, but he was still too fragile. Instead, she held his hand in hers and tried to soothe him. It was the longest hour Jack ever endured. He felt ashamed at his relief when the tow truck arrived and he hurried out ahead of Holly to look after the matter.

He was embarrassed further when Holly demanded that she pay for the boost. Jack accepted the fifteen dollars that he told her it cost.

When Jack arrived back in his own apartment parking garage, he shut off the car and sat for a moment, then reached for the sun visor. He removed the picture that Holly had given him at the hospital when she told him about Charlie's paralysis. It was Charlie taking his first steps. *Will you ever walk again?* He placed the photo back in the sun visor and went to his apartment.

Natasha wasn't about to let him retreat into his own thoughts. Dinner had barely started when she looked at him and said, "Okay, what the hell is going on? Are you upset with something I said or did? Talk to me!"

Jack looked at her and said, "It's not you."

"Then what is it?"

Jack's anger flooded his brain. *Doesn't she appreciate what I've been going through?* He put his fork down on the table and said, "Let me tell you about what has happened in the last week and a half! A husband is murdered because he had my name. I take down a bunch of speed labs and an old man is murdered because the price of speed went up! I help catch the guy who did that but let another fellow get his skull bashed in the process!"

Jack paused and returned Natasha's stare. He felt the anger drain. "It seems that the harder I work, the more grief I bring on everybody," he added, quietly.

Natasha was accustomed to grief and sorrow. Anger too. It didn't matter that Jack was her husband, the man she loved. She was a professional, as was her response: "Consequences are not always easy to predict. Could you ever have predicted that Holly's husband would be murdered?"

"No, but..."

"But shut up and listen!"

Jack opened his mouth to speak, but then closed it.

"So that was not your fault. Do you think whoever did that should get away with it?"

"No."

"Good, because that person is a psychopath. Hope you stop him before it happens again."

*Me too. Stop him dead.*

"As far as the labs go, how many kids might be dissuaded from taking the drug because the price has gone up? Can you tell me those consequences of your actions?"

"Of course not."

"Now, letting a man get his skull cracked open is a little different. You told me before that you might have been able to stop it — so why didn't you?"

"I was angry. Angry that people like him sexually exploit young girls."

"Makes me angry as well."

"Still don't know if what I did was right."

"Do you want to take a poll? Maybe half the world would say you were wrong. Maybe they all would. That doesn't really matter. It's what you think that counts. It is what you have to live with that is important."

Jack thought about it for a moment, then said, "That's not true. Your opinion counts a great deal."

Natasha smiled slightly and said, "And it damn well should. I know you see the world in all its ugliness. Violent, unpredictable, unfair, and often unjust. You're a really compassionate guy. You base your actions on your own experiences ... through your own eyes. I have faith that you will continue to do what is morally right. You're a turkey, but you haven't let me down yet."

Jack looked down at his plate and reflected upon her words, conscious that she was still staring at him. He looked up, gave a grim smile, and said, "Thanks."

Natasha smiled back and then said, "Now, want to ask me about my day? Being a doctor in a clinic on the east end ... a pansy like you wouldn't last ten minutes!"

It was early Friday morning and not yet light when Jack and Danny met Lance in the cemetery.

"The next ship arrives Tuesday," said Lance. "One metric tonne. I'm in charge of stashing it."

"Details," said Jack. "Precise."

"Well, as I told ya before. We already paid $3 mil U.S. up front. That was on the first boat. Carlos put that toward this shipment when they lost the other one in San Diego. When this one arrives, Brutus and a couple of strikers will make the second half of the payment."

"Where?" asked Jack.

"He hasn't picked a spot yet and I might never know where. My job is to see that the dope is stashed. Tomorrow I'm gonna talk with one of my guys and tell him to rent a storage locker. On Tuesday, we'll have an Econoline van at the dock. Once it's loaded, I'll have three guys take it to the storage locker and stay with it overnight. Next day it'll be split up and sent out on deliveries."

"Who will you order to get the locker?" asked Jack.

"One of the strikers. Maybe Silent Sam or Dragon."

"John Dragonovich?" asked Danny. "I thought he had his full patch."

"Not yet," replied Lance. "He's only been striking for a year and a half. He's got at least another six months to go, and that's if he's lucky."

"Use Silent Sam," said Jack. "He's the one who was busted with the labs. If there is any heat, they'll be looking at him."

Lance winced and said, "Ouch! I was afraid you would say that. If you take down the stash site, I'll be burned for sure. Only me and Silent Sam will know where the locker is until it is stashed. Then nobody calls or leaves the place until the next day when the deliveries go out."

"Thought you said there would be three guys with it?" asked Jack.

"Yeah, to ride shotgun and sit in the locker overnight. But two of 'em won't know the location until they get there."

"What about Damien?" asked Jack. "When will he pop his face in for a look?"

Lance shook his head and said, "Not a chance. He's paid his dues. He won't be anywhere near the money or the coke. When it's done, I'm supposed to drop by his house and let him know."

"This much coke and he doesn't even want to see it!" said Jack. "He has to! The club will clear about $15 mil on this! You telling me he doesn't even want to see it?"

"That's what I'm tellin' ya. There is no way he'll be around any part of the action."

"Then see to it somehow! I want him nailed!"

Lance's voice revealed his exasperation. "You tell me, then. How do I do it? You want me to hog-tie him and throw him in the van with the dope?"

Jack's silence told Lance that he knew involving Damien wasn't possible.

Danny was feeling slightly euphoric as he and Jack walked back to their car. "This is great," he said. "Don't think we've ever taken down this much blow before. At least not in B.C. Wait til the narcs hear about this! We just have to figure out a way to protect our friend. Maybe do the ship as soon as it docks."

"We're not telling the narcs," said Jack.

"Christ, you're right. There's a leak…"

"Not the leak. Damien."

"Damien?"

"I want him."

"Can't be done. You heard what our friend said."

"We have to!" yelled Jack. "I can't go on with this hanging over my —" Jack caught himself and didn't finish.

Danny looked silently at Jack, then said, "Go on. What is hanging over your head?"

Jack stopped walking. He stood with his head hanging down for a moment, then whispered, "I owe Damien a favour. One get-out-of-jail-free card."

Danny's face slowly grew redder as he realized what the favour was.

"God damn you! You found Bishop! Damien told you … then you…" Danny didn't finish the statement. He didn't want to hear an admission of murder.

Jack stared at Danny for a moment and then said, "It seemed like a good idea at the time. I just wasn't thinking about the consequences. Damien did me a favour and I promised I would do one for him someday. I'm keeping my word."

"How? By tipping him off to something?" yelled Danny. "That won't solve anything!"

"No. I'm going to catch him and then let him go. It's what the courts do anyway."

"Well, la-de-da! That's just great, isn't it?"

Jack didn't respond.

Danny's frustration was still evident in his voice. "Tell me how you plan on getting evidence on Damien, seizing a tonne of coke, and then letting him go without the brass freaking out? If you did pull it off, the brass sure as hell wouldn't let you drop any of the charges!"

"It's simple. Only you and I take the dope. We get the evidence to connect Damien, then I let Damien off and say we're even."

Danny wondered if he was supposed to laugh, but the look on Jack's face said he wasn't joking. "You're bloody insane! Damn it, Jack! I can't sleep at night as it is. I'm still having nightmares about bikers trying to ambush us ... people dying! There's no way. You'll get us both killed!"

"There's a way," said Jack. "A way to protect our friend, too."

Danny knew that he would be sorry if he asked how. *Jack will only sucker me in to helping.* He turned his back and walked toward the car.

Jack trudged silently behind.

After several steps, Danny spun around and said, "So what do you have in mind?"

# *chapter thirteen*

On Saturday at noon, Jack and Danny followed
Silent Sam and watched him rent a large storage unit
that was three-quarters of the way down a row of simi-
lar units. When he left, Jack rented the unit next to it.
Moments later, Jack and Danny went inside their unit
to look at it more thoroughly.

The storage unit was made to accommodate a truck
and had a garage door at the entrance, along with a nor-
mal-sized door beside it. The inside walls were con-
structed of cement blocks that went from the floor to
the ceiling. There were no windows but there was an
overhead light.

"Perfect," said Jack. "They have an electrical
outlet."

"Now what?" grumbled Danny.

"To the Spy Store. Now you get a lesson on video
and audio installation and recording. We'll also need

bolt-cutters, a couple of short-range walkie-talkies, a drill, and a masonry bit."

"And balaclavas," said Danny.

"Right."

"Shotguns too."

"Of course. I'll also pick up a couple of industrial-size plastic pails, some springs, and duct tape. That should be it."

"One more thing you forgot."

"What's that?" asked Jack.

"Extra life insurance."


It was nine o'clock on Tuesday night when Silent Sam opened the overhead door to the storage locker. Jack and Danny watched and recorded the event through their camera set up in the adjacent unit. Silent Sam held something inside his jacket. When he stepped inside, they saw that it was a Mac-10 machine pistol.

Dragon then backed an Econoline van into the unit. Silent Sam closed the overhead door before Dragon stepped out, along with another biker nicknamed Pan-Head. All three men carried Mac-10s. They walked to the back of the truck and opened the door, out of sight of the surveillance camera.

Jack and Danny looked at each other.

"This won't work if they stay in the truck," whispered Danny.

Danny was right. They needed the element of surprise. The Brushmaster shotguns with the folding stocks that they carried were deadly weapons in a close situation, but the spray of bullets from three Mac-10s would easily outgun the pump-action of the shotguns.

They both breathed a sigh of relief when the bikers brought out a folding card table with chairs and set them up in front of the truck. Luck was on their side.

Jack waited until after the storage locker was closed for the night, then crept out and used bolt-cutters to take the padlock off the front gate to the facility. Minutes later, he rejoined Danny and quietly said, "It's time. Grab the balaclavas."

Jack and Danny crept up to the door leading into the biker's unit. They held their shotguns at the ready.

"On the count of three," whispered Jack.

The noise and sight of two masked men bursting through the door with shotguns panicked everyone.

"Move and you're dead!" yelled Jack.

Silent Sam lurched backwards, toppling his chair over as he crashed to the floor, while Dragon remained where he was, with his mouth and eyes opened wide. Pan-Head paused, then scooped his weapon from beside the table and tried to bring the barrel around to fire.

He was too late. Jack leaped forward and with a quick reverse thrust of the shotgun slammed the stock against the side of Pan-Head's face, breaking his jaw and cheekbone while sending him crashing to the floor. He then stepped on the Mac-10, pinning it to the floor. He needn't have bothered. It was almost a minute before Pan-Head regained consciousness. When he did, his two friends were lying sprawled face-down on the floor beside him.

While Danny provided cover, Jack plastered strips of duct tape tightly across Dragon's and Pan-Head's noses and the tender skin around their eyes. He then bound their hands behind their backs.

Jack pointed at Silent Sam and said in a loud voice, "Okay, I'm gonna tape you up real good, and then you're gonna be goin' for a ride."

Jack peeled off a strip of pre-cut tape from the roll. All but the ends of the strip had been taped face to face

with another strip of tape. The end result was a cover over
Silent Sam's eyes that was twice as thick but not sticky. He
then bound Silent Sam's arms behind his back, wrapping
the tape around the shirtsleeves covering his wrists.

With the three bikers trundled up on the floor, Jack
turned to Danny and said, "Okay, check out the truck."

Danny did so, noting that the keys were still in
the ignition. He went to the rear of the truck and
returned with two kilos of cocaine and set them down
at Jack's feet.

"Good," said Jack. "Now go get *the device*. Be
fuckin' careful you don't drop it!"

"You're tellin' me!" replied Danny, disappearing
out the door.

Moments later Danny returned and set two plastic
pails upside down a short distance from each other on
the floor. On the outside bottom of each plastic pail was
a bed spring. A short section of the spring protruded
inside the pail through a small hole that had been drilled
in the bottom. Holes cut in the sides of the pails allowed
a short stick to be used as a cross-bar to provide a base
for the springs to maintain pressure.

Danny then placed a kilo of cocaine under each pail.

Jack set a walkie-talkie on the floor halfway
between the two pails, then carefully helped Pan-Head
to his feet and guided him over to a pail. He taped his
ankles together and then sat him down on the spring.

Pan-Head tried to speak but his broken jaw told
him that wasn't such a good idea. His question was
answered seconds later, when Dragon's ankles were
bound and he was placed sitting on the other pail.

"What the fuck is that under my ass?" asked Dragon.
"What are you guys doin' to us? What am I sittin' on?"

Both Pan-Head and Dragon quit squirming when
they heard Jack's voice from the other side of the room.

"I suggest you sit still. The bombs have been activated. They have both a spring and mercury switch. I strongly suggest that neither of you move — in fact, I wouldn't even fart."

Pan-Head was the first to break out into a sweat. Then again, he was in a lot of pain.

Jack trundled Silent Sam into the front of the truck and made him squat on the floor under the dash before taking off his balaclava.

Danny closed the door after Jack pulled out and then crept back into their own unit to monitor Pan-Head and Dragon.

"They're fuckin' gone," said Dragon. "They took Silent Sam with 'em. Jesus fuck, man! What the fuck should we do?"

Pan-Head's panicked response was unintelligible to Danny, but apparently Dragon understood, as he said, "For sure I won't fuckin' move! You quit yappin' too!"

Jack pulled over and parked the van a short distance away from the gate to Damien's house. He put his balaclava back on and removed the tape from Silent Sam.

"I left a walkie-talkie with your two buddies back at the locker. It's short range so the cops can't pick it up. Tell Damien to go and get the walkie-talkie. When he does, he'll receive a personal message. He'll also be told how to defuse the bombs. If he doesn't show up in exactly ninety minutes, your two friends become hamburger."

Silent Sam hurried toward Damien's house as Jack drove away.

Danny's earphone crackled a few minutes later and he whispered a reply. "Yeah, Curly and Moe are still sweating it out. Both look like they took a dip in my pool. You deliver Larry?"

"It's done. Wish I was a fly on a wall when he explains this."

Jack parked the van in a prearranged spot and quickly got in his own car, drove back, and parked a few blocks away from the storage lockers. He walked the remaining distance.

Danny smiled and gave Jack the thumbs-up sign when he quietly entered their unit.

Damien used the full ninety-minute allotment before he showed. When he did, he had Lance, Rellik, and Silent Sam with him.

"Damn it, our friend is with them," whispered Danny.

"I was afraid he might show up," replied Jack. "Try and disguise your voice, but if it doesn't work, we'll have to come clean with him later."

Rellik was first to gingerly open the side door and peek inside. "Jesus fuck! I don't believe it!" He pushed the door all the way open and gestured to the rest of the group that it was okay to enter.

Jack suppressed a snicker when he saw Damien look at the tire tracks leading to the empty place the van had been parked, then at his two men sitting on plastic pails.

Damien shook his head in disgust as he walked over to Dragon's pail. The holes holding the sticks were large enough that Damien was able to peer inside and see that the springs were tied to the sticks with pieces of wire.

"Who's there?" Dragon nervously asked.

"I'll tell you who's here!" roared Damien, grabbing Dragon by the front of his shirt and jerking him off the pail.

Jack looked at Danny and whispered, "Get ready."

Danny quietly got in the car and picked up the walkie-talkie while a din could still be heard coming from the unit next door.

Jack watched as Lance peeled the tape off Pan-Head, who held his jaw and moaned. Dragon was freed next as Damien picked up the walkie-talkie, then paced back and forth, angrily stating that he could not believe this.

Danny waited for Jack's signal. He wished Jack would use the walkie-talkie but agreed that Damien might recognize his voice. He saw Jack wave to him and squeezed the transmit button and said, "Damien, are you there? Anyone copy?"

"Yeah, this is Damien! Who am I talking to?"

"One of the people who relieved you of something heavy."

"You think you can get away with this?"

"Please don't interrupt. It's not as bad as you think. We're willing to sell it back to you if you are interested."

Damien lowered the walkie-talkie and looked at his men. "Whoever ripped us wants to sell it back to us! Our own fucking coke!"

His walkie-talkie spoke again: "As a gesture of good faith, I've left a kilo under each pail. You can check to see that I am sincere and honest."

"Honest!" yelled Damien, gripping the transmit button. He took a couple of deep breaths, then said, "Just a minute," and released the button. Seconds later, Damien picked up one of the kilos of cocaine.

"So," crackled the voice that Damien so badly wanted to identify, "I'll give you a sale price — $10 million. I'll be in touch soon."

"How? When will you contact me?" asked Damien. There was no response.

Damien's face was menacing as he gripped the kilo in one hand and looked at Rellik and said, "Whoever did this is dead! These fucking guys think they can rip us off and then sell it back to us! They are fucking dead!"

He looked at Lance and said, "Who fucked us? Who knew about the stash?"

Lance swallowed, then said, "Just me and Silent Sam. Dragon and Pan-Head weren't supposed to know until tonight."

Silence descended as Damien looked around the room — as did everyone else.

"Who fucked us?" said Damien. "Who is responsible?"

"They wore masks," said Dragon. "We couldn't see who it was. Then they duct-taped us all."

"That's right," said Silent Sam. "We didn't have time to grab our pieces. Once we were taped we were screwed."

Damien stared back at his men. One face revealed the guilty party. He turned to Rellik and gave a subtle nod of his head to indicate who was responsible.

Rellik looked at Silent Sam. At first he was confused by what Damien meant. Then he glanced at Pan-Head's and Dragon's red-speckled faces. The answer to who was behind this was as plain as the nose on Silent Sam's face.

Silent Sam subconsciously put his hand up to his face. It dawned on him why his tape had not felt sticky.

Danny stepped up to the viewer with Jack just in time to see Silent Sam make a dash for the door.

The blast from Rellik's pistol echoed like a cannon inside the room.

Silent Sam would remain forever silent.

"Damn it, Rellik!" said Damien. "You shouldn't have killed him until we found out who he was working for. Couldn't you have just capped one in his ass?"

"Sorry, boss. Thought that's what you meant," replied Rellik, looking embarrassed.

"Clean it up!" Damien looked at Lance and said, "Come on. We're out of here."

Jack heard Danny's breath coming in pants and saw that his mouth was opened wide, while his eyes stared at the cement wall in front of him.

"What is it?" whispered Jack. "You okay?"

Danny blinked his eyes a couple of times, then said, "We committed murder."

"What did you think was going to happen? That he'd be asked to leave the club?"

"Jack … his brains are oozing out onto the floor." He gave Jack a glazed look and added, "Doesn't this bother you?"

"Not really. I'm glad this worked. Don't look at it as killing him. Look at it as saving our friend."

Danny shook his head and said, "I don't think I can handle any more of this shit."

"You've handled it before."

"As I said, I'm still having nightmares. This won't help."

"Danny, I'm sorry. I didn't realize this would bother you that much."

"Well it sure as hell does!"

"Keep your voice down," said Jack, glancing quickly at the monitor. He looked at Danny and said, "I couldn't figure out any other way to pull this off, but I'm done now. Tomorrow I'll look after the dope. On Thursday I'll show Damien the evidence. If I hadn't owed him, he'd be looking at spending the rest of his life in jail for this. The deal between him and me is over."

"You think Damien will see it that way after what we did?"

"Why not? We seized the dope and have proof of his involvement. It might be considered a little dirty, but..."

"A little dirty?"

"This business is. If I hadn't owed him, I would have done the same thing, except he would be in cuffs right now."

"And Silent Sam? How would that have looked in court?"

"If you fly with the crows, expect to get shot at."

"That's what you would tell a judge — or a homicide investigator?"

"Guess it would be better if I said 'Gosh, I just thought they would ask him to resign.'"

# *chapter fourteen*

It was five in the morning when Jack stopped watching the monitor and went to nudge Danny, who was sitting in the car.

"Wake up," he whispered.

"I was never asleep," replied Danny.

"That's right. You weren't snoring. The janitorial service is packing up next door. We'll give them a few minutes' head start, then skedaddle before the owner arrives and sees his busted padlock and comes snooping."

"The sooner the better." Danny saw Jack check his BlackBerry and added, "Now what?"

"It's from our friend. Wants to meet us. Says it's urgent."

"Gee, I wonder what he has to tell us," said Danny sarcastically.

"We better meet him. Could be interesting to hear what Damien had to say."

"You still want me to follow you out to the farm and give you a ride back after you drop the van off?"

"You bet. It won't take long. Ben took his loader out yesterday and dug a pit. He already had some brush to burn so it won't take long to layer it in. Speaking of which, I wonder what I owe him for a barrel of gas?"

"You could just give him a kilo or two as payment."

Jack ignored the comment and added, "I don't want to arrive until after Marcie has gone to school. Ben doesn't want Liz to know either. We may as well meet our friend while we're waiting."

"I suppose the notion of having any sleep just never occurs to you."

"You're the one complaining about nightmares. Don't sleep and you won't have them."

"I have them when I'm awake too," replied Danny somewhat sullenly.

Minutes later, Jack had only driven a few blocks away from the storage locker when his BlackBerry alerted him to another message. Jack continued driving but handed his BlackBerry to Danny and said, "That'll be our friend. Bet he wants to change the meet."

Danny read the message and smirked.

"What is it?" asked Jack.

"If it's from our friend, he has pretty strong feelings for you ... but he sure has you pegged right!"

Jack grabbed his BlackBerry back and read the message: *Love you, Turkey!*

Lance took one look at Jack and Danny and said, "Holy fuck! I can't believe you did that!"

"Did what?" asked Jack.

"Don't hand me the bull! I was close enough to Damien to recognize Danny's voice. I couldn't believe it!

I was afraid you'd reneged on our deal and were gonna come bustin' in and arrest us when Damien picked up that key."

"I don't renege. Hadn't expected you to be there. Otherwise we would have had Damien."

"Fuck, if I'd known what was goin' on, maybe I wouldn't have. I was at Damien's tellin' him that the deal was done and went without a hitch. All of a sudden we hear Silent Sam screamin' into the intercom."

"Any heat in your direction?" asked Danny.

Lance gave Jack a glance and said, "No, you took care of that with Silent Sam. Rellik put one through his head-bone."

"Yeah, we saw," said Jack.

"You had it videoed?"

"Of course."

"Fuckin' Damien and a murder on film and you let 'im off all because of me! I never would have believed it!"

Danny gave Jack a sideways glance as Jack looked at Lance and said, "A deal is a deal. I was just fulfilling what I promised."

"Man! If I ever had a doubt about trustin' ya, it's gone now." Lance paused for a moment, then added, "Just remind me to never get on your bad side. I don't want to end up like Silent Sam."

"We just have to catch Damien again. Next time without you being so close to the action."

"I'd tell ya that it's impossible to nail him, but I said that before and was wrong."

"What did Damien have to say about it later?" asked Danny.

"He's hot. I've never seen his face that red. The pulse in his temple was just a-jumpin'. I only got about three blocks away from the locker when he told me to pull over so we could go for a walk and talk. He was really pissed at me for havin' a striker that screwed us."

"How pissed?" asked Jack.

"Well … not bad, cuz it wasn't me who sponsored him into the club. It was Petro. As far as the stash being ripped, Damien is more pissed off at himself. It was his idea to have things go the way they did." Lance looked at Jack and added, "Well, not the way they did, but the way they were supposed to. You know, with puttin' the stash in a locker and then splittin' it an' sendin' it out the next day."

"So now what?" asked Jack. "What about the next ship?"

"That's already left Colombia and should arrive in about ten days. I expect things will be done a little different then."

"Damien won't be stashing it all in the same spot," suggested Danny.

"I'm not so sure Damien will even be involved. He's worried. He knows he fucked up bad."

"How so?" asked Jack.

"This was the biggest single deal the club has ever done. Usually we try and keep stuff like this separated, you know, so not everyone can be connected. But this was so fuckin' big that every chapter in Canada had to chip in. There are gonna be a lot of pissed off people. Damien figures he might lose his position over this. Maybe even get the boot altogether."

"Who do you think would replace him?" asked Jack.

"A guy from Quebec we call The Toad. He's been here often in the last few weeks meeting with Damien."

"Ugly?" asked Danny.

Lance chuckled, then said, "That too, but the name came from his younger days, before he joined the club.

From his not-so-secret ingredient in makin' the special brand of acid that he was selling."

"You figure he could replace Damien?" asked Jack.

"He was runner-up last year."

"I think I saw him that day," said Jack. "Ugly, with a heavy French accent. Short and scrawny. Not what you expect for a biker."

"That's him. But he has other assets. He's intellectual, sneaky, vicious, not much of a conscience. Sometimes makes for a wicked combination."

When the meeting was over, Danny waited until Lance had left before turning to Jack and saying, "Looks like you just replaced Damien with a sociopath to run the biggest organized crime family in Canada. Is this what you call progress?"

Jack sighed and said, "Consequences are not always so easy to predict." It was what Natasha had said to him. At the time he'd thought it had made him feel better. *Now it just feels lame.*

"Yeah, I guess," replied Danny. "Sorry, didn't mean to sound like I was upset. I'm just really tired."

*Me too. Tired of screwing up.*


Damien sat at his kitchen table and closed his eyes as Vicki massaged the back of his neck and shoulders.

"What is it, Papa Bear?" she asked.

Damien gently reached for her hand and guided her around to sit on his lap. He glanced at the kitchen clock.

"You want to go out for dinner? Just the two of us?" suggested Vicki.

Damien shook his head. It had been forty-two hours since he had walked into the storage locker and discovered they had a traitor. A lot had happened. A lot that Vicki did not know about. He heard the muffled sound of the entertainment centre coming from another room. Briefly, he wondered what Buck, Sarah, and Kate would think of their dad when they found out. Would it change their image of him?

He whispered in Vicki's ear, "I'm finished. Out. Maybe a couple of months ... but then I'll be gone."

"What are you talking about?"

Damien put his finger to his lips to tell Vicki to lower her voice, and then whispered, "I screwed up. Cost the club millions. We're going to have to sell off some of our assets to pay back what I lost."

Vicki's eyes revealed her concern. "How? What happened?" she whispered back.

"Business. We had a traitor. Got ripped. My fault."

"Everybody makes mistakes. Don't —"

"Not like this. I've already been replaced. In the next couple of weeks The Toad will oversee ... will get a good opportunity to enhance his status. After that, a new election."

"You can beat that guy! You have before."

Damien shook his head. "Not this time. I won't even bother to run. It's time to retire. This is a sign. I've been a target too long. Up until now we've been lucky."

"Oh, Papa Bear," said Vicki, giving him a hug. "You're tired. I know you haven't slept in two or three days. Maybe if you rest..."

"Yeah, maybe," replied Damien, while checking an incoming message on his BlackBerry. He expected it to be Rellik, who had also gone without sleep in the last forty-two hours. It wasn't. He recognized the sender and knew it was urgent. He was directed to take a short walk away from his house.

* * *

Cecil Hinds knew his work well. He was a member of the Combined Forces Special Enforcement Unit of British Columbia. CFSEU was an independent police agency set up by the government to fight organized crime. It was composed of police officers from various agencies. In the last two days there had been a flurry of activity through coded messages being transmitted in and out of Damien's estate.

Hinds decided to cruise through the neighbour-hood and record various licence plates parked within a few blocks of the estate. The more cautious criminals would sometimes park and walk the remainder in an effort to avoid identification. This evening, he was rewarded for his efforts when he saw Damien walking away from his house.

Hinds manoeuvred his car a block behind Damien and watched through binoculars. He knew that it wasn't a casual after-dinner stroll. Damien walked fast and his physique implied that he was not on a fitness program. Damien was also being extra observant. *Something is definitely up.*

Hinds reached for his radio to call for support. He knew that Damien's experience eliminated the chance of being able to follow him with only one car without being detected.

The response Hinds received indicated help would arrive in twenty-five minutes. *Not soon enough*, thought Hinds, as an SUV pulled alongside Damien and he quickly got in.

Hinds watched as the SUV drove past him. He knew he had been lucky. The driver hadn't seen him, which was good, because Hinds recognized him. It was Jack Taggart. *What the hell is he doing with Damien?*

Hinds recalled reading a memo a couple of weeks earlier from the RCMP Anti-Corruption Unit requesting notification of police contact with Satans Wrath. *Jack, you son of a bitch, what are you up to? Following you by myself is out of the question.*

# chapter fifteen

"What's up?" growled Damien, as soon as Jack picked him up.

"Got something to show you. I've rented a motel room," replied Jack.

"What is it?"

"Has to wait until we get there. You'll see. Trust me."

"Trust you? That's a good one."

The rest of the drive was made in silence, with the exception of Damien's grumblings that Jack could have rented a room a little closer to Vancouver, rather than halfway to Chilliwack.

When they entered the motel room, Jack tossed an attaché case onto a small table near the window. Damien quickly walked through the unit to ensure they were alone and then took a seat at the table.

Jack pulled the other chair out and spun it around backwards before sitting down with his arms resting on the back of the chair as he faced Damien.

"Well? Get on with it," said Damien. "I'm a busy guy. What's this about?"

Jack stared briefly at Damien and then said, "It's about how I no longer owe you a favour."

Damien leaned back in his chair and folded his arms across his chest. "I'm listening. How did you reach that conclusion?"

"I've just saved you from going to jail. Even here in B.C., I figure you still would have received a long enough sentence that Buck, Sarah, and Kate would all have graduated before you got out."

Damien let out a grunt, then sneered and said, "Bullshit. I haven't done anything to go to jail for."

"I'm not bullshitting you, so please do me a favour and don't bullshit me. I find it insulting."

Damien paused and the sneer disappeared from his face. "Okay. What evidence do you think you have?"

Jack stared intently at Damien. He felt his body tense, ready to fight. "I have a lot of evidence," he said tersely. "In fact, if I was to weigh it, I would say it was about two kilos short of a metric tonne!"

Damien stared back in disbelief. "It was you?" he uttered.

Jack nodded and pointed to his attaché case and said, "Go ahead, open it. You can watch it on video — including the murder of Silent Sam."

"So this is how you pay back a favour?" said Damien, rising to his feet and shoving the attaché case off the table like it was poisonous. "You cost me my position in the club!" he roared.

Jack remained seated. Keeping his voice even he said, "I would have done the same thing if I hadn't owed you a favour. The difference is that someday you won't be looking at pictures of your grandchildren from a jail cell."

Damien stared down at Jack. His breath came in pants and it took him a moment to regain his composure. He then bent down to pick up the case and Jack quickly stood and backed away.

"I'm not going to hit you with the fucking thing," said Damien, sitting back down in the chair.

Damien was quiet for a moment and Jack readied himself for a fight. He discovered that Damien was more cerebral. A wry smile appeared on his face and he said, "You've got me. Checkmate. I concede your ... point."

Jack slid his chair a little farther back and then sat down.

Damien stared at him and said, "I never thought it would end like this. A bullet in the back from an Indo maybe, but not from your side. I underestimated you. Wish I had Bishop's murder on film."

"I only have one copy of Silent Sam's," replied Jack, gesturing to the attaché case. "After we watch it, you can destroy it. Then we're going for a ride where you can see that something else is destroyed."

The drive to the farm was made in silence. Jack parked on an access road and used his flashlight to navigate through a short stretch of bush and into a field that was being cleared to make pasture.

Damien looked down into the pit, where 998 kilos of cocaine had already been slashed open and mixed into a pile of brush. The smell of gas permeated the air as the last of it glubbed out of a barrel that Jack rolled along the top of the pit.

The men watched in silence as the flames crackled and roared to a great height. Then Jack handed Damien a set of keys and said, "These belong to you. An Econoline van that I've got parked nearby in the driveway of an abandoned farmhouse. You can drive yourself back to the city."

Damien accepted the keys and said, "I guess one good thing came out of all this."

"What's that?"

"Not being top dog. I'm no longer a target. Who knows, maybe I'll even be able to take my wife to bed without wondering who is listening."

"Unless, of course, you continue your criminal career."

Damien let out a snort and said, "I'm talking about other people. People with ambition. You got lucky. It won't happen again. You mean nothing to me."

"So you agree that I no longer owe you a favour?"

Damien didn't answer for a moment, and Jack caught the look in his eyes as the flames flickered, casting shadows of light and darkness across his face. *He really does look like the devil.*

Damien glared at him and said, "Yeah, but don't ever ask me for another one. If you do, I'm liable to kill you myself."


Cecil Hinds had his surveillance team hiding near Damien's estate waiting to video Jack and Damien together when they returned. He sat in his car with his hands in his jacket pockets. The weather had turned unseasonably cold for May, forcing him to shut the car off. Any exhaust coming from a parked car would quickly gather attention from those who were wary.

There was one obvious conclusion that Hinds drew from the covert method the two men used to meet. Hinds was a good cop. Like all good cops, he hated criminals … but like all good cops, he hated dirty cops more.

Hinds was slightly disappointed when Damien reappeared four hours later driving a rented Econoline van and alone. *Interesting. Why the van, and what part did Taggart play?*

It was nine o'clock the next morning when Hinds found out what the van had been used for. A striker for Satans Wrath had returned the van to the rental agency. Minutes later, Hinds field-tested the powdery residue found inside. Positive for cocaine!

The chief officer in charge of CFSEU met with Assistant Commissioner Isaac within the hour. Moments later, Legg was also summoned to the meeting. Taggart had just become the Anti-Corruption Unit's top priority.

"Where are we with the pictures you sent to Mexico, Harry?"

Legg squirmed slightly in his chair and replied, "We passed them on to the LO in Mexico City a week ago Monday. We haven't heard back yet."

"Today is Friday. That makes it eleven days. Why the delay?"

"The liaison officer indicated that the Mexican authorities won't be eager to admit if they made a mistake. If Bishop's death was not accidental, it would cause them embarrassment. It's a delicate matter. The LO is trying to be discreet and go through the back door on this."

Isaac pointed his finger at Legg and said, "You tell the LO to forget about being delicate! I don't care who is embarrassed! Tell him to send it through channels immediately. If there are any problems, I'll be talking with the Mexican ambassador myself!"


Danny checked his watch as he walked with Jack through the cemetery. It was early afternoon but some people were getting a jump on the weekend. Rush hour had already started. "You figure we'll be working late?" he asked.

Jack glanced at him and said, "Guess it depends on what our friend has to say. Hoping to make it home for dinner?"

Danny nodded. "I need a break. I've been on edge all week over … the storage locker thing. I'm glad things worked out for you with Damien last night, though."

"Me too. Now if we could just find out who sent Connie that note I'd be happy."

"Wish she had a lead," said Danny. "Everyone in the office is jittery. Hell, even the building, for that matter."

"It's starting to get on my nerves, too," replied Jack. "Let's make this quick with our friend, then pop back to the office and head home. Natasha should get home around five-thirty. I want to be waiting for her with a bottle of wine when she does."

"Sounds good to me," replied Danny, reaching for his cellphone to call Susan.

"Hey, babe!" said Danny when she answered. "I'll be home for dinner. Jack and I are taking the weekend off. How about taking a couple of steaks out of the freezer and not eating until after we put Tiff and Jimmy to bed?"

Susan felt relief and joy flutter through her body. This was the Danny she had married. Not the bone-weary, stressed-out, and depressed man she had been putting up with for the last couple of weeks. "I'll be glad to," she replied, "except it's cold and windy. You'll freeze your butt off if you barbecue."

"Do we have any wine in the house?"

"A bottle of Pinot Noir."

"Perfect. Then between you and the wine, I don't expect to notice the cold. See you around five-thirty."

* * *

Jack saw Lance pacing back and forth as they approached. *Not a good sign. He's not the type to be easily upset.*

"What's up?" asked Jack as they met.

"You guys have really done it this time," replied Lance. "Damien is really in shit. Basically a vote of non-confidence. The club is out $6 million U.S. Damien has to cough up $1.5 million of his own bread as a penalty."

"Where will he get the money?" asked Danny.

"Don't know. Probably from the Caymans, but he could just slap a mortgage on his house."

"Is he still boss?" asked Jack.

"In name only. The Toad is taking over in the interim until we do a proper election. He's going to handle things personally for the next shipment. This time the dope will be split up before it ever leaves the port."

"Which will be when?" asked Jack.

"The Toad arranged for the $3 mil down payment to be made a couple of days ago. The ship is due to arrive in about a week. The Toad is arriving here again tomorrow, along with a couple of his own guys. We pay the other half as the ship is unloaded."

"Where does The Toad stay when he's here?" asked Jack.

Lance shrugged. "Different hotels and motels. No place for long."

"Anything else?" asked Danny.

"Think that's about it," replied Lance. "You guys screwed Damien good. I expect things might be a little different around here with The Toad."

Danny checked his watch again and thought about Susan. *To hell with Damien! Let's go!* He looked at Lance and said, "Stay in touch. We want to know every move The Toad makes."

"You got it," replied Lance, turning to walk away.

"Not so fast," said Jack. "What else is going on?"

"About what?" asked Lance, turning to look at Jack. Jack stared back but didn't speak.

Lance returned his stare, then swallowed and said, "Oh, yeah. Guess I should have mentioned it. Noon yesterday, Damien called a meeting with Whiskey Jake, Rellik, and me."

"What about?" asked Danny.

"About who ripped off our dope. Damien is pissed. Anyone we know dealing pounds or kilos who didn't get it from us is getting whacked. Damien wants names. I gave him two guys and Whiskey Jake knew four. Rellik's crew has already taken care of three of them. The other three will be next. I think Rellik has a few names of his own as well."

"You what!" shouted Danny. "Jesus Christ! You can't be working for us and tossing out names of guys to be murdered!"

"Thought you might be pissed," said Lance, "but what was I supposed to do? You guys put me in this position. You wanted me to become prez? Well, now I am. With power comes responsibility."

"Yeah, but..." Danny stopped as Jack held up his hand.

"I understand," said Jack. "Don't worry about it," he added, while placing a hand on Lance's shoulder.

"Don't worry about it!" said Danny, as his face took on a mottled effect.

"I appreciate that you're in a tough spot," continued Jack, speaking quietly to Lance. "Know that we won't do anything to jeopardize you, but at the same time you don't have immunity from any other cops. All I can promise is that we won't help them."

Lance nodded that he understood.

"Now," added Jack, "give us whatever details you have. Who, when, where."

* * *

Susan prepared a baby bottle for Jimmy. *If I want him to go quietly to bed tonight I better wake him soon.* She glanced at Tiffany, who had been on her riding toy for an hour. Her feet sounded like a galloping centipede as she raced around the table on the linoleum floor while working her arms to steer. *She'll sleep tonight!*

Jimmy let out a high-pitched scream and Susan abruptly stopped what she was doing. It was a sound that all mothers instinctively knew. It wasn't a cranky cry. He was in pain, and she ran to his crib.

Jimmy was lying in his crib on his back, his face red and contorted in pain. Susan reached for him as she noticed a bloody pinch mark on his cheek. At less than three months old, Jimmy wasn't even able to roll over.

"Jimmy! What…"

Susan pulled the blanket back but never succeeded in picking up her baby. She felt a man's hand choke off her windpipe and heard him say, "Now be quiet, my little bird. I don't want to hurt your baby again."

Ten minutes later, Susan found herself duct-taped to a kitchen chair. Her mouth had been taped but not her eyes. She believed there were at least four men, maybe five. They all wore ski masks and latex gloves. Two of them had their jackets undone and she saw pistols stuck in their belts.

Tiffany started to cry behind her and she twisted in her chair but was bound too tight to see. Moments later her crying stopped; Jimmy still sobbed from his crib. *What have they done! What have they done to my Tiffany!*

As if reading her thoughts, one man partially spun her chair so she could see that Tiffany was being held by a man who had his hand over her mouth.

None of the men had spoken a word except the one who grabbed her. His eyes were dark brown, maybe black, and he spoke with a British accent. She saw him nod at a man behind her, who then dragged her chair over and sat her facing her patio door.

Susan looked past their barbecue and at a metre-high above-ground pool that Danny had set up in the yard. The yard was well treed but Danny had built their fence extra high for even more privacy.

*What do they want? Is it Danny? Are they waiting for him?* She glanced at the clock on her oven. It was 3:45. *An hour and forty-five minutes before Danny...*

"Now then," said the man with the British accent, bending over her. "I suppose you are wondering why we are doing this. The reason is rather simple, really. You have befriended a particular policeman who has taken it upon himself to bring an overzealous approach to his work. A chap by the name of Jack Taggart."

He stared into her eyes. Susan stared back, too afraid to move.

"There is no use denying your friendship to this man. As I recall, you had him over for dinner not long ago. I believe you served him Yorkshire pudding. An excellent dish. Something I rather fancy myself."

He motioned with his head and another man carried Tiffany into view. Her mouth was now taped, as were her hands behind her back. Her ankles were also bound. Susan wriggled and tried to shout through her own tape. The only sound she made was a murmur.

"Now, as punishment for your friendship with Officer Taggart, I have decided to kill one of your babies. You can decide which one!"

\* \* \*

Danny kept his thoughts to himself until they returned to the office. Once they parked and got out of the car he couldn't contain himself any longer.

"Damn it, Jack! He's a party to murder! We can't let him be doing this! Throwing out names for people to be murdered! This isn't right!"

Jack leaned back against the car and folded his arms across his chest. "So what do you expect him to do? If he doesn't act like one of the pack, it won't take them long to figure out what's going on. Then he's dead."

"Then maybe we should drop him as an informant!"

"What? You've got to be kidding! After all the work we went through just to turn him ... forget it! It's our job to find out what is going on. You can't send a poodle into a wolf pack. We need him. Next to Damien, he's the most valuable source we could ever get."

"And what's it gotten us? You've seen The Toad's file. He makes Damien look like a choir boy! We haven't accomplished squat! All we've done is made things worse."

"How is taking down boatloads of coke and costing the club $6 million making it worse?"

Danny didn't reply, so Jack added, "This is still the beginning. We're barely started. With our friend in the position he is in, we can really do some damage to these guys."

"I don't know," said Danny. "I don't know how much more of this I can take." The anger had gone from his voice. He sounded tired and beaten.

"Things don't always turn out the way you figure," said Jack. "When you first start this job you envision yourself wearing a white Stetson and riding in to catch bad guys. You tend to think things are either black or white. That's a fantasy. In real life, if you're effective in this job and expect to survive, then your Stetson tends to get a little grey after awhile."

"Yeah? Well I think your fucking cowboy hat has turned black!"

Jack was quiet for a moment, then said, "You're tired ... I'm tired. It's almost four. It'll take you half an hour to get home. Go now and I'll tidy up in the office. Spend some time with your family and get some rest. Let's both just calm down and we can talk about it on Monday."

Susan gasped and her eyes widened with terror when she saw a third man appear, holding Jimmy in his arms. She tried to scream but sucked saliva into her lungs and gagged and coughed as the tears streamed down her cheeks.

"I'm thinking that your little one would fit in your outside grill ... then again, I don't know if I have a match. Hmm, let me think. Perhaps the pool? Yes! Perfect! Which baby do you choose? Tell me now ... or I will presume that you want them both killed."

Susan continued to cry and shake her head.

"Oh, how silly of me. You can't talk." He took Tiffany from the other man's arms and held her up and said, "Shall I drown this one? Or ... oh, I see by the way you are shaking your head that you've obviously chosen the little one."

It was almost four o'clock when Susan watched the man carry Jimmy out into the backyard. He flipped up a corner of the pool's blue plastic cover and turned and looked at her. Seconds later, she watched as he dropped Jimmy into the water. Briefly she saw the shape of his body wriggling at the bottom of the pool before disappearing from view. The man waved at her and then they all left.

# chapter sixteen

"Hey, babe! I'm home." Danny didn't get a response but he heard a thumping sound coming from his kitchen. He entered and saw Susan, taped to a chair that was lying on its side. She was banging her head against the floor. Tiffany was taped to the pedestal of the kitchen table.

He drew his 9mm and rushed over to kneel by Susan. She stared up at him. He expected her eyes to look frantic. They didn't. They looked glassy ... lifeless. He grabbed the telephone on the kitchen counter and dialled 911 while covering off the entrance to the kitchen with his pistol. He was conscious of Susan's methodical banging of her head on the floor. *Sorry, babe. Just a few more seconds ...Tiffany crying and squirming ... everything is going to be okay.*

Danny gave quick instructions into the telephone, and then left it off the hook as he knelt beside Susan and peeled back the tape from her mouth.

"Jimmy!" she choked. "They killed our Jimmy!"

Caution disappeared in a flash as panic sent Danny racing across the kitchen toward Jimmy's room.

"No!" cried Susan. "Outside," she added softly. "They drowned him half an hour ago."

Danny turned abruptly. He saw the blue cover on the pool flipped back and drooping over the edge.


Assistant Commissioner Isaac thought about the meeting he'd had a few minutes earlier. Inspector Crana was sharp. His position on the Vancouver RCMP Drug Section demanded it. Isaac brooded over what he had been told. *No, the narcs hadn't heard of any large influx of cocaine hitting the streets this week. It was the opposite. Many major players were pulling a disappearing act.*

Inspector Crana had assured Isaac that he would tell his people to canvas all informants and sources to find out what was going on. He would also check with VPD to see if they had heard anything unusual.

Isaac was just putting on his raincoat to head home when Inspector Crana called.

"Sir, I checked with VPD. Their Vice Unit doesn't have anything, but their Homicide does. Three high-level cocaine dealers have been murdered within the last two days. A couple more are missing. The dealers don't appear to be connected with each other."

"Are they affiliated with any groups? Satans Wrath, Indos, Russians…"

"No, sir. Not that anyone knows of. It might be coincidental."

"I don't think it's coincidental," replied Isaac, with a noticeable edge to his voice. "You said earlier that many major players were pulling a disappearing act. What do they know that we don't? Get on this!"

Isaac thought about it as he drove home. *Taggart has a secret meeting with Damien, who then returns in a van that had been used to transport cocaine. Now dealers are being murdered?* Isaac shook his head in frustration. There always seemed to be one common denominator when people were murdered. *Taggart!*

Jack was also on his way home when he received a call on his cell.

"Jack! What's going on?"

He recognized Connie Crane's voice. "Hey, CC. I was just thinking about you. Anything new on whoever sent the note? I've been in contact with Holly and —"

"Forget Holly! What the hell is going on with you and Danny?"

"What are you talking about? I'm just on my way home. Danny left over half an hour ago."

"You haven't heard? He didn't call you?"

"Who?"

"Danny! Damn it! There was a home invasion at his house this afternoon. Bunch of guys. Tied up his wife and toddler, then decided to kill their baby and dropped him into the swimming pool. He didn't call you?"

"No." Jack heard his own voice but for a moment it sounded mechanical, like someone else was speaking. "Where are they?" he heard himself ask.

"BCCH. I'm on my way there now. I want to talk to you."

Jack hung up and quickly dialled Danny's cell.

Eventually Danny answered, "Yes."

"Danny? Is that you? It's Jack. I don't recognize your voice. What —" The line went dead. Jack redialled but found that Danny's phone was shut off. He called Natasha and was relieved to hear her answer.

"You okay?" asked Jack. "Where are you?"

"Sure, I'm okay. Just about home."

"Danny and Susan had a home invasion this afternoon. Someone —"

"A what? Are they okay?"

"I don't know. They're at BCCH. I'll be there in a couple of minutes. I'll call you, but watch yourself. I don't know what is going on."

Jack parked at the emergency entrance and ran inside. Moments later, he located Danny and Susan at the intensive care unit talking to an I-HIT investigator. Danny and Susan numbly stared at him as he rushed up.

"I just heard. Got here as fast as I could," stammered Jack. "What —"

"Get away from us," said Susan, her voice sounding raspy and bitter.

Jack felt stunned. His mouth opened to speak but no words came out.

"You heard her, Jack! Get the fuck away from us!" screamed Danny.

"Danny ... I don't understand. Why..." Jack stopped and stepped back when he saw Danny clench his fist and pull his arm back.

Both men stared at each other for a moment, then Jack turned and walked away. He was conscious of walking past Holly, who had stepped out from Charlie's room to see what the commotion was about.

The I-HIT investigator caught up to him and said, "Maybe you should hang around in the waiting room near the front doors. Connie should arrive soon. She'll want to talk with you."

"What happened? I heard they drowned Jimmy."

"Not pronounced yet, but he was in a backyard pool for about thirty-five minutes. Doesn't look good. All I know is that it had something to do with you. The guy who did it told Susan it was because she was your friend."

"What about Tiffany?"

"That the other one? She's being examined by a doctor. Don't think she has any ... physical injuries. Victim Services have been notified."

"I'm going home to my wife. Tell CC she can call me there."

It was five-thirty when Jack got back in his car. He called home and Natasha answered.

"I'll be home in forty minutes. Don't let anyone in until I'm there."

"Jack? What happened? Are they okay?"

"I'll talk to you when I get home. I ... can't talk right now."

"Jack? What —"

Jack hung up and tossed the cell down on the seat as his body shook with each sob. He leaned forward and crossed his arms over the steering wheel to make a pillow for his head. Minutes later, he sat up and reached for the ignition. The keys slipped from his fingers onto the floor. He slumped over to pick them up, then clenched them in his fist and sat back in his seat breathing heavily.

Time passed and Jack realized he was staring at the edge of Charlie's picture protruding from underneath the sun visor. It reminded him of another picture. A picture of Jimmy that Danny and Susan had given him when he was first born.

The tears dripped off his cheeks as the images of both infants vied for his attention.

It was forty-five minutes later when he found the energy to answer his cellphone.

"Jack! You son of a bitch!"

Jack recognized his sister's voice and panic set in. *Not her too! Not again!* "Liz! What is it? What's happened?"

"You know perfectly well what happened! It's all because of you!"

"Marcie ... Ben ... are they okay? Tell me!"

"Marcie doesn't know. But how could you do that to us? Ben's been freaking out. He wouldn't tell me until just now. How could you? What if the dope dealers come back here looking for the stuff?"

Jack breathed a sigh of relief, then said, "They won't. It's all been burned. You're completely safe."

"Don't you think having both my children murdered last year was enough?"

Jack swallowed, not knowing what to say.

"You tell us this Bishop fellow is dead, and we think, gee, maybe now we can get on with our lives. But no! You have to involve us in something like this!"

"Liz, I'm sorry. It won't happen again. The person who I did this favour for ... helped me find..." Jack paused, then said, "I promise, I'll never do anything like that again."

"That's why you and Danny came out to visit the other morning! I thought it was strange. Tell him that I'm not impressed with him either."

"Liz, something has happened to..." Jack coughed and tried to regain his composure. "I do need a favour. I hate to ask you now, but..."

"Haven't you been listening to what I just said?"

"It's Natasha. I ... never mind. I'm sorry."

Elizabeth paused and then said, "A woman problem maybe I can handle. What is it? Are you okay? Jesus, I didn't mean to come down so hard on you. Your voice..."

"I'm worried that Natasha is in danger."

"Your job?"

"Yes."

\* \* \*

It was seven o'clock when Jack arrived home.

Natasha met him at the front door and said, "What the hell is going on? Why did you hang up on me?"

"I was at the hospital. I'm sorry, I just couldn't ... oh, Jesus, it's my fault," replied Jack.

Natasha was startled by the tone of his voice but more shocked when she looked at him. Grief and anguish carved deep etches into his face. It was obvious he had been crying. She forgot her anger and hugged him, then held his hand as she led him to the living room and sat him down on the sofa to face her.

"Talk to me," she said softly.

The words poured out. Everything that had happened within the last three hours. When he was finished, Natasha placed one hand on his shoulder and said, "You mean you still don't know that Jimmy is going to be okay?"

"No. I'm sure he's not. Even if they manage —"

"Nobody has told you!"

"Told me what? What are you talking about?"

"Jimmy is going to be okay. I was going frantic. Had to find out what was going on so I called the hospital and spoke with someone I knew. Danny and Susan are in shock, but Jimmy seems fine."

"No, he can't be. It's not possible. He was underwater over half an hour. His brain will be ... if he lives ... he'll be..."

"No, we don't think so. He is alive and not showing any signs of neurological damage."

"It can't be. I was told he —"

"Let me speak. Normally, drowning suffocation causes a lack of oxygen resulting in death in only a few minutes. An exception to this rule appears in victims who have been suddenly submerged into ice-cold water, resulting in the slowing of body functions while diverting blood only to the heart, lungs, and brain. Some of these people have survived without any physical damage for up to an hour underwater. It's known as the mammalian dive reflex. If someone gradually becomes hypothermic then this reflex does not apply."

"But Jimmy is just a baby!"

"Babies are born with the mammalian dive reflex. They naturally hold their breath when submerged. Also, being less than three months old means his blood is still oxygen enriched from being in the womb."

Natasha embraced her husband. She felt the moisture on her neck from his eyes. The telephone rang and he tried to move to answer it. She held him a moment longer before relenting.

"Jack. CC here. Just to let you know that it sounds like O'Reilly's baby is going to be okay."

"I know."

"How did ... oh yeah, your wife."

"How are they doing?"

"Pretty shook up. Got two guys providing security for them at the hospital. We'll stash them at a motel later. Everyone else in your section is being warned to be cautious. In the meantime, who do you know with a British accent that is psycho enough to do this?"

"A British accent? Nobody. I can't think of anyone."

"Susan said that one of the guys spoke with a British accent. He also knew she had you over for dinner last week."

"He what?"

"Yeah, commented to her that he was going to kill her baby because she fed you Yorkshire pudding."

"How did he know that?"

"That's what I'm asking you. Who knew what you had for dinner that night?"

"Nobody. She invited me when I was leaving the funeral and I went straight..." Jack paused. *The funeral! The annoying wrong number calls ... the green van with the open window ... I never saw anyone enter it after the funeral ... sitting inside ... waiting...*

"Jack?" asked Connie.

"Someone with a British accent called me a couple of times at the funeral for Holly's husband. Said it was a wrong number. That was when Susan invited me. I think she said then what we were having!"

"You sure?"

"Positive. Tell me you were there doing your thing?"

"I was. Videoed everyone I could see who attended. Meet me at my office."

Jack hung up, then looked at Natasha and said, "I want you out of here. Go out to the farm. Take next week off work. These people are murdering people I'm connected —"

"Jack, I can't. I've got patients to look after next week."

"Aren't you paying attention? Everywhere I look or go people are getting murdered! Three nights ago I saw a guy get his brains blown out! Today someone tried to kill Susan's baby because she fed me dinner! Can you believe it? Dinner! I can't take this anymore! I'm not losing you, too!"

Natasha looked at him calmly, then said, "I didn't hear about someone losing the contents of his cerebellum."

Jack sighed, then said, "Okay, that one doesn't count. Just bad guys killing bad guys. But this other stuff ... Danny and Susan. Someone did that because they're ... they *were* my friends. I want you someplace safe until this is over."

Natasha shook her head and said, "Jack, you should have looked in a mirror when you came home tonight. You need me. We're a team. I'm not leaving you alone while —"

"If I need help, I'll get someone. I'm sorry, but that doesn't include you. You don't invite me in to assist with your patients. I need to have a clear head. If I'm worried about you then I might make a mistake."

Natasha thought for a moment, then in a whisper said, "You've made your point. Call your sister, I'll pack."

"She's expecting you. I'll stay and then follow you until I know you're not being followed. I'll call you as often as I can."

Twenty minutes later, Jack and Natasha embraced and kissed each other in the underground parking lot beside their respective cars.

Natasha looked at Jack and said, "I know you desperately want to catch who did this, but ... I've got a bad feeling. I want you to promise me that you'll take care of yourself."

"I promise. I'll take care of myself — and I will take care of whoever is behind this," he said bitterly.

# *chapter seventeen*

---

Jack met CC in the I-HIT office and said, "Check this number out. I got it off my phone bill. It's the number the Brit called me from when I was at the funeral."

"Good work!" replied CC. Her enthusiasm was cut short moments later when she discovered that the number belonged to a cellphone that had been reported lost or stolen. The owner was elderly and had no criminal history.

"Too much to ask for, I guess," replied Jack. "Show me the video."

Jack and CC then watched the video of the funeral. He saw himself walking away from the service and then answering his phone. They both studied the crowd but there was no indication of anyone calling him.

"I received two calls," said Jack. "Keep watching."

The video remained focused on those who were leaving and it became evident that the second call Jack received was not on film.

"Damn it," said CC.

"I remember a green van pulling out from the curb and cutting off someone in traffic about the time Susan invited me. The driver's window was open. You must have recorded plates."

"We did. Nothing really stood out. Nobody with a record for violence, but a green van sounds familiar. Hang on."

A moment later, Jack saw where a pan of the camera had captured the back of the green van parked on the road outside the cemetery. The driver had his head out the window and was looking toward the service. He looked dark, perhaps Indonesian.

"The plates ... did you run them?"

CC froze the frame and zoomed in for a close up. "No, I'll show you. Too muddy. The last two numbers, one might be a three, maybe an eight, but we couldn't make it out."

"The rest of the van isn't muddy," muttered Jack. "That was done on purpose. Run it under all combinations. See if one of them matches."

Several minutes later, Jack and CC received the information. None of the numbers matched a green van, but one of the numbers did match a stolen plate.

"That's him!" said Jack. "He was there when Susan invited me!"

"Lousy picture," commented CC. "Just his profile. Pretty grainy when I zoom in any further."

"There's something about this guy..."

"He look familiar?"

"No, but let me think. There's something else ... Elvis!"

"What?"

"Elvis, from Anti-Corruption! He was doing some work for me recently. Said he heard a guy with a British accent speaking to a lawyer who works on retainer for Satans Wrath. Described him as maybe being Indo."

"That's incredible!" CC's mouth dropped open as she stared at Jack.

Jack frowned and said, "Not that incredible. Elvis saw the guy but didn't identify him."

"I don't mean that! I mean the part you said about ACU working for you!"

Jack surprised himself by laughing. *Too much stress, not enough sleep. Still, it felt good.* He dialled his cell and felt relieved when his call was answered.

"Laura, it's Jack. I need —"

"Forget it, Jack! Not tonight. Operators are *not* standing by. Stall it or get someone else. Elvis and I are celebrating our fifth wedding anniversary."

"Not you, Laura. Elvis. I need to speak to him. It's about what happened to Danny and his family this afternoon."

"Your partner? O'Reilly? What happened?"

"Put Elvis on. He can tell you later."


Less than an hour later, Elvis confirmed that the man in the green van was the same man who had met Lawrence Leitch in the park and had been shown the bogus report given to Molen.

"What bogus report?" demanded CC.

Jack explained how Molen was supplying information to Satans Wrath through Leitch's secretary.

"So she gave it to Leitch, who then showed it to this guy in the park?" asked CC.

"Exactly," said Jack.

"Maybe we should bring Molen in and grill him," Elvis suggested.

Jack shook his head. "I don't think Molen knows

him. I'm not sure Satans Wrath even knows who it is. My guess is that Leitch is playing both sides of the fence. Working for the Indos and the bikers. You bring Molen in and that might just spook everybody."

"Another fake report then?" suggested CC.

Jack and Elvis exchanged glances, and then Elvis said, "We already did that, but I think Molen burned us. I'm not sure another one would work."

"Sounds like you don't have anything to lose by trying," said CC. "I want this guy bad. What he did to..." She stopped as she thought of Susan's horror. She felt her body begin to tremble and knew she couldn't articulate that subject without losing control. *If I'm going to cry, it won't be in front of these two guys!*

CC gave Jack what she hoped was a tough and angry look. He looked back and slowly squeezed his eyes shut and opened them. *He's telling me he feels like crying too.* CC felt slightly embarrassed. *He's a man and not afraid to reveal his emotions in front of me, and here I am a woman and trying to act tough. What the hell has happened to this world?*

"Guess you're right," said Elvis, staring at the video. "This is Friday, so we've got the weekend to come up with another report. If Molen has burned us, it won't take long to find out."

"The one who knows is Leitch," said CC. "How about doing surveillance on him and hope he leads us to the Brit?"

"That's part of the problem," explained Elvis. "Last time when we gave Molen the dummy report, he acted kinky. Later we saw Leitch just BlackBerry a message and then burn the report. I don't think these two will get together any time soon. Also, Leitch is a lawyer, so good luck on trying to get a wiretap."

"CC is right," said Jack. "Leitch is the key."

"He's one key," said Elvis. "How about Satans Wrath? What's the head honcho's name?"

"Damien," replied Jack.

"Do you seriously believe, with all the lawyers in this city, that it is just a *coincidence* that Satans Wrath and the Brit use the same lawyer?" asked Elvis. "Come on! That's who ultimately got the report from Leitch. He has to know what is going on."

"I agree there's some connection," said Jack, "but I'm certain Damien doesn't know about it. He would never authorize someone to mess with a cop's family like that. Not to mention this same person killed someone else thinking it was me. Damien wouldn't make that mistake."

"Sounds like you think you know him pretty well," said Elvis.

Jack noticed Elvis studying his face closely as he responded. "We met last year when his guys screwed up. I think I know him well enough."

"You haven't talked to him since?" asked Elvis.

"Haven't needed to, but what I'm saying is that Damien knows what I look like and who I'm married to. They wouldn't kill Holly's husband by mistake."

"I tend to agree with Jack," added CC.

Elvis looked at them both, then sighed and said, "Leaves us with trying another scam on Molen come Monday." Then he looked at Jack and said, "Unless you have any other ideas?"

"Try your idea. It could work."

"But if it doesn't?" said Elvis. "What then?"

Jack's eyes narrowed. "I suppose CC will just have to keep doing surveillance on Leitch and hope she gets lucky."

CC didn't respond. She didn't believe he meant that any more than he did.

# chapter eighteen

It was eleven o'clock Sunday night when Jack parked beside the cemetery and waited for Lance, who arrived twenty minutes late and got in Jack's car.

"Sorry, I'm late," said Lance. "Was with The Toad. Couldn't get away."

"Not a problem."

"Where's Danny?"

Jack turned on the interior light and told Lance what had happened. Jack could tell that Lance was uncomfortable, but it was because of the light and not because he knew anything about the Brit.

Jack turned the light off with a promise that if Lance could identify the Brit before he did, then his debt would be considered repaid.

Lance was quiet for a moment, then said, "I'm not so sure I like that deal."

Jack was surprised. "You would prefer to go with

our earlier agreement and work for Club Fed for another four and a half years?"

"I was just thinkin'. Anyone who did what that guy did … I'd like to give him to you for free." He pointed his finger at Jack and added, "And it's four years and five months. I know my math."

"Hey, I'll be glad to get a free one from you."

"You think I'm fuckin' nuts? I'd like to give him to you for free, but I sure as hell won't! I hate being a rat! The faster I pay you back the better I'll feel."

Jack reflected upon his past debt with Damien. *I know exactly how you feel.*

"I'll keep my ears and eyes open," continued Lance. "If I get a whiff of anyone matching that description, you'll be the first to know. Kinda agree with you, though. I think that fuckin' Leitch is working both sides. If Damien finds out he's doin' that, there'll be one less lawyer in the city." Lance chuckled and said, "Bet that doesn't exactly worry you much."

"It would if we didn't find out who the Brit is first."

Lance nodded and said, "Gotcha. But in the meantime, we got a shipload of coke comin' in and I've been assigned to oversee the unloading. The Toad wants at least four vehicles to haul it away. Two hundred and fifty keys each. None of it will be going to the same place so there's no way of rippin' it all off. If you try to take it down at the dock, then I'll get busted."

"What about the cash?"

"The Toad is looking after that personally. He doesn't want it and the dope in the same place at the same time. He's going to hand it off to the Colombians at some motel. The Colombians will confirm they got the money and use a cellphone to tell someone on the ship to unload."

"Why is The Toad so paranoid about bringing the money to the dock?"

"Doesn't want to have all the eggs in one basket. He said the Colombians don't want the money near the dock either."

"What motel?"

"Hasn't been picked yet. It'll be my job to take The Toad and find a suitable motel. A few hours before the deal, he'll take a few of his guys and the money and go to the motel. Nobody but him and me will know which motel until he gets there with his guys and calls the Colombians."

"So where does Damien sit on this?"

"On his ass at home. This is all The Toad's plannin'."

"Who handles Leitch … or the Brit if it does turn out to be someone working for Damien?"

Lance shrugged and said, "The way Damien feels, that end may fall by the wayside. I know this isn't the news you want to hear, but once The Toad takes over, you may never find out."

"Then The Toad can't take over," said Jack.

"Hey, man! If you bust The Toad at the motel then I'll be burned to a crisp — probably literally."

"I won't burn you."

"So what are ya gonna' do? Nothin'?"

Jack looked at Lance and said, "I'll play it by ear." He thought to himself, *I'm going to squash a toad!*

On Monday morning, Jack was a little curious when his boss was twenty minutes late for work. Louie was usually half an hour early.

Jack's curiosity was answered when Louie showed up on a pair of crutches with a cast on one leg. Before Jack could ask, Louie gruffly said, "Saturday. Ladder slipped cleaning my gutters. Broke in three places. Enough said. What's new with you?"

"Not much since I called you Friday night."

"Molen getting another report?"

"Yes. I-HIT is helping with surveillance too, but we're not optimistic."

"Your friend doesn't know who the Brit is?"

Jack shook his head. "Met him last night. He doesn't know." Jack waited until Louie nodded in response, then asked, "Have you heard from Danny? How are they doing?"

"We talked briefly. He's taking stress leave. I think they're planning on going someplace for a while. He's talking about quitting. I suggested he take time off and think about it. No need to rush into a decision right away."

"Where are they staying?"

"He had the option of staying at a motel but elected to return home. He's adamant about not returning to work. As he said, he's complying with the note so he doesn't think he's a target now."

"What about Jimmy?"

"Apparently seems okay. Lucky little bugger. What do you think about Danny quitting?"

Jack sighed and said, "Can't say I blame him. I was wrong to be around him after CC got that note. I should have stayed away from everyone."

"The note targeted everyone in the office. We have no choice but to continue working. Danny's pretty upset. Not thinking too clear. Who would? He mumbled something about your cowboy hat turning black. What was that all about?"

Jack tipped his head back, took a deep breath, and then slowly exhaled. "Guess he has me pegged as one of the bad guys."

Louie studied him closely for a few seconds and then said, "Like I said. He's upset. I'm going to talk with Isaac. Hate to lose a good man. Maybe I can arrange to get him transferred into some admin position for a while."

It was after lunch when Isaac reviewed the report submitted by the Anti-Corruption Unit noting that Jack had lied about not having met Damien since last year. *Not a big issue in itself, but...* The name of the ACU investigator caught his eye and he summoned Staff Sergeant Legg.

"This report you submitted this morning," said Isaac, gesturing to the paper on his desk.

"Yes, sir. Just a short memo. Perhaps nothing, but after the report from CFSEU about Taggart and then him telling Elvis that he hadn't met with Damien since last year ... I just thought I should keep you informed. It will be more ammunition to use after we hear back from the LO in Mexico."

Isaac nodded and said, "It was Elvis he said this to?"

"Yes, sir. Connie Crane from I-HIT was present as well."

"Isn't Elvis married to Laura Secord from Drug Section?"

"Yes, sir."

"She was the female operator who worked with Taggart on that homicide involving the war veteran."

Legg shrugged his shoulders and replied, "I don't know."

"Well I do know." Isaac leaned forward, clasping his hands on his desk. He then said, "For your information, O'Reilly is being transferred forthwith to an administrative position. It would not be ... unusual ... for him to be replaced. Intelligence is extremely busy right now. Under the circumstances, I would endorse an immediate transfer. It would appear that Taggart has a good working relationship with Laura Secord, don't you agree?"

Elvis was not pleased with Molen's response, or actually his lack of response, to the new report. He didn't make any calls and didn't leave during the lunch break. Surveillance teams monitoring Leitch and his secretary had nothing to report. It was almost four o'clock when Elvis was summoned into his boss's office.

"Did you happen to mention to your wife that Taggart could be dirty?" asked Legg.

"No," replied Elvis. "We try not to discuss work at home. I did ask her if she suspected any of the narcs of being dirty and she said no. Why do you ask?"

"O'Reilly is being transferred immediately to an administrative position. I heard through the grapevine that Laura may replace him."

Elvis sat quietly.

"How do you feel about that, should it happen? What with Taggart being under investigation by our office?"

Elvis shrugged.

"Do you feel apprehensive about the prospect?"

"That would indicate that I doubt Laura's integrity, which I don't. So, no. I'm not apprehensive."

"Would Laura confide in you if she discovered something that wasn't kosher?"

"You mean if Jack is dirty, would she burn him?"

Legg nodded.

"Without a doubt ... but I'm sure she won't take the job if you're asking her to spy."

Legg smiled, shaking his head. "For goodness' sake, I'm not suggesting that! I just want to make sure that this doesn't cause any undue stress on your marriage.

Also to ensure that if Laura did discover something she would confide in you so as to alleviate any accusations of her covering something up down the road."

"If it was anything serious that our section should know about, she would most certainly talk to me about it. She's my wife. I would do the same if the situation were reversed."

"Exactly. At which time you would follow through with your responsibilities and discuss it with me. Then we could ensure that she would be protected against any undesirable accusations concerning her own conduct."

"That goes without saying. I know Laura. If Jack is dirty, she will be the first to nail him to the wall."

"Good. That is all I expect. We have no proof that he is dirty. This Mexican thing could be a coincidence."

"It's been two weeks since we sent the photos," noted Elvis. "We should know soon enough."

Legg nodded, then said, "At this point, I would suggest you don't say anything to Laura. Taggart is clearly astute when it comes to reading people. Obviously, he has to be; I'm sure his very survival has depended upon it. With that in mind, we couldn't expect Laura to successfully hide that knowledge. Some inadvertent sideways glance or perhaps a hesitation in her voice might be all it would take to tip Taggart off."

"I understand," replied Elvis. "Not to mention, we don't know if Taggart is dirty. False allegations and rumours harm innocent people."

"Exactly. This conversation is just between the two of us. I'm telling you this as a friend, which is why you need to ensure that you discreetly report anything of consequence to me. It is imperative that Laura doesn't become implicated in anything untoward. She has an excellent reputation for being professional. I'm certain, once this is over, she would understand completely should you decide to tell her then. That would be your decision, of course."

"Of course."

Legg waited until Elvis left his office before calling Isaac.

"Everything is in order, sir. I feel confident that Elvis will cooperate fully."


Elvis rejoined the surveillance team just as Molen left the office. They followed him to a liquor store and watched as he bought a bottle of Canadian Club. Then he drove straight home.

At nine-thirty, Elvis received a call on his radio.

"Just got a good look at him through the binos from the back alley. He's sitting by himself at the kitchen table. Looks like the whiskey is three-quarters gone."

"Copy," replied Elvis. "Let's shut it down. Nothing is going to happen tonight."

"Going to haul his..." The officer paused, conscious of radio procedure, then continued, "... haul his butt in tomorrow?"

"Ten-four. Be a good time to try. He'll be tired and hungover."

# *chapter nineteen*

It was eight o'clock the following morning when Elvis consulted with Jack about his belief that Molen knew the game was up.

"So you want to grab him?" asked Jack. "If he doesn't roll, it could still heat up my source and we wouldn't be any further ahead."

"That's why I'm talking to you. I won't do it without your okay."

"You said he has a problem with the booze?"

Elvis nodded and said, "Sat by himself last night and drank most of a bottle of whiskey. I'd say he was an alcoholic. Divorced years ago and his boss said he doesn't appear to have any friends."

"How nervous do you think he is?"

"Very. I don't think he could handle the pressure of an interrogation. We've already got him dead to rights on the first delivery."

"Then do it. It's worth the risk if by some chance he knows something about the Brit."

"Your person can take the heat?"

"With the way Molen is, Satans Wrath wouldn't expect him to last long. They may think he was drunk and blabbed something."

"Good enough," replied Elvis. "I'll grab him as soon as he comes in."

Elvis was just walking away when Jack said, "Elvis, if he resists, put one through his skull for me!"

Elvis thought about Jack's comment as he waited in his office for word of Molen's arrival. Jack's response was like most cops' when it came to one of their own being dirty. *He seems genuine, but then again, he is an operator...*

Two hours later, Elvis found out why Dick Molen had not arrived at work. A postal worker had become suspicious at the sound of a car running inside a garage with the door closed.

Jack went down to the cafeteria to have a morning coffee and sat with a few acquaintances who had been in the lineup ahead of him. A few glanced around nervously. Soon they all made feeble excuses and departed, leaving Jack sitting alone.

*Gee, guys. My wife is out of town. How about inviting me home for Yorkshire pudding?* Jack left his coffee unfinished. *Can I blame them? The Brit is laughing at all of us.*

Jack returned to his desk just as Elvis arrived.

Elvis told him about Molen and then commented, "Carbon monoxide. I'm surprised he didn't eat his gun."

"Maybe was too hungover and afraid the noise would kill him," replied Jack. "Did he leave a note?"

Elvis shook his head.

"You sure it was suicide?"

"Doors were all locked from the inside. No sign of forced entry anywhere. His right hand has bloodied knuckles and splinters of glass. It matches a smashed picture on his wall."

"Picture of what?"

"Himself. When he graduated from Regina."

Jack thought for a moment, then said, "Other than saying he hated himself, it would have been nice if he told us what he had passed on."

"You'll have to presume it was everything he ever knew," said Elvis.

"I wonder if Satans Wrath will show up at his funeral to pay their respects."

Elvis rolled his eyes in response and then said, "It's too bad, though. Waste of a —"

"Yes!" interrupted Jack. "Too bad we don't know who the Brit is ... and too bad the dirty narc wasn't sitting beside Molen."

Jack met with Lance and told him about the self-destruction of The Mole.

"Thanks for the heads up," said Lance. "Normally I would be a little concerned, but right now, with Damien getting the boot, I think it will hardly be noticed. Especially with the action that The Toad has on the go."

"I need to find out who the Brit is," said Jack. "When Damien finds out that The Mole is dead, ask him if there could be a leak."

"*Me* ask *him* if there is a leak?"

"Question him about who else has contact with Leitch. Ask him if he ever used a go-between."

"Fuck! I am the leak! I don't want him to even start thinking about that."

"Do it. If he's going to suspect anything, he will regardless of what you say. It's better if you're on the inside pointing a finger rather than being quiet and being pointed at."

Lance took a deep breath and slowly exhaled, then said, "Okay. I'm meeting him tomorrow night, along with The Toad. I think I'll be told exactly when the ship arrives. If Damien knows about The Mole by then, I'll do it."

"Good. I'll see if I can get it in the news. Meet me here at five-thirty Thursday morning to let me know what is happening."

"How about four-thirty? If the ship is arriving in the next couple of days I'm liable to be busy."

"Make it five. The cemetery has a security guard check it three times a night. He does his last drive-through around four-thirty."

"How do you know that?"

"I've seen him. Know his schedule pretty well."

Lance studied Jack's face for a moment, then asked, "Is this where your niece and nephew are buried? You come out here at night?"

Jack hesitated and glanced at another part of the cemetery, then replied, "My work is often nocturnal. Other nights I just have trouble sleeping."


Jack returned to his office. One didn't have to be overly observant to notice that various colleagues avoided eye contact with him as he made his way to his desk. A couple of standard greetings that Jack gave were answered either with a grunt or a turn of the head and pretense of a cough. *It's like I'm walking around with a chicken under each arm and a sign that says I've got the avian flu...*

That night Jack called Natasha from his apartment. He was tired and intended to speak for only a few minutes, but it was over an hour before he hung up. He realized how much he missed her. His bed seemed very empty that night.

The following day was no different at his office, except this time he packed a sandwich and ate lunch at his desk. It was better than sitting alone in the cafeteria.

He was more than a little surprised to see Laura enter the room with a smug look on her face and sit in Danny's chair.

"What gives?" Jack asked. He then said, "You might want to close the door. Being seen with me isn't too popular these days."

Laura glanced at the open door and her smile vanished. "Elvis told me. I know about Danny. I want to get whoever is responsible."

"Me too. Real bad."

"How could someone do that to a baby?" she said, her voice wavering.

Jack saw some tears well up in her eyes, but then she regained her composure and said, "Staffing called me in this morning. Said they were looking for someone to replace Danny and asked if I was interested."

Jack waited, but when Laura didn't continue, he asked, "What did you tell them?"

"I said, 'Not a chance! Do you think I'm a lunatic!'"

Jack looked at her for a moment, then said, "Oh."

Laura looked surprised and said, "Oh, man ... you really think I said that? Jack ... I was joking! I'm sorry. Are you okay? This has really gotten to you, hasn't it?"

Jack paused, then said, "Yes. It has."

"Guess I can understand that."

"So did you accept?"

"I stalled them for an hour. I wanted to speak to you first. If I can help nail this crud, I'll feel like my life as a cop is complete. I figure working with you is the best option."

"Working with me maybe isn't ... look what happened to Danny. Are you —"

"Hey! I'm hoping he will come after me. I'll be bait if you want me to." When Jack didn't respond right away, she added, "Besides, you look like you could use a friend. Come on. I'll make a good partner. Just tell me what you want."

"I don't know what I want right now."

"Yeah? Well stand up, I know the first thing you need," she said, while coming around from behind the desk.

Jack slowly stood up and Laura said, "If there was anyone I've ever seen who needs a hug, it's you." She hugged Jack and gave him a kiss on the cheek.

Jack closed his eyes for a moment. Her embrace felt good. It made him feel less alone.

Laura stepped back and said, "Well? Do you want me as a partner or not?"

"Yes, I do."

"I can start next Tuesday after the May long weekend. Gotta run. Have to let Elvis know I spoke with you and that you agreed ... after I performed a sexual favour."

Jack smiled, then replied, "I don't need any heat from Elvis. I can get into trouble easy enough without that."

Laura was almost out the doorway when Jack said, "Laura!" He waited until she turned around and then said, "Thank you."

She smiled and replied, "We'll get him, Jack."

Jack thought about her after she left. *She offered to be a friend ... but would she ever be a good friend? Danny's a good friend ... or was.*

Moments later, Louie hobbled in on his crutches and asked, "Wasn't that Laura Secord who just left? What did she want?"

"Staffing offered her Danny's position. She asked what I thought."

"What did you say?"

"I'm pleased. She starts six days from now."

Louie frowned and said, "How do you know she's not the dirty narc?"

"The day we took down those labs she was on a plane coming back from Bangkok. It's not her."

"I see." Louie paused for a moment and then said, "You know her hubby works for Internal."

"I know. Anti-Corruption."

"Doesn't concern you?"

"She's okay."

"I retire in two months. You know that."

"I know, in July. Looking at those crutches, maybe you should retire now, but what's that got to do with Laura?"

"It means I won't be around to cover your ass!"

Jack smiled and said, "I appreciate that."

Louie gave him a hard look, then said, "Hope you've learned a few things over the last couple of years."

"Louie, you've been the best teacher I could have had. I'd be lying if I didn't admit I'm sorry to see you go."

"Don't get fuckin' mushy on me. Your assessment isn't due until after I leave. Won't do you any good to suck up to me. Just hope you know what you're doing."

"I trust my instincts," replied Jack. He thought about his comment as Louie left. *Funny ... "I trust my instincts" ... that was what Spider said just before Laura slammed his face into a table and arrested him.*

# chapter twenty

It was five-fifteen in the morning when Jack heard his name whispered and saw Lance stand up from behind a tombstone.

"What's up?" asked Jack. "Any news on the Brit?"

Lance shook his head. "The news about The Mole came up. Damien said there was heat on 'im. I asked about a leak. Damien said it was only Leitch, his secretary, Pussy Paul, Whiskey Jake, and me that knew. He said the leak probably came from The Mole when he was pissed. If Damien had someone else dealing with Leitch, he would have told me."

Jack hadn't expected Damien to know, but felt disappointed just the same. "You're sure everything was okay? Maybe Damien is just playing you."

"Don't think so. I was given my assignment for the ship. It arrives tomorrow night. It's a good time for us. Friday of a long weekend. Cops and port authorities won't want to take time to nose around. If anyone suspected me of being a leak, I wouldn't have been told."

"What is your job when it arrives?"

"The Toad is gonna have me at the dock to oversee things there. Will happen in the early evening. The Toad will hand the money off at a motel called the Spotted Owl."

"Never heard of it."

"It's by an industrial area out in Burnaby. Not far from the Labatt Brewery. Only The Toad and I know the location right now. Even Damien doesn't know the name of the motel. The Toad is running things really tight. The strikers won't even know until they're with him and arrive at the motel."

Jack nodded.

Lance stared at him briefly, then said, "So, like, you can't do anything or I'll get —"

"Trust me. Where's the money now?"

"Don't know. The Toad has it stashed with a couple of his guys. Around nine o'clock tomorrow night The Toad will BlackBerry the name of the motel to the Colombians. They will arrive and weigh the money to make sure it's all there."

"Can't these guys afford money counters?"

"Too slow. Should be about thirty-five kilos worth of Canadian hundreds. A little more or less doesn't really matter. Then the Colombians send a message to the ship and we unload."

"Canadian? What's with that? Thought they would demand American?"

"Yeah, The Toad said he was surprised when he found out too, but that's what the Colombians wanted. It works out to about $3.5 million Canadian. It's a hell of a lot easier for us. The Toad said they plan on buying some business up here to make things easier to connect with us. Probably have a mom and pop and couple of kids operation someplace."

"That's a lot of money for a mom and pop operation."

Lance shrugged and said, "That's just The Toad's guess. Maybe it'll be a few more than that. I don't know."

"So the Colombians are coming off the ship and going to the motel?"

"No. I guess some of them are already here. I don't know how many for sure, but I think only a handful. Probably looking to scout out the business front. A couple will be at the dock and two are supposed to wait and go to the motel when The Toad calls 'em."

"You haven't met any of them?"

"Nope. From what The Toad says, they barely speak English. All this was arranged by The Toad previously so we don't expect any problems."

"Just two Colombians for all that money?"

Lance chuckled and said, "That's what I asked. The Toad said that these Colombians treat that like you and I would a hundred bucks. We're paranoid as shit about it and they just laugh. I think the fucking cartel deals in truckloads of cash. This is just peanuts to them."

"A lot of peanuts."

"No shit. But I guess if you try an' rip 'em for fifty bucks they'll slash your throat."

"A matter of honour."

"Yeah, I guess. I can only wonder at how much their organization is rolling in."

"How many of your guys will be protecting the money?"

"The Colombians agreed that they won't be packin' when they come to the room."

"You can bet they'll have weapons close by."

"Yeah, for sure. But not with them. They go to the room and consent to a search. Then The Toad makes a call and the money is brought in. We're not worried about a rip. It went smooth with them last time." Lance paused, then added, "Not counting what happened at the storage locker after."

"Right," replied Jack. "We won't count that. How far away do you think the money will be?"

"Last time we brought it in a van. This time we rented adjoining rooms. Once the Colombians are frisked, The Toad will just rap on the door. Things should go smooth. We've already established a trust with each other. Unless, of course, you do something…"

Jack arrived back at his office. Louie arrived for work an hour later and motioned for him to come in.

"Anything going on?" asked Louie.

"No," said Jack. "I just talked with my friend but he doesn't know who the Brit is. Doesn't think Damien knows either."

Louie nodded and said, "Too bad. Nothing else happening?"

"No. That was it."

Louie looked at Jack closely, then said, "Maybe just as well. You need a rest. I want you to take some time off. We'll find out who the Brit is sooner or later."

"I'd rather it be sooner."

"All of us would. The thing is, he obviously knows what you look like. It would be better for everyone concerned right now if you weren't around. Maybe take a week or two off. You should be with Natasha."

"I'm okay … and there's no way this guy is going to start dictating who works in this office and who doesn't."

"Have you thought about Natasha? Cooped up at the farm? She must be worried sick about you. I'm not telling you to run away and hide. Just take a holiday. Maybe I-HIT will nail him in the meantime."

Jack sighed and said, "I'll think about it over the weekend. Monday is a holiday so I should be rested by then."

"Why not take tomorrow off too? In fact, you should take off now."

"It's only eight-thirty in the morning."

"Yeah, and you've already put in ... what? Four hours? How many more hours in the last couple of weeks? You're a newlywed for God's sake. Start acting like one and go see your bride."

Jack thought for a moment, then said, "Thanks, Louie. I appreciate what you're saying. I've got some paper work to do. I'll leave at noon."

"Good."

"Anything further from Danny?"

Louie frowned and said, "I spoke with him briefly, tried to be supportive. Don't think he wants to talk to any of us right now. They're all getting counselling. I think we should just butt out for now."


Jack called Natasha and told her that he would be out to the farm shortly after lunch. She said she was pleased, but he heard the irritation in her voice. He knew he couldn't hold her off much longer from getting back to the clinic.

At noon, Jack stopped at a café for lunch before driving out to the farm. The café did have one thing going for it, thought Jack, as he dabbed a greasy french fry into some ketchup. It was clean and the service was friendly. Unfortunately, it was just a little too busy for Holly to be able to take the time to visit with him.

He watched as she greeted the customers and gave them all big smiles. Sometimes her lips trembled slightly, revealing her real thoughts. It had been less than a month since her husband had been gunned down. Pretending to be happy ... trying to get that extra quarter or loonie for a tip. *Welcome to hell.*

Jack left a twenty on the table and nodded politely to Holly as he left. He was barely out the door when she came running after him.

"You forgot your change," she said.

"No, that's for you. It's your tip."

Holly shook her head. "You don't drop a twenty on someone for a seven-dollar burger. I don't take charity," she said, thrusting the twenty toward him.

"It's not charity. It's just a tip."

Tears filled to the brim of her eyelids and she said, "You think you can buy off your guilt for twenty bucks? Forget it! What you ate is on me!"

Jack didn't know what to say. It occurred to him that she might be right.

"Get the two men who killed my husband and shot Charlie," she said, "then you can leave me a tip."

Jack nodded, then reached over and slowly took the twenty from her hand. "You'll be getting this back soon," he said. "That's a promise."


Natasha waited until she climbed into bed beside Jack, and then whispered, "How much longer?"

Jack pulled her close and she lay with her head on his chest. "I may get a break tomorrow night," he replied.

"I don't like the sounds of that," said Natasha. "You going to be wearing your black turtleneck?"

Jack paused. Natasha was catching on. The black turtleneck was what he often wore at night — usually when he was doing something he shouldn't be doing. He chose to ignore her question and said, "If all goes well, I may find out who the Brit is in the next few days. Getting tired of being a farmhand?" he added, hoping to change the conversation.

"Incorrect answer, officer. Your failure to respond would indicate a *yes* to the turtleneck question. As far as changing the subject goes, Liz and Ben have been great. I enjoy being around Marcie, too, but I miss you and I also need to get back to the clinic."

"It's just not safe. Not after what happened."

"What is going on tomorrow night? Can you talk about it?"

"Basically, the Brit knows a lawyer by the name of Leitch who works on retainer for Satans Wrath. The bikers don't know about the Brit, but I know Damien could find out who it is if he wanted to."

"How? You're not planning on owing him another favour?"

"Shhh. Ben and Liz are in the next room."

"You're not…" whispered Liz.

"No. I've used up any favours with him."

"Why would he find out, then?"

"A character nicknamed The Toad is taking over the club. I want Damien to distrust The Toad. Then I want him to think that The Toad, Leitch, and the Brit are working together. It won't take him long to find out who the Brit is, providing I can get him back into power. When he does, my friend will know and then so will I."

"How will you do all this?"

"I'm working on that."

"What if you do and Leitch refuses to tell Damien?"

Jack chuckled, then said, "Damien isn't a cop."

"Meaning?"

"He can be more persuasive."

Natasha looked up at Jack's face, then replied, "Oh … I see."

## *chapter twenty-one*

It was seven-thirty on Friday night before The Toad and two underlings showed up at the Spotted Owl. Jack was parked in a lot across the street and watched the motel through binoculars. He had seen The Toad last year when he interrupted an executive meeting at Damien's house, but he glanced at a photo just to be sure.

Jack smiled as he recalled the event. He had intentionally interrupted the meeting on the pretext of returning some colours that had belonged to some bikers who had been killed. Damien was cordial and offered him a beer. The Toad was not pleased and voiced his objection in a thick French accent. An accent that Jack soon hoped to mimic.

Jack now saw that the two underlings each carried a sports bag.

Jack smiled. *Very expensive sports bags.*

The Toad entered one room while his two cohorts entered the room beside it. Moments later, The Toad opened his door and Jack saw one of the other two bikers behind him. It was obvious that their rooms had an inside adjoining door.

Two hours later, Jack saw an old beat-up white van with tinted rear windows slowly drive through the motel parking lot. The curtains moved slightly in The Toad's room as someone peeked out.

The two men inside the van paid close attention to all the other parked cars. Eventually the van parked. Jack steadied the binoculars on the top of his steering wheel and watched. The two men talked with each other for a moment, then the passenger bent over out of sight. Seconds later, both men got out of the van. Their complexions told Jack that they were the Colombians. The driver then opened the rear door to the van and removed an object wrapped in a garbage bag.

*Scales! Lance was right. This is going to be fast.*

Both men then walked over to The Toad's room and knocked on the door. Seconds later, they disappeared inside. Jack threw the binoculars down and grabbed a roll of duct tape and his balaclava.

Moments later, Jack was inside the van. A quick search under the dash located two handguns. Each with a silencer. Jack put them back, then squatted on the floor in front of the passenger seat and peeked past the seat to the rear. It gave him a view of the motel through the back windows of the van. He gripped his 9mm and waited as the seconds slowly ticked by. He was conscious of a strong odour of coffee in the van. *As if my nerves aren't frayed enough!*

Jack hadn't needed to hurry. Almost forty-five minutes passed before the door to The Toad's room opened again. One Colombian carried the scales and a sports bag, while his friend carried the other sports bag. They paused at the door and the driver shook hands with The Toad.

Sweat dripping from Jack's face made a wet spot on the vinyl cover of the seat and he wiped it off with his sleeve as the two Colombians approached the van and opened the rear door. Jack ducked down and heard the sports bags and scales slide across the van floor. He waited until the door slammed shut before quickly making his way into the back of the van and hiding behind the passenger seat.

The passenger door then opened, but the man didn't get in. Jack heard the sound of numbers being pushed on the man's cellphone. The driver's door then opened and the driver stood looking across the seats at his partner.

Panic gripped Jack's brain. He had hoped the two would quickly enter the van and drive away. His hiding spot behind the passenger's seat was not large enough to conceal him completely. He had purposely picked the passenger's seat believing that the driver would be focused on his keys and the ignition upon entering the van. *Not standing there with the door open staring in!*

Jack held his breath but was conscious of the noise his heart made. It seemed loud inside the metal walls of the van. He stared at the driver's face, waiting for his eyes to wander to his location. It was dark, but not so dark that he couldn't be noticed. Outside, he heard the passenger talking in Spanish.

The passenger then yelled, "Okay, amigo! I see you!"

Jack sucked in a mouthful of air and his grip tightened on his gun before he realized that the man, in his broken English, was saying good bye to The Toad.

Seconds later, both men got inside and the driver quickly drove out of the lot. They were barely out on the street when Jack saw the passenger bend over to reach under the dash.

"Okay shit-heads! Don't move!" screamed Jack, while leaping forward and sticking the barrel of his pistol into the passenger's ear.

The driver panicked, hitting his brakes and causing his passenger to slam face first into the dash. The movement threw Jack off balance and he waved his pistol back and forth at both their faces while regaining his footing.

The driver started yelling at his passenger in Spanish but stopped when Jack yelled, "Shut up or die! Keep both your hands on the steering wheel!"

Jack grabbed the passenger by the back of his collar and jerked him back into his seat. "Hands behind your head! Now!"

"Señor! No understand!"

Jack made a motion with his own hand behind his head and the passenger clued in.

Jack pointed to a side street and said, "Drive!"

The driver made the turn and then pulled over to the curb as directed. Jack held the roll of duct tape between his knees and peeled off a pre-cut strip and handed it to the passenger with his free hand.

"Do it yourself! Over your eyes! Now!"

Moments later, Jack ensured that both Colombians were securely blindfolded. He then took out his cell and punched several numbers, pretending to make a call.

"Hey, Toad! Worked just like you said! We're just down the street. Hurry up."

The driver muttered something under his breath. Jack didn't know much Spanish, but he heard The Toad's name being used. *Questioning the legitimacy of The Toad's parentage, no doubt.*

"Shut the fuck up!" Jack ordered, before allowing himself a moment to take a few slow deep breaths.

Jack then guided the men to the rear compartment of the van and made them sit on the floor. He taped their hands behind their backs and their ankles together, before knocking on the rear window.

Jack opened the rear door of the van and said, "Hey, Toad. What took you so long? Look at this ... I did good, yes?"

Jack then stuck his head around the back of the van door and lowered his voice and put his hand over his mouth and gave a guttural, "*Oui!*" He then leaned back inside the van and said in his normal voice, "Here, I'll pass you the money."

Jack slid the sports bags across the floor of the van, then gently lowered them to the ground outside where they could not be seen from within. He then said, "Yeah, I'll sit with 'em for ten minutes just in case they get a call. Don't worry, I'll make sure they say the right thing! If they don't, I'll see it in their eyes. Besides, *mia hablo Espanol!*"

Jack then closed the rear door and ripped the tape off the men's eyes and mouths. He took the cellphone out of the passenger's pocket and held it close to the man's face. "If this rings, amigo, you say everything is okay ... or else you die!"

The men stared back at him. The driver's wide eyes and the sweat glistening on his forehead revealed his fear. The passenger was different. His eyes looked dark and angry.

Jack put their phone in his jacket pocket and sat on the floor of the van. He frequently looked at his watch while he waited, ignoring the stares from his captives. After ten minutes he used his own cell to place another fake call.

"Toad ... what's taking you so long? Thought you would have called by now."

Jack pretended to listen for a moment, then said, "The ship's unloaded?" He glanced at his two captives and added, "You want me to kill 'em now?"

The passenger no longer looked angry. His eyes widened and he whispered to his friend.

"Hang on," continued Jack, "why not do it in another hour? This street is basically deserted." Jack paused, pretending to listen, then said, "No…" while reaching around to his hip and pulling a hunting knife out of the scabbard. "I'll slash their throats like you said. No noise, but that's not what I meant. This street is deserted so it's not like any of their friends will find us. There's no rush. Why not wait an hour just to make sure our guys are far away from the ship?" Jack paused again and saw both men with their mouths open, straining to hear every word. "I disagree! Toad, if we just … Toad? Toad?"

Jack cursed and shoved his phone back in his pocket. He stared at the two men while slapping the blade of the knife against his open palm.

"Señor. Please. I have children to feed," pleaded the driver.

"Shut the fuck up," said Jack, getting to his feet. "Both of you, slide together back to back. I'm gonna tie ya together instead o' killin' ya."

They did as directed and Jack wrapped several strands of duct tape around both men's chests, tying them together. He then used his knife to cut the end of the tape. A flicker of the passenger's eyes told him it was noticed that he had placed the knife on the floor of the van while pretending to ensure that his captives were bound properly.

"Señor … thank you for letting us live," said the driver.

"Fuck that," said Jack, while taping their mouths again. "I'll be back soon to finish the job."

Jack went out through the rear door of the van and slammed the door behind him. He grabbed both sports bags and went back to his car and waited. It didn't take long before he spied the two Colombians creeping through the parking lot toward The Toad's room.

Jack adjusted the focus on his binoculars and saw that each held a pistol. He watched as one stepped back from the door, raising his foot to kick, when the door unexpectedly opened in front of him.

A biker stood for a moment, with an ice bucket in his hand and his mouth drooped open. Jack didn't hear anything but saw the biker's head jerk and knew where the first bullet struck him as his body crumpled to the floor. The Colombians ran inside. A few seconds later, Jack saw one Colombian casually look outside before closing the door. Several minutes passed, and then the Colombians left the room and went to the parking lot. They tried two different vehicles before finding the one that the keys matched.

Their search for the money was fruitless, and Jack chuckled out loud as he watched them gesture and point in anger before running back to where they had left their van.

Jack drove out of his parking spot and saw the van enter the main street and then drive off in the opposite direction. A minute later, Jack parked behind the motel and went to his trunk and put on some latex gloves and a toque. He walked around to the front of the unit and stepped inside. One biker was sprawled on his back on the floor. One eye was open, but the other eye had been replaced by a bullet hole. The second biker was sitting in a chair, slumped face-down on the table. Blood oozed out of his forehead.

The Toad was still lying on top of the bed, partially propped up with pillows. His chin was resting on his chest. Jack went over to check his pulse but realized that The Toad had taken two bullets to his heart.

*I wish whoever taught the Colombians to shoot would teach me.*

Jack went to the rear of the unit and opened up a bathroom window overlooking the back of the motel. Seconds later, his cell vibrated. He was expecting a call, but his nerves were taught and his body surged with more adrenalin.

"You told me to call when it was done," said Lance. "Did I wake ya?"

"No," replied Jack. "It's only eleven. I was just getting ready for bed," he said, glancing at The Toad. "How did it go?"

"Smooth as shit. Went down just like I told ya."

"Good. Glad it went okay."

"Man, I was a little nervous. Appreciate you sitting this one out."

"Yeah, well … maybe next time. What are you doing now?"

"Goin' home and gettin' some rest. Do you want the details?"

"Later. We'll meet next week and you can tell me then."

Jack shut off his phone and bent over the bed. *Okay, Toad. Hibernation time.*

# *chapter twenty-two*

It was after midnight when Danny answered the phone on his bedside table. He saw Susan as she walked in and stood in the doorway. She had been sitting in a chair in the children's room.

"Danny ... sorry to wake you, but I need help."

Danny looked at Susan and said, "It's Jack."

Susan didn't reply but stood and stared at her husband.

"What do you want?" asked Danny as he spoke to Jack but continued to look into Susan's eyes.

"I need a friend right now. A *good* friend. Tonight, before the sun comes up."

Danny paused as Jack's cryptic message sunk in, then said, "Forget it! I don't want you calling..."

"Please, Danny," pleaded Jack. "Just listen. I'm really close to identifying the guy that did this to your family. He was at the funeral for Holly's husband.

That's how he ID'd us. Elvis identified him as the same guy who met Leitch in the park. Looks Indo and has a British accent. I've got a plan. I'm going to trick Damien into identifying him for us."

"No," said Danny quietly.

"You don't get it! We can nail him within the week! He won't be trying to kill any more babies!"

"Damn it, Jack! *You* don't get it! I don't care if you catch him! I'm done! I want out!"

"Danny ... you're just ... probably PTSD," said Jack, speaking rapidly. "Try to calm down and think about —"

"You're fuckin' right I'm stressed! So is my whole family! All I want is to get Susan, Tiff, and Jimmy the hell away from here — and from you!"

"Danny, I'm sorry. I —"

"Don't ever call again!" Danny said, before slamming the receiver back down.


It was after one o'clock in the morning when Laura drove past a cemetery and then spotted Jack parked nearby on a quiet street as per his directions. She parked and then hurried over and joined him.

"What's up?" she asked, glancing around. "You got the eye on someone?"

"No, it's not surveillance," replied Jack. "I lied."

"You lied? Three or four days before I'm even supposed to start working with you and you're already lying to me?"

"I just thought it would be easier to explain once you got here."

Laura studied him briefly, then said, "Well, I'm here."

Jack took a deep breath and slowly exhaled, then said, "The other day you offered to be my friend."

Laura nodded.

"What I need right now is a *good* friend."

Laura looked at Jack but didn't reply.

"Do you understand the difference?"

"Don't know what you're getting at. Sorry. Maybe I'm not awake yet."

"A friend is someone who would help you move."

Laura nodded.

"A good friend is someone who would help you move a body."

Laura snickered, then said, "Yeah, right. Good one. So what's really going on?" She saw Jack's face partially illuminated by a streetlight. It was a face that looked desperate. A sense of dread overtook her when she realized he was serious. "Does this have something to do with who tried to kill O'Reilly's baby?" she asked.

"Basically," Jack replied.

Laura didn't speak for almost a minute.

Jack didn't interrupt her thoughts. What he was asking her was to risk everything she had.

Finally she spoke. Her words were a whisper. "If this is about the guy who attacked the O'Reilly family, then I could be a good friend."

"Are you sure?" Jack asked. "I know you. I remember when I worked an operation with you in Alberta. You made me stop the car to rescue a gopher that was snagged on something."

"That's cuz gophers don't kill babies."

Jack nodded, then said, "Okay. We don't have much time."

"Who, when, and where?"

"Right now ... and he's in the trunk."

"You're not serious!"

Jack quietly handed her the keys and sat in the car while she went to look. She saw the man's body wrapped in a yellow plastic police emergency blanket. A shovel was also in the trunk.

"Oh, man," she mumbled, then got back in the car. "You killed the guy?" she asked.

Jack shook his head, then replied, "No. He was already dead when I found him."

"And he's the piece of shit who likes to kill babies?"

"No, but he is a piece of shit. He's a — he was — a member of Satans Wrath. If he disappears, I expect we'll find out real fast who tried to drown Jimmy and murdered the guy who had my name."

"What is going on?" asked Laura. Her voice sounded quiet but firm.

Jack quickly explained what had happened, along with his plan. Laura glanced into the back seat at the two sports bags, then reached over and unzipped one of them. She dug her hand briefly through a few of the layers of bundles of money before zipping the bag closed.

"If The Toad and the money are missing," continued Jack, "it will look like The Toad ripped everyone off. I've already found a fresh grave. We'll just make it two for the price of one. It won't take long, but I need you to distract the security guard when he comes by."

"Are you on medication?" asked Laura, sounding serious.

Jack shook his head and said, "I'm not crazy. This will work. Once I spread the rumour that The Toad was working with the Brit, it won't take Damien long to find out. When he does, my friend will also know. My friend thinks Leitch launders money so it would fit that he could be involved in the rip along with The Toad."

"Have you tried following Leitch?"

"Ask Elvis about that. They did, along with I-HIT. They got burned. Leitch would have warned the Brit. Whoever this guy is, he has to have a lot of clout to get

Leitch to show him secret police reports before the bikers even see them. You can bet he'll be extremely cautious. I doubt that any future surveillance on Leitch
would be successful."

"But your friend could find out through Damien?"

"If Damien knows, then my friend will know. I want
to put all the heat on The Toad and spread the rumour
that The Toad, Leitch, and the Brit are in cahoots. With
The Toad gone, Damien should step back into power. In
the unlikely event my source isn't made privy to the Brit's
identity, Damien might be willing to help me. He'll think
it's in our common interests. He'll want the money and
revenge, and we want the Brit."

"Really?" said Laura. "Damien might help you?"

Jack caught her suspicious look and said, "He's
helped me before."

"Sounds interesting."

"Don't even go there."

Laura studied Jack's face for a moment, then said,
"So how do you get Damien to think the heat was on
The Toad? He's not stupid."

"I'll put word out that we were working on The
Toad when he led us to the Brit and Leitch. One of our
narcs is supplying info to Satans Wrath."

"I know. Elvis told me."

"If the info comes to Damien through the dirty
narc, he'll be inclined to believe it's true. Especially with
The Toad and the money disappearing. To protect my
friend, I'll indicate my informant is a hooker who was
servicing The Toad. I'll say she saw The Toad meet with
the Brit who then met with Leitch that day in the park.
Damien won't know what to think."

"What about the Colombians?"

"They barely speak English. Everyone will be confused. It doesn't really matter. What counts is that

Damien will grab Leitch and find out who the Brit is. I know this isn't exactly by the book, but..."

"By the book? Oh, man! It is in the book. The Criminal Code of Canada! We'll both end up in the crowbar hotel."

"Not if we're careful. But I understand. If you want to back out, go ahead. This is the only plan I could come up with to protect my source and find out who the Brit is."

"So you plan to lie to everyone about this hooker and the park thing?"

"Satans Wrath have too many of their own sources and are always developing new ones. I don't believe in telling our people anything that isn't necessary for them to know."

"Did it ever occur to you that you might have a trust issue?"

"I always have a trust issue."

"Glad you recognize it. Maybe there's a twelve-step program you could take."

"There is. I can walk past a dozen tombstones of people who died because someone trusted the wrong person."

Laura decided to ignore the remark and said, "So when you do find out who the Brit is ... what then? Turn him over to I-HIT?"

"Something like that."

"What do you mean, 'something like that'?"

"Put yourself in Susan's position. Imagine being tied to a chair while you watch your baby being tossed in a swimming pool ... then being left there to watch for the next half-hour."

"I've thought about that," said Laura quietly. "Often."

"If that doesn't get you, then think about Holly's

dead husband and a toddler by the name of Charlie spending the rest of his life in a wheelchair."

"So what are you getting at?"

"We have no solid evidence on the Brit to link him to anything. Just a picture of a guy in a van looking out while I'm getting a call on my cellphone. Even if he was convicted, do you really think that ten or fifteen years in jail is enough for what he did?"

"So what are you saying? That we should just shoot him?"

"Personally I think that is letting him off too easy." Jack thought briefly about two other murders. His niece and nephew. They were killed by bikers, but someone else — Bishop — gave the orders. He looked at Laura and added, "We don't even know if the Brit is responsible. He could be working for someone else."

Laura stared back at him without speaking.

Jack waited for a moment, then said, "All I'm saying is we can cross that bridge together when we come to it. Who knows what opportunities will arise along the way."

"Opportunities? Like what?"

"Take tonight. I didn't expect to get this lucky, with the bad guys killing each other and me ending up with $3.5 million. Believe me, I understand your concern."

"This wasn't luck. You orchestrated what took place tonight."

"I didn't know for sure the bikers would get whacked. As long as I had the money, it would make The Toad look bad. My plan still would have worked as long as Damien was suspicious of The Toad."

"That aside, when the time comes to cross that bridge you spoke of, what then?"

"If you are going to be my partner, we'll discuss it then."

Laura sat in silence.

Jack waited briefly and then said, "Today was a chance to give Satans Wrath a good kick in the balls. Besides losing the money, we've just cut off their Colombian connection."

Laura gestured to the sports bags in the back seat and asked, "What do you plan on doing with that?"

Jack sighed, then admitted, "There was another reason I did this tonight."

"You wanted to pay off your Visa?"

"I couldn't stand the idea that the bad guys had this much money while Holly can't even afford to buy a wheelchair. In a little while, when things cool down, $1 million goes anonymously to her. Later, in dribs and drabs over a year, the rest to spinal cord research."

"That should make Holly happy."

"It's not that much when you consider the expenses she's going to have. Even if she buys the most modest home, she'll still be lucky if she has enough left over to cover expenses for the rest of Charlie's life."

Laura nodded, then said, "Considering what she lost — her family, her baby — nothing could compensate for that."

"You got that right."

"The Colombians will still want the rest of their money back."

"Let Satans Wrath figure that out. They've still got the coke so it won't take them long to repay. Maybe they won't even bother. They'll know the Colombians won't deal with them again."

Laura remained silent.

"So that's the story. Do you want to help me … or arrest me?"

Laura continued to remain silent.

Jack stared at her, then said, "I can't take the stress any longer." He withdrew his gun and dropped it in her lap and said, "I'm exhausted, burnt out ... and this conversation is killing me. If you want to call and have me busted, go ahead."

Laura sighed, then said, "This is absolutely nuts. Maybe it's not too late. Let's haul the body back to the motel. We can't be doing this. It's wrong."

"What's wrong about it? The guy is even getting a proper burial — almost."

Laura glanced at her watch and saw that they didn't have much time. *Even taking the body back could land us both in jail.* She thought for a moment and then said, "Just a minute," and went to the trunk and took another look.

"What were you doing?" Jack asked when she returned.

"Small calibre that plugged him. Hardly any blood," she said, while handing Jack his gun back. "Obviously wasn't your piece."

"I told you I didn't shoot him."

"So you said, but you also lie to people. Let's take him back. There's still time."

Jack tried to wipe the sleep and stress from his eyes, then turned on the interior light and said, "Take a look at the picture stuck in the sun visor."

Laura removed the picture.

"That's Charlie taking his first steps. I want you to imagine him in a wheelchair, maybe for the rest of his life. I want you to picture his mother. Stuck with raising a paraplegic baby and another child who is only four years old."

Laura looked at Jack.

"Don't look at me! Look at the picture! Right now there is no cure, but research indicates that spinal cord repair and regeneration is possible. A cure for paralysis could be as close as ten years away, but it takes money! Tell me again that what I am doing is wrong! You really think we should turn this money over to the politicians! Come with me now if you're not convinced. We'll go to BCCH and I'll introduce you to Charlie face to face! After that you can drop in and have a tea with Susan O'Reilly."

Laura was silent for a moment, but her hand shook as she held the photo. Then she put the photo back and said, "You know how to get to my underbelly, don't you?"

"Yes ... because my feelings are the same as yours."

"You're lucky I was stationed in Alberta. I know the expression 'shoot, shovel, and shut up.' Looks like the shooting is done. Time now to shovel and shut up."

"You're sure?"

Laura ignored him and continued, "There is one condition. If we find the Brit, we turn him over to I-HIT."

Jack took a deep breath and then let it out. "Thanks. I agree. From what Danny says, you're probably right on that account."

Moments later, Laura followed Jack's car in her own through the cemetery gate and along a narrow path lined with tombstones. He parked over a small hill, near a grave laden with flowers. They both got out of their cars to talk.

"This one is fresh," said Jack. "I'll have to remember exactly how the flowers were laid, as well as how the sod was re-laid. It shouldn't take me long to shovel and I've got spare blankets so the dirt won't show."

"Too bad you didn't find a fresh hole. Bury him a little and have the coffin go on top."

"I've checked. They have liners that go inside with a cover on top. Someone would know if it was tampered with."

Laura glanced at Jack and said, "Out of curiosity, how long have you really been planning this?"

"As I said, I didn't know what was going to happen until tonight."

"Then … do you have other people buried in here?"

Jack nodded.

*Oh, man…*

"My niece and nephew."

"Oh! Right," she said, and then blurted, "I heard Bishop was killed in an accident in Mexico."

"Yeah, I heard that too. Come on. Help me with the blankets and flowers. Maybe the sod, too. Then get down by the gate and park at the entrance. Security came through when you first arrived. We should have about three hours. I should be done by then, but if I'm not, you stop him."

Laura nodded and said, "I'll be the grieving lady in distress. I should be able to handle it."

Jack opened the trunk and turned to Laura and said, "Welcome to your first shift on Intelligence. Looks like you and I are about to become good friends."

Laura gave Jack a hard look and said, "Don't make fun of this. Would your wife stick by you if she knew what you were doing?"

"She wouldn't be happy, but I think she would agree with it."

"Maybe that's because she doesn't work in Anti-Corruption."

Her words were not lost on Jack. *It's easier to be brave when you don't have so much to lose.* It occurred to him that Laura might be one of the bravest people he ever met.

In Colombia, Carlos flung his telephone against the wall and swore. *Because Damien lives in Canada, he thinks he can spit in my face!* His orders were clear. Retaliation would be immediate!

\* \* \*

Jack had made two serious miscalculations. First, he had presumed that Carlos was a businessman and relatively sane. Second, he knew Damien as a pragmatist and had expected him to react calmly and logically to a situation that would see his power restored.

# chapter twenty-three

It was taking Jack much longer than he had expected. More than three hours passed before he lifted The Toad out of the trunk and placed him in the grave. He was exhausted. It would take at least another hour to finish.

He was just starting to shovel the dirt back in when an arc of headlights over the hill and the sound of a horn at the gate caused his body to tense.

Laura pretended she didn't notice the small white car with *SECURITY* printed on the door as it slowed down on the street before turning in and parking behind her. She discreetly unbuttoned the top two buttons on her blouse, then held her face in her hands and started crying.

Moments later, the beam from the security guard's flashlight hit her face. Her mouth and eyes opened wide with apparent shock. Her elbow hit the horn as she scrambled to roll the window down.

"Miss, what are you doing here? I'm going to ask you to move your car immediately. You're blocking the entrance."

"Oh, sir. I'm sorry," she sobbed. "Can't you just drive around me?"

"It's pretty tight," he replied. "Still, would you mind explaining to me..." He stopped when his flashlight beam fell upon Laura's sleeves.

Jack had provided her with surgical gloves to help roll back the sod, but they had not protected her arms. Now she saw dried mud on both sleeves.

"I want you to step out of the car, now!" he ordered.

*Oh, man...*

Laura stepped out and the security guard shone his flashlight over her body, then saw that her shoes were also muddy. He held the flashlight above his head and slowly shone a beam of light across the cemetery grounds. "What have you been doing in here?" he demanded.

"I'm sorry," sobbed Laura. "I'm sure I killed it. I don't know what to do," she wailed.

"You what?"

"The cat," said Laura, pointing down the street toward the corner of the cemetery grounds. "Down there, by the culvert. I was driving and it just ran out in front of me." She put her hand on the guard's arm and added, "I tried to stop! But I ... just couldn't. I heard the noise of its little head under my car. My God, it was sickening. I can't bear to think about it!"

"Oh!" said the guard as he shone his light toward the corner. "I didn't ... I'm sorry. Take it easy. It's not your fault if..."

"I, I pulled in here and ran back. I thought I heard it down in the culvert. I reached in, but I couldn't find it. It's so dark and dirty down there. I don't know what to do. We can't just leave it there!"

The security guard allowed his flashlight to pan Laura's body one more time before saying, "Come on, hop in with me. Show me exactly where. We can use my flashlight to look."

Laura rode with the security guard and directed him to park down the block.

"It's almost four-thirty in the morning," noted the security guard. "You always out this late?"

"Not usually. My girlfriend organized a singles party. By the time I helped her clean up, it was pretty late. She wanted me to sleep there. Wish I had."

"Really?" The security guard's tone revealed his interest as he adjusted his rear-view mirror lower than it should have been. "Meet anybody interesting?"

"No," said Laura glumly. "Just the usual beaters, cheaters, and bottom feeders. Sprinkled with a few who were either emotionally or physically gimped. Then there were a couple of gays and lesbians. Wasn't for me. The men I did talk to were wussies." She then glanced at him and said, "Isn't your job dangerous? Working out here all alone at night?"

The first rays of sunlight were visible on some scattered clouds to the east when Jack slowly drove past Laura and the security guard. They were still parked at the end of the block and Laura was drinking out of a Thermos cup.

Fifteen minutes later, Laura parked behind Jack and walked to his car. She turned her back briefly as she remembered to do up the buttons on her blouse, then got in.

"What took you so long?" she asked. "If I had to

sit another minute with that wannabe cop I'd be digging him a hole in there!"

Jack allowed himself a grin, then said, "Sorry. It was a lot tougher to do than I thought it would be."

"Oh? So this is the first time you've done this?"

Jack ignored the question and said, "Let's find a washroom to clean up. Then go sit on the Spotted Owl."

"Speaking of that, how come you're not dirty?"

"Had an old pair of coveralls in the trunk. Bought them last year for Danny when he had to do surveillance from a pile of garbage."

"Would have been nice if you had thought to provide me with a pair," she said, gesturing to the dried mud on her sleeves. "Not to mention, my shoes are ruined."

It was six-thirty when Laura used the binoculars to scan the motel from a lot across the street. "How long, you figure?" she asked.

"There's a bloody smear on the sidewalk outside the door. Someone should notice."

Damien thanked Vicki when she poured him another cup of coffee, then went back to reading the morning paper. It was nine o'clock in the morning. Buck and Sarah were still in bed, but Katie was up and chatting with excitement about going to an afternoon birthday party. Vicki had promised to take her shopping for new clothes for the event.

Damien leapt from his chair when Katie toppled her glass of orange juice, sending the liquid over the edge of the table.

"Sorry, Dad! It slipped!"

"It's okay," he grumbled. "Quit talking and get a cloth."

Vicki smiled at her husband and said, "It's a pretty big event. Not every day that your *much* older friend turns nine."

Damien rolled his eyes, then said, "Right. Older by what? Five months?"

"We'll leave in a few minutes, honest," said Vicki, kissing Damien on his forehead as he sat back down.

Damien received a message on his BlackBerry. It was from Lance. The message was coded but told him that the shipments had gone as planned last night.

*Is this good news or bad? Good news is I'll be getting my money back. Bad news is there's little doubt as to who will be the new national president.*

"See ya in about two hours, Papa Bear," said Vicki, giving him another kiss on the top of his head.

"Goodbye, Daddy."

Damien wrapped one arm around Katie and gave her a hug and then a kiss. "Tell Mommy that she's not to spend more than five dollars on you," he said.

"Daddy!"

Damien chuckled, but his joy turned sour as soon as Vicki and Katie left. *The Toad isn't the type to want anyone with brains around who could question his actions once he takes over. Surprised he isn't here gloating right now.... Hope his hangover kills him.*


Vicki found a place to park, then opened her door to get out. She was thinking that her life had been blessed. Her family was happy and healthy, and her husband had climbed his way to the top of the ... corporate ladder. She smirked when she thought of it as a corporation. *But that's what it is, isn't it? An international corporation continuing to expand around the world.*

*This thing with the new mortgage and The Toad ...
somehow it would work out. It always did.*

She had turned in her seat and placed one foot out
of the Hummer when a man's fist buried deep into her
midriff. The air exploded from her lungs and her body
doubled over as the force of the punch rammed her
backwards across the seat.

Vicki gasped for air as she tried to scream, but the
man's fingers and thumb formed a claw to dig deep into
her throat and squeeze until she felt her windpipe begin
to collapse. She lay still, hoping he would stop. He
stopped squeezing but kept the pressure on her throat.

Vicki saw other men moving about. She saw a man
gripping Katie by the throat. Katie's bulging eyes briefly
stared down at her as she was dragged out of sight to
the rear of the Hummer.


"Think we've got action!" said Laura. "The maid stopped
her cart outside the door."

"Too bad," replied Jack. "I was just starting to
doze off."

"She's kneeling down and looking up ... now she's
standing ... knocking." Laura passed the binoculars
over to Jack.

"Using her pass key," he said, then lowered the
binoculars. "Guess you don't need binos to see that!"

The maid ran across the parking lot to the office.
Jack and Laura looked at each other and then slumped
low in their seats.


Vicki and Katie were gagged, blindfolded, and bound,
with their wrists taped together behind their backs.
Vicki guessed that her Hummer had been driving for

half an hour before it stopped. Then she heard the sound of a large overhead door close.

Moments later they were both hauled out and the tape was ripped from their eyes. Vicki saw that they were in a small warehouse. The strong smell of coffee was in the air and burlap sacks were piled on various pallets.

Two men held Vicki and Katie by the arms and roughly jerked them along to a pallet that contained only a few bags. Then they were shoved and fell beside each other onto the pallet. The two men stood over them, watching as Katie cried and choked through her gag.

Then two more men approached. One was carrying bolt cutters. The other rolled Vicki over onto her stomach and then grabbed her hands. She tried to scream but the gag prevented any real noise as she twisted and rolled her body. She managed to roll over, digging her fingers into the sack for support and kicking upwards with her feet.

The men stood up, then looked at each other and laughed. They spoke to each other in Spanish.

Vicki did not know these men. Perhaps it was better that she didn't.

They were hand-picked from an army of desperate, violent men who wanted a share of the narco dollars. Carlos did not pick them because of their limited knowledge of English or even their willingness to do anything he asked. He picked them because they were likely insane. They inspired terror and would do anything asked of them. It was simply human nature to pick people who are like you — albeit not as intelligent.

Seconds later, both men were on her again. She fought and kicked hard. Katie got to her feet and kicked one of the men. He punched her hard in the mouth and she fell to the ground and didn't move.

Vicki quit kicking. Tears blocked her vision and she allowed herself to be rolled back over onto her stomach. She was conscious of the taste of coffee beans on her lips from where a sack had been torn. She felt a man's grip on her fingers and the cool metal of the bolt cutters as the pinchers tightened on her finger. For a brief instant, her brain refused to accept that the sound she heard, like celery being crunched, had come from her own body. For a moment it was as if her brain had detached itself from her body. She heard her own muffled cry as if it came from someone else, but then she felt incredible pain and knew the voice was hers. She squeezed her eyes shut, trying in vain to block it out.

# chapter twenty-four

Connie Crane and her partner arrived at the motel and a uniformed officer waved to them from the doorway of one of the units.

"Call came in about forty minutes ago," he said as they approached.

Connie glanced at her watch and replied, "About nine-thirty, then?"

He nodded and stepped aside to allow them to enter.

Connie did a brief examination of the room while her partner fished wallets from each of the two victims. One had a pistol in his belt, and Connie saw a Mac-10 pistol lying on the bed in the adjoining room.

The radio response to their inquiries came back within seconds. Both victims were listed as probationary member of Satans Wrath out of Montreal.

"Gee, that's a big surprise," said Connie sarcastically.

"What the hell are they doing out here?" her partner asked.

"Dope deal gone bad," replied Connie.

"You find dope?"

"No, but this door is open to the adjoining room. There's a blood smear in the bathroom and it looks like a third guy escaped out the back window. These two yo-yos were killed instantly so it wasn't them moving around."

"Could be dope. They have lots of firepower."

Connie nodded and said, "That's their number one money-maker. Three guys — bikers — in adjoining rooms with only a double bed in each. They weren't here to sleep. Probably using the other room as either security or to stash the money or the dope. Being from Quebec even fits. Last year Intelligence discovered that assholes from Satans Wrath in Quebec were running speed out here."

"Who would have the balls to waste a couple of these guys?"

Connie glanced around the room, then replied, "No sign of forced entry. I bet whoever did this was known to them. They didn't even have their guns out. Alert the hospitals to be on the lookout for anyone coming in with potential GSWs. Let's see if we can find who did this before the bikers do."

Fifteen minutes later Jack walked into the motel room. "Hi, CC. Want some help?" he said.

Connie turned around in surprise. Jack was already in the room and she saw Laura looking in from the doorway. "Careful! We're still waiting for Forensics to arrive."

"Hi, Connie," said Laura. "There's a blood smear on the sidewalk."

"We know." Connie looked at Jack and asked, "How the hell did you hear about this and get here so fast? It's Saturday morning of a long weekend," she added.

"A source I've known for a long time told me that three Satans Wrath members from Montreal were in town to do a major dope deal this weekend. An executive of the club known as The Toad and two strikers. Apparently they were to hand off three or four million bucks to buy dope."

"Three or four million!" said Connie's partner. "I guess that could give someone the balls to do this!"

"Recently I turned another informant — a hooker — who knows The Toad. We were meeting her when we heard your radio transmission about the two strikers. She has been servicing The Toad since he arrived. She said that back on the second of May, she was with The Toad and saw him meet some dark-skinned guy on Robson Street. She says the dark-skinned guy then walked across the street to a park and met with Lawrence Leitch. He's a lawyer that Satans Wrath uses."

"I know about that!" said Connie. "We were working with…" She paused and looked at Jack and said, "Wait a minute, that was almost three weeks ago! You telling me that some hooker can remember an exact date that long ago?"

Laura leaned against the doorway and watched. *This ought to be good.*

"Definitely," replied Jack, his face expressionless as he stared at CC. "She said she remembered it because of something she had said to The Toad the day before and he joked to her about it as they drove past the park."

"Which was?" demanded CC.

"She had said, 'Hooray, hooray, it's the first of May — outdoor screwing starts today!'"

Laura snickered to herself, more at the sincere look on Jack's face than his words.

"Oh," replied CC, eyeing Jack warily. "I was there that day with" — she glanced at Laura — "your husband. That was over the Molen incident. This Toad is tied in with the guy we call the Brit? The same son of a bitch who attacked the O'Reillys and murdered Holly's husband and shot their baby?"

"Has to be," said Jack. "The Toad told my inform-ant to wait for him in the car. She said he was acting really kinky and paranoid. She followed him and only caught a quick glimpse of the action."

"Damn it! I was there that day. I didn't notice any hooker or The Toad," said Connie.

"How would you have known?" replied Jack. "It's not your fault," he added, while stepping over to look at the face of the biker lying on the floor. He looked closely at the biker who was sprawled face-down on the table.

"Be careful," said Connie. "Forensics hasn't —"

"Just making sure that either of these two isn't The Toad. They switch identities like most people change underwear. They're not. No money here, I take it?"

Connie shook her head.

"There's a rental out front. Could be theirs."

"It is. We already checked. No bags of money."

"Sure, you say that now," said Jack. "I'll be watch-ing. If you two retire next week I'm coming after you."

Connie grinned and replied, "Don't I wish." Her face then became serious and she asked, "Any sugges-tions? Can your sources help us out? We think one guy was wounded and escaped out the bathroom window."

Jack rubbed his chin and thought for a moment, then said, "Maybe The Toad decided to retire early. The bikers probably had security out front. Bet that's why he slipped out the back."

"But who would have shot him?" said Connie. "There's some blood on the bedspread and a smear on the bathroom wall. Neither victim had a gun in his hand."

"Who says he was shot?" said Jack. "This guy sprawled out on the floor ... maybe he saw it coming and got a punch in. The Toad might only have a broken nose."

Connie considered this and then said, "Guess that's possible." She paused, then asked, "Your hooker friend have any leads as to where he might be?"

"I'll check. You should call the narcs right away and tell them what I told you. This much action should have their sources talking. Tell them I have a hooker close to The Toad. Maybe something will click with them. If The Toad is running off with the club's money, he won't be sticking around long. Maybe one of the narcs will know something to identify the Brit. If we find him, I bet we find The Toad as well."

Connie looked carefully at Jack as she digested what he said.

"We'll head out now," said Jack, moving toward the door. "Tell our source to get to work."

"Not so fast, Jack!" said Connie.

Laura felt a lump in her throat. *Oh man ... I knew we couldn't pull this off!*

"What's the problem?" asked Jack.

"Your DNA," said Laura. "It'll be all over the room now. We'll need a sample for elimination."

Laura had wondered why Jack had moved around the room. Now she knew.


Jack and Laura were just returning to their car when Jack received a call on his cell.

"You said you wouldn't bust our guys! I'm dead! I'm fucking dead!"

Jack recognized Lance's voice and said, "Your guys weren't busted."

"Bullshit! I just left the motel. There are cops all over the place! The Toad's not answering or returning calls!"

"I know. I'm at the motel now. I was notified about it through Homicide."

"Homicide?"

"The maid checked the room this morning. Both strikers are dead and The Toad is missing. Looks like he took the money and split."

"You've got to be fuckin' kidding me!"

"We should come and meet you and talk about it."

"Danny back in action?"

"No," said Jack, glancing over at Laura. "I've got a new partner. You can trust her."

"It's a *her*? Oh fuck!"

"She's a ... good friend. Trust me."

"Yeah, like I have a choice."

On their way to meet Lance, Laura asked, "How long do you think it will be before Damien hears the whopper you just told Connie?"

"Wish we knew who the dirty narc is. Regardless, the club is out a few bucks. Not to mention two dead strikers and a missing toad. The heat will be on. I bet Damien hears the story by Monday or Tuesday. The friend I'm about to introduce to you will hear when Damien finds out."


Jack introduced Laura to Lance. He was polite but mostly ignored her. Bikers tended to view women as property. Not as anyone you would listen to, let alone take orders from. At the moment he had too many other things on his mind to worry about Laura.

"What the hell happened? Who whacked 'em? Where's The Toad?"

"We don't know," said Jack. "You called me last night to say everything was okay. That it was a done deal!"

"It was! I don't know anything about this!"

"You said nobody knew about the motel except you and The Toad," said Jack accusingly.

"And the Colombians," said Lance. "But that don't make sense. They were already paid before I..." Lance stopped and glanced at Laura.

"She knows," said Jack. "I trust her. You're going to have to do the same."

"Yeah, well ... anyway. They were paid before the ship was unloaded. So why would someone kill 'em?"

"Have you talked with Damien? Maybe The Toad is with him."

"Not yet. Guess I better send him a short message, then drive over to talk details."

"Do it, but first call the motel office and see if they'll tell you what happened."

Lance understood, and a couple of minutes later a clerk at the motel admitted that two guests had been murdered.

"Good," said Jack. "Now tell Damien you went to look for The Toad and saw cops all over and called the motel. Call me as soon as you're done meeting with him."

After Lance left, Laura suggested, "Home to bed?"

"Think you can sleep?"

"I might. When I get really stressed I feel like my whole system shuts down. All I want to do is close my eyes."

Jack nodded, then gestured toward the back of the car and said, "Right after I stash what's in the trunk."

"Three-point-five. You're going to have a lumpy mattress."

"Actually ... I rented a storage locker the other day."

"I knew it! How long have you been planning all this?" she said, letting her exasperation show.

"The storage locker was for something else a couple of weeks ago."

"*Something* else?" She paused, then asked, "You have a freezer in there?"

Jack smiled, then replied, "You are tired. If I had a freezer in there I wouldn't have had to call you out last night. Great idea, though. Maybe I should get one and extend the rental."

"If you do, get a new partner while you're at it. No wonder Danny is on stress leave."

Laura had meant it as humour but saw the look on Jack's face and was embarrassed. "I'm sorry," she said, "that was a dumb thing to say."

"Not your fault. I just feel bad about how things turned out between me and Danny."

Jack noticed that Laura was silent as he drove her back to her car. Then he saw that she was shaking. "Cold?" he said, turning up the heat.

"It's not the cold. I'm scared."

"Of what?"

"Of what I did! Helping you!"

"Now it hits you?"

Laura opened and closed her fists a few times to try to regain control.

"Afraid we'll get caught?" asked Jack.

"A little. More worried about whether or not I did the right thing."

"When we catch the Brit you'll feel like you did the right thing."

Laura sighed and said, "I know. I'm not blaming you. I made my own decision." She paused a moment and then added, "Although it bugs me that you made me look at Charlie's picture. I feel manipulated."

"Kind of late to change what we did now."

"I'm not saying we should. I'm just not sure what we did was right."

Jack felt the acid in his empty stomach as he worried about Laura having second doubts. He glanced at her and said, "What we did was right." He then paused and said, "Sorry about the manipulation. Won't let it happen again."

"Yeah, right. As if I really believe that. You're an operator."

"You're an operator too."

"Exactly," Laura said, and then smiled.

"Were you just jerking my chain?"

"About having second doubts? Yes. You should have seen your face. But not about the manipulation part. I don't like being manipulated. I was just getting even."

Jack smiled. "Are we even?"

"Sure. Now how about we get some sleep."

"Let's have brunch first. It would be better if you relax a little before going home. I know this great little café. Excellent service as long as you don't try to leave a tip."

It was almost noon when Damien received a text message from Carlos. *A cold phone is at your front house. I will talk at you in one hour!*

Damien chuckled. Carlos's attempt to use English slang sometimes sounded funny.

*My front gate perhaps? Probably means a delivery service will bring me a cool phone.* Damien went to his communications room and checked the television monitor near the front gate. Vicki's Hummer was parked there, but she was not in the driver's seat.

*Maybe she's picking a package up from the ground. I've warned her about packages!* He zoomed the camera in on the Hummer. *Where's Katie?*

He paused as he received a text message from Lance. *Two bros from Q were murdered last night at the motel. Coming over.*

Damien stared at the Hummer. It was still deserted. He ran from the house.

# chapter twenty-five

Connie Crane called her boss and briefed him on the double homicide. She spoke of Taggart and Secord's involvement and said that Drug Section was canvassing their members for any leads.

Randy hesitated when he hung up. Any reason for calling the assistant commissioner on a Saturday had to be extremely serious. He soon knew he had made the right decision.

Isaac listened to the details with a keen interest and thanked Randy for updating him. Isaac then called Staff Sergeant Legg and ordered him to contact Elvis immediately.

Elvis took the call and listened carefully as Legg explained the situation.

"I don't really know anything," said Elvis. "She's not home yet."

"It's after twelve. You haven't heard from her?"

"She called about an hour ago. Said she was going to have a bite to eat with Jack and would be home after. That's all I know."

"What time did she start working last night?"

"We were asleep. I didn't really check the time. It was late, after midnight for sure."

"She didn't mention why she was called out?"

"I asked her if it was undercover. I thought she said surveillance, but I'm not sure. I was half asleep. Do you want me to ask her?"

"A little gentle prodding might not hurt."

"She should be home any minute. I'll ask."

"Be discreet! As I said before, we'll just keep this between the two of us. The road to hell is slippery and steep. Let's make sure Laura doesn't reach that part."


Damien stopped when he reached Vicki's Hummer and looked around. Nobody was in sight. Something was wrong. Really wrong.

It was with a sense of dread that he opened the driver's door and looked inside. He felt relieved to see that it was empty, except for a plastic bag on the driver's seat. He peeked inside the bag and saw that it was just a cellphone, partially wrapped in a rag. The keys hung from the ignition. He parked the Hummer in the garage and brought the plastic bag inside to the kitchen table.

*What the hell is going on?* He took the cellphone out and set it on the table. He picked up the rag and saw a small blue jeweller's box in the bottom of the bag. He was about to set the rag aside but something caught his eye. The fabric had pictures of Disney characters on it. They were panties that Vicki had bought for Katie during the Easter break. They had been slashed off with a knife.

Damien felt the bile from his stomach burn his throat. He abruptly grabbed the jeweller's box and opened it. He saw Vicki's wedding ring. It was still attached to her finger.

Elvis greeted Laura as she came through the door, then gave her a warm kiss and a hug that lasted longer than normal.

"Everything okay?" she asked.

"Just missing you," he said. "That was a long shift. I didn't think you were supposed to start working with Jack until Tuesday."

"He needed a hand."

"Something couldn't wait?"

"A lot of action right now. Some bikers just got wasted in a motel."

"Some?"

"Two guys. Both with Satans Wrath. Drug deal went sideways. Jack has a good source. He introduced me. Pretty heavy stuff." Laura turned away and headed for the bedroom. "I'm going to shower and go to bed."

"You're not on Homicide. How come you were called?"

"We found out about that later. It was Jack's source we were meeting. We knew a major deal was going down. Just didn't know where until we heard Homicide radio it in."

When Laura finished her shower, she was about to get into bed when she saw a penny on her pillow. She paused, then slipped on her housecoat and walked into the kitchen where Elvis sat in a chair staring at her.

"What's wrong?" he asked.

"Nothing," she replied.

"You're avoiding looking at me. Can you talk about it?" he said, then saw the tears in her eyes. He rose quickly and wrapped his arms around her. "What is it? What the hell happened?"

Laura wiped her eyes with her fingertips and then said, "Everything is okay."

"Bullshit," said Elvis quietly. "I'm your husband. Talk to me."

Laura sighed, then said, "Jack has a picture ... he just got me to do something."

"To do what? What is it?"

"To meet someone."

"This informant?"

"Not about that. The mother. This baby's mother! The ... oh, the picture was of a little guy taking his first steps. His name is Charlie. He was shot last month when his dad was killed."

"The one in the news?"

Laura nodded. "Now Charlie is paraplegic. His mom is a waitress. Her name is Holly. Now she's trying to raise a four-year-old and Charlie by herself."

"Why the hell did Jack introduce you to her?"

"He's become friends with her. She's really a nice lady. I'm glad I got to meet her."

"So she showed you the picture?"

"Actually Jack did, the first time. She gave it to him a while ago. He keeps it tucked in his sun visor."

"The first time?"

"When we were working. I looked at it again just as Jack dropped me off. My choice." Then she started to cry and added, "What kind of human being could do something like that!"

Elvis pulled her close so that Laura's head was on his chest. "I don't know," he murmured. "I just don't know."

They stood for a moment, hugging each other, then Laura said, "We're going to get the fucking asshole! That's for sure!"

Her words shocked Elvis and he stepped back. It had been about four years since he last heard her swear. Then she had said *shit*.

"One shift with Jack and you're learning a new vocabulary?" he asked.

Laura blushed and said, "Sorry. I didn't hear that from Jack. His methods of investigation are ... rather unorthodox, but he acts like a gentleman." She smiled and added, "I came up with them sweet little cuss words all on my own."

"Think maybe I should wash your mouth out with soap," Elvis chided.

"Not now, I'm too tired," she said, kissing him quickly before heading back to the bedroom.

"Hon!" yelled Elvis. "What did you mean when you said that Jack's methods were unorthodox?"

"Don't worry about it," she replied. "He just thinks outside the box. I'm looking forward to working with him. I suspect we'll become — actually, we already are — good friends."

Jack flopped on his bed and called Natasha, who was still out on the farm.

"Sorry, sweetie," he said. "It was a long night. I don't have the energy to drive all the way out there. I need sleep."

"Hey, turkey! How did it go?" she asked. "Have you identified this British person yet?"

"No," Jack admitted. "But we're a lot closer."

"We?"

"I called Laura. She came out to help."

"Good! So you're not on your own, then?"

"No. She's my new partner."

"Think she will ever be as good as Danny?"

"I trust her. She's not afraid to get her hands dirty."

Lance saw the pain in Damien's eyes. It had been less than fifteen minutes since Damien found the package, but the driveway was already filling up with vehicles. A state of war had been declared, and every available soldier and resource was being alerted. Damien's house would be packed with loyal followers within the hour.

Buck and Sarah were inside battling each other over a computer game. The children ignored the two strikers who stood warily at the doorway. They had been taught since birth not to ask questions about Dad's work, especially inside the house.

Damien and his upper echelon met in hushed tones outside by his pool. The word had gone out to every source who might know something.

Pussy Paul was the first to break the news when he hung up his cell and said, "Our rat-narc came through. Both strikers dead. Nobody knows where The Toad is and the pigs are looking for him. They think he skipped out with the money."

"How did the feds know about the money?" Damien snarled.

"That fuckin' Jack Taggart is involved. He was working on The Toad. Has some whore as a rat. Had info about him doin' the deal. Also says The Toad has something to do with some dark guy with a British accent. They figure if they find that guy, they might find The Toad."

"Who the fuck is that?"

"Don't know. Taggart, or I guess it was the whore, said that The Toad met with this dark guy about three weeks ago. Said The Toad was with him in a park and that they met Leitch."

"Leitch? That doesn't make sense! He doesn't know The Toad … at least as far as I know."

"Isn't that around when you got the info on the Indos?" asked Pussy Paul.

Damien paused, then said, "Yeah, I think so. Leitch handed it off to me … in a park."

"Kind of fits," said Pussy Paul.

"I wouldn't believe anything Taggart says," replied Damien.

"Who the fuck would? Can't see him lyin' to the other cops, though. This came through one of them. Someone they trust."

"What whores was The Toad hanging out with?" asked Damien.

"None that I know of," said Lance. "Him and the boys from Quebec kind of kept to themselves in that department."

"I can't believe this!" roared Damien. "What the hell is going on?"

"Maybe you'll find out more when Carlos calls," suggested Lance.

"Yeah, maybe … but something stinks."

An uneasy silence descended over the group as everyone's eyes focused on the cellphone that Damien had placed on the patio table.

The sudden flurry of activity at Damien's had not gone unnoticed by the Combined Forces Special Enforcement Unit. A hidden camera recording licence plates and the coming and going of vehicles relayed the information directly back to the CFSEU office. It didn't take long before Cecil Hinds arrived with a surveillance team to watch.

A young woman slowly sauntered past Damien's gate but continued to stroll for several more minutes before speaking into the transmitter hidden inside her sleeve.

"Go ahead, Nicole," said Hinds. "What ya see?"

"Counted four moving around just inside the gate. Two had their hands inside their jackets. Pretty sure they're packin' heat. They're paranoid. Really eyeballed me good and weren't giving wolf whistles."

"Heads up, people," said Hinds. "In case any of you haven't heard, two of these guys were found shot in a motel this morning. Looks like we might have a war. If you don't have your vests on, put 'em on now!"

# chapter twenty-six

Damien tried to force himself to be calm. *Think! Don't say anything to get them hurt any more than they already are. Keep your cool.* He knew he was too terrified at the moment to express anger. That would come later.

The cell rang and vibrated on the patio table. Damien stared at it as it rang again. *Sound calm ... don't reveal what you think!* On the third ring, he snatched it up.

"Damien, here."

"Are you laughing now, Damien?" said Carlos, sounding facetious.

"I'm not laughing, Carlos. Why —"

"You think you can rob me? To spit in my face and be safe? No place in the world is safe for you!"

"I did not rob you! Why have you done this?"

"My men were robbed! You are the hombre responsible! It was your men!"

"I wasn't even involved in —"

"Do not talk! You will listen!"

"Carlos, you don't understand! I —"

"Your *puta* — that whore you call a wife — every time you speak at me now, she will lose something ... what you say ..."

Damien listened as Carlos spoke briefly in Spanish to someone in the background before continuing.

"She will lose something ... like her tit! Now you understand, gringo? *Si* or no?"

"Yes. *Si*!" replied Damien.

"*Bueno*! You listen. Now, business! I have decided to charge you only $7 million Canada and $3 Americano. That is what you owe me and I am honourable man. If you do not think your wife and girl are worth that, then shut up the phone now!"

Damien held the phone. The seconds that went by seemed like an eternity. Panic flooded his brain out of fear that there would be an accidental disconnection. Finally Carlos spoke again.

"On Monday, I will call. You will bring $3.5 million Canada to where I say. Any *policia* or any of your hombres go with you ... then we will find out how many parts your wife and girl can lose before she both dies. We also find out if your girl is old enough to enjoy a man. Do you understand me, Damien? You say now. Yes or no!"

"Yes."

"On Wednesday, you will pay another $3.5 Canada. After, I tell you how you make last payment!"

The line went dead, but Damien hung onto the phone, too stunned to be bothered by the dial tone. Then he turned to his men. His voice was barely audible when he said, "Carlos didn't get his money last night. Vicki ... Katie ... he will kill them if we don't pay."

"That fuckin' bastard is dead!" yelled Rellik.

"He says we still owe him $3.5?" asked Lance. "How much time do we have?"

"He wants $7 million Canadian first, then a final payment of $3 mil U.S."

"What!" roared Whiskey Jake. "We only owed him $3.5! And that's if he didn't already rip us off! Maybe he's got The Toad on ice too!"

"If he had The Toad and the money, I can't see why he would do this," offered Damien, lamely. "He wants me to deliver $3.5 on Monday, then again on Wednesday. After that he'll tell me when he wants the rest."

"The extra money," said Lance. "He's charging us for the first boatload! The one the fucking DEA took down in San Diego!"

Damien's brain was racing ahead to Monday. He pointed his finger at Whiskey Jake and Lance and said, "The dope from last night! Sell it fast!"

"We'll never get the cash in time," said Whiskey Jake.

"Give it away at cost!" said Damien. He clenched his teeth, causing the tendons in his neck to stand out. Then he said, "Just get the cash we need by Monday!"

Whiskey Jake's voice showed his concern. "The load is worth over $20 million. Stall for a couple of weeks and we'll have it all."

Damien grabbed him by the front of the shirt with both hands and shook him like a dog with a rat and yelled, "There is no fucking stalling!" He then used one hand to grab Whiskey Jake by the crotch and yelled, "If Vicki loses any more parts, so will you! Understand?"

The look on Whiskey Jake's face indicated he understood. Damien released his grip and his voice returned to a normal level but did not hide his deadly intention. "Get to work. Four strikers with Buck and Sarah at all times. I'm leaving."

"Where are you —" Lance started to ask.

"None of your business," replied Damien, as he ran into the house.

Jack was almost asleep when he received the phone call from Damien. Moments later, he rushed to the parking garage where his car was parked. There was no missing the urgency in Damien's voice when he said he wanted to meet immediately. *Hope he used a cool phone...*

Lance entered Damien's house in time to see that he had just finished making a call on the cellphone that Carlos had provided. He spotted the 9mm tucked in Damien's belt — something his boss had not carried in years.

"I'm coming with you," said Lance. "It's not safe."

Damien shook his head and said, "This is something I need to do alone. Start selling the fucking..." Damien stopped when he realized he was inside the house, then said, "You do what you were told to do!" He rushed toward the door to the garage but stopped and ran back to the kitchen. He grabbed a small picnic cooler from the fridge and then ran to the garage.

On a normal day, Damien might have spotted the surveillance team and taken appropriate action. Today was not normal. His mind was on his family as he drove.

Cecil Hinds watched as Damien parked his car in Stanley Park. Part of the surveillance team remained with the car while others followed Damien on foot.

"T-1 is carrying a small cooler," reported Nicole. "Maybe meeting someone for a picnic."

"*Who* is the big question," replied Hinds. "Stay with him, but give him lots of room."

* * *

Damien didn't mince words when he sat beside Jack on a park bench, placing the cooler between them. "I need a favour. Now!" he said.

Jack was surprised. "I don't owe you any favours! We're even! A tonne of coke and a murder makes us more than even!"

"This isn't about that!" said Damien, harshly. Then his voice softened and he said, "I mean I would like a favour from you. I'd owe you this time."

Jack was caught off guard. *Why would he come to me, even if two of his guys were murdered? Is he hoping I can locate The Toad?* He eyed Damien and the cooler curiously. *He's more agitated than I expected. Thought he would be happy that the heat's on The Toad. And the cooler ... what's that all about?* Jack cleared his throat, then said, "Last time we met you said you would never give me another favour. Remember?"

"I remember."

"So why should I believe you would ever pay me back?"

"Because I'm telling you I will! I gave you one on credit! I'm just asking for the same!"

Jack nodded, then said, "You can do me a favour first. An easy one. Your lawyer friend, Leitch, deals with a guy who has a British accent. Looks Indo. I want him."

"I don't know who that is," said Damien, his face reddening.

"He's connected with your club!"

"If he is, I'll find out! I just don't know right now!"

"He knows The Toad. He met with The Toad and then with Leitch three weeks ago. They were all paranoid, so something was going on!" Jack studied Damien's face closely as he spoke. *What I'm telling him ... his face ... he already knows! Thought it would take another few days.* Jack stared at Damien and then said, "The Toad works for you. Call him and ask."

"We tried! Nobody knows where the fuck he is! That's what I want you to do! Find him!"

"You want me to find The Toad? He had something to do with a couple of your strikers getting shot in a motel last night, didn't he?"

"Are you going to help me or not? First tell me that! You help me find The Toad and I swear I'll find out who this British guy is!"

Jack leaned back and briefly massaged the back of his neck. "Okay," he said. "I'll take you at your word, but tell me what's going on."

Damien handed Jack the cooler and said, "Open it!"

Jack placed the cooler on his lap and heard the sound of ice moving around inside. He opened it and looked in. A plastic bag containing a girl's panties lay on top of the ice.

"Under them," said Damien. "Look under them."

Jack dug deeper into the ice and found another plastic bag. It contained a human finger.

"What's this?" said Jack.

The words spilled out of Damien. He told of the ransom and his fear that he didn't have time to raise the first payment by Monday.

Jack felt stunned as he stared at the finger. *I did this. I may as well have chopped it off myself.*

"Your wife is a doctor, right?" said Damien, pointing at the finger. "Can —"

"I don't know. I'll call her," replied Jack, quickly punching the numbers on his cell.

\* \* \*

The surveillance team from CFSEU scrambled to get into position to see what was in the cooler.

"Anybody see what was in it?" asked Hinds into the radio.

"No, the lid blocked my view," came the reply. "By the look on their faces it must be something important."

"Damn it," mumbled Hinds, reaching for his cell.

Jack spoke with Natasha and quickly told her about a kidnapping. He said the husband did not want any official police involvement or any record of the incident. He then told her where they were.

"I'm coming in. I can be there in an hour," she said.

"I don't want you around until after I find the Brit," said Jack. "It's not safe."

"I'm done living my life in fear out here."

"Natasha! Listen to me! It's obvious he'll murder you the first chance he gets!"

"We'll talk about it later. Stay there, I'm on my way."

Jack put his phone away and said, "She'll be here within the hour."

Damien stared at Jack for a moment, then asked, "So what was that all about? Why do you want this Brit? You think he wants to murder your wife?"

Jack told Damien about the Brit but changed the story to say that a source of his identified the Brit in the park with The Toad and Leitch.

"And this guy tried to make your partner's wife decide which one of her kids was going to die, just because she made you dinner?"

Jack nodded. "Who the hell would do that? You must know him."

"I don't! Maybe he was hired by someone I do know, but I can't think of who that would be."

"You doing anything with the Indos?"

"Not me. And he met with The Toad ... it doesn't make sense. The Toad would never get involved in something like that! He was at the election last year when we were deciding whether or not to waste you. He voted against the idea. Same as everyone else."

"Maybe The Toad doesn't know about it. Could the Brit be someone Leitch is using to pass on messages to The Toad?"

"But if they were all in the park together, why didn't Leitch just deal with The Toad personally?"

"Maybe The Toad wanted to keep his liaison with Leitch secret. Maybe he didn't want to risk someone seeing them together."

"Possible, I guess."

Jack decided to change the subject and asked, "Why $7 million in Canadian and then $3 in American?"

Damien shrugged and said, "Doesn't really matter. If we can't find The Toad and get the money back by Monday, Vicki and Katie are..." He stopped, unable to say what he was thinking.

"You're telling me that you have all that coke and can't come up with $3.5?"

"In a week, easy. But not in two days. Maybe half, I don't know. But look what Carlos has done. You really think he'll accept half?"

Jack glanced down at the cooler. It made him feel ill. He said, "I'm not so sure it's even about the money. He runs one of the biggest cartels in Colombia. This is chump change to him. What he's doing ... he's a psychopath. This is entertainment for him."

"I figure the same. That's why I want you to find The Toad for me. You said you have a source close to him. I don't care who that is. I just want the money before Monday!"

"The Toad likes a little female companionship," said Jack. "I know someone. I'll see what I can come up with."

Damien nodded and said, "Thanks, I appreciate it." He then took the cooler and placed it between his feet. For a while, both men were silent, absorbed in their own thoughts. The cooler eventually became a magnet for their eyes.

"They're in this because of me," said Damien, fighting back tears. "I thought the club was everything. How could I have been so fucking stupid?"

Jack didn't respond. His own emotions were boiling to the surface as he stared at the cooler.

"After all these years of being in charge of the club, this happens ... and who do I turn to for help? A fuckin' cop." Damien paused, trying to regain control of his emotions before saying, "How could this have happened to me?"

"It didn't," said Jack. "It happened to Vicki and Katie."

Both men returned to their own thoughts. Jack thought about Damien. *I always saw him as a monster. Now he looks like any worried dad or husband would. Scared because the people he loves are being violated. Angry at himself because it was his lifestyle that put them there.*

Jack then thought about his own actions. *Charlie paralyzed ... his dad murdered. A war vet murdered because I made the price of speed go up. The O'Reillys. Now this! Consequences of my actions. What have I done?*

"What have I done?" said Damien.

Jack looked at Damien in shock. *Was I thinking out loud?* He saw the tears in Damien's eyes as Damien leaned forward, placing his elbows on his knees while covering his face with his hands. His body started to shake.

"I think they've raped Katie," he said, choking out the words. "She's only eight years old."

Jack had forgotten about the panties. He picked up the cooler and examined them. "These have been sliced off," he said.

"I know. Oh, God, please ... what have they done to her? I know I don't deserve a break ... but if you really exist, why would you..."

"She may not have been raped," said Jack. "They were probably cut off because her ankles were bound together. He sent them to terrorize you."

Damien sat upright and looked at Jack. "You really think so?"

"Cop's point of view." Jack shrugged.

"You've dealt with this kind of thing before?" asked Damien.

"Not really. I've been thinking a lot about the psychopathic mind, though. Especially since my partner's family was attacked. Picture a mother tied to a chair for half an hour staring at a swimming pool that her baby had been tossed in."

"Christ," came Damien's mumbled reply.

"We're dealing with" — Jack paused to look at Damien — "real monsters. You help me catch mine and I'll help you with yours."

Damien nodded and said, "If The Toad met this British or Indo, you can bet he was involved in ripping off the cash. I'm not sure where Leitch fits in. He once offered to ... help me with my finances. I don't entirely trust him, so I said no. Maybe The Toad is using his services."

"How long has The Toad been dealing with him?" asked Jack.

"That's just it! I didn't know the two even knew each other."

"But you will find out who the Brit is? Maybe through Leitch?"

"I'll deliver him to you like pâté on a plate!" Damien nodded toward the cooler and started to shake. "I just have to make sure they're safe, first. That's all that counts."

Natasha hurried toward the park bench. She saw the tears in her husband's eyes as he tried to console the large man sitting beside him. "Jack?" she asked hesitantly. Both men sat upright and then stood. Their faces became masks. Hiding any appearance of weakness. As a doctor, it was a sight that she had seen often, but it was not something she respected. *Be who you are, not what you think others expect you to be.*

"Natasha," said Jack, "this is ... an associate of mine. He needs help. His wife and daughter have been kidnapped. They sent this back," he added, gesturing toward the cooler.

"My name is Damien, Mrs. Taggart," he said, handing her the cooler.

Natasha set the cooler on the park bench and looked inside. She examined the bag containing the finger quickly and then said, "Good, it's not frozen. You did the right thing. Any amputated digit should be quickly cooled, but not frozen or placed directly in any solution. I'll take it to my clinic. It should be wrapped in a saline-soaked swab, then sealed in a plastic bag and placed on ice."

She glanced at Damien and saw the anguish on his face. "There have been recorded cases where digits have been successfully reattached up to twenty-four hours later if the amputated part was quickly cooled."

Natasha knew by the looks on their faces that this did not appear likely. "Barring that, a prosthesis could be made from an impression cast of this finger, making an exact match…"

Damien stared down at his feet.

"I'll get going now," she said, then looked at Jack and asked, "See you at home after? It's almost four o'clock. I'll make dinner."

"Wish you would reconsider. The Brit is —"

"And if you never catch him, do we spend the rest of our lives hiding? As I said, I'll see you back at our apartment."

Jack argued with Natasha a little more, but it was to no avail. Neither paid attention to Damien, who opened the cooler one more time.

Jack knew he had lost the argument and handed the cooler to Natasha. Both men watched as she returned to her car.

"She's pretty headstrong," said Damien, watching as Natasha placed the cooler in her car.

"Yes."

"Why not stash her at your sister's place out on that farm? At least until we get this Brit. Believe me, I'll find out who he is."

"She was at the farm. Now she wants to get back to work."

"How come you don't have cops protecting her?"

"She's a doctor. She sees walk-in patients alone. If she was protected, that couldn't be done. With our people, it would have to be all or nothing. Plus everyone in our office has been threatened. There's no way everyone could be protected. If I complain about it, they just transfer us up to Baffin Island or someplace. We'd rather take our chances here."

Damien paused, then nodded his head and said, "Okay. I see the problem. You guys play by the rules too much. I'll have a couple of the boys watch over her.

Once word goes out that she's protected by the patch, nobody will try anything."

Jack couldn't help but chuckle at the prospect. "Hell no! All I need is for the brass to hear..." His thoughts were interrupted when he spotted a familiar car pull out into the traffic behind Natasha. He looked at Damien and said, "We've got heat."

Jack noted that Damien held the urge to look. He was a professional. "You sure?" he asked, looking directly at Jack.

"I'm sure. Anti-Corruption. Someone must have spotted us together and called them. With Bishop's body being found and now me meeting with you ... this isn't good."

Damien swore under his breath, then said, "I wasn't thinking too clearly today when I drove to meet you. Bet it's my fault."

"Too late to worry about that now."

Damien stared at Jack for a moment and then said, "Anti-Corruption?"

"Think of it as the heavies in Internal Affairs."

Damien raised his eyebrows and said, "Bishop ... can they connect you?"

"Natasha talked to a Mexican cop just two blocks from where Bishop lived. I didn't know until later. Now being seen here with you ... I'm going to be taken down!"

# chapter twenty-seven

For Hinds, the minutes ticked by while urgent calls were exchanged between Isaac and the bosses at I-HIT, Anti-Corruption, and CFSEU.

Isaac then made a decision and called Staff Sergeant Legg back.

"This may be a long weekend here, but it's not in Mexico!" said Isaac. "I want a response from Mexico no later than Tuesday. Tell the LO to do it in person! A dinky little village like that, Mexican time or not, it shouldn't take long to find out. Tell the LO if I don't have his report on my desk Tuesday morning, he'll be protecting our sovereignty in the Arctic!"

"And in the meantime?" asked Legg.

"Tell CFSEU or whoever is watching Taggart they can do a loose surveillance today but then back off. I don't want Taggart heated up until we hear back," replied Isaac.

\* \* \*

Surveillance teams split up into three groups. One watched Natasha carry the cooler into her clinic and then depart a short time later with the cooler and return to her apartment.

Damien, followed by a second team, went straight home.

Hinds elected to follow Jack and noted that when he returned to his car, he immediately used his cellphone.


Jack called the home number of his colleague who worked with the DEA in San Diego.

"Hello?" said a feminine voice.

"Sally! It's Jack Taggart calling from Canada. Is Jim-Bo around?"

"Sorry, Jack. You got another ship for him?"

"No. Something else."

"He's out of the country. I expect him home Tuesday or Wednesday. Can it wait?"

"I suppose. I was just looking for some background info on someone. Have him call me when he gets in. He's got my cell."

Jack casually glanced in his mirrors before pulling out into traffic. He did not see anyone. Ten minutes of driving passed before his rear-view mirror reflected a car that had passed him earlier. *These guys are pretty good...*


The surveillance team followed Jack to the downtown core of Vancouver.

They soon found themselves driving along East Hastings, where Jack entered a parkade. Moments later, he was spotted entering the Black Water Hotel.

"Inside coverage," ordered Hinds. "Who's available that our target doesn't know?"

Hinds found a volunteer and soon he had a whispered report from inside the bar.

"Target sitting by himself. Ordered a beer."

A half-hour ticked by before Hinds received an update. "He's just been joined by a woman. Looks like a hooker. He's buying her a drink."

"Are you close enough to hear?" asked Hinds.

"Negative. I'm getting enough heat as it is. Whatever they're talking about, they don't look happy."

A short while later the volunteer reported, "Target getting up. Think he's leaving. He tried to give the hooker a twenty. She shook her head and gave it back. Personally I think twenty was too much. She's ugly. Okay, Target is heading for the front exit. I've lost the eye. He's yours."

Hinds saw Jack come out of the bar and the surveillance team was soon mobile again.

Jack arrived home at suppertime. His BlackBerry buzzed as he walked into their apartment. It was a message from Lance: *Damien's wife and daughter kidnapped by the Colombians over the rip. SW having a sale to raise money! No time to meet. Tomorrow?*

Jack was too tired to respond to the message now and closed the door behind him.

Natasha immediately met him at the entrance, picking up the cooler off the kitchen counter as she passed it.

"This Damien is the monster you've been after?" asked Natasha. "The guy who has sanctioned what? Forty, fifty, sixty or more murders? Anyone from young prostitutes to suspected informants!"

"Yes, that's him," admitted Jack.

"Now you're consoling him and had tears in your eyes! What's that all about?"

"He's a monster, but ... I found out there are bigger monsters."

"Take a look in the cooler!"

"I did. I thought you were leaving that at the clinic. Didn't you take the finger and —"

"I did leave the finger at the clinic. By the way, it smelled of coffee."

"Coffee?"

"That's not what I'm showing you. Take a look in the cooler!"

Jack looked inside. He saw a 9mm.

"Guess Damien figures you should protect yourself. Good idea."

"Like hell it is! What is going on?"

Jack sighed and said, "I'm going to pour a martini. Then we'll talk."

Moments later, Jack and Natasha were sitting on their sofa and sipping on martinis as Jack told her everything leading up to her arrival at the park.

"So you're upset because you feel responsible for them being kidnapped."

"I am responsible. I feel horrible! Him trying to protect you makes me feel worse."

"I can't work with security hanging around. It will freak the patients out."

"I know. Wish you would give it one more week at the farm."

"Not an option. Can't Damien tell you today who the Brit is?"

"That's another problem. When I gave him the story about a connection between The Toad, the Brit, and his lawyer, I didn't know his wife and daughter had been kidnapped. He might do a lot more than talk with Leitch."

"Didn't you think that to start with?"

"I expected Leitch might get slapped around a bit. Not now. This is different."

"These are consequences you'll have to live with. Damien too."

"You're comparing me with him? He's the devil! Tell me you don't think that?"

"I wasn't saying that. Sounds to me like you were thinking that on your own."

"Oh," was all Jack said.

"But if he is pure evil, why were you so upset in the park?"

"I feel bad about his wife and daughter."

"You had your arm around his shoulder. You feel bad for him too."

Jack was exasperated. "I'm just not thinking clear," he snapped. "This is Saturday night. I haven't been to bed since Thursday. I'm just —"

"You're just ... compassionate. You care about people. Don't blame that on being tired."

Jack looked at her for a moment, then sighed and said, "There's more. Anti-Corruption were at the park. The Homicide Team too. They followed you and me after."

Natasha was shocked. "Mexico? They know?" she whispered.

Jack grimaced and said, "It doesn't look good. Me meeting with Damien ... they may have figured it out."

Natasha grabbed Jack's arm and said, "I won't let that happen to you. I'll say I —"

"You won't say anything! Trust me! Tomorrow I'm going to start fixing things. This time without being watched."

\* \* \*

Sunday morning was quiet. There was little traffic when Jack pulled out onto the street. It didn't take long to establish that he was alone. His meeting with Lance was brief.

"The club can only raise $1.5 million at the most," Lance said. "We're still $2 million short. Damien is screaming at everyone. Shit has really hit the fan."

"Any sign of The Toad?" Jack asked.

"No, but Damien thinks Leitch might know where he is. He called him on his cell to meet him. Leitch is away until Tuesday. On some houseboat up in the Shuswap."

"Damien going to wait until Tuesday?"

"Nope. He's sending Rellik and his crew up there this afternoon."


Damien received Jack's urgent text message just before noon. He ensured he was alone before going to meet Jack outside the bus depot.

Jack came directly to the point. "My source saw The Toad take two sports bags into this place last night. He came out without them. Said he had to give them to a friend who was going on a trip."

"Sounds like bullshit," growled Damien.

"It is. My source rented a hotel room later with The Toad, just for an hour. She got a chance to look in his pocket. Found two locker keys and told me the numbers. I think I know where the money is!"

Damien was elated. "Thank you, thank you," he kept repeating.

"The Toad said he wouldn't see her for a week or two because he had to go out of town. Looks like she's out of the loop. At least for now."

"The fucker is leaving," said Damien. "She'll never see him again!"

"That's what I figure. Once he comes back here for the money, I'll bust him."

"What!" Damien yelled. "You can't do that! I need the money!"

"I know. I was going to give it to you. I just need The Toad to get the keys."

"Fuck the keys! My guys can handle it. I'll have someone check to make sure it's there. Then I'll have some guys wait and grab him when he shows."

"Then you'll politely ask him who the Brit is?"

Damien allowed himself a quick smile and then replied, "Yeah ... of course. But right now the important thing is my family. I need to make sure the money is there." Damien then paused and said, "It's been at least twenty-four hours since..." He held up his hand and wiggled his ring finger. "Guess you can tell Natasha to throw it out."

Jack patted Damien on the shoulder and then replied, "She said that it could be used to make an impression. An exact match."

"Yeah, right. Exact. You really believe that?"

"My wife doesn't bullshit."

Damien stared at Jack for a moment and then simply replied, "Good."

"Which reminds me," said Jack. "Open the glovebox. She really appreciated the 9mm but said to give it back."

Damien retrieved the gun and said, "You sure?"

"Positive. I gave her a little .32 Beretta a few months ago. After that thing with Bishop last year."

"I should have known. Makes sense. Smaller and easier for a woman to shoot."

"Also registered to her. The problem is she usually refuses to carry it."

"At least you had the foresight to try and protect her. Maybe if Vicki had one, she would still have her finger."

"Or be dead."

Damien slowly nodded. "Guess that's a good possibility too."

Jack took a deep breath and slowly exhaled, then said, "Okay. I agree with what you intend to do. Just two things. First, send me a message to confirm that the money is there. Second, I want you to meet me tomorrow after you do the drop. Agreed?"

"Not a problem," replied Damien. "If we grab The Toad I'll tell you who the Brit is immediately." He pointed his finger at Jack and said, "Don't try and follow me when I make the drop! I'm going to do whatever Carlos asks, and that includes going alone!"

Jack was on his way home when Lance sent him a message. *Rellik's crew on their way to the bus depot. Got a tip on The Toad.*

Jack smiled. Two hours later he received another message. This time from Damien. *Got the $. Thanks again. TTYL.*

The LO was finally able to rouse his Mexican contact, who complained about being called on a Sunday. Promises of another lavish dinner and expensive hotel room with his mistress seemed to appease him. He didn't understand the urgency. Then again, he had never seen snow.

Early Monday morning, the LO heard back. They were in luck. A report identified a policeman who is certain he saw Jack and Natasha on the day Bishop died. Yes, arrangements had been made. They could leave immediately and the LO could talk to the policeman in person and show him the photos.

# chapter twenty-eight

Normally at eight in the morning on the Monday of a long weekend, Jack would be enjoying the comforts of his bed. Not today. He had already been up with Natasha for an hour and a half. Neither one spoke much as they went through the motions of drinking coffee.

Expecting to be arrested any moment tended to numb the brain as well as the taste buds.

Jack received a message from Damien. He was surprised that the call came so early but was glad to be doing something. Anything was better than waiting.

Damien met him in a parking lot at Burnaby Lake and they took a stroll along a path.

"Any heat?" asked Jack.

Damien shook his head and said, "None that I could see. Fucking Carlos called at four o'clock this morning."

"Time zones," said Jack. "They're a couple of hours ahead of us."

"I made the drop two hours later."

"How and where?"

"I put the money in my trunk and drove to the industrial area near the harbour at the end of Clark Drive. I left my car unlocked and went for a walk as instructed. Came back an hour later and the trunk was empty."

"Really wish I had been there," said Jack.

"Forget it! Nobody does anything until they're safe!"

"I know. I understand. I take it that The Toad still hasn't shown up at the bus depot?" asked Jack, pretending to look suspiciously at Damien.

"No. Our guys are still there, but I don't think it looks good."

"Why not?"

"If he ripped us, I can't see him hanging around. Leaving the money this long ... I got a feeling that he may have spotted us. I'll keep the guys there for a while longer, but something doesn't smell right."

"Well, at least you got the money."

"Not all of it. There was only $2.5 in the locker. One mil was missing."

"I didn't think that it might not all be there," said Jack. "You obviously had enough, though?"

"Yeah ... just barely. Which leads me to think that The Toad had an accomplice. The extra million could have gone to the guy you call the Brit, or maybe Leitch, too."

"Sounds logical. Looks like we both want to find him. Have you talked with Leitch?"

"He's out of town until tonight. That can wait. I want to find my family first."

"Was there anything else in the shipping container with the coke?"

"No. That was all we were getting."

"I mean legit."

"Legit? Yeah, there were sacks of coffee. Why?"

Jack thought of the van he had been in outside of the motel. *It reeked of coffee. Natasha said Vicki's finger also smelled of coffee.*

"What are you thinking?" asked Damien.

"I don't know, just trying to find something that might add up. How about Wednesday? Figure you can come up with another $3.5?"

"Someone says they got the cash to invest in a bargain. Looks like Wednesday won't be a problem. The market is going to be flooded for a while … bargain basement prices. Maybe a good thing. Put more of the competition out of business."

Jack and Damien returned to the parking lot and stood for a moment, scanning the area.

"No heat," said Damien.

"That we can see," replied Jack.

"When do you think it will happen?"

Jack let out a deep breath and then said, "Let's just say I'm not looking forward to tomorrow."

"Can they make you for it?"

"I don't know. Things could get pretty hot."

Damien nodded, then asked, "You ever been to Merida, Mexico?"

"No. Why?"

"There's a hotel there called the Angeles de Merida. Suggest you check it out on the web today. Don't use your own computer. Do it at library or internet café. I gotta go. Talk with you later."


It was just before noon when Jack called Laura's number. Elvis answered.

"Hi, Elvis. It's Jack. How are things?"

"What do you want?" Elvis obviously wasn't in the mood for small talk.

"Is Laura there?"

Elvis paused and then replied, "I'll get her."

Jack thought about the sudden change in Elvis's attitude toward him. *Guess I would be upset too, if my spouse was working with someone about to be arrested.*

"Hi, Jack! What's up?"

Laura was friendly. *Means Elvis hasn't told her.* "We need to talk. How about we meet and I buy you lunch?"

"Not with —"

"No, not with Holly. Just the two us. Stuff happening that you need to know about."

"Where and when?" asked Laura.

"Know the Gillnetter Pub on the Mary Hill Bypass?"

"Good spot. One hour?"


Jack brought Laura up to date on the kidnapping and told her how he had returned all but $1 million to Damien.

"That's awful." She thought for a moment and then added, "You must feel awful."

"I do."

"Have you notified I-HIT yet?"

"Can't. Damien would never cooperate. All he wants is to get his family back. No cops involved."

"You trust him to tell you who the Brit is when he finds out?"

"He'll tell me. It won't be long. He's already paid the first instalment on the ransom. Second instalment will be made on Wednesday."

"Will he be short of cash then too?"

"No. The coke is practically being given away to raise the money in time."

Laura nodded.

"You on board with this? With what I just did?"

Laura nodded.

"Good. I appreciate your view. Thanks."

"After the other night, this seems like small potatoes. I was afraid you were going to tell me to buy rubber boots and a pickaxe."

"At the moment I agree with Damien. What's important now is to get his family back. I think we can help. I have a theory."

"To find them … if they're still alive?"

Jack grimaced and then nodded.

"If they're dead, it would explain why Carlos won't let Damien talk," said Laura. "So he can't verify if they're still alive."

"I considered that, but I think they're alive. He'll want Vicki and Katie alive so he can use them to make Damien come crawling to him — literally."

"For a guy like that, I would be willing to do the digging. What's your theory?"

"The Colombians wanted the money in Canadian funds. I think they're already established here. Likely in the coffee industry."

Laura reflected on it briefly and then said, "Would look legit. Good for laundering. Who is going to count cups of coffee, let alone figure out how many sacks of coffee are sold versus the money collected. Even sending the money back to Colombia would look legit!"

"Natasha said Vicki's finger smelled of coffee. I'm thinking she could be stashed in a warehouse where the coffee is stored."

"We should check Customs and see who is picking up the shipments."

"Exactly. I also want you to check out a company registered to the plate I scooped off the van at the motel. It smelled of coffee too. We might get lucky and find a match."

"Today is a holiday so…"

"I know. I don't think you'll find much out before tomorrow, but get on it as soon as you can."

Laura took a sip of Rickard's Red and then a bite of calamari. "I bet you're right about the coffee connection. It all ties in. Find the warehouse and we find his wife and daughter."

Jack nodded.

"But then what? We can't raid the place ourselves. We'll need to call out the troops."

"I know. We'll do it anonymously. It might even be in VPD's jurisdiction. I'll talk to Damien about it then. All he wants is his family back. Our Emergency Response Teams are better trained than anyone he has." Jack took a bite of a chicken wing and then added, "They haven't killed as many, but they're better trained."

"Then we're set."

"Sort of."

"Sort of?" Laura put her fork down. "What else? You're holding something back!"

Jack looked at her and said, "I know I've dumped a lot of crap on you in a hurry."

"No kidding! Officially I don't even start until tomorrow."

"And I want to thank you for being the person you are. There are only a few people I trust in this world. I trust you."

Laura nodded and said, "Thanks. Now quit avoiding the subject. What else should I know?"

Jack sighed and said, "Tomorrow things could go bad for me. Something unrelated to this."

"Bad? In what way?"

"I'm under investigation. On Saturday, when I met Damien in the park and Natasha showed up ... I spotted ACU following Natasha when she left with the cooler."

"They're working on you?"

"I recognized the car ... didn't see who was driving. When I left, others followed me. I'm sure I-HIT is involved as well."

Laura became silent as she thought about her marriage.

"I don't want you to panic," said Jack. "Don't worry about the shoot, shovel, and shut up incident. If worse comes to worse, I will always deny you were with me. If I get grabbed, I want to make sure that you follow through on this stuff. Do what you can to save Damien's family."

"Why, Jack? Why would they be working on you?"

Jack returned her stare for a moment, then said, "They think I had something to do with Bishop's death. The day I was told about it, someone followed me out to my sister's place to see if I would tell her."

"Wondering if she already knew?"

"Exactly."

Laura looked at Jack but didn't speak. She didn't want to make him lie to her, or worse yet, hear something that she could be asked to divulge.

"Once Damien's family is safe, I know he'll identify the Brit," said Jack.

"Sounds to me," said Laura quietly, "that you have bigger problems to worry about than the Brit."

"Other people have problems too. Charlie's going through life in a wheelchair because his dad and I had the same name."

"Not your fault."

"Perhaps. Then there's Danny and Susan. They're

so traumatized I don't think they'll ever get over it. I don't blame them that they hate my guts."

"They need time."

"Something I may not have. This thing with Vicki and Katie ... I don't have a bigger problem than them. Someone has to save them. I'm counting on you."

"I'll do what I can."

"Don't come in to the office tomorrow morning or answer any calls except from me. Go straight to the port and start looking at shipping invoices. If I get grabbed, I don't want them grabbing you too. Vicki and Katie can't afford any delays."

"Sure, fine," said Laura harshly.

"What's wrong?"

Laura leaned back in her chair and said, "Men! What is it with you guys? I was hoping you were different!"

"How? What do you mean? We don't have time to sit around the office. I'll deal with it while you investigate."

"Not that. What you did in the last two days without me! Partners should work together. I want to catch the Brit, too. Hope he resists ... that would make it easy. But the point is, you went off and did all this stuff on your own while keeping me in the dark. If you don't want me as a partner, then keep doing what you're doing!"

"It's not that! It's Elvis. I don't want to jeopardize your marriage! How do you think he feels right now? Even if he wasn't following me on Saturday, he —"

"He wasn't. He was home with me."

"Even so, ACU is a small office. He must know what's going on."

"I'm sure he does." Laura studied Jack's face closely and added, "I'm not going to interfere with his job."

"Exactly. So now you know why I hesitate to put you in the middle."

"Asking me to do my job is not putting me in the middle. I do what I think is right — just like Elvis does."

"Would he think hiding The Toad's body is right?"

"Of course not, but that is not your concern. Let me deal with that. I'm still not sure if that was right either, but I did see your point. If you arrested anyone, you would have burned Lance and that much cash would never remain a secret."

"Please, never use his name."

"Sorry ... your friend. Speaking of which, I hope he's not a *good* friend of yours."

Jack smiled and then replied, "He's disposed of a few bodies, but I didn't help."

"What's his motive? Staying out of jail?"

"He tried to murder me once ... thought I was a dope dealer ratting out to the cops."

"And you let him off the hook for that?"

Jack nodded. "It was worth it. Now he's president of the west-side chapter."

"Meaning you ... we ... have to dance around a lot of grey areas with him. At least we do if we want to know what is going on."

"Exactly."

"Little things, like hiding corpses and that."

Jack smiled. "Sounds like you're a natural for this work."

Laura massaged her forehead with her hand and then looked across the room at the waitress and yelled, "Leisa! Another round, please!"

It was late Monday night in Mexico when the RCMP liaison officer met with the police officer and showed him pictures of Jack and Natasha. Yes, he was positive it was them. There was absolutely no doubt.

Communications in Third World countries are not up to the standards of other places on the planet, but the LO's report would still arrive on Isaac's desk before noon tomorrow.

# chapter twenty-nine

Early Tuesday morning, Jack embraced Natasha warmly before reluctantly pulling away.

"Don't worry," he whispered. "Everything will be okay."

Natasha used the cuff of her sleeve to wipe away her tears. "I'm scared," she said.

"I'll call you as soon as I know anything. If you're questioned, remember what happened."

"But details," she said, "what if I'm asked about little things?"

Jack faked a smile and said, "That's where the tequila comes in. How can they expect you to remember anything about our honeymoon? Other than that I was the best lay you ever had!"

Natasha smiled in spite of her fears. "You're such a turkey!"

* * *

Jack arrived at work and listened to his voice mail. Louie had a doctor's appointment and would not be in until later. He had barely put the phone down when he was approached by Staff Sergeant Legg from the Anti-Corruption Unit.

"Come with me," said Legg.

"Why?" asked Jack. "I haven't had my coffee yet."

"My instructions come from Isaac. Forget having coffee!"

Jack was taken to an interrogation room consisting of a small table pressed against a wall and three chairs seated in a semicircle around the front of the table. Randy Otto was already in the room.

"Bosses from I-HIT and Anti-Corruption," said Jack. "To what do I owe the pleasure?"

"Take a seat," said Randy.

Jack grabbed a chair and swung it around, then sat facing over the back of the chair. Randy and Legg exchanged glances, then sat down facing him.

"I take it you want me to assist you with something important?"

"Drop the act," said Legg. "You know why you're here!"

"Actually, I don't," replied Jack. "I did, however, spot one of your cars following my wife Saturday afternoon. Would you care to explain? Is she a Russian agent?"

"Jack, this isn't a game," said Randy. "It's serious. Isaac has taken a personal interest. Do yourself a favour — drop the comedy act."

"Sorry, Randy. Bad habit. I use humour to alleviate stress."

"Have you been meeting Damien?" asked Legg.

"You know I have. He was with me in the park on Saturday when you followed Natasha."

Legg looked frustrated and said, "Just for the record. I wanted you to say it."

"Sorry. Yes is the answer."

"Why?" continued Legg.

"It's highly confidential."

"Believe me," said Randy, "Isaac has given us full authority to hear about anything you're involved in."

Jack nodded, looking pensive as he reflected upon this information. Then he answered, "I'm trying to turn him into an informant."

"Yeah, right," said Legg sarcastically. "Why was your wife meeting him?"

"She was picking something up from him. In the cooler he handed her."

"Which was?" asked Legg.

"He had been to her clinic a few days ago. He was told to come back and give her some sort of specimen. When he mentioned that he knew me, Natasha told me about it. I didn't like the idea of him meeting my wife alone. I made him hand the specimen over to her when I was around."

"What kind of specimen?"

"You would have to ask my wife about that. She wouldn't tell me. Doctor-client privilege was all she would say."

"You were seen looking in the cooler," said Legg.

Jack sighed, then said, "You're right. I did." He paused and said, "I know I'm in trouble."

Legg hid his satisfaction. *He's folding already.*

"Please don't tell my wife," continued Jack. "I was just curious. I think it was a stool sample, but I'm not sure. She'll be mad as hell if she thinks I was snooping into her business."

Randy let out a soft chuckle, bringing him a glare from Legg.

"I used the park as an excuse to talk to him while waiting for Natasha. It was a good opportunity to build trust and get him to confide in me."

"Bullshit!" said Legg. "You don't turn the top guy of Satans Wrath! That's who you want to nail! You turn informants to catch him!"

Jack looked surprised, then said, "Oh! Is that how it's supposed to work?" He pointed his finger at Legg and said, "Perhaps *you* would think that. Not coming from an intelligent background ... oops, Freudian slip ... I mean from an Intelligence background." Jack paused when Randy frowned, then said, "Sorry. I do understand how you might think that."

"I think that because it's true!" said Legg, harshly.

"If it's true, then why was I meeting with him?"

"You're working for him!"

"Working for him?" said Jack, as his eyes widened. "I'm shocked that you would jump to that conclusion. Absolutely aghast! Mortified to think that you would accuse me of that! There is no way that —"

Legg pounded his fist on the table and said, "Think I haven't seen this routine before? Act surprised, show concern, deny, deny, deny!"

Jack leaned back and slowly shook his head while staring down at the floor.

"Think about it, Jack," said Randy, "do you really expect us to believe that you could get the national president of Satans Wrath to turn on his own club?"

"His own club? Damien would never do that!" said Jack.

"Precisely!" said Legg.

"It's the Indos he's concerned about," said Jack. "I was suggesting to him that it's in our mutual interest for the police to arrest them."

"That's enough," said Legg. "I tried to be good to you. Give you a chance to come clean. A chance to use your head and make yourself look a little better. Maybe even show some remorse. Hell, who knows? A murder beef could even be dropped down to manslaughter if you played your cards right."

"Murder? What on earth are you talking about?"

"We've got a surprise for you," retorted Legg. "Mexico! You've been identified! The LO left us a message. His report should be arriving any minute."

"I don't understand," said Jack.

"Don't you think we figured out that Damien told you where Bishop was hiding?" said Legg. "You killed Bishop while you were on your honeymoon. Now Damien owns you!"

"You're wrong! It was just a coincidence that I was in the country at all!"

Legg ignored Jack's denial as he continued, "And you show up at the motel on Saturday morning with a bullshit story that an informant told you about The Toad and a huge dope deal!"

"Well, that part is true. I did go to the motel. What does that have to do with anything?"

"Nothing with you is true! Who's your informant? I need a name and an address now!" said Legg, sliding a writing pad across the table.

"I don't disclose the names of my informants!"

"You will if you don't want me to read you your rights and put you in jail now!"

Jack glared at Legg for a moment, then grabbed the notepad and scribbled a name and address before tossing the pad into Legg's lap.

Legg looked at the name. "This is it? A first name and an apartment address? What's the phone number?"

"Doesn't have one." Jack looked at both men and said, "Check it out. Take CC from Homicide. She'll verify it."

"Yeah? Well you can sit here until I do!" said Legg. He left Randy in the room with Jack and went to another room and called Connie Crane.

"Don't know anything about it," said Connie. "If Jack thinks I'll lie for him, he's mistaken!"

"Could it be an alias? Maybe somebody you used to deal with?" asked Legg.

"Possible, but I've never handled a source with Jack. I'm kind of busy right now."

"Isaac wants this done now. Are you going to tell him you're too busy?"

Seconds later, Connie hurried from her office to meet Legg.

Pussy Paul and Rellik arrived at Damien's estate as ordered. It was raining and both men soon wished they had brought umbrellas. Damien was the only one who had one as they strolled along the manicured path that led past the koi pond in his backyard.

"What did you find out?" Damien asked Pussy Paul.

"He should be in court all day. Up until about four."

"Good," replied Damien. "Meet him at the courthouse as soon as he's finished. Tell him we have a new source in the prosecutor's office. Tell him we know that the cops have a tap on him … including payphones."

"The fucking pigs are buggin' our lawyer?" said Rellik.

"No," replied Damien. "I think Leitch is two-timing us. He might be doing something with The Toad."

"The fucking Toad!" said Rellik. "I've still got guys at the bus depot."

"Cancel them, except for two. I doubt he'll show, but if he does ... make sure he's taken care of."

Rellik nodded.

"It's possible that Leitch is using a go-between. Some dark guy with a British accent. Bait him," said Damien, directing his order at Pussy Paul. "Tell him our rat at the prosecutor's read something to indicate it involved a meeting he had with the guy in a park. Then leave."

"Got it," said Pussy Paul.

Damien pointed his finger at Rellik and said, "Have your team standing by. If he meets The Toad or anyone who fits the description of the other guy, grab 'em."

Rellik made a motion with his hand, imitating firing a pistol.

"Not yet. I'll want to talk to them personally. Someplace private," said Damien.

"Wet Willy's?" suggested Rellik.

Damien nodded and said, "That will do."

"Should I bring a talking stick?"

Damien was silent for a moment. The thought of it churned his stomach ... but then an image of Vicki's finger came to mind. He looked at Rellik and said, "Do what you have to do."

Legg knocked on the apartment door while Connie Crane stood to one side, keeping an eye on a couple of junkies who entered a room farther down the corridor.

"You sure this is the right place?" asked Connie.

Legg rechecked the piece of paper from his pocket and said, "This is what Taggart wrote."

A moment later, someone was heard moving around inside and Legg knocked again. Eventually the door opened as much as the chain lock would allow.

Connie caught a glimpse of the woman who stared back at them. She wore fishnet nylon stockings, small satin shorts that allowed the cheeks of her ass to hang out, and a tube top that advertised her nipples.

"Vice?" she croaked. "What the fuck do you want?"

Legg shook his head and said, "Not Vice. RCMP. Are you Ophelia?"

She nodded.

"We'll make it brief," continued Legg. "If you don't want to come with us, then just talk to us now. Will take less than a minute. Do you know Jack Taggart?"

The hooker paused, then quickly closed the door.

Legg looked at Connie and was about to ask what they should do when he heard the chain being removed. Then Ophelia opened the door and glanced nervously down the hallway.

"Yeah, I know Jack," she tried to whisper, but her voice was raspy and it still sounded loud. "But tell him I'm not working for him anymore. The jerk said he'd never tell anyone."

It was a voice that Connie knew she recognized ... but from where?

"You know a guy called The Toad?" asked Legg.

"Yeah, I've been talking to Jack about him. Fuck! If someone found out, I'm dead!"

"No, it's nothing like that," said Legg. "We just want to ask you a few —"

"I know you," interjected Connie.

The hooker glared at her and said, "No ya don't."

"I recognize your voice. Ophelia, we talked on the phone. It was me you spoke to about Spider."

Isaac listened as Randy told him about Ophelia saying she was Jack's informant.

"Taggart still in interrogation?" he asked.

Randy nodded and said, "Staff Legg just got back and is with him. I just came out to tell you about this hooker. It's the same hooker who solved that homicide for us. With the war veteran."

"So Taggart did have an informant," mused Isaac. "Guess he doesn't lie about everything."

"I don't think he has her anymore. She was pretty upset that he divulged her identity."

"So be it," said Isaac. "I feel bad about that, but this takes priority. Once we get the confirmation report from Mexico, I want you to —"

Isaac was interrupted by his secretary, who brought in the report and said, "You told me to bring this in immediately, sir."

Isaac quickly read the report, then grimaced and said, "It seems the Mexican police would like to have Taggart return. I'm delivering this message in person. Bring him to me!"

Minutes later, Randy reappeared in Isaac's office. Isaac glanced up as Jack Taggart entered, followed by Legg. Isaac immediately arose and came around from behind his desk and walked directly up to Jack.

Legg saw the angry look on Isaac's face. That's when it occurred to him that Taggart might be armed. He placed his hand on Taggart's forearm while nodding to Randy to do likewise.

"Damn it, Harry! Let go of the man's arm!" ordered Isaac.

Legg quickly pulled his hand back in surprise.

Isaac looked at Jack and said, "I owe you an apology and I believe apologies should be made in person."

"Sir?" said Jack.

"I'm afraid I made some presumptions that turned out to be false," said Isaac. "With your association with

Damien, coupled with Bishop's death in Mexico at the same time you were in the country ... well, it aroused my suspicions."

"Sir, that was just a coincidence. That is what I have been trying to tell —"

Isaac raised his hands, gesturing for Jack to stop. "I know. I just received a report from our LO. The day Bishop died, you were on the opposite side of the country. A place called Merida."

"Sir!" said Legg. "What proof is there of that? Even if he was booked in a hotel, it doesn't mean that he didn't —"

"Don't interrupt!" said Isaac. He then looked back at Jack and continued, "There's more to it than that. Something that makes me even more ashamed of my actions."

"Sir?" asked Jack.

"An incident near the hotel you were staying in. It took place the same morning Bishop died..."

"The Angeles de Merida?" asked Jack.

Isaac glanced at the report in his hand and said, "Yes." He then looked at Randy and Legg and said, "That morning, five thugs jumped a policeman in an alley. They credit Taggart with coming to his rescue and saving his life."

"Oh, that," said Jack. "It was really nothing. I barely remember the incident."

"Well, they do! They have a report on it. They wanted to honour you with an award, but you left before they could get their act together. They said they tried to locate you but weren't able to. Speaking of which, you don't use credit cards much when you travel, do you?"

"I find I can negotiate better rates at some places using cash. Especially in Mexico."

Isaac nodded. "Well, they would like to see you get recognition for it. Later, at a more appropriate time, I'll be presenting you with a letter of commendation."

"Thank you, sir. I really appreciate that, but now I am kind of busy. May I get back to work?"

"You certainly may."

Isaac waited until Taggart left his office before turning his attention to Randy and Legg.

"Do you think he was sincere?" asked Isaac.

"Sir?" responded Legg.

"Taggart ... do you think he was sincere?"

"I certainly think so," replied Legg. "This is rather embarrassing. I'm afraid I may have been a little overzealous in my questioning."

"There is an addendum on the report from the LO," said Isaac. "Take a look."

Both Randy and Legg leaned over Isaac's desk and read: "The policeman who claims to have been rescued by Jack Taggart arrived at the meeting on a new Yamaha motorcycle. Unusual, considering the low salary of policemen in the area. This may be coincidental, but it should be noted that Satans Wrath has a history of influence with the Mexican authorities. Undoubtedly, this is the very reason that Sidney Bishop fled to this country."

"If Taggart is innocent," said Isaac, "I do not wish to be embarrassed any further ... so be careful."

"Sir?" asked Legg.

"Don't close the file on him yet," said Isaac.

It was late afternoon when Pussy Paul met with Leitch and passed on the information that he was the subject of a police wiretap. Leitch's concern was immediately evident on his face. Pussy Paul was barely out of sight when Leitch used his BlackBerry to send Ray a text message to arrange a meeting.

It was the last message Leitch would ever send.

# chapter thirty

Laura drove into the office parking lot and picked up Jack, who stood waiting for her.

"How did it go?" she asked. "You didn't call me this morning, so I figured..." Her voice trailed off as she waited for a reply.

"You figured right," replied Jack. "Everything has been cleared up. They discovered I was on the opposite side of Mexico when Bishop died."

"Really?" said Laura, looking surprised.

"What have you got?" said Jack, changing the subject. "On the phone, you said you had a good lead."

Laura nodded and passed Jack her notebook as she drove. "It took awhile, but between Customs and company checks, I finally hit pay dirt. Take a look at the last entries. You were right about the van. It is registered to the same company that picks up shipments of coffee from the dock. I've found seven different addresses associated with them."

"Perfect!" said Jack, while scanning the addresses that Laura had written in her notebook. "Let's go! Find that van and I bet we find Vicki and Katie!"


Leitch sat on the park bench and warily watched the faces of various people as they passed him. He didn't think any looked like police officers. He was right.

Leitch stood when Ray arrived, and the men walked while Leitch divulged what he knew about the police wiretap.

"Does it really matter, ol' chap?" asked Ray. "We have never spoken of any illegalities on the phone. Why are you so worried?"

"I didn't think you wanted anyone to know that you were here. Obviously the police are aware of your presence!"

Ray smiled, then patted Leitch on his back and said, "You gringos ... you really do worry too much. They were bound to find out sooner or later. We will buy them. Do not worry."

"It is not as easy in this country," said Leitch. "Some can be bought, but it is much more difficult. Bribery ... killing those in the judiciary ... it is not the same as in your country."

"Still, they must be reasonable," said Ray. "My brother has an expression. Silver or lead. Reasonable men will take the silver. If not, they will die. Either way, it is not a problem."

Leitch felt less anxious as he walked with Ray back to the parking lot — until he discovered he had been duped.

\* \* \*

Jack peered through the window of the premises. It was a small unit in the middle of a commercial mall where the businesses appeared to be wholesale outlets. The door was locked and there was nobody around. It was a few minutes past six o'clock and the other businesses were also closed for the day.

"This place is like the last," said Laura. "What's inside? Half a dozen chairs and a coffee machine? From the outside, you wouldn't even know this was a coffee shop."

"It's not," said Jack. "It's a laundromat. Got any dirty fifties on you?"

"Not on my salary. No back rooms?"

"They wouldn't be here," replied Jack.

"Four down, two to go," said Laura. "Want to grab a burger first?"

Jack shook his head.

Damien lay down on the back seat while Lance and Whiskey Jake sat up front and drove through Damien's gate. Several minutes passed before Lance indicated that they were not being followed. Neither Lance nor Whiskey Jake had been informed about what they were doing. Damien's instructions were brief and Lance drove as directed.

Rush hour traffic was over by the time they arrived at Wet Willy's. The automatic car wash was closed and looked to be deserted, but Lance knew otherwise. He spotted a striker sitting low in the seat of a parked car at the front of the business. Two more of Rellik's men sat in a truck at the back. Security remained where they were while the three bosses were ushered in a rear door.

The lights were on inside, but tarps hung from both doors, giving the appearance that the business was in darkness.

Rellik nodded to them as they entered and gestured to the two men who were tied spread-eagled and face-down between the inside rails of the car wash. Both men were naked except for the band of duct tape wrapped around their mouths.

"This how you wanted 'em?" asked Rellik.

Damien nodded.

Both men turned their heads and stared up at them. Lance recognized Leitch. His face was thin and pointed, making his wide eyes look almost comical. His hands were tied close to the soles of the feet of the man in front of him. Lance didn't recognize this man, whose dark eyes stared up at him.

"Leitch dancing with the Indos?" asked Whiskey Jake.

Damien shook his head, then looked at Rellik and said, "Show them."

"Found this in his Mercedes," said Rellik, while handing Lance and Whiskey Jake a Colombian passport. The meaning became startlingly clear.

"This ... Ramon. He's Carlos's brother!" said Lance.

Damien nodded. "They call him Ray."

"Dealing with The Toad," said Whiskey Jake.

"Probably," said Damien. "We do know he was dealing with Leisure Suit Larry here!"

Leitch mumbled something inaudible while pleading with his eyes.

Damien turned his attention back to Rellik and said, "I don't know what the fuck is going on, but right now all I want is my wife and daughter back. They do any talking?"

Rellik prodded Leitch in the ass with the toe of his boot and said, "Larry says that Ray is just a client. Says he didn't know that he had anything to do with us."

"Liar!" screamed Damien, stepping between the rails and kicking Leitch hard in the groin.

Leitch's body arched and bucked against his restraints. Despite his gag, his scream and whimpering echoed through the room.

Damien savagely kicked Leitch again and saw Ray looking back over his shoulder. Leitch's body became a quivering mass after the third kick.

Damien continued to stare into Ray's eyes, then walked up and ripped the tape from his mouth.

"Where are they?" Damien asked. "My wife and daughter — what have you done with them?"

Most men would have told, but Ray was no stranger to torture ... only he had always been the one to inflict the pain. He knew his life would be worthless once he talked.

"I — I don't know," he said. "I had nothing to do with it."

Damien looked at Rellik and said, "Get on with it!"

Rellik grinned down at the two victims and said, "Gentlemen, let me introduce you to the talking stick!"

Ray gasped when he saw Rellik pick up a length of broken broom handle with a spiral of barbed wire wrapped around the end. He held the stick close to Ray's face and slowly examined it.

"Please ... no ... sir," pleaded Ray. The reason for his nakedness and face-down position had become evident to him.

Rellik stepped between Ray's legs and slowly twisted the end of the stick between his buttocks. The barbs drew thin red lines of blood.

"Please, no!" screamed Ray. "You must believe me! My brother is the boss. He controls everything. Everything! It was his men … I don't know where they took your family. Please, call him. He will pay big money for me. Big money…"

Damien held up his hand, gesturing for Rellik to stop, then held out the cellphone that Carlos had supplied him earlier. "His number," said Damien. "Give me his number and I will hold the phone so you can talk to him!"

Jack scanned the warehouses in the industrial area that Laura was driving through. It would be dusk in another hour, but there were still a few trucks moving about.

"This looks good," said Laura. "Independent warehouses. Trucks and vans coming and going."

Jack saw the address they were looking for. He also noticed something else. "Keep driving! Don't slow down or look!"

"Someone eyeballing us?" asked Laura, as she drove right past.

"There's a guy sitting in that pickup out front."

Laura caught sight of the truck in her rear-view mirror. It was backed into a parking stall. "People getting off work. Maybe waiting for someone," she offered.

"Or standing six," said Jack.

"Did you get a plate?"

"No front plate. Find a place to park where we can watch. This could be it."

Laura parked where they could watch the warehouse through binoculars. The pickup truck remained out front.

Jack received a call on his cell and handed the binoculars to Laura.

"Hey, Johnny Canuck! How you all doin' up there?"

"Jim-Bo! How are you? Heard you were out of the country."

"Just got in. Tried to do a sting on the head honcho of a Colombian cartel. Didn't go well."

"Carlos?"

"No. The Diego Ramirez cartel. He's in close competition with Carlos, though. They were at war with each other up until a couple of months ago. Looks like they settled on a truce for now. Ramirez operates out of Cali, while Carlos operates out of another city just north of Cali called Buga."

"Were you successful in nailing Ramirez?"

"Naw. We tried to set up a sting on him. He has a weakness for redheads. Got a CI close to him and tried to sucker him out of the country so we could grab him. Didn't work. Ramirez is smart. Cultured too. Speaks perfect English and generally pretends to be a gentleman. When it comes to cocaine distribution, Ramirez is about even with Carlos. He's a major player. We've been after him for years. Same as Carlos. Both top drug lords we'd like to put behind bars."

"What can you tell me about Carlos?"

"He's the opposite of Ramirez. Relies on terror to stay where he is. Not that Ramirez is averse to torture and murder, but he generally tends to be more subtle and will give someone time to reflect upon how much money could be made. Carlos's organization is more inclined to offer a smaller bribe while they stick a gun in the person's face and pull the trigger if they refuse. That's if Carlos is feeling nice. Otherwise he tortures them to death."

"Nice guy."

"Yeah. Real nice. Sally said you all called. Was it about Carlos?"

"Yes. I want to know everything about him. Particularly in regard to kidnappings."

"I can tell you that you don't want to be on the receiving end. His organization has snatched lots of people. Usually they're found mutilated. The guy is a real psycho. He's got lots of enemies. Never leaves Colombia and always travels with at least thirty bodyguards. Well connected, too. The asshole always wears a green beret. I think he does it to relate to the militant factions down there that he hires to protect his labs. We've tried for years to get evidence to extradite both him and Ramirez. So far, no luck."

"A fellow up here owes Carlos money. His wife and daughter were grabbed for ransom."

"Yeah? Well tell the guy he probably won't be seeing them again ... at least not alive."

"Appreciate it if you don't tell anyone about this call. The guy confided in me but doesn't want the police involved."

"I hear ya."

"Speaking of which, someone tried to kill me and murdered the wrong guy by mistake. Then almost murdered my partner's — I mean my ex-partner's — baby."

"Jesus Christ! You all right?"

"I'm still above ground. You never mentioned my name to anyone over that ship I gave you, did you?"

"Not a soul. In the warrant I just listed you as a reliable CI. Haven't told anyone, including my people."

"Didn't think so. The guy I'm after is dark-skinned but has a British accent. I figure he's Indo."

"British accent?"

"Yes."

"Carlos has a brother by the name of Ray. Ramon in Spanish. I thought he was in Britain. He got his masters at Cambridge in business administration. We figured he was going to return to Colombia and help Carlos launder money."

Jack stared at his phone for a moment, then yelled, "That's it! Carlos knows! It is retaliation for what I told you!"

"Jack ... I'm sorry. If it is Carlos, I still don't know how he could have found out about you."

"It has to be! You said he's a psychopath! Ray is here! I know it! He's doing his brother's bidding!"

Carlos listened to Ray gasp and choke out the words, describing where he was and what had happened. Damien heard the outrage as Carlos screamed into the phone.

Damien then spoke into the phone and said, "So, Carlos! If you want to see your brother again, you'll let my family go. You've got five minutes and then the next call I get better be from my wife!" He hung up before Carlos could reply.

The minutes crawled by and everyone in the car wash remained silent as they waited. Three minutes later, the phone rang. Damien smiled with satisfaction as he answered.

"I have telled my men to move your whore and bastard girl," said Carlos. "If you hurt my brother, he will not be able to tell you where they are."

"Let me speak to them," demanded Damien.

"You will not speak to me in that manner," replied Carlos. "You understand. I have two peoples. You have one."

"I have your lawyer," said Damien.

Carlos laughed and then said, "I no care about him. I bought him for nothing. One hundred thousand dollars Canada. He then talk to me. He tells me all about you. Who can trust hombre like that? Kill him if you wish. He is not important."

Damien glanced at Leitch and cursed silently, then demanded, "Let me speak with my wife. I want proof that they're alive!"

"You will have talk soon, amigo. I have told my men. You will get such a call in one hour."

"Good. Then..."

"But you have now attacked my family. My ... what you call honour. One of your family is die because you make more mistake. In one hour you can tell me which one!"

"What do you mean!" Damien yelled before realizing that Carlos had hung up. He quickly redialled. No answer.

Damien looked at his men, who stood waiting for instructions. He had none.

# *chapter thirty-one*

Jack gripped his phone and listened intently as Jim-Bo spoke.

"If it is Carlos, he's untouchable," said Jim-Bo. "So will Ray be, if he makes it back to Colombia."

"We've got activity," said Laura, looking through the binoculars. "The warehouse door is opening."

Jack looked up and saw a van pull out of the warehouse. "Gotta go, Jim-Bo," he yelled into the phone before grabbing the binoculars from Laura.

Seconds later, Jack knew they were at the right place. "That's the same van that was at the motel the other night," he said.

"This place is it!" said Laura, excitedly. "Vicki and Katie ... they've got to be inside that warehouse!"

They watched as the van screeched to a stop beside the pickup, then the driver of the pickup ran over and got in the van. Moments later, the van raced away.

"Maybe I can figure out a way to peek inside that place," suggested Laura. "Pretend I'm lost or something."

"They took the lookout," said Jack. "Something's not right."

"Maybe he wasn't a lookout."

"Maybe. We can always come back later. Follow the van. They might lead us to some other place."

It was dusk when the van turned off the Lougheed Highway onto Pitt River Road. Laura was stuck in traffic and Jack said, "It's crossing the Red Bridge."

Laura found an opening and quickly started to cross the bridge spanning the Coquitlam River, then abruptly slowed down.

"Watch it!" said Jack.

"Too late," said Laura, "we're on the bridge. Going to have to pass them."

Laura watched the van in her rear-view mirror as she drove past. "They're turning off," she said. "Small parking area by the bridge."

Laura drove for a moment before parking on the side of the highway. "What do you figure? Meeting someone?"

"Yeah, maybe someone with a British accent," said Jack tersely. "Come on, we'll go on foot."

Damien sat on the floor, resting his elbows on his knees and holding his face in his hands. *You can tell me which one.* The words echoed in his brain. *Taggart's partner's wife ... she had the same option. This isn't just an idle threat!*

Three-quarters of an hour passed before Damien got to his feet and spoke quietly with Whiskey Jake and Lance. Lance went outside as Damien looked at Rellik and said, "Untie him!" while gesturing to Ray. "Give him back his clothes. Wallet, passport — everything!"

"What about Leisure Suit Larry?" asked Rellik.

The hope in Leitch's eyes disappeared when Damien said, "Leave him as is."

Ray quickly dressed and Damien handed him the cellphone. "When your brother calls, tell him I'm setting you free. You can just walk out of here."

Damien saw Lance return and said, "You tell the boys outside to let him go?"

"I told them," said Lance. "You want me to call a cab too?"

Damien nodded and said, "Tell them to be here in half an hour."

"Yellow or City?"

"I don't give a fuck! There's a phone book in the office. Use it!"

Damien looked at Ray and said, "Nobody will follow you. When you know you're safe, call your brother and let him know. Your Mercedes is still at Stanley Park. I'll give you your keys back."

Ray's dark eyes gleamed. He was back in control again. There was one thing he was certain. He knew his brother ... and what would happen when he was freed. Damien would pay dearly for this intrusion. He would never see his wife and daughter again. In a few years, when Damien thought he was safe, he would also die. *But what choice does Damien really have? Not to release me will mean that both his wife and daughter will die. Of course, they will anyway. But how can you live with never knowing for sure?*

Ray stared at Damien, who returned his stare briefly before looking down. Damien was beaten. He knew what was about to happen and there was nothing he could do about it — but beg. Something he was likely willing to do right now.

The Carlos cartel was no stranger to kidnappings. Ray knew that his brother looked at it as entertainment. It instilled terror and maintained the position that Carlos had hacked out for himself. *Damien will suffer the fate of many others. He will listen to his loved ones die...*

"*Hola*!" answered Ray when Carlos called.

Ray spoke with Carlos in Spanish, then looked at Damien and asked, "I may leave now?"

Damien peered out from the tarp covering the front window, then replied, "The cab just arrived. Go. Leave the phone so that your brother can call me. When you know that you are safe, use a payphone to call your brother. He can then call me on this phone."

"I can't believe you're letting him go!" shouted Lance. "This is not the way to do this!"

"It is not your family!" yelled Damien. "You are not in charge! I am!"

Ray paused as Lance mumbled an apology. Carlos heard the angry exchange of words and laughed. He then gave Ray instructions: "Make sure you are truly free," he said in Spanish, "then call. The men are waiting at a place to dispose of two packages but should not wait long. Leave quickly! Do not go home. Do not get your car. Go to the airport!"

Ray hung up and handed the phone back to Damien. He almost felt sorry for him but glanced at Leitch and thought of the indignity he had suffered himself. Almost sorry ... but not quite.

Moments later, Ray gave the taxi driver one hundred dollars to ensure that they were not being followed. He earned his money. His expertise as a city cab driver was evident as he followed orders and whisked down back alleys and ran red lights.

Ray watched carefully to ensure that they were truly not being followed before instructing the driver to pull over by a payphone where he would make two calls.

His first call would be to Carlos. His second call would be to order a taxi from a different company. Even if they were watching the airport, he knew he would be safe once inside. He glanced at his watch and wondered how many hours it would be before he arrived at the Aragon International Airport in Cali. Once in Cali, it was less than an hour's drive to his home turf of Buga.

Vicki did not have any religious beliefs, but now she prayed that her ride in the van was to their freedom. Her hands were still bound in tape behind her back and her ankles were also bound. Pain radiated up her arm from her severed finger and she wondered how long it would be before the infection killed her ... if she lived that long.

More tape covered her eyes and mouth. She knew that Katie had been bound in the same manner. Both had been bound that way shortly after their arrival at the warehouse. Neither had received any food, water, or bathroom breaks in the last eighty-four hours. Vicki had lost control of her bladder. From the smell, she knew that Katie had defecated. Their only comfort had been to lie back to back on the burlap sacks and touch each other's fingers.

The van stopped and they waited for a while. She could hear the men speaking to each other. Eventually she was dragged out of the van. She felt men's arms reach through her own arms and drag her over the ground, scraping her knees as she went. She could hear the sound of water and wondered if she was going to be drowned. She moaned when her knee came in contact with a protruding stone in the path. Other men grunted behind her and she knew that Katie was also being dragged along.

A few minutes later, Vicki was placed sitting on her knees. She heard the sound of a cellphone being dialled, then a man spoke in Spanish. Fingernails scratched her face and the tape was ripped from her eyes. She blinked as flashes of light and shadows mixed. She saw that she was kneeling in front of a river. Seconds later, the band of tape was ripped from her mouth.

"Numbers! What numbers?" a man said, then slapped her across the face.

She blinked her eyes and saw the man holding a cellphone toward her face.

"Your hombre! What numbers?"

Vicki tried to speak, but her throat was swollen and no words came out.

The man cursed in Spanish and was about to slap her again when someone else intervened, grabbing her by the back of her head and shoving her face into the river.

*They're going to drown me now ... my poor Katie...*The water suffocated her and she started to choke as her head was brought out, then repeatedly dunked again. Finally she found the words and pleaded, "No, please. Don't kill us! She's just a child. I —"

She was brought back to her kneeling position and the man with the cell demanded, "Your hombre. His phone. Talk to me the numbers!"

Vicki then understood what was being asked and quickly gave Damien's cell number. As the man dialled, the other man spoke in Spanish on another phone.

It was good that Vicki did not understand Spanish as the man verified his instructions from Carlos. He was to slash Katie's throat as Vicki spoke with her husband. Vicki would then receive the same treatment.

Vicki looked at Katie as she knelt beside her. The tape had been torn from her eyes but she was still gagged and bound. Vicki saw the bewildered look in her eyes as she looked around. The look of bewilderment turned to pleading when she looked at her mother. Vicki had thought the two of them had used up their well of tears in the last few days as their brains slowly went numb. She was wrong.

# chapter thirty-two

Jack slapped at a mosquito on his face as he and Laura made their way along a narrow path leading through dense bushes and trees that followed parallel to the river and would eventually lead them to the Red Bridge.

"Dusk ... prime time for these little vampires," whispered Laura, slapping her own neck.

"There it is," said Jack, pointing to the upper structure of the bridge as they neared.

"Wait here in the bush. The parking lot should be close. I'm going to take a look and see if they've got company."

Laura waited a moment and then Jack returned.

"Didn't see any other vehicles except theirs," said Jack.

"Maybe that's why they're waiting," suggested Laura.

"Using themselves for mosquito bait? Let's sneak

a little closer and see if we can get an eye on what they're up to."

A minute later, they heard men's voices and crouched behind some scrub brush and peeked out. The bridge had numerous large cylindrical cement pillars in a cluster on each side to support the bridge. The pillars themselves were in the ground on each side of the river. The sandy recourse went out from the pillars and then dropped off sharply in a small bank down to the river. The men were standing in a group close to the river but some of them were blocked from view by the pillars. The bush had been mostly cleared around the base of the bridge and Jack and Laura could not get any closer without being seen.

Damien's hand shook as his fingers stumbled over the button to answer the cellphone.

"So, Damien, my brother is free," gloated Carlos.

"Let my family go," said Damien. "Please ... I beg you. Let me speak to them."

"You telled your man that you were in charge. You are not in charge. I want to hear you say I am boss."

"Please, your brother is —"

"Now! Then your woman can talk at you!"

"Carlos is in charge!" yelled Damien to his men. "He is the boss!"

Carlos laughed, then said, "*Bueno*! Now I will tell my man to let your woman speak at you on your own phone. Keep this phone close so we can still talk."

Seconds later, Damien's personal cellphone rang and he raised it to his other ear.

"Damien," gasped Vicki.

"I'm sorry," cried Damien. "I'm giving them everything they want. Are you ... is Katie?"

"I've been told to tell you," said Vicki, "we are tied up. Katie … me … we are on our knees."

Damien heard Carlos shout a command in Spanish, and Vicki's voice became a gurgle.

"Now," said Carlos, "you will pay for what you have done. Your woman can tell you how you pay!"

Vicki gasped and coughed, then said, "I don't know why he did that. He choked me. I … Damien! He has a knife! He's cutting Katie's neck…"

Damien listened as Vicki screamed. His other ear picked up the sound of Carlos laughing and cheering.

"Your girl is die, Damien! Now your *puta*! Listen to her…"

Jack heard the sound of a woman's voice and then saw one of the men yank Vicki into view by her hair and drag her to the top of the bank where she kneeled on the ground. At the same time, another man yanked Katie into view and placed her beside her mother.

"It's Vicki and Katie!" whispered Jack. "One guy is holding a cellphone up to Vicki's face. They both look like their hands are tied behind their backs. Ankles bound too. "

"We're too far away to get the drop on them … there's four of them," said Laura.

"I'll call for backup," said Jack. "We can just sit tight until —" Vicki's scream interrupted his thoughts, and he looked up in horror as he saw one of the men yank Katie's head back by her hair. A flash of light reflected off the blade of a knife on Katie's throat. Vicki screamed.

"Police! Drop it!" screamed Jack, leaping to his feet. The men looked up in surprise as Jack sent a bullet zinging above their heads and into the river bank on the opposite side.

Two of the men reacted by pulling out their own pistols as Jack and Laura ran towards them, trying to use some of the bridge pillars as cover. The men fired a volley of bullets that thunked into trees and ricocheted off the cement pillars. The distance was too great for a handgun to be really accurate, but fear instinctively drove the Colombians to fire rapidly.

A couple of the men crouched behind the pillars as Jack and Laura came closer.

"Die, you bastards!" screamed Jack, as he and Laura let loose with their own volley of shots. Shots that quickly improved in accuracy as the gap narrowed.

Jack stumbled over an old firepit, skinning his hand, but then regained his footing and raced ahead to catch up with Laura as she crossed the final few steps of the clearing.

One of the men yelled something at them in Spanish, then turned and pointed his gun at Vicki while looking back at Jack and Laura for a response. His meaning was clear. The response wasn't what he expected. Instead of backing off, Jack stopped, took aim, and fired. The man leapt backwards as the bullet zinged past his ear.

"Vamoose or you will die!" screamed Jack. "Run and we let you go!"

"Locos!" yelled one of the other men to the others.

*That's right, I probably am crazy,* thought Jack.

One of the men yelled at a colleague in Spanish. They violently shoved Vicki and Katie, causing them to scream as they tumbled down the bank and into the river where their screams coldly stopped. The four men bolted through the pillars to the far side of the bridge toward a path that would lead them back to their van.

For Jack and Laura, the choice was obvious. If they pursued the men, Vicki and Katie would drown.

* * *

Damien heard the scream and then the sound of shots as both phones went dead. "No!" he cried in anguish. "No!" he yelled again, and then he kicked Leitch hard in the ribcage. Leitch choked and gasped in pain.

Lance was quick to shout instructions into his own cellphone. Seconds later, the striker left his taxi and moved into position. Ray was just calling another taxi to take him to the airport as Rellik's crew arrived.

Twenty minutes passed before Ray, blinded, bound, and gagged with duct tape, was dragged back into the car wash. Perhaps knowing what was in store for him, he risked being shot and put up a fight when he was approached. It did little to delay his capture but did result in a blow from a steel pipe that broke his arm.

Ray, again stripped naked, was being tied face-down to the railing when Damien knelt in front of him and ripped the tape off his eyes and mouth.

"You couldn't do it, could you?" said Damien. "Let my wife and my daughter live. You could have just walked away and released them. But no, you had to kill them!"

"It wasn't me," pleaded Ray. "My brother ... he is sick. I would not have hurt them. Please. You must believe that!"

"And was it your brother who cut off my wife's finger?" yelled Damien.

"His idea. Yes! It was all Carlos!"

"But Carlos wasn't here, was he?" screamed Damien. "It was you who did it!"

"No. It was men who work for Carlos. Not —"

"And who do you work for?" snarled Damien, picking up the roll of duct tape.

Ray's eyes bulged as Damien wrapped the duct tape around his mouth. He then shut his eyes tight as Damien ground his foot into his broken arm. The resulting scream could be heard through the tape.

Damien looked at Leitch and said, "And who do you suppose gave Carlos that idea?"

Leitch mumbled through his gag and vehemently shook his head from side to side. Two of his ribs were broken and breathing was painful.

Damien's cellphone rang. He paused, then looked at his men. "Carlos ... wanting to gloat. He can fucking wait!" he roared, while walking back and kicking Leitch in the face. Blood splattered from Leitch's broken nose onto Damien's shoe.

"Wrong phone," said Lance, as the ringing persisted.

"What do you mean?" yelled Damien, while stooping to use Leitch's shirt as a rag to wipe the end of his shoe.

"It's not the phone Carlos sent you. It's your private one!"

Surprise registered on Damien's face and he quickly took the phone from his pocket, then held it in the palm of his hand and stared at it as it continued to ring. For a moment, he was afraid to answer. Afraid of what he would hear ... but he had to know.

It was Vicki. She was hysterical and crying but said that she and Katie were alive. Then she cried, "They were going to kill us! We were saved by —"

The phone went dead and Damien stood in a stunned silence for a moment, then turned to his men and said, "That was Vicki. They're alive!"

"Where are they?" asked Whiskey Jake.

"I don't know. The line went dead," he said, as the arrival of hope coincided with the return of panic.

"They let them go!" said Lance.

Instantly Ray's eyes portrayed his relief and he mumbled a prayer.

"Maybe," replied Damien. "She said they were going to be killed, but then weren't. Then the line went dead."

A moment later, Damien received a text message on his BlackBerry: *They're both okay. We're on our way to VGH. -JT-*

Damien looked at his men. He felt his knees tremble and it took him a moment to comprehend.

"Damien?" asked Lance. "What is it? What's going on?"

"They weren't let go," he said simply. "They were rescued by a cop ... Jack Taggart. They're on their way to the hospital."

Bile immediately flooded into Ray's mouth. He choked and swallowed rapidly to keep from suffocating.

"Taggart! How the fuck did he get his nose into this?" growled Whiskey Jake.

"Yeah," quickly added Lance, wondering who was talking with whom. He glanced down at Leitch and Ray and felt a wave of fear.

"Whiskey Jake, you come with me," ordered Damien. "Rellik, you find out everything these two fuckers know. What they know about each other, Carlos, The Toad ... how many guys are working for them ... everything!"

"Will do, boss."

"But keep them alive until I come back," added Damien, before turning to Lance and ordering, "Arrange for a security team to cover off the Vancouver General, then meet me there."


Jack sat in the Emergency waiting room, off by himself. Laura remained in the car outside in the parking lot. She agreed that the fewer Satans Wrath members who knew what she looked like, the better it would be.

Jack didn't have to wait long before three strikers he recognized from the west-side chapter entered the hospital and quickly scanned the waiting room and the corridors. One of the strikers then went back outside to wait near the entrance. The other two set up a vigil inside.

Several minutes later, Jack saw Whiskey Jake and then Damien enter behind him.

Damien's eyes met his, and he stood as Damien approached. He was conscious of the two strikers moving toward him, but a flick of Damien's hand sent them both away. Damien then said something to Whiskey Jake, who took a seat in the waiting room while Damien spoke with Jack.

"Where are they?" asked Damien. "What happened? How...?"

"They're going to be okay," said Jack. "They're both being examined right now. Give the doctors a few minutes, then you can see them."

"You said they're okay?"

"Vicki did lose one finger and she has an infection, but other than that, she'll be okay."

"Katie! What about Katie?"

"She wasn't sexually molested. She is missing two teeth from being punched in the mouth. I understand they're baby teeth so ... anyway, she'll be okay. They're both dehydrated and in shock, but that's it."

"They punched her in the mouth! She's only eight years old," seethed Damien.

"She tried to rescue her mom when they attacked her with bolt cutters."

"How? How did you find them?"

"My partner tracked them down through Customs declarations and shipping invoices for coffee. We had just found their warehouse when we saw a van leaving in a hurry. We decided to follow the van. It was just luck. We didn't know Vicki and Katie were inside. We followed the van to a spot along the river in Coquitlam. That's when we realized what was going on. There were four guys. They got away but we managed to save Vicki and Katie."

Damien let out a deep sigh, looked at his watch, then said, "Everything go okay with your trip to Mexico? I heard you were a hero."

"Yeah, thanks."

"Well, tonight you really are one." He looked at his watch again and said, "That's it. I'm not waiting out here. I'm going to see them. I'll send you a message in the morning. We'll talk then."

Jack nodded, then said, "There's one more thing. I found out that Carlos has a brother by the name —"

"Ray," said Damien. "Yeah, I just found out. He's the one with the British accent. Leitch was two-timing me behind my back. Don't worry about Ray. He won't be bothering anyone again."

"You … *got* him?" asked Jack.

Damien nodded.

Jack wondered if Ray was dead and used his finger to make a slashing motion across his neck to convey what he wanted to know.

Damien shrugged, then said, "Yeah, sure if you want to do it personally. I owe you big. If you want to kill him, that's fine."

Jack realized the mistake and said, "No! That's not what I meant. I just wondered if he was still alive?"

"Oh! Yes, he's being questioned as we speak." Damien paused, then said, "I presume you had something to do with a shipload of coke that was taken down in San Diego?"

Jack nodded and said, "That's why Ray tried to kill me. Only he botched it and killed the wrong guy. Acting on orders from Carlos, I presume?"

"Maybe," said Damien. "Either that or following a suggestion from their lawyer — Leisure Suit Larry."

"Leitch?"

"It would be his style. He recently recommended that someone from your toxicology department be killed to jeopardize some court cases. I believe her name was Lucy."

"Lucy! Who did he say this to? Is there a contract on Lucy's —"

"No. He suggested it to me. I nixed the idea immediately ... but I'm not Carlos. You cost him a lot of money in San Diego. He would agree to have you killed if he didn't think of it himself."

"I didn't exactly advertise my involvement."

"No, you were waiting to nail me with the second ship," said Damien bitterly.

Jack nodded and said, "Speaking of that, nobody in my office knows about tonight either. I was grilled this morning about Bishop. I would like to be prepared before I go to work tomorrow morning. Anything you learn from Ray would be appreciated."

"I'll see what I find out. I'll send you a message around four tomorrow morning. We can meet then," said Damien.

"I don't start work until eight. We could do it at seven," said Jack.

Damien shook his head and said, "That doesn't work for me. If you want to know what Ray said, answer back at four."

"I would like to ask him a few questions myself," said Jack quietly.

"Such as?"

"Whose idea it was to try and kill me and Danny's baby. Was it Carlos or Ray? Also, I want to know how Carlos found out I was involved with the first ship."

Damien nodded and said, "I'll ask, then let you know."

"One more thing. Ask him who the four guys were who kidnapped your family and where they can be found."

"That," said Damien, pointing his finger at Jack's chest, "is my business." He turned to walk away but paused and said, "We're just like you guys on this one."

"How so?" asked Jack.

Damien sneered and said, "We're making sure that Ray doesn't say anything without his legal counsel present."

*His legal counsel?* Jack realized what Damien meant and watched him walk away. He thought about the early morning hour when Damien said he would call. *Certain tasks are better accomplished in the dark ... like body disposal.*

Jack checked his watch. That was six hours from now. He left the hospital and got in the car with Laura and told her about the conversation.

"You think they've got Leitch and the Brit?" she asked.

"Positive. The way things are going, I bet they'll both be dead in less than six hours."

"We better reach out to our friend and see if he knows where they are!"

"Whiskey Jake is with Damien. I'm sure our friend is involved and unable to call. He could be with Rellik right now."

"So what should we do? Set up on Damien? You can bet he is going to take a personal interest in this."

"Personal! Oh, it's personal all right. Just ask Holly or Charlie or Danny and Susan! This is personal! It's also personal for Damien!"

"Jack, relax," said Laura quietly. "You don't have to convince me it's personal. Danny's baby convinced me of that. If the both of them are found with a bullet in their head, I won't exactly lose sleep over it, if that's what you're thinking."

"Good. Then let's not lose sleep. Go home and rest. I'll call you as soon as Damien contacts me."

Laura stared intently at Jack and then nodded in agreement.

They were just pulling out of the lot when Jack received a text message from Lance.

"It's our friend," he said, reading the message. "Says we need to talk. Urgent. He is on his way to meet Number One."

"He's on his way here," said Laura. "We could meet him a block away before he arrives."

Jack shook his head. "We don't need him telling us tonight what is going to happen. I'd rather he tell us tomorrow."

"Good point," replied Laura.

Lance wasn't too surprised when he received a message back asking, *On your way to VGH?*

Lance quickly typed, *Yes.*

Lance was shocked when his next message asked, *The two interviews over?*

Lance paused, not sure how to respond. Then simply typed, *Yes, but not finished.*

*You safe?*

*Yes.*

*We'll meet tomorrow.*

Jack put his BlackBerry away as Laura said, "Yes, but not finished?"

"They're still alive."

"That's what I figured," said Laura.

A few minutes later, they stopped at a traffic light and Jack noticed that Laura was starting to tremble.

"You okay? Your body is shaking."

She turned the heater on high and said, "I'm cold."

"I know how you feel," said Jack. "I get ... cold too, when I've been shot at. It's funny. You think it would happen at the time, but with me, it seems to come later when I'm actually safe."

"I guess that's when we finally have time to think about it. How do you handle it?"

Jack let out a sigh, then said, "Natasha says it's something you need to be aware of and control. Emotional shock, acute stress disorder, PTSD — whatever the label, it basically boils down to someone being exposed to a life-threatening event. A reaction to something that causes intense fear, helplessness, and horror."

"Like back at the river."

"For Vicki and Katie ... yes."

"You trying to tell me you weren't afraid? Horrified at what almost happened?"

"Definitely, but not helpless. Neither were you. When we were running toward them, I slipped and fell. It didn't slow you down any. You continued right on."

"I was too afraid to turn around. Thought I would get a bullet in the back."

"Or too angry. Either way, you're not what I would call helpless. Remember that. You made decisions. You were in control. As long as your brain has control of something, anything, you are not entirely helpless."

Laura gave him a grim smile, then continued to drive. After a moment she turned the heater off and said, "Thanks."

"You may not know it yet, but there might be times when this job could become stressful. We have to watch out for each other."

"It could get stressful!" yelled Laura, while punching Jack on the shoulder. "Well, please let me know if you think that might happen!"

They both laughed, harder than they would normally have, as their bodies and minds leapt at the chance to relieve some tension.

"Does Natasha prescribe something for it? The stress, I mean?" asked Laura, while glancing in the rearview mirror at her mascara.

"A three-olive martini works for me. Care to join me?"

Laura shook her head. "Thanks, no. Elvis will be wondering what happened. We've already logged in fourteen hours today. All I want to do now is close my eyes."

Laura was almost home when she drove past a liquor store, then slammed on her brakes and backed up.


Jack was relaxing on the sofa talking to Natasha when the phone rang.

"This stuff is awful!" said Laura. "How do you drink it?"

"Ah ... you are wise to phone the master martini maker," replied Jack. "It is actually an acquired taste. For beginners, I recommend..."


Elvis saw Laura's hand tremble as she slid a martini across the kitchen table toward him. He took a sip, grimaced, and then said, "So, you set the alarm clock for four?"

Laura nodded.

"Pretty early."

Laura took a swallow but held the glass with both hands to try to stop it from spilling.

"Are you going to tell me about it?"

Laura peered at him from over her glass but didn't reply.

"Something bad happened today ... or tonight."

Laura put her glass back down on the table and her eyes opened wider as she feigned surprise.

Elvis's face reddened and he said, "Don't lie to me, Laura! Don't give me that act surprised, show concern, deny, deny, deny routine. You narcs do it so much that it has become a joke in our office. If you don't — or can't — tell me, fine, but respect me enough not to lie to me."

Laura's face went blank for a moment, then she started to cry. Elvis put his arms out to her. She quickly rose and then sat on his lap and held him tight.

"I respect you," she sobbed, "and I love you more than anything. What happened today … I really love you. This … I can't talk about it. Everything will be okay. Just trust me."

Elvis held her but didn't respond. *What is going on?*

# chapter thirty-three

It was quarter to four in the morning when Damien, Lance, and Whiskey Jake arrived back at the car wash. Leitch and Ray lifted their heads and turned to stare. They were still naked and tied face-down to the railings on the floor, with gags in place.

Leitch's eyes were wide with fear. His face was bloodied, but he still had hope. He grunted and whined as he tried to plead. White blisters on the soles of his feet were explained by the cigarette butts lying beside them.

Ray's eyes were dark. His experiences had taught him that pleading might only prolong the inevitable, delaying the welcome relief of death. The smell of burnt hair lingered in the air from more personal places where a cigarette lighter had been applied to his body.

"What did you find out?" asked Damien.

Rellik tapped Ray in the ribs with his boot and said, "Ray, here, was acting on orders from Carlos. They found out that Jack Taggart was involved with the first shipment that the cops grabbed in San Diego."

"How?"

"They have sources in the phone companies. They did phone tolls of the U.S. cop who got the search warrants. They found several calls back and forth between him and Taggart. Right before the bust, during the bust ... and a call after. Good idea. Something we should be doing."

"Why the fuck didn't Carlos tell me? Would have been nice to know, seeing as we had two more shiploads coming!"

"They figured they had taken care of the problem before the next ship went out, except they whacked the wrong guy. That's also where Leisure Suit Larry here came in. He told Ray that you weren't prone to killin' cops ... not even broads that work in the cops' labs. They figured if you knew, you might back out of the deal."

Damien knelt close to Leitch's face and said, "You will soon discover that killing people is an option I am not always opposed to."

Leitch grunted and whined as Damien stood to face Rellik again.

"What about The Toad? Where is he?"

"They both deny knowing him."

"I was told that they were both in a park with The Toad."

"Maybe someone bullshitted you?" suggested Rellik.

"Same person said that these two knew each other. That info was good."

"I was pretty thorough, boss," said Rellik. "I really don't think they knew him. At least, not under that name."

Damien thought about this, then asked, "What about trying to drown the cop's kid?"

"Ray says that Carlos figured they could neutralize the cops by messin' with their brain cells. Scare 'em all into doin' nothin'. After that, he said somethin' about giving them a choice of silver or lead."

Damien looked at Ray and said, "For your information, the cops in Canada are paid a fuck of a lot more than the cops where you come from. They're not easily bribed here, and if you offer them silver or lead ... I guarantee they'll give *you* lead!"

"There's another thing with Leisure Boy," said Rellik. "Ray paid him a hundred grand to backstab us. Leisure Boy gave him reports from the rat cop before we even saw 'em. Also set up companies for Carlos to launder money here."

"Maybe that was The Toad's interest in Leitch," suggested Lance. "Using him to move the money out of Canada for him!"

Leitch shook his head from side to side and let out a muffled protest. It brought him another kick in the ribs from Damien, who then asked, "How many guys they got here?"

"Twenty-one people," said Rellik. "But only four besides Ray that got balls to do stuff. The rest are mom and pop types used for laundering."

"Names and addresses?"

Rellik nodded and said, "Phone numbers, too. The four tough asses live in a rented house together. Got someone watching it now. Don't think anyone is home yet. Ray has his own apartment. We got someone lookin' in it now."

"Anything else?"

"Yeah. Before we got Ray, Carlos was planning to have you personally deliver the last payment down to Colombia. Wanted to see if you would give your life to save Vicki and Katie."

Damien stared down at Ray for a moment, then said, "Untie his arm. The one that's broken. He can still use it to hold a phone."

Rellik untied Ray's wrist, and a moment later Damien punched in the numbers on the cellphone. He waited until Carlos answered and then said, "Carlos, your brother wishes to talk with you." He handed the phone to Ray and said, "I'll let you say goodbye."

"Carlos!" screamed Ray, then rapidly spoke his native tongue.

Rellik's face betrayed his wishes as he looked at Damien.

Damien stared briefly at Rellik and thought, *You disgust me.* He then said, "Yeah, go ahead. Do your thing. Leitch first."

Ray looked back in panic as Rellik put on a pair of coveralls and surgical gloves before picking up the broken broom handle. He held it with both hands and closely examined the spiral of barbed wire, then looked down at Leitch's upturned face and grinned.

The high pitch of Ray's voice made it almost unrecognizable as he relayed the details of what was happening as Rellik twirled the broom handle slightly between Leitch's buttocks.

Leitch's body writhed and squirmed against the restraints while he emitted muffled screams. Rellik then thrust deep and Leitch's eyes and fists closed tight as his body arched. His scream was muffled by vomit. A moment later, his body went limp.

Rellik slowly pulled out the broom handle, then walked around and knelt in front of Ray, holding the bloodied implement close to Ray's eyes. He looked at Damien and said, "I better tape his mouth."

Damien nodded and took the phone from Ray, who pleaded until Rellik applied the tape.

Rellik then looked at Ray and said, "For you, I will not be so kind. It will be much slower."

Damien held the phone close to Ray's mouth. The gag that Ray wore did not block out the screams broken by the intermittent whimpering of a dying man. In the background, the sound of Carlos's voice could be heard on the phone as he alternated between pleading, offering money, and then screaming when Ray quit speaking.

Damien put the phone to his mouth and said, "How does it feel, Carlos?" before smashing the cellphone on the floor and grinding it with his heel. He then hurried out of the building.

Lance followed and stood silently as Damien vomited before getting in the car.

Jack was awake when he received the text message from Damien. They were to meet at six o'clock.

Jack called Laura and asked, "You awake?"

"Already showered."

"We meet him in an hour and forty-five minutes. I'll pick you up. It's on the way to the meet."

"An hour and forty-five! He could have let us sleep longer."

"I'll buy you breakfast. Something other than olive soup."

Elvis's eyes were closed, but he was awake when he heard Laura rummaging in the bureau dresser. She then went to the bathroom.

He listened to the sound of her refilling the bullets in her clip ... and then the backup clip. *What the hell happened yesterday?* Moments later, he felt her warm kiss on his cheek, then she was gone.

* * *

Jack and Laura were just pulling into a coffee shop parking lot when Jack received another text message. It was from Lance.

"Our friend is still up," said Jack. "Better cancel breakfast. We don't have much time."

"Cemetery?" asked Laura.

"You trying to pick up another date? Forget it. We're using a parkade."

Twenty minutes later, Lance climbed into the back seat.

"The Brit is Ray," said Jack, before Lance could speak. "Carlos's brother."

"Yeah, I fuckin' figured you knew that," mumbled Lance. "I thought I was about to be done with all this bullshit of havin' to work with you, until Damien met ya at the hospital last night. Thought he would tell ya. Didn't know you two were so tight."

"Actually we figured it out before then," replied Jack. "So what happened? I know Damien had both Leitch and Ray grabbed."

"They were more than grabbed."

Lance recounted what happened and Jack and Laura listened quietly to the grim fate of Leitch and Ray. When Lance finished, he stared quietly at Jack for a moment and then said, "So you knew that Ray was the guy before Damien talked to ya in the hospital?"

Jack nodded.

Lance frowned and said, "Shit! I was close to winning this time."

"Winning what?" asked Laura.

"An agreement with your partner here. He said if I could identify the Brit before he did, I wouldn't have to work for ya anymore." Lance looked at Jack and said, "Okay, I better go. I'll be in touch when I need to be."

"Don't bother," said Jack.

"What ya talkin' about?"

"We're even," said Jack. "As far as I'm concerned, you've more than repaid your debt. This is the last time I ever expect to hear from you."

Lance's eyes opened wide. "You mean it?"

"I mean it," said Jack, while extending his hand over the back seat.

Lance was quick to shake his hand and then said, "Man, you don't know what a relief this is! Don't take it personal — you've been real solid with me — but not seein' ya anymore is ... well, better than winnin' the lottery."

"You're president of the west-side chapter," said Jack. "Think about it. If you don't want to see me, don't look in your rear-view mirror!"

Lance paused as he thought about what Jack said, then laughed. When he got out of the car he turned and automatically said, "See ya around." He then took two steps and said, "What the fuck am I sayin'? I ain't never seein' ya again!"

Laura waited until Lance left the car before saying, "You're cutting him loose at a time like this?"

Jack shrugged and replied, "I don't really like it either, but fair is fair. I've put the guy through enough. Besides, right now I want Carlos and he can't help me with him."

"Your call," replied Laura. "Right now I'm too sick thinking about what Rellik did. A bullet in the head is one thing, but this ... I feel nauseous."

"I feel the same way," replied Jack.

"And we're supposed to meet Damien in less than half an hour! He's as demented as Carlos is! "

"It made Damien sick. Neither of us has thrown up."

"Yet."

Jack nodded. *I won't be sick ... but my nightmares are going to become wilder.*

"Rellik ... sticking that up a person's bum!" exclaimed Laura. "You heard our friend. He enjoyed what he did! What kind of person would do that?"

"A psychopath, just like Carlos."

"And you think we should talk to Damien? Rellik wouldn't have done it if Damien didn't let him."

"You can't show weakness when you're the lead wolf. Besides, we can use Damien to catch Carlos. That is who made this personal for us."

"Yeah, he made it personal, and I would like to see someone put a bullet in his head. But he's too protected. I think we should go with who we can catch. Concentrate on Rellik and Damien. Which is why I wish our friend — or ex-friend now — was still working for us."

"I want Carlos!" said Jack, feeling agitated. "Who do you think is worse? Carlos, who is responsible for the murder of Holly's husband, turning Charlie into a paraplegic, and trying to drown O'Reilly's baby ... or Damien, for murdering the people who kidnapped and mutilated his wife and daughter?"

"I know what you're saying, but..."

"But what?"

"After what we just heard? I won't sleep as long as Rellik's above ground! I can picture him grinning as he did it! His long stringy red hair, that thin face and chipped front tooth. I can feel myself vibrate with anger, just thinking about him."

"You've been studying photographs."

"He stands out. Now in more ways than one. I'd love to get the chance to double-tap two into his chest." She then became silent, imagining the horror of what went on inside the car wash.

Jack drove out of the parkade toward their rendezvous with Damien and then said, "Maybe when it comes to protecting our families, certain actions are made without much rationalization."

"You condoning what they did?"

"No. Definitely not. Damien's a monster. No doubt. But he does have a human side to him. Can't say the same from what I know about Carlos."

"Carlos lives in another country protected by an army. He's untouchable. Damien might not be. I think you're making a mistake. Let's nail Damien ... or at least Rellik. That's who I really want. Ray is dead. We're going to have to forget about Carlos."

"Nobody is untouchable."

Laura paused, then conceded, "You're right, but neither are we."

"Are you that upset that Leitch and Ray are dead?"

Laura sighed and then said, "Not that they're dead. Upset with how they died. Wish he had just shot them instead. Treat them like you would a rabid dog. Don't torture them. Just shoot them and be done with it."

"Oh, I see. Your philosophy. Shoot, shovel, and shut up!"

Laura smiled and said, "Yeah, maybe that is becoming my philosophy. Right now I'm just glad it's over."

"Over? It's not over!" The anger flashed across Jack's face as he reached to the visor and threw Charlie's picture down on her lap. "Look at that and tell me it's over! Call Susan O'Reilly and tell me then that it's over!"

Laura felt stunned, then said, "I meant over as far as who attacked Danny's baby. That was Ray. He's dead."

"Ray was a pawn!" said Jack bitterly. "Carlos calls the shots. As long as he's alive, there will be more victims. Think about the ones you and I know ... imagine how many others there are."

Laura looked at Charlie's picture.

"Carlos has the power to continue his terror," continued Jack. "When he's dead, then we can say it's over," he added quietly.

"Jack, you said it yourself. He lives in Colombia. Surrounded by his own army. DEA have tried unsuccessfully to extradite him for years. There's no way."

Jack gave Laura a hard look. "There's always a way ... but I need a partner who thinks like I do."

"And how do you think?"

"Not afraid to play dirty."

"Like torture?"

"I agree with you on that philosophy, but I do consider Carlos to be a rabid dog."

Laura looked at Jack for a moment, then asked, "You already have a plan, don't you?"

"Yes."

Laura waited, but Jack didn't elaborate. *He's not going to tell me unless I agree to help.* Laura glanced at Charlie's picture one more time. *Oh man!* She looked at Jack and asked, "Do I need to buy rubber boots and a shovel?"

"Maybe."

"If it was for Rellik, I'd buy them right now, but Carlos? How can we?"

"My plan won't work without you."

Laura sighed and said, "I figured that. What's your plan?"

"It's really quite simple," replied Jack.


Jack left Laura sitting in the car as he walked along the path meandering through New Brighton Park. Damien, freshly showered and clothed, was on time.

"How are Vicki and Katie?"

Damien took a deep breath and slowly let it out

before saying, "They're going to be okay. Thanks for asking."

"They're both traumatized," said Jack. "They're going to need special help."

"I know. They'll get it."

Damien extended his hand and said, "I should have done this last night in the hospital. I want you to know I wasn't ashamed to be seen shaking your hand ... I was just too upset to think about anything other than seeing them."

Jack accepted the handshake and Damien said, "Thank you. I will never forget what you did. You saved my family twice."

"Twice?"

"First time on Sunday when you found the money."

Jack shrugged and said, "You helped me become a Mexican hero."

"That was one favour. You saved two of my family. Then did it again yesterday. Figure I owe you three more favours."

"Yesterday I wasn't alone," replied Jack. "My partner was actually the one who found out where they were being kept."

Damien nodded.

"How are you going to explain Vicki's injury?" asked Jack. "They'll know it's not fresh."

"Accidentally chopped it off when she was backpacking in the wilderness. Was a two-day hike to get back out. Katie said she fell."

"Their clothes aren't what you would call hiking clothes."

"The docs know it's not true ... but they also know who we are. All they needed was an excuse to write down on some form. They're too afraid to call the police."

"Good thing you didn't try and pull that stunt with Natasha."

Damien grinned and said, "I know better. She'd probably slash my throat with a scalpel."

"You find out the answers to my questions?" asked Jack, choosing to ignore the remark.

"Yeah, I did."

Jack listened closely as Damien told him everything he had found out. He didn't mention how Leitch and Ray died. He summed it up by saying, "There are some details that are best left unsaid. If I was psychic, I might make a prediction that Leitch and Ray are deep-sea diving. Bet they remembered their weights but forgot their tanks."

Jack gave Damien a long, hard stare. He realized he was holding his breath and slowly exhaled. He then asked, "So now what? You know Carlos is going to come after you."

"Yeah, I know. But what was I supposed to do? By the time I figured out who Ray was, it was too late for apologies. Besides, Carlos was going to kill me anyway. He wanted me to make the last payment myself in Colombia. Once I did that, he would have whacked me and my family."

"So what will you do? Take your family and hide? Carlos is not going to let this drop. Especially when he finds out … what you did."

"He already knows. I let Ray talk to him just before … a certain procedure."

"His revenge could be swift," noted Jack. "He's already set up here laundering money through coffee companies. He'll have guys looking for you or anyone else you know."

"I know. I don't know what to do. It's not like I'd ever get a chance to nail him first. All I wanted to do was save my family."

"You're not the only one who wants Carlos. He made this personal for our side. I want him!"

Damien's thoughts were still on his own family and he said, "I've got guys guarding my house. I thought of moving everyone to some other country, but with Carlos's money and connections, it would probably be just a matter of time."

"Witness protection program?"

"Fuck you. I'm not testifying on anything. I'd take my chances with Carlos first."

"If I told you a way to get to Carlos, would you help?"

Damien eyed Jack suspiciously and then said, "Maybe. What are you thinking?"

"You would have to pretend to be my informant and —"

"Not a chance! I'm not being a rat to —"

"I said pretend! You won't say anything we don't already know or would find out."

Damien looked at Jack curiously and then asked, "What's your plan?"

"It's really quite simple. There's another cartel in Colombia that rivals Carlos's. It's called the Ramirez cartel. With your connections, I bet if we were in Colombia, you could connect with that cartel in less than a week."

"Diego Ramirez. He lives in Cali."

"You've heard of him then?"

"I've been to his villa for dinner."

"Perfect."

Damien grunted and said, "His prices were a little steep." He then glanced around and added, "But I guess, ultimately, not as steep as Carlos's."

"Is Carlos based out of Cali too?"

Damien shook his head and said, "Nope. A small city called Buga. It's less than an hour's drive north of Cali."

"Close enough," said Jack thoughtfully.

"Close enough for what?"

Jack looked at Damien closely, then said, "Time for you to meet my partner, then we'll discuss strategy."

"Fine by me. I want to shake O'Reilly's hand, too, for what you guys did last night."

"O'Reilly's busy looking after his own family. My new partner is Laura Secord."

Damien's face registered his surprise, then he said, "Jesus. A fucking broad?"

"A fucking broad? This is from someone who once told me that there could be a 'certain degree of verisimilitude' to what I say? The same guy who asked why cops tend to 'lard on the tough talk'?"

Damien stared at Jack but didn't respond.

"You sound like you think I'm one of the bozos who work for you!"

Damien frowned and said, "That's upsetting. I think you might have a point. Sometimes it's hard to think you're not just some guy from another chapter."

"That kind of scares me," said Jack, wondering if Danny was right. *How close am I to being one of the bad guys?*

"You trust her? Your new partner?" asked Damien.

"She's the one who found your family last night. She's smart ... pragmatic. I trust her. Something I don't feel about too many people."

"If Carlos finds out I'm in Colombia, he'll slowly skin me alive. I mean that literally."

"Do you want Carlos or not?"

"It's either him or me. Do I really have a choice?"

"Then let's do it. Come on, I'll introduce you to Laura. Your life will be in her hands. I suggest you don't call her a 'fucking broad'."

* * *

Damien shook hands with Laura. The meeting was brief as Jack quickly reiterated what Damien had just told him. He then told them about his plan to trap Carlos.

When Damien left, Laura looked at Jack and said, "Find me a ladies' room. I shook hands with him. I know it's psychological, but I need to wash."

"Likewise," said Jack.

"Then your plan says we go to the office and lie to the people who are on our side?"

"Exactly," said Jack.

"Oh, man..."

## chapter thirty-four

Anti-Drug Profiteering investigators arriving at work were greeted by Jack and Laura, who had called a meeting. Randy Otto from I-HIT also attended. They listened attentively as Jack and Laura described the Carlos cartel and outlined the Colombians' money-laundering activity orchestrated by Ray and Leitch through a chain of coffee shops.

Jack paused as different investigators hastily wrote notes, then he looked at Randy and said, "Yesterday, while I was being detained in the office, Laura did some checking and found several businesses and a warehouse that the Colombians have invested in."

"I've made copies for all of you," said Laura, sliding sheets of paper across the table.

"Laura and I met our informant early this morning," said Jack. "Last night things went sideways. Leitch was skimming money that he shouldn't have. Our informant says Leitch met with Ray last night and then disappeared."

"The Colombians teaching Leitch a lesson?" asked Randy.

"Excellent guess," replied Jack. "It shouldn't take long to verify. Find Ray and you may find Leitch. If all this is true, and I believe our informant is reliable, evidence of the money laundering is likely in Leitch's office or in a safety deposit box held by his secretary."

"It won't take long to find out if Leitch is missing," said Randy, checking his watch. "He should be at work by now. Someone toss me a phone book and I'll call his office."

"I suggest everyone jump on this," said Jack. "As soon as the Colombians know we're on to them, they'll head for the border."


Randy quickly learned that Leitch had not shown up to work and had missed a scheduled meeting with a client that morning. His girlfriend reported that he hadn't come back to his apartment last night.

Four hours later, Leitch's secretary went to her bank and tearfully turned over records to ADP involving the laundering scheme. It didn't take them long to search the warehouse and several businesses. It was apparent that the Colombians had already fled.

Bloody bolt cutters with traces of human tissue, along with blood on sacks of coffee beans, were located at the warehouse. The investigators submitted the evidence for DNA examination and believed that Leitch had paid the ultimate sacrifice for his crime. Later the DNA was found not to match, but that did little to undermine the Colombians' violent reputation.

* * *

Elvis watched Laura as she quietly ate her dinner. Her eyes were distant and her face was without expression.

"Seems you did well today," he said.

"Yeah, it tastes good," she replied.

"I'm not talking about the chops *I* just cooked. I heard what you and Jack did at work today."

The focus returned to her eyes. She leaned back in her chair and asked, "What do you mean? What did you hear?"

"I was talking to someone in ADP. Heard they've frozen $2.4 million in Colombian drug money. Not bad for your ... second official day at work."

"Oh, that. Yeah, it's a good start."

Elvis noticed that Laura's eyes returned to some distant view. A view that he wanted to see.


"Menu?" asked Holly, while pouring Jack a cup of coffee.

"No, thanks. Just on my way home for supper. Natasha's expecting me."

"You just pop in to say hi?"

"Came to ask you a question."

Holly took a seat in the booth across from him and said, "Go ahead."

"Do you believe in capital punishment?"

It was a question Holly hadn't expected, and the surprise registered on her face. "I never really thought about it before, but ... yes, I believe in it now. Why? It doesn't really matter. Even if you catch the guys, it's not done here."

"People don't always know what is done and what isn't." Jack reached in his pocket and took out a twenty-dollar bill and said, "Remember this?"

"That the same one?"

Jack nodded.

"I told you I wouldn't accept it until you caught the guys."

Jack nodded, stood up, tossed some coins on the table, and said, "This is for the coffee." He then ripped the twenty-dollar bill in half and dropped one piece on the table. "I'm working on the second half. Appreciate it if you keep this between the two of us."

Holly sat in a stunned silence as he walked away.

The following day, Isaac summoned both Jack and Laura into his office and gestured for them to take a seat.

Isaac smiled and said, "I've been apprised by ADP and I-HIT about the intelligence you two gathered this week. A lot of money and assets have already been frozen. It would appear that you're responsible for destroying a major organized crime family before they could get too established. Well done!"

"Thank you, sir," said Jack and Laura in unison.

"However," said Isaac, "there are still a few loose ends. For one, that lawyer is still missing and presumed murdered. For another, when it comes to the Colombians, it is obvious that none of the main players have been apprehended."

"I warned our units that they would likely flee for the border once the investigation started," said Jack. "Unfortunate, but not really anyone's fault. I think the Colombians took that precaution after Leitch was kidnapped."

"Your informant in this matter, is it the same person you cultivated last year with O'Reilly?"

"No, sir. This one just came on board yesterday,

but obviously his information is proving to be both valuable and accurate."

"Obviously," said Isaac. "Who is it?"

Jack paused to take a deep breath and slowly exhaled before saying, "It's the national president of Satans Wrath."

"What?" yelled Isaac.

"His name is Damien," continued Jack.

"I know his name! Why ... how ... why is he talking to you? This is absurd! I don't believe it. How did you ever convince him to cooperate?"

"I had approached him the other day, trying to find out if he would tell me anything about the Indos. He wasn't all that cooperative, but it must have got him thinking. He contacted me and we set up a meeting with him yesterday morning. He said he wants to retire, but the club won't let him."

"He's the national president. Can't he quit when he wants? This has to be a trick!"

"He's the boss for Canada," said Jack, "but the club is international. There are still people above him. Some with grandiose ideas."

"You expect me to believe that he would turn on his own club? After all these years?"

"No, and he made it clear that he won't. He's willing to cooperate to expedite his own interests, which would also benefit us."

"How so?" asked Isaac, leaning forward in his chair and looking closely at the two faces in front of him.

"He's been ordered to import tonnes of cocaine into Vancouver from Colombia."

"Why him?"

"B.C. basically has the lowest sentencing rate in the world for drug traffickers. Not only is this the safest place to set up an international distribution centre, but cargo leaving here doesn't get the same scrutiny it does in Third World countries."

"That I understand, but why is Damien cooperating?"

"He simply wants out. He's fifty-three years old and has a wife and three children. His values are changing and he doesn't like to be pressured into doing anything. He's also worried about the new anti-gang legislation."

"Section 467.13 of the Criminal Code. That hasn't even been tested here yet. I understand that won't be before the courts until almost Christmas."

"I know, but Damien is a visionary. He wants to retire now while things are still good. He thinks that if a major dope deal or two went sour here, then some other location would be selected instead and he would be free to retire."

"Is that why he handed over the Colombians?"

"Yes. He wants to slowly extricate himself from everything. He's been ordered to go down to Cali, Colombia, and order a tonne of cocaine. He is willing to take us along, providing we don't burn him and seize the ship before his own people get involved."

"From the Carlos cartel? The man we think is responsible for the lawyer's disappearance?"

"Satans Wrath think they're too hot now with how they mishandled this business with Leitch. He's been instructed to meet with the Diego Ramirez cartel. Damien has met with him before but opted for Carlos because he received a better price at the time."

"How do you know he's not blowing smoke? Trying to set us up somehow?"

"He appears to have been straight with us about Leitch and the Colombians."

Isaac nodded, then asked, "And is he willing to let

us do what it takes to monitor him and make sure he's on the level?"

"He said he would allow that, as long as we promise never to burn him. He'll give us the ship, the dope, and all the bodies we can snag as long as we keep him out of it and promise to seize it before his guys unload it."

Isaac shook his head and said, "I never would have believed he would turn."

"It's a once in a lifetime opportunity," said Jack. "Won't cost us that much, and if we take him to Colombia we'll find out pretty quick if he is being straight with us."

"Corruption among the Colombian police forces is rampant. We can't risk that someone down there might tip off Ramirez that Damien is working for us, if, in fact, he actually is."

"Sir, the Colombian government has formed an elite police squad that is proving to be trustworthy. To provide extra safety, we wouldn't have to tell everyone down there what is going on. As long as the LO has a few people he can trust, we can make it look like we're targeting Damien. If Ramirez is tipped off, it would still make Damien look legitimate."

"If we don't do this," said Laura, "I suspect Damien will simply go ahead and import tonnes of cocaine without our knowledge."

Isaac let out a deep breath, then said, "Okay, I'll approve it."

"Sir, I don't anticipate his cooperation unless Laura and I go along as his handlers. We've built up a trust."

"That goes without saying." Isaac then pointed his finger at Jack and Laura and said, "But I want full electronic surveillance on him from the time he lands until he returns."

"He won't be able to wear a wire when he meets with Ramirez. They are bound to sweep for bugs."

"Then how will we know he's not deceiving us?"

"We've already discussed this with him. Laura and I are both operators. I could play the part of Damien's financial consultant and Laura could play the part of his mistress."

"He'll agree to that?" said Isaac, sounding surprised.

Jack and Laura both nodded their heads.

"It would also provide the appropriate cover and protection for us to stay in the same hotel as Damien," said Laura. "We could monitor him closely and pass on information to our people. As Jack said, it would be safer if not everyone knew who we really were."

"I agree. Get on it, but I still want you to bring some equipment with you. If there is a chance to record any of this, it could later prove valuable. I'll leave it up to your discretion if you think an opportunity arises where it is safe to use it. You'll need to have Damien sign the waiver forms before you go, giving permission for electronic monitoring between the three of you. It will give you a chance to appraise his integrity, even if you decide not to use it. If he refuses to sign it, then I would look at it as a sign that he is trying to deceive us."

"I'm sure he won't object, sir," said Jack, "as long as there is no chance of it being detected."

"Good. You better get started. I'll notify Drug Section myself. I'll have them send a team and contact our LO in Bogota to meet you in Cali."

"Thank you, sir," said Jack.

Isaac looked pensive, then said, "You will both have to tread carefully. Heed the advice from the LO. Colombia averages over a hundred kidnappings a month, mostly Colombians, but some foreigners as well. Safety comes first. If something doesn't seem right, I want everyone back here, pronto."

"Yes, sir," they replied.

On the way out of Isaac's office, Jack leaned over to Laura and whispered, "I hope Elvis likes redheads!"

Isaac waited until Jack and Laura left his office before placing a call to Drug Section. They would send a team of four.

Isaac then called Staff Sergeant Legg in the Anti-Corruption Unit. They would be sending representatives as well, in advance and on a separate flight. Elvis would not be one of them.

Isaac also informed Legg that waiver forms giving permission for electronic monitoring would be signed, with Jack believing that he was in control of whether to use it. Legg smiled. *Dirty pool, perhaps ... but legal.* In view of this, it was decided that they would also send two men from a more technical unit. Men whose training and reputation indicated they could plant a bug up your butt without you knowing it.

## chapter thirty-five

It was eleven o'clock at night when Jack, Laura, and Damien checked into their rooms at the Intercontinental Cali Hotel under fake names. Their flight from Vancouver had taken ten and a half hours. It took another hour to clear customs and then half an hour to rent a car. Despite this, with the two-hour time difference and an added boost of adrenalin, none of them felt like sleeping.

They adjourned to the hotel bar and all ordered a local beer called Aguila. Jack noticed that four members from the Vancouver RCMP Drug Section were already seated in the bar, but they pretended not to know each other. Jack and Laura were scheduled to meet with them the following morning upon the arrival of the RCMP liaison officer stationed in Bogota.

"Narcs?" asked Damien, with a nod of his head toward the other table.

Jack nodded silently.

"They get to pack pieces?"

"Not allowed," said Laura. "None of us have any authority to pack heat."

"Trust me," said Jack, "the local authorities covering us will be armed to the teeth."

"You, I sort of trust," said Damien. "The local authorities, I don't!"

"Tomorrow, when we meet Ramirez ... how much do you trust him?" asked Laura.

"Diego? Well, he sounded okay when I called him last week. A little surprised but seemed friendly enough."

"We've got to do this fast," said Jack. "In and out quick."

"Just like a boy losing his virginity," said Damien. "You don't have to tell me. Can you imagine what Carlos would do if he knew I was here? Fuck!" He glanced at Laura and said, "Sorry about that ... but think about it. Carlos is less than an hour's drive away. I'd be happy if we could fly back tonight!"

"Any chance of us meeting Ramirez someplace public?" asked Jack.

"I doubt it," said Damien. "His place is probably safer. Lots of bodyguards and less chance of some rival trying to take him out. If he did agree to a restaurant, his guards would kick everyone else out and the whole place would be jittery."

Jack looked into Laura's eyes and knew they were both thinking the same thing. If anything went wrong tomorrow, there would be no hope of a cover team being able to extract them — at least, not alive.

"Down here, you also got to really watch for bikes," warned Damien. "Small ones, like Yamahas or Suzukis, with two riders. One guy drives and the other one shoots. They can disappear in traffic before the victim hits the ground. Real pros."

Jack took a sip of beer and thought about the men who killed Holly's husband. He knew the sound of motorcycles would haunt her for the rest of her life.

"I'm going to call it a night," said Laura. "I want to give Elvis a call before I turn in."

Jack nodded. He would call Natasha as well. *Tell her how much I love her ... but try not to have her worry...*

It was nine o'clock the following morning when Jack and Laura went to a room two floors above where they were staying to meet with the other RCMP investigators.

Jack shook hands with the RCMP liaison officer, who introduced himself as Jean-Louie. He knew Jean-Louie by reputation as being a top-notch undercover operator before taking on the job of foreign liaison officer. He was also fluent in French, English, and Spanish.

Jack felt the firm handshake and saw the flash of a smile as Jean-Louie's eyes met with his.

"I know you by reputation," said Jean-Louie. "Old-school operator. Not too many of us around. I'm glad our paths have finally crossed."

"Likewise," replied Jack.

Jack watched as Jean-Louie shook hands with Laura. He admired him for the work he was doing. His own paranoia of working narcotics in Colombia for only a day or two was bad enough. It was hard to imagine how Jean-Louie could handle the pressure on a full-time basis.

Jean-Louie then gave a thumbnail sketch of Diego Ramirez and the local area. Ramirez controlled an army of men in Cali, which was located in the Valle de Cauca, the heart of Colombia's cocaine business.

A short distance away to the north, a place the locals called Norte del Cauca was home to several militant factions who protected the cocaine labs in return for an infusion of cash to support their war with the Colombian government. Over a thousand people in this vicinity had been murdered in six months because of rivalry in the cocaine trade.

Ramirez owned a chain of stores selling leather goods, including shoes and jackets. He was also known to be heavily invested in the petroleum industry in Costa Rica, where he laundered his money. In short, he was one of the top drug lords around and had been targeted unsuccessfully by the DEA for years.

Jean-Louie said he basically trusted the special police unit that came with him to provide protection in Cali, but even they would be kept in the dark about the real identity of Jack and Laura.

"And our friend, obviously," said Laura.

Jean-Louie nodded, then pointed his finger at Jack and Laura and said, "Under no circumstances are you to leave Cali! It will be difficult to provide cover here, but the city is big enough that they are used to strangers. Nearby cities, like Buga and Palmira, are infested with spies. People who are the eyes and ears of various drug lords. Any cover team put in these areas would be quickly identified and you would be executed ... quickly, if you were lucky."

"Our friend says Ramirez lives on the northwest edge of the city," said Jack. "That is where we intend to meet with him. From what I understand, Ramirez is not anxious to leave his own place. Travel elsewhere should not be a problem."

Jean-Louie reached for his briefcase and said, "I'll show you some aerial photographs of his estate. He's situated on forty acres with the best security money can buy. He has a tennis court, a couple of pools, and it is even reported that he has a bowling alley in his home."

"Sounds like he is managing to eke out a living," said Laura, before smiling.

"This guy is big," replied Jean-Louie. His voice was serious and there was little doubt that he was worried. "I'll get guys in the vicinity to try and follow in the event you drive someplace, like to a restaurant or something. Just remember they can't get too close. You'd be dead if they're spotted. As far as being at his place ... nobody could ever get to you in time if something did go wrong. So understand that you'll all be on your own when you're there."

"We understand," replied Jack. "Our friend did call Ramirez before we came down. He was told to go to a shoe store here in Cali first where he was to place a call to arrange to meet."

"I read the reports on Satans Wrath's past involvement with the Carlos cartel," said Jean-Louie. "If Ramirez isn't available, maybe your friend could look him up. He's not quite as sophisticated as Ramirez, but personally I believe he would be a worthy target. His reputation is rather ugly."

"Carlos drew too much heat when he took out that lawyer in Vancouver for skimming money," said Jack.

Jean-Louie wasn't easily dissuaded. He responded, "I-HIT is looking for four guys connected to Carlos for the lawyer's disappearance. Also his brother, Ramon. I'm sure they're back here now. If your guy is still tight with Carlos, it might be a good chance to find out."

Jack shook his head and replied, "Satans Wrath doesn't want anything to do with them. They're too unpredictable. Ramirez is our target. We'll go with our friend in a few minutes to the shoe store and let him reconnect. We can then let you know when and where."

Jean-Louie slowly nodded and then said, "Good enough. It's your call. We'll cover you when you go. I was told you're playing the part of your friend's money launderer?"

Jack nodded and said, "I know enough to pull it off."

"And you?" said Jean-Louie while looking at Laura. "I understand that you're pretending to be the mistress?"

"As much as I hate bikers, I think I can manage the role," replied Laura.

"You recently dye your hair red?" asked Jean-Louie.

Laura frowned, then replied, "Why do you ask?"

"Ramirez has a reputation for loving redheads. I just wondered if you did it to impress him."

Laura shrugged and said, "Not really. I just thought I would try a new look."

Jean-Louie would have accepted her explanation but saw her glance at Jack when she answered. *She wants to know if Jack approved of her response. They are hiding something.*

"There is one more thing," said Jean-Louie. "You have your cell so I'll give you a cool number in Canada that is on call-forward back to me. If there is a problem, pretend you are calling your colleague in Canada. Try and let me know what is going on, but be aware that they might have the equipment to monitor both ends of the conversation."

"Understood," said Jack. "If I want the cavalry to arrive, I'll ask how Charlie is. Otherwise, just play it by ear."

"Good enough. If I hear *Charlie* I'll send the teams in with guns blazing, although I doubt they could get to you in time."

As Jack wrote down the phone number, Laura said, "You know, Jack, I've had a migraine all morning. Would you mind if I skipped going with you to make the call? I need to lie down for a couple of hours."

"Not a problem," replied Jack. "It's just a phone call. Besides, our friend wants to go into the store alone. He doesn't want to include either of us until he gets permission from Ramirez to introduce us. You and I won't do our thing before this afternoon."

Jean-Louie watched as they left. *Laura's eyes look bright and alert. Her reputation says she's dedicated. Too dedicated to be put off by a headache while in Colombia, of all places!*

Jean-Louie returned to his own room and sat on the bed for a moment. Then he took a deep breath and slowly exhaled before reaching for the phone. He hoped his gut instincts were wrong. He hated dirty cops.

A team from the Anti-Corruption Unit were only minutes away. The call was brief. Jean-Louie would pair off the RCMP narcs with the Colombian team to cover Jack and Damien. ACU would monitor Laura. Room bugs had not picked up anything of value yet, although Damien was prone to talking in his sleep.

Laura waited until she knew that Jack, Damien, and the cover team had left the hotel before putting the "Do Not Disturb" sign on her door and heading to the lobby. Soon she found a taxi driver who spoke *a leetle English* to take her to the northwest part of the city. She wanted to find a motel on the outskirts, someplace isolated. The taxi driver smiled. For such a beautiful woman, he understood the need for discretion. He knew a few such places.

Eventually Laura settled for Maria's Cabinas. The taxi driver waited patiently while Laura went inside the *officina* and rented three cabins grouped in a cluster. Only one unit would be used, but Laura didn't want anyone else hit by a stray bullet when Carlos died.

On her way back to her hotel, she had the taxi stop at a *pharmacia*. In the event the team was back from covering Jack and spotted her entering the hotel lobby, the pills she carried to relieve her migraine would explain her absence.

She entered the hotel lobby and did not see anyone she recognized. Moments later, she got off the elevator and paused in the hall and knocked on Jack's door. There was no answer so she entered her own room and closed the door behind her. She took a few steps and abruptly stopped. Her room had not remained empty in her absence. She was in trouble and she knew it. Before she could move, a sharp knock landed on her door.

# *chapter thirty-six*

Jack parked the car a couple of blocks from the shoe store and lagged behind Damien as they walked. He used his cellphone to discreetly take a picture of Damien from behind, then another of his profile as he crossed the street. The third picture was of Damien passing a newsstand. Today's headlines were taped to the wooden structure in the background.

When Damien entered the shoe store, Jack remained outside while he placed a call and sent the three pictures.

As discreet as Jack tried to be, his actions did not completely escape the sharp eyes of Jean-Louie. He was not sure that Jack had actually taken pictures, but there was no doubt that he had made a phone call. Jean-Louie's thoughts were interrupted when he received a text message from the Anti-Corruption team who were detailed to follow Laura:

*Information just received. Reference
the four men associated to the Carlos
cartel sought in the disappearance of a
Vancouver lawyer. These men connected
to a warehouse near Vancouver where
spent bullets were recovered from a
wooden beam used for target practice.
Lab matched these bullets to the same
gun used in the unsolved murder of a
man in Surrey last April. The victim was
named Jack Taggart. His one-year-old
child, Charlie, was left a paraplegic as a
result of the murder. Believe this murder
was a botched assassination attempt on
Cpl. Jack Taggart. If there is any indication that Cpl. Taggart is connecting with
the Carlos cartel, have the Colombian
police arrest him immediately and
detain for interrogation.*

Jean-Louie read the message carefully. The name
*Charlie* did not escape his attention. In a way, Jean-
Louie was pleased with the message. *Jack and Laura
are not dirty ... at least not in a moral sense. But if they
think they can seek justice on Carlos, then they are
fucking insane!*

Carlos was inclined to dismiss the telephone call. It was
not possible. But when he studied the three pictures he
knew that he was wrong. Damien was here! He had the
nerve to come to Colombia to hire an assassin to kill him!

Carlos had been busy plotting to send a team of
professionals to Canada to seek revenge. Fantasizing
about how he could inflict the most pain before killing

Damien had become an obsession. *Now Damien shows up in my own backyard!*

"I understand that you would like to ... speak with this man," said Jack.

"Very much," replied Carlos. "Face to face!"

"I would expect a fee to arrange this. Say $1 million in American?"

"You show me where he is and I will agree to that."

"I also want your assurance that you will never come after me or my family again."

"For this, you are my amigo."

"Good. I am told he will only be in Colombia tonight. I have someone close to him. He fears you. He said he would never be taken alive."

"I want the last face he sees to be mine!"

"I will know later where he is staying. My friend may be in a position to assist. I am told he always likes to take a shower after having sex. Perhaps my friend will signal when he is in the shower. Do we have a deal?"

"*Si*, Señor Taggart. We have a deal! How may I contact you?"

"I will contact you. I suggest you have people standing by. Time is of the essence. It will have to be tonight or early tomorrow morning."


Damien left the shoe store and met with Jack.

"Went great," said Damien. "They tracked down Ramirez and I spoke with him on the phone. He invited all three of us to his villa for lunch. I declined. It's noon now. We need more time to get organized, so I said we would be there at two."

"Excellent. Good work."

"Everything okay out here?"

"Perfect," said Jack.

* * *

Jack and Damien entered the hotel lobby just as Laura stepped inside the elevator. They caught the next elevator, and moments later Jack knocked on Laura's door. He saw the movement as she checked the peephole, then opened the door.

Jack saw the look of concern on her face as she held her finger to her lips.

Damien, standing behind Jack, did not see Laura's finger and asked, "You sneak out and rent a place to use?"

Jack grabbed Damien by the arm but was too late. Both men silently followed Laura inside the room.

Laura pointed to her pillow.

Jack saw the coin and picked it up. *A Canadian penny!*

Damien frowned and looked at Jack and Laura for an explanation. Jack used a piece of hotel stationery to write "We're bugged."

Damien briefly closed his eyes and slapped his forehead. His question to Laura was a serious mistake.

"So, I didn't really hear you," said Jack, while turning to face Laura. "Were you able to sneak out and rent a place without anyone knowing?"

Laura was startled but saw the slight nod of Jack's head.

"Yes, I did," she said. "Three of them. A place called Maria's Cabinas."

"Good," said Jack somewhat loudly. "I feel bad not letting anyone know, but it is for our own protection. Jean-Louie may trust his people, but I don't. If anything goes wrong and we need a safe place to hide, that will be it. You pay cash and use a fake name like I told you to?"

Laura took a deep breath and slowly let it out. She

then replied, "You bet. How did it go with you? Did you connect?"

"Went smooth," said Damien, glancing around the room and wondering if video had also been installed. "We've been invited to meet Ramirez at his villa at two."

"I better let Jean-Louie and the narcs know," said Jack, looking at Damien. "Why don't you grab a table in the restaurant downstairs for lunch. Laura and I will pay them a quick visit and then come down."

When the trio left the room, Jack turned to Laura and said, "I thought Elvis was still at home?"

"He is. I talked to him last night. He took the call on the first ring. He wouldn't lie to me about that!"

"What the hell is going on?" growled Damien. "Who is Elvis?"

"Laura's husband. Works Anti-Corruption," said Jack.

"You've got to be kidding!" said Damien, looking at Laura.

"He's a great guy." Laura shrugged.

"Yeah? Well who are you working on?" asked Damien.

"Enough," said Jack. "She's solid. We wouldn't have been warned if it hadn't been for her husband. Someone is suspicious. You can bet they've got bugs in at Maria's Cabinas and everywhere else they can."

"I'm used to that," grunted Damien. "Now you know how it feels. Shouldn't change anything."

"We're in too deep to back out," said Jack.

"Good," said Damien. "Besides, what could really go wrong? All you do is make a phone call and we head for the airport. Let Ramirez take care of loose ends."

Laura rolled her eyes and thought, *What could go wrong? Oh man...*

* * *

Jack and Laura both forced themselves to smile when Damien stopped at the guard house at the entrance to the Ramirez estate. One guard, carrying an M16A1 automatic rifle, checked their faces carefully while another guard used a telephone. Moments later, the electronic gate opened and they were allowed to proceed.

The estate was treed with a variety of pine, teak, and palm trees. The long driveway that eventually meandered up to the mansion was lined with palm trees. Jack and Laura caught glimpses of guards, with M16s slung over their shoulders, patrolling the grounds.

Jack grimaced. Jean-Louie was right. *We're on our own.* He exchanged glances with Laura and Damien. He knew they were thinking the same thing. *All we have is each other...*

Introductions were made inside the front entrance to the mansion. Above their heads hung a chandelier that was slightly larger than a Volkswagen.

Ramirez was cordial, spoke excellent English, and his eyes sparkled when he met Laura. Jack guessed that he was about sixty years old. He was a tall, solid-looking man with grey hair that contrasted sharply with his dark skin. He had a long ponytail that made his balding head more obvious. Despite the heat and the humidity, he was dressed in a long-sleeved silk shirt and slacks. Leather sandals adorned his feet.

They were ushered out to the rear of the mansion, past an Olympic-sized pool where a bevy of young and beautiful women either lay on lounge chairs or cooled themselves in the water. Most wore thong bikinis and some had elected to go topless.

Minutes later, they took a seat in a gazebo and drinks were offered. Both Jack and Laura chose a Chilean Riesling, while Damien settled for a beer. Ramirez also chose the Riesling.

Conversation was light until after the waiter poured the wine and placed an Aguila beer in front of Damien. As soon as he had left, Ramirez looked at Damien and said, "So, amigo, you have brought ... your friends with you on this trip?"

"They're acquainted with the business," replied Damien. "Jack here is good with numbers."

"Numbers?" asked Ramirez.

"I am like a gardener," said Jack. "I know how to make them grow ... safely."

Ramirez laughed, then raised his glass to salute Jack. As he took a sip, he paused to look at Laura and asked, "And you, my *beautiful* lady. Why is it that you are here?"

"Oh, I'm just here to help murder you," said Laura.

Ramirez's eyes widened and he spit wine from his mouth while signalling to a nearby guard who quickly dropped his weapon from his shoulder.

"Christ!" said Damien.

"Oh! I'm sorry," said Laura, looking at Ramirez. "I take it that Damien has not explained that part to you?"

Ramirez gestured for his guard to wait while Damien quickly explained the situation. When he was finished, Ramirez looked at the three of them and said, "So ... this worthless dog, Carlos, he has hired a beautiful woman to lure me away to be murdered."

Jack studied Ramirez's face as he spoke. His words were calm, sounding matter-of-fact. His face revealed his true feelings. Despite his dark skin, there was a noticeable redness, and the tendons in his neck protruded slightly more than usual. He was clearly angered.

"We've rented a place nearby," said Jack, "called Maria's Cabinas. We thought we would tell Carlos that Laura had lured you there."

"This does not seem right to me," said Ramirez, while scratching his chin and frowning. He looked at Damien and said, "I have heard that after we last met you went to Carlos to do business. Is that correct?"

"That's correct," replied Damien. "His prices were a little better than yours."

"So why do you not still do business with him? Why come to me?"

"When he saw Laura, I think it gave him an idea. Obviously this was something he intended to do but had not yet figured out how, until now."

"You have not answered what I asked! Why do you not work for him?"

"His price was cheaper ... but my instincts say not to trust him. He only thinks of himself. He wants to have Laura in the room with you when he and his men decide to attack. He wants her to stand in the window and give a signal. When I mentioned I was concerned for her safety, he threatened me." Damien then clenched his fist on the table and added, "I will not be threatened ... by anyone!"

Ramirez appeared unimpressed and said, "But Carlos would know that I would not travel to such a ... rendezvous ... without protection," said Ramirez.

"He thought if you believed that Laura was my woman," said Damien, "so as to be discreet, you would not surround yourself with bodyguards."

Ramirez did not respond and looked perplexed.

"You do not think that I would be worthy of such a rendezvous?" asked Laura mischievously.

Ramirez blushed, then chuckled and said, "For such a beautiful lady as you," he said, "I would meet you in

Carlos's own bedroom." Ramirez paused and added, "After he was dead, of course!"

Everyone laughed. Ramirez then excused himself from the table for a few minutes. When he returned, he asked, "Whose idea was it to rent a place in Cali — Maria's Cabinas?"

"Mine," said Jack. "I thought it would be convenient for you. I have not told Carlos about it yet."

"So it is you who talks with Carlos?" asked Ramirez.

"Carlos wanted you to think you were having an affair behind Damien's back. As it would appear that the situation does not involve me, it would be easier for me to converse with Carlos."

"I do not think that he would dare try to do this so close to where I live. If he made a mistake ... the road back to Buga would become very long. I will pick another location. Palmira would be good. He will feel safer there."

"Palmira?" asked Laura. "Where is it?"

"Cali, Buga, and Palmira ... think of it as a triangle on the map," said Ramirez. "Buga is to the north and Palmira is to the northeast. All three cities join each other and are all less than an hour away. Buga belongs — no, *used* to belong — to Carlos. I enjoy the business in Cali. Palmira will be a good spot. He will not be so suspicious there."

"I spoke to Carlos this morning," said Jack. "I told him that tonight was the only opportunity. I was afraid that if we stalled, he might choose some other means. He is expecting me to call and let him know."

Ramirez nodded and said, "The sooner we take care of this problem, the better it will be. Allow me a couple of hours to make some arrangements, then you can call Carlos."

"I would prefer to call him from our hotel," said Jack. "I could appear to be more open with him then.

Perhaps you could phone me later and give me a location to tell Carlos?"

"The three of you will be my guests for dinner tonight. Seven o'clock. You will phone him after that. It will give me time to make preparations."

Jack knew that the dinner invitation, like the call he was to make, was an order and not a request. He nodded in agreement and said, "Perhaps I will tell Carlos that you are having a party tonight. I'll tell him that Damien is drunk or has passed out. Laura will say she has a headache and ask you to escort her home. He will understand."

Ramirez smiled and said, "Very good, my new friend. Very good."

For the next half-hour, the conversation around the table was light. Ramirez bragged about the abilities of his chef and the various paintings and statues he had acquired. Jack saw that his eyes frequently glanced in Laura's direction and knew that something was on his mind. Soon it was revealed.

"Have you dyed your hair?" asked Ramirez abruptly, looking at Laura. "It is not real?" he added, sounding disappointed.

"My natural hair just has red highlights. I did dye it, just on the pretense of enticing you."

"Ah," said Ramirez. "That is most unfortunate. Highlights, as you say, is how I do prefer it. That is a secret that my enemies do not know. Perhaps, for me, that is a good thing. Come, I will walk you all to your car."

They walked to the front of the mansion and were just approaching their car when Ramirez said, "Jack, walk with me for a moment."

Jack, Damien, and Laura all raised their eyebrows at one another, then Jack did as instructed. Ramirez walked with Jack until he was just out of earshot and then said, "Laura. She does not really belong to Damien, does she?"

"No, she doesn't," replied Jack.

"I see her look at you sometimes ... like perhaps you are her boss? She does not look at you like a lover. Am I correct?"

Jack felt uncomfortable. Ramirez was more observant than he had expected. He also did not want to put Laura into a position where it would appear that she was for sale. He replied, "She looks to me because she values my opinion. But you are right. She belongs to no man, although there have been men who have belonged to her."

Ramirez chuckled, then said, "*Perfecto*!" He smiled as he walked with Jack back toward the car.

As they neared the car, Jack noticed a security guard answer his portable radio. Seconds later, he barked an order in Spanish. Another guard quickly levelled his M16 at Damien, who was leaning against the driver's door of their rental car. A second guard pointed his weapon at Laura, who was standing a short distance away where she had been watching a gardener prune some rose bushes. Jack heard a noise behind him and knew that a third guard was covering him.

Ramirez looked startled and the guard spoke to him rapidly in Spanish. The word *policia* was used as the guard gave a sweep of his arm to indicate the three guests.

The eyebrows furrowed on Ramirez's face and his dark eyes looked like black marbles. He looked at his three guests and said, "A man has climbed a tree just outside the fence to our property. He is watching with binoculars. My guards believe it is a policeman! You have come to try and trap me! Yes?"

Damien's hands were behind his back and he slowly used his fingers to feel for the door handle. *My only chance ... keys are in the ignition ... if I can get it started ... keep my head down and crash the gate. Maybe the Mounties will try to run and distract them...*

Laura glanced around. *No place to run ... gardening shears in this guy's hand ... won't stop an M16 ... oh, man! Elvis, I'm sorry.*

"A policeman!" Jack exclaimed, then let out a chuckle that he hoped sounded genuine. "This is great news!" He then whispered to Ramirez, while conscious of the end of a gun barrel nuzzling his back.

Ramirez looked up, then said, "Of course!" He barked out a command and the guards quickly shouldered their weapons. He smiled and walked over to the gardener. A moment later, he bowed slightly as he handed Laura a freshly cut rose.

Damien was the first to speak as he drove Jack and Laura through the gate and out onto the street. "What the fuck just happened?"

"I said it was obviously someone who worked for Carlos. I suggested he show some affection toward Laura, so Carlos would think his plan was working."

"We can thank Jean-Louie for almost getting us killed," said Laura angrily. "I thought he said he was going to keep the troops far back!"

Jack expected Damien to voice his anger as well, but he remained strangely silent. *Perhaps just thankful to be alive ... at least, for now.*

# chapter thirty-seven

Jean-Louie breathed a sigh of relief when Jack, Laura, and Damien drove out the gate from Ramirez's driveway. Seconds later he knew his worries were not over. Two motorcycles, each containing two men, departed as well. They were followed by four SUVs that were all packed with men. It was soon apparent that Ramirez had ordered his three guests to be followed.

Jean-Louie quickly conferred with his Colombian counterpart. *Being naturally suspicious is one thing, but this many men? What the hell happened in there? Yet, if Ramirez wanted to kill them, he would have already done so.*

Jack saw one of the narcs in a car that was driving past them. The narc made eye contact with him and slowly gestured with his head to look behind them.

Jack nodded that he understood and the narc disappeared in the traffic ahead.

"We've got a tail," said Jack.

"Damn it," replied Damien. "With all these strange streets and traffic, I've been too busy to notice."

"Think we should lose them?" asked Laura.

"No," replied Jack. "Ramirez is paranoid enough. Drive easy back to the hotel. When it's clear, we'll slip up the stairs and thank the narcs and Jean-Louie for heating us up. Also want to kick whoever was up that tree in the balls."

Jean-Louie was adamant. None of his people had climbed a tree or even left their vehicles. He slammed his fist on the coffee table and said, "We know that Ramirez's grounds are infested with guards! Only a fool would do such a thing!"

"Perhaps the fools were us," suggested Laura.

"What do you mean?" asked Jack.

"Perhaps Ramirez made up the whole story, just to see our response."

"He is cunning," said Jean-Louie. "That is one scenario I hadn't considered."

*Or perhaps a different police unit,* thought Jack. He looked intently at Jean-Louie's face and then asked, "Are there any other police units that could have been watching us?"

Jean-Louie stared briefly at Jack, then replied, "No operational units that ... were in the vicinity of Ramirez's estate without our knowledge. I am positive that the tree climber, if he actually existed, was not a policeman."

Jack and Jean-Louie briefly stared at each other. Now, without actually saying it, they each knew there was another police unit involved, but apparently not at Ramirez's place.

"I would suggest that you use extreme caution," said Jean-Louie.

Jack nodded, then said, "Thank you. I will."

"At first I was more concerned when so many men and vehicles appeared to be following you," said Jean-Louie. "I was relieved when I learned that three of the SUVs headed northeast out of the city. The other SUV was last seen heading north. Right now there are only two motorcycles, each with two men who are hanging around the hotel here."

"Not totally unexpected," said Jack. "We'll do the tourist thing this afternoon. Buy Laura a new pair of shoes from his store. Maybe even lounge around the pool. Wouldn't hurt to try and catch a few winks. I suspect this party we're going to might last all night."

"I don't like the idea of the three of you going back in," replied Jean-Louie.

Jack shrugged and said, "We certainly felt welcome this afternoon, although it was a little uncomfortable when he said someone was watching. Partying with him will make him trust us more."

"Besides," said Laura, "I expect lots of people will be coming and going from the party. It wouldn't be the time for him to try anything serious, even if he was suspicious."

"If he wasn't suspicious," said Jean-Louie, "he wouldn't have four goons outside watching."

Jack, Laura, and Damien arrived promptly at seven o'clock. Jack and Damien each wore slacks and a golf shirt. Laura wore an emerald green silk blouse and a white skirt. Her new high-heeled shoes were also an emerald green.

A servant nodded politely and gestured for them to follow. Ramirez was at a desk in his study. He was not unfriendly, but his demeanour had changed considerably since the afternoon. As they entered, he complimented Laura on her choice of shoes — and on which store she had purchased them in.

"You were watching me?" asked Laura, portraying anger.

"Do not be offended," Ramirez replied. "Cali can be a dangerous city. I have many bodyguards. It was no inconvenience to ensure that no danger came to you. As you are my guests, I feel it is my responsibility."

Jack studied Ramirez's face as he spoke. *Subtle intimidation or a need for absolute control? Likely both.*

Ramirez dismissed any further comments from Laura simply by turning to Jack and saying, "You will call Carlos now."

"Now?" asked Jack.

"Yes. Here, with me. You will say that I will be with Laura in Palmira tonight. Tell him that you will meet him in front of the church at the main plaza in Palmira at eleven o'clock. Say you are in my house and do not have time to talk now, so he cannot ask many questions."

"There is no need for me to meet him," said Jack, feeling a rush of acid to his stomach. "I can simply phone him."

"No," said Ramirez. "You will meet him. He will be less suspicious then. Many of my men are already in place."

Jack and Laura exchanged a look. Each thought the same thing. *A simple plan has just become complicated and dangerous.*

"In front of a church in a plaza," said Jack. "It does not sound like a good place. Lots of people could get hurt or he might escape."

Ramirez smiled and shook his head. "We will not kill him there. His car, a Mercedes, it is bulletproof and heavily protected. Personally, I prefer my Land Rover. It also has such protection but is more suited for the roads in Colombia."

"Where do you intend to do this?" asked Jack, feeling irritated that Ramirez could be so casual about planning a murder.

"You will take him to a villa on the edge of the city. It is a good spot. The driveway to the villa goes over a small bridge. When he enters the villa, I will have a truck block the bridge. More men will be inside the villa and also in a shed outside. He will not escape once he is over the bridge."

"I think I should come to Palmira as well," said Laura.

"Definitely. I intend for you to come," said Ramirez. "You will leave your car here and all three of you will come with me," he added, while getting up and walking around his desk to face Jack. "Call Carlos now!" he ordered.

Ramirez watched closely as Jack dialled, and then he placed his head close to the phone so he could listen. Out of the corner of his eye, Jack saw Laura move closer to the desk, her hand within grabbing distance of a thin knife used as a letter opener.

"Carlos! This is Jack."

"What news do you have for me?" demanded Carlos. "Tell me where the pig is!"

"I am a short distance from him now," said Jack, looking at Ramirez, whose face indicated a rise in blood pressure. "I do not have time to talk. He will be with the lady in Palmira tonight. I do not have the address now. I will meet you at eleven o'clock in front of the church at the main plaza in Palmira and show you where he is."

Carlos let out a tirade in Spanish that Jack did not understand. He felt his muscles contract as the rage showed on Ramirez's face.

Carlos then said, "*Si*, amigo, we will meet in Palmira!"

Ramirez stepped back when the call ended. His face was contorted in anger and he reverted back to his Spanish tongue as he let loose with a barrage of obscenities while looking at Jack.

Laura turned her back to the desk but put her hands behind her and picked up the letter opener. *Two bodyguards in the room ... if I can take out Ramirez while Jack and Damien jump the other two ... oh man!*

Ramirez then spun toward Laura and said, "I am sorry, Laura. For what I have said. I hope you do not know such Spanish words."

Laura smiled sweetly and said, "I'm ashamed to admit that I haven't learned Spanish."

"That is okay. I am ashamed of the words I just spoke," replied Ramirez. "It is unbelievable what he said he will do to me with ... a stick." Ramirez paused momentarily, then said, "Very barbaric. I do not understand such rage. I thought he and I had an agreement. He is a lunatic."

"He really is," said Damien in agreement.

Ramirez looked at Laura and said, "Do you know that he always wears a little green tam? He pretends he is a soldier. He is not. He is just a lunatic."

Laura let out a deep breath. She then thought of Rellik with his stringy red hair and chipped front tooth. *How could Ramirez understand such rage? Perhaps if he had a brother and knew Rellik, he would understand. Carlos isn't the only lunatic who should be put down!*

Laura gently laid the letter opener on the table and stepped away when Ramirez said that they would have dinner now.

On their way to the table, Laura whispered to Jack, "Think maybe you should call Jean-Louie? Have them pull us over when we leave? Ramirez isn't going to let us take our car but if we let Jean-Louie know, then…"

"Not a chance. We're this close to Carlos. I'm not going to let him slip through my fingers now. You stay close to Ramirez. He'll be protected. He's not the type to risk his neck."

"Yeah, he's really different than you. Probably smarter."

Jack chose not to respond.

The dinner, consisting of a main course of garlic buttered prawns and wild rice with mushrooms, would normally have tasted succulent. Neither Jack nor Laura felt like eating. The anticipation of tonight's activity did not seem to affect Damien, who was pleased to accept a second helping.

"Tell me, Jack," said Ramirez, "Damien said that you are not with his club, but that he has hired you for your knowledge of money."

Jack nodded.

"What would you propose that I do as an investment strategy for your country?"

Jack took his time to chew and then swallow a prawn before replying, "I would presume that a man of your calibre would already own a bank someplace — perhaps in the Grand Caymans?"

Ramirez smiled and said, "Perhaps more than one."

"Your official business is inspired by leather. Shoes, jackets … correct?"

"Yes," Ramirez replied, then looked at Damien and said, "Officially, of course!" then laughed.

"Then," said Jack, "I would propose you open a chain of such stores in Canada. You could get a tax break by borrowing money from your own banks while paying yourself interest. Naturally, the paper trail would be hidden through different companies so that the government would not know you owned the banks. On paper, it would appear normal that you would send large amounts of money back to the banks as well as to shoe or leather distribution companies in Colombia."

"Your government would give me a tax break?" exclaimed Ramirez.

"If you have to borrow money to invest in a company in Canada, it is expected that you would deduct such an expense from your cost of doing business. On paper, you would say that you are selling a large volume of expensive leather goods. You would only send a few high-quality and expensive items for show. The rest would be of a very low quality. Practically worthless. Once these cleared customs, the poor-quality merchandise could be destroyed. As long as large amounts are being imported, it would appear that they are being sold and money is being sent back to order more and pay for loans."

Ramirez beamed, then looked at Damien and said, "You have picked your people well." He then glanced at Laura and added, "Very well." He raised a glass of Pinot Blanc. Everyone followed suit and gave a silent toast.

"Perhaps," said Ramirez to Damien, "some of the shipping containers of shoes might contain a much more expensive product."

"That," said Damien, "would depend upon how expensive it is for me!"

Ramirez smiled and replied, "We will talk after dinner."

At eight-thirty, a man arrived and stood quietly in the doorway. Eventually, Ramirez excused himself from the table to talk with him.

When Ramirez returned, he smiled as he sat down. "I have just been informed," he said, "that Carlos's Mercedes, three vans, and two SUVs have left Buga on the road to Palmira. It is estimated that he has thirty men with him." Ramirez paused to sip his wine and then said, "So many men. Carlos is a coward, is he not?" He added, "Does he think that I am Superman?" and laughed.

Jack, Laura, and Damien also laughed politely.

"Now," said Ramirez, "we have one hour before we should leave. I recommend the dessert tonight. Grilled banana with a rum glaze topped with ice cream."

"Sounds good," said Damien.

"Ah, my friend," said Ramirez, looking at Damien, "after tonight I will give you the best price I have given anyone."

"That sounds good, too," said Damien. "After dessert, let's discuss it further and I will call my men in Canada to arrange the details."

Jack glanced at his watch and looked at Laura. *What will happen when I meet Carlos? One thing is for sure … Damien will keep right on going — with me to thank for bargain prices!*

# chapter thirty-eight

Jean-Louie received the report that Ramirez's Land Rover, accompanied by three Hummers, was leaving the estate.

"What do ya think?" asked one of the narcs.

Jean-Louie didn't respond as he dialled Jack's cell.

"Hey, Jack! How are you, my friend? This is John calling from Canada. I hear you are out of the country someplace?"

"John! Good to hear from you," replied Jack, relieved that the Land Rover he was in had tinted windows. "I am out of the country. Partying with a friend," he said, smiling as he glanced at Ramirez. "They really know how to have a good time here. They're even providing limo service to the guests. How's it going up there?"

The call was brief, but when Jack hung up, Ramirez looked at him and said, "No more calls ... for any of you."

Jack glanced at Laura and Damien, who stared ahead in silence. There was no mistaking the icy tone in Ramirez's voice. The remaining half-hour trip to Palmira was made in silence.

As they approached Palmira, Jack looked around and realized that their small convoy had become well spaced. None of the Hummers were in sight.

Ramirez watched Jack, then smiled and said, "You are observant, my friend. If Carlos has men watching for me to arrive in Palmira, it is better if he thinks I do not have security."

Ramirez might have been right. At the outskirts to the city an SUV appeared to follow loosely behind them. It only took minutes for Ramirez's driver to lose him in traffic.

"The dog does not want to alert the chickens too soon," observed Ramirez, wiping the palms of his hands together in anticipation. He looked at Jack and said, "They will rely on you to tell them where I have gone. We will park my Land Rover at the villa to bait the trap. I have another vehicle there too."

Ramirez paused to take a call on his cell. When he hung up, he said, "Good! Carlos's Mercedes and two of his vans have been seen driving near the church."

Jack realized that he was holding his breath and slowly started to exhale. *I almost feel disappointed that he showed up. Great time to think that this isn't such a good idea!*

A short time later, they slowly drove past a row of buildings. Most were homes, with about half of them in darkness. Others had a few lights on, including the occasional porch light.

Some noise and a bustling of activity came from one building in the centre of the block with an Aguila sign above the door. The street had no sidewalks, but a few people could be seen walking along the edges of the road. Just past the bar, the road turned to dirt. The Land Rover slowed and turned onto a single-lane bridge that spanned a creek, marking the entrance to a driveway.

The dirt driveway led up to a modest two-storey building. They parked and Jack walked around the villa. With the exception of a small mango grove behind the home, there were few trees for protection. A short distance away from the side of the villa was a small shed where some of Ramirez's men waited. It was a perfect place for an ambush.

"What do you think, my friends?" asked Ramirez.

Damien smiled and slapped Ramirez on the back and said, "I like it. You have done well!"

"Good. When it is over, I will have my men pile the bodies like a monument. It will be a symbol for those who cross me!"

Damien smiled and said, "I think your competition will get the message."

"We will go to the plaza now," replied Ramirez.

"I would like to stay here," said Damien. "If one of your men would lend me a gun, I would like to be here when Carlos arrives."

"But it is not your fight," said Ramirez, looking puzzled. "It is me he wishes to kill! Besides, it is too dangerous. Carlos will enter the villa, and then my men will switch on the lights when they climb the staircase. There will be much shooting."

"It was me he insulted," replied Damien, "when he told me to risk Laura's life. I consider it a matter of honour to take part in his execution. I hope he sees my face when he dies."

Ramirez stared intently at Damien but did not respond.

"I could hide out here, under the bridge," said Damien. "If Carlos tries to run back, then I will be waiting."

Ramirez relented, shrugging his shoulders and said, "As you wish!"

"Speaking of shooting," interjected Jack, "should I be forced to go with Carlos into the villa, let your men know that as soon as the lights go on, this gringo will drop to the floor. They'll have about two seconds of surprise to shoot everyone standing. Make sure they know who I am!"

Ramirez chuckled and said, "Don't worry. I will tell them not to shoot you!" He then spoke with his men and Jack watched as Damien was handed a snub-nosed, five-shot .38-calibre revolver.

"It is all that is available," said Ramirez. "It will not penetrate Carlos's car, but maybe if any of Carlos's men escape you will find a use for it."

Jack pondered over Damien's unexpected decision as he and Laura were driven back to the centre of the city. *A true survivor. If things go wrong he has a chance to escape.*

Twenty minutes later, Ramirez ordered his driver to park in an alley before turning to Jack and saying, "Walk to the end of the street. You will see the steeple. It is only two blocks away. A couple of my men will be watching."

Jack nodded.

"Do not worry," said Ramirez. "If you must go with him inside the villa, my men have been told not to shoot the gringo."

"If Carlos knows that it is a trap, it will not be necessary for me to worry about *your* men," replied Jack.

"By the time that happens, Carlos will be dead. He must trust you, or he wouldn't have asked you to carry out this mission. I am sure that you will be permitted to remain outside. Perhaps you could wait in the bar down the street."

Jack nodded silently.

"You seem troubled," said Ramirez, looking at him closely. "Perhaps there is something I do not know about? Between you and Carlos?"

Jack shook his head and said, "I'm just the cautious type." He then glanced at Laura and said, "If need be, apologize to Natasha for me, will you?"

Jack saw the Mercedes parked between two vans in front of the church. As he approached, four men surrounded him. Jack recognized two of the men and felt the dampness spread down his shirt. They were the ones he robbed outside of the Spotted Owl Motel. *Hope they don't recognize my voice.*

"With me, señor!"

Jack felt the barrel of a gun nudge his kidneys. He tried to smile and nodded politely as he followed. The side door of the van opened and a sharp jab from the barrel told him to step inside.

The search was thorough and did not take long. One of the men took Jack's cellphone, then he was allowed to dress himself before being hustled out of the van. He was then brought to the Mercedes, where the rear door opened on the passenger side and he was shoved inside.

"I am Carlos," said the short, squat man sitting beside him. He wore a green beret and a light jacket that was open to expose a pot-belly.

Thoughts of Charlie flashed across Jack's mind. He thought of Holly and the terror that Danny and Susan were still living with. *Wonder if I could grab his throat and squeeze the life out of him.*

Carlos's eyes peered at him from under the beret. Jack knew that his hatred showed, but for a brief moment he didn't care.

Carlos barked out a command in Spanish and a burly man sitting in the seat in front of him turned to face him, while reaching into his waistband. At the same time, the driver reached into his shoulder holster while staring at Jack through the rear-view mirror.

"You have my money?" snapped Jack, pointing his finger at Carlos.

"You do not talk at me in such manner!" roared Carlos.

Jack stared back. He knew his actions were not professional. *I'm supposed to make this guy like me, or at least not appear as a threat.* He sat back and looked down in submission.

Carlos appeared to relax and then said, "After Damien is dead, you will be paid." He gestured to the two men in the front and said, "You tell my men to drive to Damien now! They come back from Canada. They speak English good."

Jack glanced quickly at the two men and then said, "I will tell you how to find the place when you let me out of the car. I do not have a gun. It would be dangerous for me to go with you."

"You will tell me now or you will die!"

"If I die, then…"

"Then my men will wait for Damien on the road to the airport," countered Carlos. "He leaves tomorrow. I can wait."

Jack looked around him. *I feel like I'm in the middle of a movie. It's all so surreal. I may never see Natasha again … Carlos might win.*

"Talk my men now!" ordered Carlos.

* * *

When the small convoy consisting of Carlos's Mercedes, three vans, and two SUVs drove past the tiny bar with the Aguila sign, Jack pointed to the end of the street and gave directions into the villa.

Carlos immediately ordered the convoy to park down a side street while one SUV left to check out the area around the villa.

Muted light from a nearby home illuminated the men's faces in the car. Carlos accepted a call on his cell and then looked suspiciously at Jack and said, "There is a Jeep in front of villa. Is that Jeep belong to Damien?"

"I think he borrowed it from whoever he hired to kill you."

"That Jeep, it look like a Jeep belong to man I were at war with."

"You're joking!"

"I am no joking!"

"Maybe tonight is not such a good idea. Is this man dangerous? The one whose Jeep —"

"Enough! I think maybe you know this man!"

"I don't. I know your reputation. I am not stupid enough to do anything to make you angry!"

Carlos stared at Jack for a moment and then said, "We will wait here until Damien is got by my men."

"You're not going in as well?" asked Jack. "I thought ... man to man ... you would wish to avenge your brother!"

"I will revenge when it is safe," replied Carlos. "There is a small bridge to the villa. I do not think it wise to cross bridge until my men have Damien."

Jack looked at the two bodyguards in the front seat and noticed four more standing outside near the car. *I'm dead!*

Carlos continued to stare at Jack and said, "You know that I told my men to kill you in Canada. Yes?"

Jack saw the distrust in Carlos's eyes. *I've got to gain control — and his trust — fast!* He smiled and said, "That was simply business. I understand that."

"That man my men shoot. The news it say his baby cannot walk. What you think?"

"I think ... I'm glad you made a mistake and didn't shoot me."

Carlos was determined. "I am told you upset that my men try to drown the policeman's baby. Yes?"

Jack shrugged and said, "It was expected that I should look upset, so I did."

Carlos leaned closer. "Tell me. What woman think when she see her baby die in water?"

Jack's mind flickered back to an undercover operation years earlier when he had purchased child pornography. The operation was successful, but he had found it humiliating and degrading to even pretend to be that kind of person. *Now I have to pretend to be worse — to be like this man.* He looked at Carlos and laughed, and then said, "I think she squirmed ... just like a baby kitten when you light it on fire!"

The shock was evident on Carlos's face, and then he sat back and laughed too.

Jack watched him laugh but also saw something else. A glimpse of a holster on the side of his waistband under his jacket.

Carlos then slapped Jack on the shoulder and said, "Yes, amigo. That is what I think too!"

"I would like to see Damien squirm when you catch him," said Jack. "Just like a kitten!"

"He will, amigo. He will squirm long time."

"But if your men kill him, we will not see that. It is better if we go with your men."

Suspicion returned to Carlos's face. "No! We wait here!"

Jack's mind raced for a solution. "How will your men catch him?"

"I send everyone to drive fast to the villa. My men call me when safe and we go see."

"Damien might be killed before you catch him. I know how to catch him alive."

"Alive? How?"

"Have some of your men sneak up to the back of the villa first. Then have the rest of your men drive up to the front really fast. The more vehicles the better. We could go too but stop at the bridge. Damien will get scared and run out the back door. Bingo!"

"Bingo?"

"You would have him! Your men could jump on him in the dark!"

Carlos thought for a moment, then said, "That is a good plan. I want caught him alive!"

"There is a small problem, but I can fix it."

"*Problema*? What *problema*?"

"Damien sometimes sets a booby trap."

"What is booby trap?"

"A grenade to go off. It could kill your men and warn Damien."

"He has a grenade," said Carlos quite simply. An item that did not surprise him.

"Give me my phone back and I will call the woman who is with him. She will tell me about the trap and she could describe what the villa is like and what room Damien is in."

"This woman. She think she work for the *policia*?" asked Carlos.

"Yes. She is an informant. She is who told me about Damien. She hates him. She is expecting me to call. She thinks the police will arrest him tonight."

"I hate him also," said Carlos. "But you phone her and maybe Damien hear her speak."

"I do this often. We talk most nights at this time. Damien thinks it is her father who calls. You can listen as I talk."

Carlos thought about it for a moment and then said, "Okay. I listen. You make mistake and you squirm like a kitten on fire a long time."

Jack was thankful that Laura answered.

"Listen closely," said Jack. "I am outside your villa right now with the top boss. We are going to wait here until after his men raid the villa and catch him."

Laura felt sick when she heard the words. "You mean he's not coming in here to —"

"That's correct," Jack interjected. "Listen carefully to what I say and please do *exactly* what I ask."

"I understand," replied Laura, wondering if Carlos was listening in to Jack's conversation like Ramirez was hers.

"From your tone, I know that you are being listened to ... correct?"

"Yes," replied Laura, shrugging her shoulders and smiling at Ramirez.

"I want a description of the inside of the villa. It is important to know which room the men need to run to. I know you can't talk right now, but as soon as you can, I want you to get a pad of paper and a *pencil* and draw a picture of the inside of the house. I am worried about the booby trap near the back door. I presume it has been set?"

Laura paused and then said, "Yes," hoping it was what Jack wanted to hear.

"When he is getting ready for bed, make an excuse to go outside. Say you're emptying the garbage. Take the paper and pencil and leave it on the bridge under a little rock. Then *get out of there*. I will draw a sketch to show the boss the booby trap and then the men will rush the house. Do you understand?"

"Yes."

When Laura hung up, Ramirez looked at her and said, "I don't understand. Why does Carlos not go to the villa? He has lots of men."

"That's the problem," replied Laura. "He has so many men he doesn't need to risk his own life. He isn't going into the villa until after."

"As long as he crosses the bridge. That is most important. Otherwise my men will have to ram his car with the truck. That might not be so good for Jack."

"No, that wouldn't be good," agreed Laura.

"And his car is strong. He might still escape."

"I need a pencil and some paper," said Laura. "Then I'll cross the creek farther down the road and come up past the villa and leave it on the bridge like Jack asked."

"I don't understand," said Ramirez. "Why did Jack say there was a booby trap?"

"We do not know what is being said between Carlos and Jack. It is best we do this."

Ramirez shrugged and said, "If you wish. I have a pen and paper in the glove box."

"Pencil and paper," replied Laura.

"There is a difference?"

"Yes."

Damien peeked out from under the bridge and saw an SUV slowly driving toward him. It stopped and two men got out and quickly ran toward the bridge as the SUV sped off.

Damien gripped the pistol tighter and ducked as the men slid down the embankment near the bridge. He watched as they scrambled to hide in some bushes.

Moments later, someone was walking on the bridge above him. He heard the sound of a stone grate on the plank above his head and caught a quick glimpse of Laura's face in the moonlight as she bent over. She then continued walking across the bridge and out onto the street. *Now what the fuck is going on?*

Immediately the two men left their hiding spot and went to the top of the bridge. Damien heard them whisper and then heard one place a call on his cell. Seconds later, they both headed down the street. Damien peeked out again and saw one of the men staying in the shadows as he followed Laura down the street. The other man was carrying a pad of paper and stopped to wait a short distance down the street.

Damien saw Laura nervously looking back as the SUV arrived again. The man with the pad of paper quickly climbed in and the SUV drove away. She stepped back and hid in the doorway of a building, oblivious to the other man who was creeping closer.

# *chapter thirty-nine*

Carlos accepted the pencil and pad of paper and quickly scanned the crude drawings. One showed the first level of the villa, with a bathroom, kitchen, and a pantry room at the rear and a dining room and television room at the front. Near the pantry was marked a set of stairs leading to the upper level.

The second drawing showed three bedrooms on the upper floor with one marked with a large *X* and the drawing of a stick man lying on a bed.

"Your *puta*, she do good," said Carlos. "Now, tell me about bobby trap," he said, shoving the paper and pencil onto Jack's lap.

Jack quickly sketched two trees that were the closest to the rear door of the villa. He then drew what he said was a fish line tied to one tree leading to a glass hanging in the crook of a branch on the other tree.

"The glass is held in place with a clothes pin," said

Jack. "He puts a grenade with the pin removed inside the glass. Below the glass is a rock. If someone walks into the line..."

"Then the glass falls and the grenade ... it go bang," said Carlos.

"You've got it," replied Jack. "A simple idea, but effective."

Carlos rolled down the window and handed the sketches to one of his men. He then gave him some brief instructions before rolling up the window.

The minutes passed and the tension reduced everyone to silence. Carlos finally got the call he had been expecting. When he was finished, he barked some orders at the driver, who flicked a switch. Jack heard the doors lock. Entering the car without permission was virtually impossible. Now, leaving the car would be up to the discretion of the driver.

"My men in place at back," said Carlos. "No bobby trap."

Normally Jack might have found Carlos's grasp of the English language amusing, but this was not the time — and he hated Carlos too much to find anything amusing about him.

From her hiding spot in the doorway, Laura watched as two vans, followed by two SUVs, roared past her down the street toward the small bridge. The Mercedes followed from behind, but the darkness, coupled with the tinted windows on the Mercedes, stopped her from catching a glimpse of Jack's face as it went by.

The first three vehicles bounced across the small bridge, causing the wooden planks to echo loudly in the night. The fourth vehicle stopped crossways at the entrance to the bridge. Four men leapt out and stood

with machine guns at the ready as the Mercedes skid-
ded to a stop in the dirt behind it.


Jack watched as Carlos, sitting beside him, screamed
instructions into his phone from the safety of the back
seat. The two men in the front of the Mercedes remained
in their seat, but the man in front of Jack had turned to
face him and made no pretext of hiding the pistol he was
pointing at Jack.

Jack tried to control his breathing and relax his muscles as he watched Carlos, waiting for the inevitable.
Waiting for when Carlos knew and turned to face him...

Jack looked across the creek and caught a glimpse
of a small army of men as they kicked open the front
door to the villa and rushed inside. *The time will be
now ... I love you, Natasha.*

Jack smiled at the man facing him from the front
seat and gave a nod of his head toward the villa just as
the lights went on in the house. The distraction didn't
work. Jack saw the man's eyes flicker toward the villa,
but he remained focused on Carlos's face, waiting for
his boss to give the order.

Instantly, automatic weapons erupted inside the
villa as men's screams echoed their terror. At the same
time, men rushed out of the shed beside the villa while
their weapons burped fire and death.

Carlos looked at Jack. His eyes burned with hatred
and his mouth opened to shout a command.

Jack gripped the pencil. The eraser butted against
the palm of his hand while the pencil protruded from
between the middle of his fingers.

Carlos reeled back in horror as Jack slammed the
point of the pencil upwards through his neck under his
jaw. His intent was to penetrate the brain but Carlos

twisted his head. Instead, the pencil skewered his esophagus and snapped in half, leaving the jagged end protruding from his throat. He tried to scream but instead his voice became an ugly wheezing sound as his body demanded air.

Jack was barely conscious of the man in the front seat raising his gun toward his head while he grasped Carlos with both hands around the back of his neck, pulling him down on top of him.

Carlos gurgled and tried to push himself upright, but Jack had partially wriggled down between the seats and held on tight. Carlos grabbed at his own throat, trying to remove the pencil.

Jack twisted and turned. For a few brief seconds, he felt fingers trying to pry his arm free from the back of Carlos's neck while the two men screamed at each other in the front seat.

Laura waited for the sound of gunfire before leaving the shelter of her doorway and running toward the Mercedes. She was thankful that Ramirez had given her a Glock 9mm for protection and reached for it in her purse as she raced forward. She knew it wouldn't penetrate the car, but if a door opened she might have a chance.

A few scatterings of citizens on the street ran past her, going in the opposite direction to escape the din of terror that unleashed itself at the far end. One man appeared in front of her and she gasped as she recognized his face. *The stringy red hair ... chipped front tooth.* Her brain tried to react to what she thought was impossible. Rellik raised his hand and she saw the gun pointed at her face — *point blank range!*

Her training took over as she instinctively crouched and started to raise her own weapon. Over the noise of a multitude of automatic weapons firing and people screaming, her brain heard him yell, "Fuckin' bitch!" and she saw the muzzle flash from his pistol.

Rellik grinned. *Good shot. Right through the centre of the forehead!*

Jack hung onto Carlos's neck with one arm while his other hand reached around Carlos's waistband. His fingers touched the leather holster and he frantically grabbed for the weapon and felt his fingers wrap around it. *Got it! ... Wait ... No! It's a cellphone! He was just packing a second cellphone!*

Jack was conscious of the man in the front seat opening his door. A second later, the door by Jack's head opened. He tilted his head and looked up just as the man took aim at the top of his skull. In a futile effort, Jack released Carlos and tried to grab at the gun. The man stepped back slightly, and it gave Carlos the opportunity to push himself upright, exposing Jack from the chest up as he lay pinned between the seats.

Jack had heard that you never hear the sound of the shot that takes out your brain. *It's not true. I hear it ... sticky pieces of skull and brain splattering down my chest ... Carlos pushing himself backwards to safety ... blackness...*

He heard the sound of a second shot, then stared numbly upwards as the light returned.

"Jesus fuck!" yelled Damien. "Don't just lie there!" he screamed, while dragging the corpse off Jack's face with one hand, holding the pistol in his other hand.

Jack wriggled out of the car backwards onto the ground. He saw the driver slumped over in the front seat and the car window awash in blood behind him. In the back seat, Carlos stared at him in terror with the broken pencil protruding from his neck. He took his hand from his throat and made a gesture to reach for the door handle. He knew it was hopeless. He was right.

Damien's third shot sent another wave of blood over the rear passenger window.


Laura saw the smile on Rellik's face when he fired. Her ears were ringing as the pistol exploded a round just above her head. She immediately fired two bullets from her own gun into his chest cavity.

Rellik's mouth gaped open in surprise and he fell backwards. Laura heard the sound of another body fall behind her and she turned to look.

*Oh man! He missed me and took out a citizen!*

Then she saw the gun in the man's hand, and the realization of what had happened took over. She looked back at Rellik, then quickly knelt down beside him.

He looked at her and his voice gurgled as he spoke.

"Why'd you fuckin' shoot me, bitch?"

"I thought you called me a fuckin' bitch and shot at me!" cried Laura.

"I said *Duck*, bitch! You ducked and..." Rellik's body convulsed and spewed blood from his lungs. Seconds later, he died without speaking another word.


Jack, followed by Damien, ran up the street and found Laura counting aloud while pumping a man's chest with her hands and then pausing to blow air into his lungs.

"This is Rellik!" Jack exclaimed. "What is he doing here?"

"You're alive!" said Laura, returning to pump on Rellik's chest.

"Yeah, still above ground," replied Jack, looking at Damien for an answer.

"Carlos ... you kill 'im?" asked Laura. She glanced at Jack, while still pumping on Rellik's chest.

"Pencil snapped in his throat. Damien finished him off," said Jack, while placing two fingers over the carotid artery in Rellik's neck. "He's dead, Laura. What the hell are you doing?" He looked at Damien and asked, "What is he doing here?"

"You didn't really think I would trust the Feds to protect me down here, did you? I had Rellik and two of his crew tag along for protection."

Laura continued to perform cardiopulmonary resuscitation until Jack said, "Laura! Will you cut this out! He's dead! We will be too if we stay out here in the middle of the street!"

Laura looked dazed as she slowly sat upright before picking the 9mm up from where she had dropped it in the dirt.

"I sent Rellik to protect you," said Damien. "Didn't know you had a piece. This other guy, he kill Rellik and then you shoot him?"

Laura shook her head. "I thought Rellik was shooting at me. I didn't know this other guy was behind me. I ... I didn't know...." Her voice trailed off and she stared down at Rellik.

"Yeah?" replied Damien. "Well, shit happens. Honest mistake. Rellik wasn't exactly one of my favourites, anyway. Guess we don't have to worry about him climbing any more trees."

"Where are your other two guys?" demanded Jack, looking around.

"They helped me take out the four guys outside of Carlos's Mercedes. I told them to take off after I waxed Carlos."

"You shouldn't have brought them here! Damn it, Damien!"

"Yeah, right. And if they weren't here, you both would be dead!"


Jack, Laura, and Damien hardly spoke as Ramirez gave them a ride back to his place. Once there, he gave them jogging suits to wear and took their bloodied clothes to be burned.

Ramirez told them that nine men who worked for Carlos managed to escape Palmira in a van. He said they did not arrive back in Buga.

It was almost four o'clock when Jack, Laura, and Damien arrived back at their hotel and hurried to their rooms before Jean-Louie and the narcs could see their jogging suits.

Jack waited a few minutes for Jean-Louie to return, then called his room.

"Went really well," said Jack. "Some details still have to be worked out, but we can head home now."

"Long night. Was starting to worry."

"Partied hearty. Helped gain his trust. Right now we're all beat. I'm going to grab three hours of shut-eye, then meet you at seven. We want to catch the morning flight back to Vancouver."

Jack then knocked on Laura's door. She came out in the hall and quietly closed the door behind her. They gave each other a hug before walking down the hallway.

"Think I could round up a drink if you want one," Jack said. "It's just that if you feel like talking, we can't do it in our rooms."

Laura shook her head and said, "One drink wouldn't be enough and forty-seven would be too many. Glad you're here, though."

"How do you feel?"

Laura didn't respond.

"You okay?"

"I don't know. Right now I just feel numb. I just killed a guy for saving my life. How do you think I should feel?"

"Numb. Same as I feel."

"I should have ordered him to drop it. I just … I was so freaked out with what was going on … then to see his face. The guy I figured for the epitome of evil. I double-tapped him without thinking. I should have known that he wouldn't have missed me at that range. My presumptions got him killed!"

"Rellik didn't save your life. Damien did. Rellik was just a soldier following orders. The fact that he was ordered to save you doesn't make him a good guy. He acts without conscience. He could have just as easily been told to torture you. Knowing his personality, he likely would have preferred that."

"I thought of that, but I still fired without weighing all the evidence. He even told me to duck! I was so convinced about him being evil that I didn't listen. What if he had been a good guy and I did that?"

"He wasn't."

"But me thinking he was…"

"We don't live in a courtroom. We don't have the luxury of taking months or years to decide whether or not a decision is right. Out here, it's survival. You reacted how you should have."

"It's the consequence of my prejudgement that is eating at me. It made me react…"

"Consequences! Tell me about it! Everything I've done lately brings about a consequence I hadn't planned on. I guess there are things we have to accept. Things we can't control. There are always consequences. You shooting Rellik was a consequence of the type of guy he was. In a way, he got himself killed. At least, his lifestyle did. It wasn't Mother Teresa running toward you!"

They walked for a little while longer, both lost in the silence of their own thoughts. Eventually they returned and stopped outside of Laura's door.

"Thanks, Jack," she said. "I'll be okay. Just need time to sort things out."

"You sure?"

Laura nodded and said, "You're a good friend. Goodnight."

"A *good* friend?"

Laura smiled and said, "Yeah. This time you're helping me bury a body ... if only in my mind." She then hugged Jack. He kissed her on the forehead and returned to his own room.


It was six-thirty in the morning when Jack was summoned to Jean-Louie's room.

As soon as he entered, Jean-Louie waved a copy of *El País* in front of him and yelled, "What is this?"

"A newspaper," replied Jack.

"What it says," snarled Jean-Louie, holding up the headlines reading *CARLOS — MORTE!*

"I don't know," replied Jack. "Haven't seen it and I don't read Spanish."

"I'll explain the grisly details," said Jean-Louie. "Sit down!"

Jack took a seat and listened.

"Norte del Valle," Jean-Louie started, then paused and said, "Early this morning, on a road outside of Buga, travellers were shocked to discover the bodies of nine men piled in a pyramid on the road."

"Wow!" said Jack. "People really play it rough down here!"

Jean-Louie stared briefly at Jack, then said, "I'm an old-school operator too, remember? Skip the concerned part and go straight to denial."

Jack stared ahead, his face frozen.

"I'll continue," said Jean-Louie. "This pyramid of bodies was only half the size of another pyramid discovered on the outskirts of Palmira. A naked man was laid face-down at the top of that pyramid. He had a broomstick protruding from his buttocks with a green beret dangling from the end. Later it was discovered that this was the notorious..." Jean-Louie paused to look at Jack and said, "The hell with it! You know who it was!" he said, flinging the newspaper down. He glared at Jack and asked, "Any comment?"

"No."

"The paper said that in both incidents the police were unable to find anyone who heard or saw anything ... but Ramirez is being linked as someone who has a previous history with Carlos."

Jack nodded quietly.

"For the record, were you with Ramirez all last night at the party?"

"He left for a little while. We thought he was picking up some more guests."

"A little while?"

"Might have been longer. Maybe a couple of hours. Everyone was partying and having fun."

"Good." *Almost believable*, Jean-Louie thought.

"What are you thinking?" asked Jack.

"I'm thinking the three of you should grab your bags and get the hell out of here!"

# chapter forty

It was eleven-thirty at night when the plane touched down on the Vancouver runway. It was an hour later when Jack and Laura cleared Customs. Damien was already gone.

Jack expected to get a taxi, but a familiar voice in the terminal stopped him.

"Hey, cowboy. How ya doing? How's your new sidekick?" asked Danny as he approached, carrying a shopping bag.

"What are you doing here?" asked Jack.

"Talked to Natasha. Heard you were coming in. Thought I'd like to pick up a friend … if you still want to call me that."

Jack looked at him, too surprised and too tired to respond.

"I know I've been an ass," added Danny.

Jack put his suitcase down and embraced Danny. "I

always think of you as a friend," he said. "A good friend."

"Thanks," said Danny, stepping back while wiping his eyes. "Your trip ... did it have anything to do with..." He paused a moment and looked nervously around before whispering, "The guys who ... tried to drown Jimmy?"

"Yes," said Jack.

"How did it go?"

"Total success," said Laura.

Danny closed his eyes and whispered, "Thank you."

"We'll talk about it over a beer," said Jack. "Just not tonight. We need to get home."

Danny nodded that he understood but looked glum as they made their way to the parking lot.

"What's wrong?" asked Jack.

"I should have been there," he mumbled.

Jack shook his head and said, "No, you should have been with Susan."

"You really believe that?"

"Beyond any doubt. Laura is my partner, but if you want to come back to Intelligence, we could maybe find another spot for you."

"Hell, no!" said Danny. "I want to be your friend ... not your partner!" He looked at Laura and added, "You've got no idea what working with him is like!"

Laura laughed and said, "I think I've got a pretty good idea!"

Danny smiled. "Yeah, if your trip was a total success, then I guess you do." He passed the shopping bag to Jack and said, "This is for you."

"For me?"

"Yeah, well, you know what they say," mumbled Danny. "Beware of geeks bearing gifts."

* * *

Laura unlocked her apartment door and stepped inside. Elvis rushed toward her, but before he could speak, she flipped a penny toward him. He caught it, then looked at it and smiled.

"How?" asked Laura.

Elvis shrugged and said, "Didn't you ever have any good friends when you were on Drug Section?"

"Yes, I had friends."

"Now, on Intelligence ... isn't Jack a friend of yours?"

"Yes, I consider him a good friend. Get on with it," said Laura quietly.

"Did it ever occur to you that I might have a good friend in the section I work in?"

"Not really. I wouldn't trust any of them."

Elvis paused until he saw the grin on Laura's face. He embraced her and felt her warm kisses on his neck. After a moment he said, "Come on. I'll unpack your bags while you put your feet up."

Laura looked at Elvis and said, "Do you know the difference between being a friend and being a good friend?"

"Sure," replied Elvis. "A friend bails you out of jail. A good friend is sitting beside you saying, 'Boy! Wasn't that fun!'"

Laura laughed.

Elvis studied her face carefully and then said, "With Jack ... does that hit it pretty close to the mark?" Before Laura could respond, he said, "Never mind. House rule. We don't discuss work."

Their next kiss was more passionate.


Natasha was in the shower but heard Jack yell that he was home. She quickly shut off the water and wrapped a towel around herself. She then saw Jack standing in the doorway. He was wearing a white cowboy hat.

Natasha kissed him warmly on the lips, then stepped back but kept her arms wrapped loosely around his waist.

"Something new for your wardrobe?" she asked, looking at his hat.

"Present from Danny," he replied.

Natasha smiled and said, "Good. He told me." She then let the towel fall from her body. "Ride 'em cowboy!"

# *epilogue*

In July 2005, Jean-Louie received three pictures of Damien from the Colombian police. They were found during a search of Carlos's home and given to Jean-Louie as a matter of courtesy. The pictures were not mentioned in his report to Assistant Commissioner Isaac, which simply stated that continual physical and electronic surveillance of the Canadian investigative team did not reveal any irregularities. Further investigation of the Ramirez cartel was not recommended at this time due to unrest in the area and an inability to provide adequate protection.

In August 2005, Satans Wrath held a memorial service on an acreage owned by one of the club members. Rellik's ashes were dumped inside his motorcycle helmet and buried. His colours were hung with distinction inside the east-end chapter clubhouse. Only a few members of the club were ever aware of how their fallen comrade had died.

In September 2005, a woman discovered a large amount of cash inside a duffle bag on the seat of her car. She turned it over to the police, who, when it went unclaimed, transferred the million dollars in Canadian hundreds to the woman's bank account. The police told her that part of a torn twenty-dollar bill had also been found in the bag. She retained it as a souvenir.

In December 2005, the B.C. Supreme Court struck down the anti-gang legislation under Section 467.13 of the Criminal Code as being too broad and too vague.

Within hours, strikers manning Satans Wrath clubhouses in B.C. received orders to purchase a total of 114 bottles of champagne. The clubhouse phones were used as a gesture to slap the police in the face. The amount ordered indicated to the police that the club had grown from their original estimation.

While most bikers celebrated the event, Damien remained worried. The decision served to advertise that B.C. was choice territory for organized crime. Competition would be fiercer. He was not upset when the Crown indicated they might appeal the B.C. Supreme Court decision.

In early January 2006, Damien was approached by two members of the Russian mafia and invited to join in a criminal venture. Damien believed there was something much more sinister to the offer, fearing the actual plan, if implemented, would result in thousands of lives being lost. He searched for a solution. Club rules would not allow him to phone the police ... but what if the police came to him?

In mid-January 2006, Laura received a carton delivered to her apartment. It contained ten pairs of expensive shoes and two pairs of knee-high boots. A note from Damien said that it was a gift from Ramirez. The